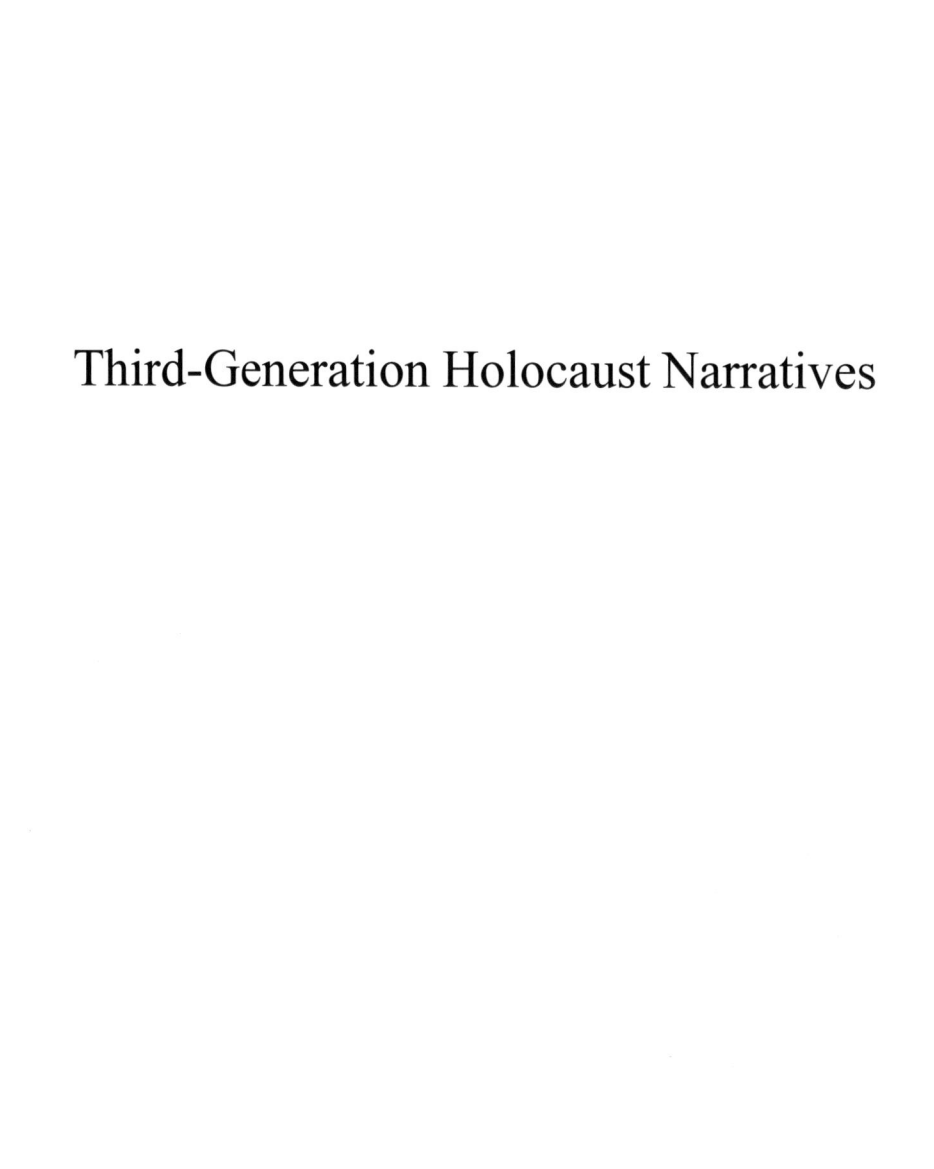

Third-Generation Holocaust Narratives

Third-Generation Holocaust Narratives

Memory in Memoir and Fiction

Edited by Victoria Aarons

LEXINGTON BOOKS
Lanham • Boulder • New York • London

Published by Lexington Books
An imprint of The Rowman & Littlefield Publishing Group, Inc.
4501 Forbes Boulevard, Suite 200, Lanham, Maryland 20706
www.rowman.com

Unit A, Whitacre Mews, 26-34 Stannary Street, London SE11 4AB

Copyright © 2016 by Lexington Books

All rights reserved. No part of this book may be reproduced in any form or by any electronic or mechanical means, including information storage and retrieval systems, without written permission from the publisher, except by a reviewer who may quote passages in a review.

British Library Cataloguing in Publication Information Available

Library of Congress Cataloging-in-Publication Data

Names: Aarons, Victoria, editor.
Title: Third-generation Holocaust narratives : memory in memoir and fiction / edited by Victoria Aarons.
Description: Lanham ; Boulder ; New York ; London : Lexington Books, [2016] | Includes bibliographical references and index.
Identifiers: LCCN 2016028388 (print) | LCCN 2016029276 (ebook) | ISBN 9781498517164 (cloth : alk. paper) | ISBN 9781498517171 (Electronic)
Subjects: LCSH: Holocaust, Jewish (1939-1945), in literature. | Holocaust, Jewish (1939-1945)--Influence. | Grandchildren of Holocaust survivors--Fiction.
Classification: LCC PN56.H55 T45 2016 (print) | LCC PN56.H55 (ebook) | DDC 809/.93358405318--dc23
LC record available at https://lccn.loc.gov/2016028388

∞™ The paper used in this publication meets the minimum requirements of American National Standard for Information Sciences—Permanence of Paper for Printed Library Materials, ANSI/NISO Z39.48-1992.

Printed in the United States of America

In memory of my mother
Anna S. Aarons
(1919–1969)

Contents

Acknowledgments		ix
Introduction: Approaching the Third Generation *Victoria Aarons*		xi
1	A Special Kind of Kinship: On Being a "3G" Writer *Erika Dreifus*	1
2	Memory's Afterimage: Post-Holocaust Writing and the Third Generation *Victoria Aarons*	17
3	A Visible Bridge: Contemporary Jewish Fiction and Literary Memorials to the Shoah *Avinoam Patt*	39
4	Storytelling, Photography, and Mourning in Daniel Mendelsohn's *The Lost* *Paule Lévy*	57
5	Life After Death: A Third-Generation Journey in Jérémie Dres's *We Won't See Auschwitz* *Alan L. Berger*	73
6	The "Generation without Grandparents": Witnesses and Companions to an Unfinished Search *Malena Chinski*	89
7	Avatars of Third-Generation Holocaust Narrative in French and Spanish *Alan Astro*	103

8   Measure for Measure: Narrative and Numbers in Holocaust
    Textual Memorials   131
    Jessica Lang
9   Against Generational Thinking in Holocaust Studies   159
    Gary Weissman
10 Simon and Mania   185
    Henri Raczymow, translated by Alan Astro

Index   199

Contributors   209

Acknowledgments

Once again, I would like to extend my enormous gratitude to Trinity University for its continuing support of my work in Holocaust Studies. Moreover, this book would not exist without the contributions of the scholars and writers whose thoughtful essays and deep commitment to Holocaust memory and literature shape this collection. I would also like to recognize the conscientious efforts of my research assistant, Megan Reynolds, whose Mellon Summer Undergraduate Fellowship provided her the time and resources to compile an extensive annotated bibliography that contributed significantly to my thinking about the design of this volume. So, too, our many conversations about the preoccupations and complexities of third-generation narratives were not only helpful in refining my own thinking on these and related matters, but were a genuine pleasure, reminding me of the value of ethical readers and listeners and the community of scholars formed from the shared enjoyment of reading good books. I would like to thank, too, the students in my Holocaust literature seminars for indulging me in our lengthy digressions on my current project and on their cheerfully tolerant, if eye-rolling, patience in pausing discussion long enough so that I might "write down that idea before I forget it."

I would also like to thank the Fundación IWO, Instituto Judio de Investigaciones, Buenos Aires, Argentina, for providing gracious permission to reprint the photograph from the Historical Archives of the Society for the Protection of Jewish Immigrants (Soprotimis) in chapter 6, "The 'Generation without Grandparents': Witnesses and Companions to an Unfinished Search." The inclusion of this photograph documents the important work of this organization in locating survivors during the early postwar period in Argentina. Many thanks to the following for granting permission to reprint the related photographs in chapter 8: Gefen Publishing House (www.

gefenpublishing.com), Karin Richert, and Zydowski Instytut Historyczny imienia Emanuela Ringelbluma, and The United States Holocaust Memorial Museum (www.ushmm.org/information/press/press-kits/20th-anniversary/milk-can-used-to-store-ghetto-archives).

My writing of the chapter on "Memory's Afterimage" was interrupted by the premature death of the novelist Ehud Havazelet (1955–2015). I had been thinking about Ehud and my indebtedness to his work and, in particular, to his novel *Bearing the Body*, as I was writing this chapter. I had the very good fortune of meeting Ehud on the occasion of the presentation of the Edward Lewis Wallant Award in recognition of this remarkable novel, and our continued association, the short stories he would send me, and the clarity and sheer beauty of his prose came to inform and enrich my own thinking about the continuing imprint of the Shoah. Ehud created in *Bearing the Body* a kaddish to history and to memory, a landscape in which, as one of his characters puts it, "another history, not his, not one he'd ever know, sifted its weight over him like ash."[1] Sadly, this same time saw the passing of American-Jewish critic and scholar Mark Shechner—colleague, fellow Wallant Award judge, and trusted friend—who was a discerning interlocutor for some of the ideas taken up in this book. Finally, I would like to thank Willis Salomon, on whose wise counsel I depend, as well as Jane Prosnit, Aaron Salomon, and Gabriel Salomon for their forbearance in listening over and over again as I sift through the past and for their reassuring trust in the importance of such endeavors.

NOTES

1. Ehud Havazelet, *Bearing the Body* (New York: Farrar, Straus & Giroux, 2007), 133.

Introduction

Approaching the Third Generation

Victoria Aarons

What is revealed in the attempts by yet another generation to untangle, to decipher, and to give literary voice to the enormity of the Holocaust? How, in other words, do we talk about the Holocaust *now*—the myriad of aftereffects and the imprint of the Shoah on contemporary life and thought? The essays in this volume set out to engage these central questions. From this wide-ranging, elastic opening spring other, equally complex, questions: What kinds of affective, temporal, geographical, and imaginative intersections and crossings are brought to bear on the project of Holocaust representation? Are we finding *something else*, something new in the literature in the decades surrounding the new millennium? How is the Holocaust viewed through the interpretive lens of the events of the twenty-first century? What kinds of configurations, patterns, and scaffolding are called upon to structure and interpret the events of the past? What motives are exposed in the contemporary literature that returns to the subject of the Holocaust? How does the tragic past run alongside of and hope to explain present conditions and anxieties? Where is the "place" of the Holocaust in a contemporary framework? Who are the custodians of memory now? What are the distinguishing features of the third generation and what makes this a useful marker in defining current trends in Holocaust writing? What, arguably, is at stake? As Paule Lévy asks in her essay in this volume, "Beyond amnesia or obsession what type of poetics of rhetoric may allow third-generation writers to mourn over people and over a world they have never known and to come to terms with a loss which, to them, has no concrete shape or face?"[1] These are just some of the guiding questions that occasion the essays in this collection and that consciously and self-reflexively shape the very narratives that we explore.

At the close of Molly Antopol's "My Grandmother Tells Me This Story," an elderly woman who in her youth escaped capture by Nazi troops through a maze of sewers, "an underground system of tunnels running from Poland to Belarus to Lithuania," to join the partisans in the forests of Belarus, tells her insistently inquisitive, American-born granddaughter: "I don't understand you. All your life you've been like this, pulling someone into a corner at every family party, asking so many questions. . . . Why don't you go out in the sun and enjoy yourself for once, rather than sitting inside, scratching at ugly things that have nothing to do with you . . . horrible things that happened before you were born."[2] In this story, which in narrative time takes place in New York in the twenty-first century, the granddaughter of a survivor of the Holocaust—a refugee who fled her small village of Antopol to join the Yiddish Underground—wants to go back in time, to wrest from her reluctant grandmother the story of her life during this dark period of history, and to fathom those "horrible things" that occurred long before the world into which this grandchild was born, an attempt to "imagine the world before she entered it" and thus to establish a traumatic origin story.[3]

Here, as elsewhere in the literature by and about third-generation descendants of Holocaust survivors, Antopol's youthful and largely inexperienced character willingly and willfully seeks out the stories of her grandparents' traumatic past and fortuitous survival. Entering into the narratives of this tragic history by choice rather than happenstance or unconscious compulsion, this granddaughter—like others of the third generation—purposefully wants to hear these stories of terror, upheaval, and loss. She wants to know the facts of the events that altered the course of her grandparents' lives and ultimately steered their survival. But she also wants the *story*, not only the factual account, but the "authorial" imprint and reflection of that experience, the narrative that gives continued meaning to the events described. And although the elderly narrator will resist her granddaughter's persistent probing with censorious exasperation—"Why don't you go out in the sun and enjoy yourself for once"—the grandmother will, in the face of such prodding assume the narrative authority, reaching back into her desperate past to reignite and mediate those "horrible things" that her granddaughter wants so desperately to know. Her story, however, is truncated, arrested at the moment of potential completion, leaving her granddaughter without the answers she fervently imagines are possible. For the reticent, disapproving survivor in Antopol's story will deny her granddaughter the completion of the story: "[N]o," she tells her persistent interlocutor, "I won't tell you the rest."[4] Instead, she admonishes her granddaughter that what she is searching for, the fate of those who vanished, who are not there to tell their own stories, is forever lost. She offers her granddaughter, instead, only the abruptness of erasure, a caesura where a narrative might have existed: "You can guess. You can go to the library and read. . . . You can waste full days in the research room, ruining your eyes scrolling through microfilm. . . . But you won't learn about what happened . . . there's just no way to find out."[5] Such Holocaust stories, generationally transferred, characteristically and inevitably are incased in silence, a gap at either end, enacting the very absence they evoke. As Andrea Simon puts it in her memoir, *Bashert: A Granddaughter's Holocaust Quest*, ultimately, for the grandchildren of Holocaust survivors, "The Holocaust is one big empty hole."[6] And here, in Antopol's short story, the grandmother confirms her granddaughter's worst fears that she has inherited a legacy of irredeemable loss that has come to shape the life she inhabits.

Despite the realities imposed by the limitations of memory and the imagination, as well as the disjunction of past and present, third-generation narratives—memoir and fiction, and the blending of both—reveal, as third-generation writer Erica Dreifus puts it in her piece in this collection of essays, "A Special Kind of Kinship" with "a past that is both personal/familial and world-historical."[7] Such consanguinity and the consequent quest for discovery will bring the third generation on return journeys—both physical and imagined—to the sites of traumatic origin. Undeterred by silence and sanctions against such a pursuit, third-generation narratives reveal attempts to comprehend, give voice to, and demystify the "unimaginable," unrepresentable fracture of the Holocaust, remaking a place for the Shoah's necessary imprint in the twenty-first century. The essays in this volume hope to capture the shared and extended shape of loss and longing generated by the continuing presence of the Holocaust if only in the imagination of those writers who enter into narrative moments of invention and calculation of that loss.

Third-generation writer Daniel Mendelsohn, in his memoir *The Lost: A Search for Six of Six Million*, will, despite his mother's injunctions, return once again to the site of his relatives' death, those who perished long before his conscious awareness of the events that catastrophically ended their lives. Such a fraught journey, doomed to incompleteness, will enigmatically form his own sense of identity and kinship. Having gone once to the small Ukrainian town, entering unknown territory—both geographical and emotional—in search of the fate of his grandfather's brother, his wife, and four daughters, Mendelsohn will return yet again in pursuit of the elusive and largely irretrievable knowledge he hopes to find. In justifying his repeated attempts to uncover the "truth," to give some sense of completion to his labyrinthine endeavors to discover the "particulars" of his unknown relatives' tragic end, Mendelsohn will defend his efforts in the face of his mother's clear misgivings: "I told her that I wanted to go back . . . because I thought that more than anything else, a return to Bolekhiv would give me a sense of an ending . . . to walk again the confusingly twisting streets of the town once more, but armed, this time, with so much more information than we had had the first time we went . . . when we had known nothing at all except six names. . . . An ending that showed how close we'd gotten, but also how far we'd always be."[8] Resigned to her son's inexplicable pursuit of such impossible, destabilizing, knowledge—"scratching at ugly things that have nothing to do with you . . . horrible things," as Antopol's character insists[9]—Mendelsohn's mother can only reply in the defended finality of her Yiddish inheritance, "an unbroken chain . . . from the present to the remotest imaginable past": "*genug is genug*. . . . My family ruined their *lives* by always looking at the past, and I don't want you to *be* like that."[10] Such warnings from preceding generations—survivors and eyewitnesses as well as the second generation, those born in the direct aftermath of the war—do little, however, to deter the third generation's attempt to discover and create narratives of the past. Such quests reveal a kind of repetition compulsion in the return and re-return, as if going back and back *again* to the place of traumatic origin will bring some kind of understanding, some kind of recognized consanguinity, a completion of the ellipsis that is, for this generation, the Holocaust.

Dissuaded neither by silence nor by such prohibitions, however, the teen-aged granddaughter, in the epilogue to Julie Orringer's novel *The Invisible Bridge*—a novel based on her Hungarian grandparents' experiences during the Nazi occupation—persists in her tenacious quest, though belatedly and in the face of the silence that has enshrouded the past: "She wanted to hear the whole story. . . . [M]aybe even now they didn't want to talk about it. But she would ask. . . . She was old enough now to know."[11] Not unlike the third-generation interrogator in Antopol's short story, Orringer's third-generation character persistently is drawn to such "strands of darker stories . . . absorbed through her skin, like medicine or poison."[12] The motivation for "hearing" the events of the story that has already been told in this extended narrative constitutes the briefest part of this epic novel, a narrative that spans decades, geographical boundaries, and generations. The narrator's desire to hear the story of her grandparents' ordeal and auspicious survival, as well as the story of the great-uncle, whose lingering presence exists only as "a photograph taken when he was twenty years old . . . just that photograph," materializes almost as an afterthought, a postscript to the exacting narrative of loss that has just taken place.[13] Coming at the novel's close, that is, after the detailed account of her grandparents' lives at war has been told, this pledge, an opening rather than an ending for the narrative that has already taken place, mimics the condition for the third generation, a generation arriving *after* such knowledge. Ironically, given their place in history, a contemporary generation is prepared "now to know," to begin again the uncontained, incomplete, and ongoing process of discovery and narration. A third wave of Holocaust transmission is poised to fill in the gaps of narration and representation, affective gaps as well as gaps in knowledge. The brevity of the epilogue in relation to the extended narrative that precedes it—standing as a cautionary sentry to the future—speaks to the way in which Orringer's third-generation narrator becomes an active participant in the memory of the history she attempts to enter and transmit. She, like others of her generation, becomes an ethical listener, one who recognizes and acts upon, as Geoffrey Hartman suggests, the "duty to listen" for "[t]he sense of the human has always to be restored."[14]

These three paradigmatic narratives—Antopol's short story, Mendelsohn's memoir, and Orringer's novel—suggest the third generation's approach to the Shoah, a pattern that makes emphatic the anxieties and uncertainties that attend such efforts to imagine onto the page the unspeakable real of that traumatic history. These works reveal the characteristic imprint of resistance, caution, and determination that becomes the motivating principle of the literature of the third generation. Patterned on the controlling trope of memory, both internally and externally structuring, such contemporary narratives find their place among the corpus of post-Holocaust literature, extending and performing the conditions of anticipatory dread and the enactment of genocide. These are narratives of collision and collusion. That is, these are works that make imperative the ethical demands inherent in reading well, in engaging in the shared exercise of reading responsibly—reading in the imagined presence of others, whose stories one only provisionally tells and hears. Bordered by the competing tropes of silence and of memory conferred, such narratives hope to give voice to absence and to pay homage to that which was so tragically lost. In these uncertain registers, third-generation narratives reanimate the past as they reckon with recurring patterns of loss. The essays contained in this collection address such issues of trauma, memory, representation, and transmission as they are played out in the discourse of and about the third generation.

Alan Astro, at the opening of his essay, "Avatars of Third-Generation Holocaust Narrative in French and Spanish," poses a definitional question that habitually arises in discussions of the new wave of Holocaust writers: "What constitutes a third-generation Holocaust narrative?"[15] All the contributors to this volume either implicitly or explicitly take up this question, circling back to it as a way into discussions of contemporary Holocaust narratives. What do we mean by third-generation Holocaust narratives? In what way might such a distinction help locate the ways in which we approach the subject of the Holocaust and the representation of its aftermath in the early decades of the twenty-first century? What makes the definitional issue such a nagging question? On the one hand, of course, "third generation" specifically refers to the grandchildren of survivors. But the specificity of this definition is arguably limiting. Avinoam Patt, in the chapter "A Visible Bridge: Contemporary Jewish Fiction and Literary Memorials to the Shoah," speaks to one aspect of the definitional problem inherent in the designation of the term "third generation": "I do not think it explains much aside from identifying an individual as the grandchild of survivors. There is so much variance between survivor families: How do we define survival? Did one grandparent, two grandparents, four grandparents survive? Did they share their stories? When? How much? What is the difference between the grandchild of survivors and a Jewish writer whose grandparents did not survive but who has taken an active interest in the history of the Holocaust?"[16] To all this definitional ambiguity, Gary Weissman, in the chapter, "Against Generational Thinking in Holocaust Studies," adds another variable that muddies any attempt to characterize a fixed identity for a third generation: "some members of the third generation will have spent significant time with their survivor grandparents and know them well, while others will know them hardly at all, and others will have grown up never knowing survivor grandparents who died before they were born."[17] That being said, while the designation of third generation may prove useful in locating the *specific* familial relationship between the writer and his or her subject, it also might suggest the motivation for such attempts to retrieve stories from the past and a metaphor for the ambiguities of historical distance and proximity. "Third generation" suggests both an ongoing chain of necessarily complicated continuity in the transfer of memory from one generation to the next and a context for the affective disruptions of that continuity.

Further, to limit the definition of "third generation" to direct familial ties—an uninterrupted line from grandparent to grandchild—does not get at the range of expression and representation found among contemporary narratives that return to the Shoah. A focus on direct familial ties neither suggests the breadth of expression nor registers the problem of moral reckoning in the prolonged aftermath of the Holocaust, the aftershocks of such an extended, ongoing rupture. Granted, one wants to refer to the third generation with qualifications. As Esther Jilovsky and many others have maintained, there is "no one homogenous definition" of the third generation.[18] And indeed, the definitional question regarding the exactitude with which we call upon the third generation opens itself up to other, equally vexing questions: How do we consider a writer, such as Mendelsohn, who goes in search, not of the grandfather he knew, but of the great-uncle he did not? And, further, how do we define "survivor"? Must one have survived the concentration camps to be considered a survivor? How do we classify those who were refugees from the Nazi occupation, those who escaped just at the moment when their worlds were closing in? Malena Chinski, in her essay "The 'Generation without Grandparents': Witnesses and Companions to an Unfinished Search," collected here, refers to the "generation without grandparents" for which "two simultaneous meanings can be distinguished. On one hand, it points to an inter-familial condition: the grandchildren of victims within a family. On the other hand, the same expression has a cultural implication, referring to all those people without a family connection but who share the condition of being grandchildren of victims."[19] Thus, as third-generation writer Erika

Dreifus suggests in regard to contemporary Holocaust narratives, in "A Special Kind of Kinship: On Being a '3G' Writer," "the generational categories and boundaries aren't quite so clear."[20] Indeed, this fluidity, this mutability and stretching of fixed limits in the range of expression reveals the rich and varied approaches to the subject of the Holocaust. This volume hopes to show that, while the term third generation raises a number of complicated issues that we take up here, it is also a useful designation from which to discuss the perspective from which this particular generation—cultural, temporal, familial, affective, imagined—approaches the Holocaust, a generation, as Lévy argues, "already removed from, yet still haunted by the Shoah."[21] This is a generation approaching the Holocaust from a position that is precariously balanced between proximity and distance, a position that characterizes this generation, this literature, the discourse about this literature, and the disposition of our time.

Thus, the third generation finds itself in the position of being simultaneously remote from and also consciously connected to the memory of the Holocaust, inheritors of the memory of the Shoah. The suspension between "proximity and distance," as Mendelsohn suggests in his memoir, poses a significant position from which and context within which this generation approaches Holocaust memory.[22] As Mendelsohn puts it: "A unique problem faces my generation . . . a problem that will face no other generation in history. We are just close enough to those who were there that we feel an obligation to the facts as we know them; but we are also just far enough away . . . to worry about our own role in the transmission of those facts, now that the people to whom those facts happened have mostly slipped away."[23] This is a generation writing at a time in history that will witness the passing of those who experienced firsthand the immediacy of the events. Direct testimony and firsthand accounts of the Holocaust as they were experienced will exist as a matter of recorded documents, voices stored in archives, rather than as the active transference of memory.

Of course, it is not simply a matter of the coming end of direct engagement with the generation of survivors that complicates the transmission of memory. There is not only a temporal distance with which a contemporary generation of writers must contend, but also a "spoken," locutionary distance that intercedes as well between the traumatic event and the re-engagement with it. These writers must contend with a discursive distance from the stories told. The telling, then, is no longer reciprocal, cooperative; that is, the current generation of writers who return to the subject of the Holocaust find themselves in a position within which they must become ethical listeners without the benefit of direct escort through the volutes of memory. Not entirely unlike those who escaped the Nazi occupation of their countries in time but were aware of their families' fates, those who, as Chinski puts it in her essay, "lived through the Shoah at a distance," in reconstructing memory, third-generation writers imaginatively navigate the gap between proximity and distance.[24] In creating such narratives, however, as Astro suggests, "the very distance implicit in the third-generation structure can allow for constructed—or perhaps even contrived—memory that is an appropriation but not a recuperation/expropriation . . . an aspect of the Holocaust as useable past, wherein we move not beyond mourning but outside of it."[25] In doing so, such narratives create sites of the imagination, imaginative spaces within which are balanced the antinomies of proximity and distance symptomatic of the ambivalence between forgetting/relinquishing, on the one hand, and remembering/retaining and finally transmitting memory, on the other. Despite such confusions and limitations, this is a generation linked by the trope of memory—all engaged in, as Jessica Lang proposes here, "the act of remembering remembering."[26]

How, as Avinoam Patt and others ask, do we "remember"? How, that is, "do we remember something we never personally experienced"?[27] Furthermore, how do we access and represent memory even as it is waning? How do we talk about remembering? How, in other words, do we enact remembering through narrative and figurative representation? The third-generation writers whom we examine here create memory "sites," narrative frames for the reconstruction of memory all the while evoking the loss that accompanies it. The unearthed knowledge is habitually measured against the limits of such knowledge, as we discover in Henri Raczymow's narrative that returns to his grandparents' lives in the small shtetl in Poland and to their son for whom the writer was named, the twenty-year-old Heinz who, "deported to the East," was arrested by the Germans and sent to the camps.[28] "What else is there to say?" Raczymow asks. Unable, in memory, to let them go, he explains: "As a child I felt a closeness to them, a physical, organic, visceral intimacy . . . and a practically secret language that we shared and that wasn't secret at all, just a mix of rough French and poor Yiddish, the same they and their son had communicated in some twenty years before I was born. . . . What else to say? What more to say? How to speak about them more, about them just a bit more?"[29] The language both of loss and found memory, like the French and Yiddish of their shared past, "an untranslatable language, with no equivalent," is, for Raczymow, a language of memory, a language of loss and felt connection.[30] Such narratives simultaneously, as Lévy writes, "give a voice to silence and a face to absence."[31]

Such "sites" of memory—discursive, imagined, reconstructed—function as *Yizkor* books, chronicles of memory, as Patt suggests.[32] In doing so, these narratives create midrashic moments of representation, reckoning, and extension. Such memory sites are brought to bear directly on Lang's discussion of Holocaust memorials in the chapter "Measure for Measure: Narrative and Numbers in Holocaust Textual Memorials" that suggests both the similarities and differences in physical and narrative memory sites and the social, public, and private spaces they inhabit. In raising the complexities in memorializing memory, Lang makes claims for the "hybridity" that "bridges the gap between Holocaust literature and Holocaust memorial."[33] Such sites, Lang argues, "undergo a process of transformation," similar to the narrative "sites" of the third generation—novels, memoirs, and the like—that navigate memory along the passage of time as we move farther and farther away from the Holocaust and from survivor memory.[34]

The essays included here draw upon a range of genres and approaches, extending beyond North America. Furthermore, while the essays collected herein focus on writers from the United States, from France, and from Latin America, they also take us back to Poland, to Germany, to Ukraine in an attempt to show the reach of the continuing legacy of the Holocaust on subsequent generations. The first three chapters establish the general preoccupations of third-generation writers, suggesting the complexities of and direction for the literature that emerges. Erica Dreifus, author of the short story collection *Quiet Americans*, establishes the premises upon which this volume is based. Writing from a third-generation perspective, Dreifus, in "A Special Kind of Kinship," sets up the complex relation that she and other third-generation writers have to the legacy of the Holocaust and the ways in which they have "recorded, transmitted, and/or transformed this history in fiction."[35] My essay, "Memory's Afterimage: Post-Holocaust Writing and the Third Generation," argues that the literature of third-generation writers is characterized by attempts to navigate the trauma of the past all the while looking toward the future. This literature, I propose, "attempts both to memorialize and to fight against the debilitating specter of the past" as the singular, defining moment of Jewish history and identity.[36] This is a literature, I argue, that is "deeply invested in a return to the past, in preserving the memory of the Shoah, all the while opening future possibilities."[37] In "A Visible Bridge: Contemporary Jewish Fiction and Literary Memorials to the Shoah," Avinoam Patt links contemporary writing that returns to the subject of the Holocaust to the evolution in American Jewish writing as reflected in the works of fiction recognized by the Edward Lewis Wallant Award, an award given annually to emerging American Jewish writers. Patt discusses the current "literary preoccupation with the Holocaust in contemporary Jewish literature" and the ways in which such writers return to history in their fiction, balancing the reach of the imagination with the historical data and source material.[38]

The next four chapters examine representative works and diverse genres from a number of different geographical locals, suggesting the broad scope of this literature and both the similarities and differences in perspective. Chapter 4, "Storytelling, Photography, and Mourning in Daniel Mendelsohn's *The Lost*," by Paule Lévy, examines the memoirist's pursuit of the unknown fate of his relatives, as articulated in this very personal narrative, as "[b]oth the story of a quest and the quest for a story."[39] In doing so, Lévy focuses on material artifacts and on the way in which photographs come to "deepen the sense of loss" that shapes this narrative.[40] Here Lévy shows the dialectics of absence and presence, memory and oblivion, trauma and recovery, established by the complex relationship between text and pictures. The next chapter, "Life After Death: A Third-Generation Journey in Jérémie Dres's *We Won't See Auschwitz*," by Alan Berger, proposes that the search for the grandparent's past becomes a means of returning to one's Jewish identity, as depicted in the structural and illustrative patterns of this graphic novel by a third-generation French writer. Here Berger suggests that the project of *tikkun olam* (repair or restoration of the world) implied in such attempts to reckon with the Shoah becomes a process of *tikkun atzmi* (repair or restoration of the self).

Chapters 6 and 7 introduce Latin American third-generation approaches to the legacy of the Holocaust. The point of departure for Malena Chinski's essay is the Uruguayan Jewish historian Graciela Ben-Dror's description of the "generation without grandparents." In her discussion primarily of Argentinean writers, Chinski, in "The 'Generation without Grandparents': Witnesses and Companions to an Unfinished Search," suggests the consequences of the Shoah for the third generation, those "dispossessed of the history of their murdered relatives" and their search that extends the reach of the imagination.[41] In "Avatars of Third-Generation Holocaust Narrative in French and Spanish," Alan Astro takes on the notion of the intersections and "confusion of generations wrought by the Holocaust" in his discussion of second- and third-generation writers.[42] In examining the representative works of French and Spanish writers, Astro shows the complexities that arise from a "merging of the generations."[43] Ending with a fourth-generation text, Astro proposes that such evocations of memory will continue into the future.

Chapter 8, "Measure for Measure: Narrative and Numbers in Holocaust Textual Memorials," extends our reading of third-generation narratives to memorial sites as the imagined spaces of memory. Here Jessica Lang demonstrates the import of those Holocaust memorials that "derive their symbolic and literal meaning through an invocation of numbers and counting . . . as a means of both representing the many and the individual."[44] Lang shows the attempts among post-Holocaust generations to calculate and memorialize the scope of the total destruction, all the while pointing to each singular loss in an act of remembrance.

Gary Weissman, in chapter 9, "Against Generational Thinking in Holocaust Studies," challenges us to reconsider such generational categories, cautioning us that "what we do out of convenience or convention should not go unexamined, nor should it come to underlie, as it has, theories concerning how the Holocaust is presently remembered, represented, and 'transmitted.'"[45] In an argument that provides a valuable theoretical and methodological context for reading contemporary texts, Weissman raises important questions about the ways in which Holocaust memory, literature, and aesthetics have been theorized and discussed over the past three decades. In doing so, Weissman articulates what the essays in this volume show: that the blurring and overlapping of generations in responding to the Shoah reflect the very tensions and ambiguities that such narratives hope to enact.

Writing from both a second- and third-generation perspective, French writer Henri Raczymow closes this volume with "Simon and Mania," a narrative that reaches back to his family's history and deep connection to his grandparents and to his memorialized kinship with the uncle he never knew but for whom, in memory, he was named. Thus the essays in this collection are framed by narratives that draw upon the ongoing legacy of the past and the haunting sense of connection—inherited, imagined, longed-for, lamented—that give rise to the richly, if provisionally, sculpted shapes of memory.

NOTES

1. Paule Lévy, this volume, "Storytelling, Photography, and Mourning in Daniel Mendelsohn's *The Lost*," 58.
2. Molly Antopol, "My Grandmother Tells Me This Story," in *The UnAmericans: Stories* (New York: W. W. Norton & Company, 2014), 84. This story is discussed in further detail in chapter 3, "A Visible Bridge: Contemporary Jewish Fiction and Literary Memorials to the Shoah," by Avinoam Patt.
3. Antopol, "My Grandmother Tells Me This Story," 84, 59.
4. Antopol, "My Grandmother Tells Me This Story," 83.
5. Antopol, "My Grandmother Tells Me This Story," 84.
6. Andrea Simon, *Bashert: A Granddaughter's Holocaust Quest* (Jackson: University Press of Mississippi, 2002), 38.
7. Erika Dreifus, this volume, "A Special Kind of Kinship: On Being a '3G' Writer," 2.
8. Daniel Mendelsohn, *The Lost: A Search for Six of Six Million* (New York: HarperCollins, 2006), 450. For a lengthy discussion of Mendelsohn's memoir, see chapter 4, "Storytelling, Photography, and Mourning in Daniel Mendelsohn's *The Lost*," by Paule Lévy, in this collection.
9. Antopol, "My Grandmother Tells Me This Story," 84.
10. Mendelsohn, *The Lost: A Search for Six of Six Million*, 452.
11. Julie Orringer, *The Invisible Bridge* (New York: Alfred A. Knopf, 2010), 597.
12. Orringer, *The Invisible Bridge*, 596.
13. Orringer, *The Invisible Bridge*, 597.
14. Geoffrey H. Hartman, *The Longest Shadow: In the Aftermath of the Holocaust* (Bloomington: Indiana University Press, 1996), 133.
15. Alan Astro, this volume, "Avatars of Third-Generation Holocaust Narrative in French and Spanish," 125.
16. Avinoam Patt, this volume, "A Visible Bridge: Contemporary Jewish Fiction and Literary Memorials to the Shoah," 54, endnote 2.
17. Gary Weissman, this volume, "Against Generational Thinking in Holocaust Studies," 165.
18. Esther Jilovsky, Jordana Silverstein, and David Slucki, eds., *In the Shadows of Memory: The Holocaust and the Third Generation* (London: Vallentine Mitchell, 2016), 5.
19. Malena Chinski, this volume, "The 'Generation without Grandparents': Witnesses and Companions to an Unfinished Search," 89.

20. Dreifus, "A Special Kind of Kinship," 5.
21. Lévy, "Storytelling, Photography, and Mourning," 57.
22. Mendelsohn, *The Lost*, 88.
23. Mendelsohn, *The Lost*, 433.
24. Chinski, "The 'Generation without Grandparents,'" 90, 92, 99.
25. Astro, "Avatars of Third-Generation Holocaust Narrative," 124.
26. Jessica Lang, this volume, "Measure for Measure: Narrative and Numbers in Holocaust Textual Memorials," 144.
27. Patt, "A Visible Bridge," 43.
28. Henri Raczymow, this volume, "Simon and Mania," 197.
29. Raczymow, "Simon and Mania," 197.
30. Raczymow, "Simon and Mania," 197.
31. Lévy, "Storytelling, Photography, and Mourning," 61.
32. Patt, "A Visible Bridge," 44, 50.
33. Lang, "Measure for Measure," 133.
34. Lang, "Measure for Measure," 144.
35. Dreifus, "A Special Kind of Kinship," 13–14.
36. Victoria Aarons, this volume, "Memory's Afterimage: Post-Holocaust Writing and the Third Generation," 20.
37. Aarons, "Memory's Afterimage," 20.
38. Patt, "A Visible Bridge," 53.
39. Lévy, "Storytelling, Photography, and Mourning," 57.
40. Lévy, "Storytelling, Photography, and Mourning," 63.
41. Chinski, "The 'Generation without Grandparents,'" 100.
42. Astro, "Avatars of Third-Generation Holocaust Narrative," 109.
43. Astro, "Avatars of Third-Generation Holocaust Narrative," 117.
44. Lang, "Measure for Measure," 132.
45. Weissman, "Against Generational Thinking," 163.

Chapter One

A Special Kind of Kinship

On Being a "3G" Writer

Erika Dreifus

I will commence with a confession: This essay has proved to be far more difficult to write than I anticipated when I accepted the editor's invitation to join the contributor roster. We have experienced innumerable fits and starts, this chapter and me. Countless dead ends. Finally, I expected that even if I managed to meet the requisite word count, and if the words managed to make it past editorial review, readers would ultimately find themselves paraphrasing the words of the late Admiral James Stockdale from that memorable 1992 vice-presidential debate: "Who is Erika Dreifus? Why is she here in this volume?"[1]

I'm only half-joking, and it might be useful to open with some answers to those questions.

Let's begin with the first—*Who am I?*—because the response offers some vital background. On my father's side, I am the elder granddaughter of two German Jews who fled their native country in the late 1930s. In their early twenties at the time, my paternal grandparents met and married in New York; my father, their only child, was born in Iowa about six months before the end of the war in Europe. (More about that shortly.) But the little family soon returned to New York, where, in due course, my father met my mother. I was born in 1969, when, at the vast ages of twenty-three (Mom) and twenty-four (Dad), my parents had been married almost three years. For my first nine years, which were spent in south Brooklyn, my father's parents were ever-present; even after my parents and younger sister and I moved to a New Jersey suburb, we rarely went more than a day without a phone call or a week

1

without a visit. My father's parents outlived my mother's; his mother was our last surviving grandparent, passing away at the age of 87 in early 2002.[2]

So much for the bare outlines of the most relevant personal history. Now, let's talk professional background. If you peruse the biographies of this volume's other contributors, you'll find an impressive array of scholars and teachers, people who have trained in the art of literary analysis and spent many years devoted to the study of Holocaust representation.

And then you find me. And the next question: *Why am I here?*

I haven't had a straightforward academic career (or, to be perfectly frank, any discernible, laddered career). I hold a PhD in history (earned in 1999; dissertation title: "Double Games and Golden Prisons: Vichy, Washington, and 'Diplomatic Internment' During World War II"); *and* an MFA in creative writing (earned in 2003; fiction focus). I cobbled together a professional existence as a lecturer (in French history), an instructor (in writing), and a freelance writer for a number of years while I waited for My Great American Post-Holocaust Novel to sell (spoiler alert—it never did). In 2007, I returned to a stable, benefits-awarding office job; I remained there until 2014, when I left for a job in a publishing start-up. And that is my primary employment as I type these words.

But along that odd road, I've crossed paths with several of this volume's contributors. For many years, my academic background gave me the access and tools to participate at least on the margins of scholarly exchange, even if I grew increasingly distant from French-history circles and drew ever-closer to Jewish studies, creative writing, publishing, and venues where those might overlap. Meantime, and helped immeasurably by the advent of the Internet and social media, I became part of a more fluid community of readers and writers, often finding myself especially "at home" within subgroups devoted to literature and writing of specifically Jewish interest.

Then, although my novel never sold, a tiny press brought forth a collection of my short stories. Published in 2011, *Quiet Americans* is my most official contribution to the growing cluster of "Third-Generation Holocaust Narratives," one manifestation of "the intergenerational transmission of memory, longing, and loss" at the heart of this book's focus. And those intertwined subjects—writings by members of the so-called Third Generation (3G) of grandchildren and the ways in which those writings transmit a past that is both personal/familial and world-historical—have interested me for a long time, especially as life and social media have slowly but steadily connected me with other "3G writers" in ways that have enhanced a sense of kinship.

IN THE BEGINNING: A "COMMUNITY" OF ONE

It was about fifteen years ago—back when I was still teaching French history at Harvard and simultaneously was a student, via distance-learning, in an MFA program in creative writing—that a Call for Papers caught my attention. For a conference to be held at the Imperial War Museum in London titled "Beyond Camps and Forced Labour," organizers sought work reflecting (what was then) current research on "survivors of Nazi persecution."[3] This seemed to offer a valuable opportunity for me to begin to synthesize some early ideas and theories generated by my own experience thinking and writing from the perspective of a "3G." I submitted a proposal and attended the conference; my presentation was prepared for publication and included with the conference proceedings under the title of "Ever After? History, Healing, and 'Holocaust Fiction' in the Third Generation."[4]

In that essay, I essentially offered myself and my family as an unofficial case study of grandparents' experience transmitted to their grandchild and then further transformed into fictional narrative. I opened with some statistics about U.S. military service during the Second World War, including statistics about noncitizen servicemen and Jewish servicemen. I noted that my paternal grandfather belonged to both groups. And I wrote:

> The story of Pfc Sam S. Dreifus is one he never articulated, the story of a Jewish refugee from Nazi Germany who was already wearing his U.S. Army uniform by the time he sat for the photograph that appears on his Certificate of Naturalization . . . who fled his home country in 1937 and was drafted into his adopted one six years later. The story of a baker, assigned not to the European or Pacific fronts, but to domestic battle in the kitchens of the prisoner-of-war camp in Clarinda, Iowa, where Pfc Dreifus supervised Germans captured at Normany while he and his wife awaited the birth of their first child.

I continued:

> It is a story that I, with the historian's tools and the creative writer's craft, have extracted from primary documents and secondary sources, and woven into fact-based fiction. It is one of my many war and Holocaust-related writings— works that include an article on my re-acquisition of German citizenship, and a novel manuscript that developed from archival documents I found while searching for a dissertation topic, and book reviews. These writings seem to expand and deepen with every paper proposal and short story sketch. This story, set in Clarinda, is titled "*Lebensraum,*" one in a collection. . . .[5]

I observed that across my fictional writings, whether I had created characters who were refugees who left Europe "in time," survivors who did not, or their children and grandchildren, I had discerned ways in which these characters "still search for psychic and physical territory, still don't feel safe, still cannot fully 'live' their lives":

> Lots of flashbacks. Lots of pain. Freud might identify quite a bit of "remembering and repeating" in my pages. He might even agree with my hypothesis: The historical research and the creative writing, the (re)constructing of the past in my own excruciatingly informed ways, help me in the process of "working through."[6]

Acknowledging that as a privileged young American growing up in the 1970s and 1980s I'd had a lot less to "work through" than had my refugee grandparents, I went on to chronicle an array of Holocaust-related anxieties that had characterized my childhood before noting a milestone: the discovery of Israeli psychologist Dan Bar-On's *Fear and Hope: Three Generations of the Holocaust*, published in English in 1995, which made me realize "that mine were not the only third-generation nightmares." As I wrote for the conference paper, not until encountering Bar-On's book "did I begin to reflect seriously on the possibility of a heritage handed to the third generation that required healing. Working through."[7]

But *Fear and Hope* was an exception. At the dawn of the twenty-first century, I was able to locate painfully little research or writing on the third generation. And I had yet to find those others who were also writing stories and novels infused by their grandparents' histories under Nazism and the Holocaust. When I revisited my own family's timeline, I realized that my birthdate and the rest of the history—my grandparents' emigrations as young adults in the late 1930s and my father's birth in the United States toward the end of Second World War—meant that I was among the "elders" of this third generation.

But I sensed that it was a matter of time. The material would come.[8] In fact, in some languages, it was already there.

A TRANSITIONAL PHASE

I wish that I could recall how, when, and where I discovered the work of Amir Gutfreund. My personal archive shows only that a review-essay in which I discussed his stunning novel *Our Holocaust* was published in 2006, the same year that the novel—in a translation by Jessica Cohen—was published by the Toby Press. But Hebrew readers had had access to the book since 2001, when it was published, to acclaim, as *Shoah Shelanu*.[9]

When I look back *now* on that review-essay of mine, I notice something: It is a transitional piece, essentially a stop between the paper-essay that I'd prepared for the London conference and subsequent publication and another significant piece that was yet to come. And I wrote it just as I was beginning to sense the emergence of an actual, vocal third generation, a group for whom I was longing in the first essay and would come to know (and write about) much more extensively in the future.

It begins with a discussion of a new edition of Elie Wiesel's *Night* (which likely needs no further explanation among this readership). It continues with an analysis of *What Time and Sadness Spared: Mother and Son Confront the Holocaust*, a sort of dual memoir by a survivor and her son (Roma Nutkiewicz Ben-Atar and Doron Ben-Atar), which extends into the third generation when the son explains the role his niece played in encouraging her grandmother to share her memories.

And it concludes with Gutfreund's book, which I introduced as follows:

> Time passes. Children grow up. Grandchildren arrive; even without knowing their grandparents' stories they may be, as Doron Ben-Atar tells us his own children were, "haunted" by that past. Like Ben-Atar's niece, who "refused to be satisfied with the familiar family narrative and forced [Ben-Atar's mother] to delve deeply into her past," the descendants want to know what happened. The survivor ages. Soon, she knows she will not be alive to tell her tale.
>
> If Roma Ben-Atar was initially reluctant to share her story, so, too, is Grandpa Yosef, one of the central characters in [*Our Holocaust*]. And if Doron Ben-Atar and his niece played key roles in peeling away the layers of their mother/grandmother's story, the first-person Israeli narrator of *Our Holocaust* proves similarly committed to learning his elders' stories and works at least as hard to discover them.[10]

There is a way in which *Our Holocaust* reads like a memoir, in part because it's narrated in the first-person voice, in part because the narrator shares his author's first name and many biographical details. The novel's brief afterword explains which characters are based on actual individuals—including members of the author's extended family—and which are "purely invented."[11] Gutfreund, who was born in Haifa in 1963, is often described as a child of Holocaust survivors, but just as Narrator Amir—son of a mother who was two years old when the war began in 1939, and a father who was then nine—describes his own family, the reader realizes that the generational categories and boundaries aren't quite so clear. That's because, in the character's words, the parents were

> young enough to recover from the Holocaust and eventually start a normal family. We children were not the "second generation" of the Holocaust—we were the second-and-a-half generation. That slight shift, just half a rung on the generational ladder, gave us a simpler, healthier life, with parents who smiled, who found it easy to love, to hug, to talk with us. But beneath the surface was an enchanted tapestry of musts and must-nots. Questions you didn't ask Mom, questions you didn't ask Dad.[12]

Most of all, in the world of *Our Holocaust*, there were questions you didn't ask the "grandparents," whether they were your biological, blood grandparents, or the ones made so by the "Law of Compression" that drafted older people, distant relatives, to fill the role. And grandparent-characters fill this book from the very first page, which begins, in fact, with the word "Grandpa." Amir (Author and Narrator) may not technically be a member of the third generation, but as I devoured the novel the role of survivor grandparents in the protagonist's life and emotional landscape seemed unlike virtually anything I'd seen depicted before.

For Amir, "the Shoah was a dual entity: there was the one declaimed at school ceremonies with torches and handmade black placards and the six million, and there was its twin, the familial one, the one that had not enlisted six million into its ranks but contained instead a vivid cast of characters."[13] The characters in *Our Holocaust* may be vivid; for the reader, they can also be overwhelming in sheer numbers, at least at first. But soon enough, clear voices emerge, especially that of Grandpa Yosef, one of the adopted grandfathers. He, whose "Holocaust trail was the longest and most intricate of all the survivors we knew," dispenses sage counsel and kindness throughout the extended family and his own Haifa neighborhood, and exerts a powerful influence on young Amir and his frequent childhood companion, Effi.[14]

Because Grandpa Yosef believes that children should not be inflicted with horrific tales from their elders' past, certainly not until they are Old Enough, Amir and Effi must work very hard to obtain this information. True, their elders cannot always contain themselves. And sometimes there's a subtle, dark humor at work in the prose:

> We liked to listen to them, although in our presence (by Grandpa Yosef's order) they did not delve too deeply into the Shoah itself. We sat at their feet, an inner ring inside the circle of tea-drinkers, enjoying a wonderful childhood in the shadow of their terrors. When Grandpa Lolek was not around they could compare stories, rate their suffering, measure their sorrow. And they could quarrel, declaring things like, "*Nu*, you, let's see you in Stutthof? Let's see you survive just two days there. . . . " As if the possibility existed—a simple matter of addressing the package correctly, and the man would be sent off to Stutthof for two days.[15]

For Amir, becoming Old Enough is "a purpose, a mission. Every year they told us stories about the war. Every year, the appropriate dose of horror. In order to climb up the rungs of horror we had to wait, restrained, until we were Old Enough. In the meantime, don't ask why. Food is Not Thrown Out."[16]

Much of the book is devoted to how Amir constructs this past before he is Old Enough. ("We tried. We harassed old people.") One summer, he and Effi engage in a gruesome game. "We played Buchenwald. We fasted and did not drink. We licked water from leaking taps, slipped behind the dining hall, stole old hunks of cheese and ate with trembling hands. We even sucked on straw, like Littman had done when he had escaped."[17]

And then the book shifts into recounting how Amir constructs this past when, as a young husband and father, he is, at long last, Old Enough. When Grandpa Yosef, perhaps sensing some of the same change of heart that we know has moved other survivors to begin to speak and to write, finally shares his whole Holocaust story. When Amir's father, too, is finally convinced to recount his early experience. When Amir collaborates with another survivor, Attorney Perl, and investigates the perpetrators more closely—and learns a terrible secret truth about his own wife's grandfather.

In a sense, one message the novel left me with was that grandchildren-authors were, at long last, becoming Old Enough. That we were, indeed, beginning to tell our stories. And that we would find each other very, very soon.

DISCERNING A COHORT, FINDING SOME "KIN"

Five years after that review-essay, much more had changed. On many levels. I see the shifts clearly when I revisit another piece of my writing: an essay titled "Looking Backward: Third-Generation Fiction Writers and the Holocaust," published online at *Fiction Writers Review* at the end of April 2011.[18]

My own work and its background was very much an interest—this was the year that my own book was published, after all. But the essay provided an opportunity for me to collect, in one place, my thoughts about *other* books, mainly novels, by writers roughly my age who—whether in front matter, acknowledgments, author bios, or easily accessed interviews—had spoken openly about their novels' roots in their grandparents' histories. Writers such as Natasha Solomons (*Mr. Rosenblum Dreams in English*) and Alison Pick (*Far to Go*). And perhaps above all, in that essay, the writer Julie Orringer and her debut novel *The Invisible Bridge*.

I couldn't exactly psychoanalyze these writers. I hadn't met them, and apart from an odd Twitter mention here and there, I had no established connections with them at that time. I didn't know the extent to which they'd sensed themselves the inheritors of Holocaust-related anxieties or traumas. Nonetheless, I sensed a kinship with them. It was a connection forged by our common pursuit: writing (largely historical) stories about the past, about the worlds our grandparents had come from and experienced, from a decidedly "close" third-person perspective.

I was impressed particularly with one exchange involving Orringer, in which the author responded to the question, "Why did you choose the Holocaust as the subject of your first novel?"

> What drew me to the story was hearing about my grandfather's experiences when he was younger. Despite the fact that I grew up in a Hungarian family, I just didn't know much about what had happened to Hungarian Jews during the war. Like a lot of families with Holocaust survivors, those years just weren't discussed in my family. My grandparents certainly alluded to them and I heard bits and pieces about their survival, but I didn't really have a sense of the whole picture because my grandparents didn't talk about it. Once I started asking them questions about what had happened, they really wanted to tell their story. They wanted the novel to be written. But initially, I didn't think I was going to write a book about the Holocaust. I wanted to write about a young man who moved to Paris who tries to study architecture and loses his scholarship, which is what happened to my grandfather. I thought his life was so fascinating and I wanted to learn everything I could about how he got by and what he studied and how he managed to live. That was the initial impetus for the book. Of course I knew that there was the weight of history behind the beginnings of that story. Because I'm a fiction writer, once I started telling that story, the experiences of my characters became different from those of my grandfather. That was when I really had to start thinking about how the war was going to affect my characters and change the course of their lives.[19]

In this response, Orringer emphasizes the fictional qualities of her narrative, including a key point about her characters' differentiation from their familial models. To be sure, the questions of an author's motivation and choice to write a fictional rather than nonfictional narrative arise when a book is "about" a subject other than the Holocaust. (For that matter, I often think back to a memorable week in my low-residency MFA program in creative writing, when it seemed that virtually every evening's faculty reading featured grandparent-related content—and none of the grandparents in question had been Jews in Nazi Europe.) But it is often especially pressing when it comes to Holocaust-related stories. It has certainly been asked of me.

In some ways, I suspect that my academic training as an historian actually turned me away from writing a family memoir or other nonfiction book. Writing fiction allowed me freedoms that don't (or shouldn't) exist in historical books. I could fuse and streamline experiences from the stories of different relatives into one character's trajectory; I could imagine emotional lives without qualifications or repeatedly inserting myself, decades post-facto, as Grand Theorizer; I could take some true accounts that had been shared with me—such as snippets about my grandparents' first trip back to Europe during the summer of 1972—even "further," dramatically, than I knew them to have gone in fact.[20]

Not surprisingly, then, I was also impressed by Orringer's response to the question "What do you think fiction can tell us about the Holocaust that nonfiction can't?"

> I would like to answer the question without the qualifier of "Holocaust." The reason I chose to write the book as a novel rather than as a book about my grandfather's experience is that fiction has the ability more than any other art form to really place the reader inside the character's experience. E. M. Forster writes beautifully about this in his book, *Aspects of the Novel* in which he writes that fiction is unique among other forms in its ability to inhabit the human psyche and do to [sic] so from within, instead of in a more distant way. I wanted to suggest something of what it would be like to be a young man, building a life at that time, falling in love, studying architecture, making close friendships, and then to have all that fall apart when historical circumstances got in the way. It would certainly be possible to do something similar in non-fiction, but when we read a piece of historical non-fiction, there's a sense of foreknowledge of what comes later. In this case, even though the reader knows what comes later, the character doesn't know and he's able to inhabit a more innocent space then [sic] I would have been able to communicate otherwise.[21]

To be sure, a lot of "outside" work is required to successfully place a reader "inside" a fictional character's experience, and Orringer has also addressed the history and historical research that informed her work. Indeed, the cohort of 3G writers would appear to constitute a robust subset of what Mark Shechner, Thane Rosenbaum, and Victoria Aarons identified—also back in 2011—as "The New Jewish Literature."

Writing from their perch as veteran judges of the prestigious Edward Lewis Wallant award, Shechner, Rosenbaum, and Aarons declared: "At no time before have Jewish writers in America turned so uniformly to history for their fictions." In contrast with many of the most celebrated American Jewish writers who "located their stories in contemporary America," Orringer and others might be seen as an exemplars of "the Jewish voice turning outward after decades of inward reflection," as fictionists whose "settings and set pieces themselves have been taken out for a walk, a test drive, as if the Jewish literary voice now has an impressive passport and has gone truly global."[22] Again, this resonates with my personal sense of writerly development, because it is so clear to me that the travels in various European countries that inspired and edified my unpublished novel and a number of my short stories were essential to those works. (The mention of "impressive passport" also brings to mind the fact that my father, sister, and I all "reacquired" German citizenship and obtained German passports during the 1990s, a topic about which I have also written.[23])

But when these 3G writers did, indeed, "turn inward," presenting 3G characters—as Orringer did in the brief epilogue to her novel—I felt an even greater sense of kinship. As a "trained" fiction writer, I had, after all, been instructed in workshop after workshop that one should never assume a confluence between author and character. But I couldn't help myself. I assumed, for instance, that my sense of affective bond, identification, and connection extended not only to the Lévis' unnamed granddaughter, a fictional creation of Julie Orringer; I assumed that I shared something inchoate with Orringer herself. Especially when I read paragraphs like these:

> There were strands of darker stories. She didn't know how she'd heard them; she thought she must have absorbed them through her skin, like medicine or poison. Something about labor camps. Something about being made to eat newspapers. Something about a disease that came from lice. Even when she wasn't thinking about those half stories, they did their work in her mind. A few weeks ago she'd had a dream from which she'd woken shouting in fright. She and her parents had been standing in a cold black-walled room, wearing pajamas made of flour sacks. In a corner her grandmother knelt on the concrete floor, weeping. Her grandfather stood before them, too thin, unshaven. A German guard came out of the shadows and made him climb onto a raised conveyor belt, something like the luggage carousel at the airport. The guard put cuffs around his ankles and wrists, then stepped to a wooden lever beside the conveyor belt and pushed it forward. A meshing of gears, a grinding of iron teeth. The belt began to move. Her grandfather rounded a corner and disappeared into a rectangle of light, from beyond which came a deafening clap that meant he was dead.
> That was when she'd shouted herself awake.[24]

I don't know if Julie Orringer herself experienced that nightmare. But for me, the sense of kinship and identification with this unnamed granddaughter-character remained powerful nonetheless, and it echoes whenever I learn that an author's writing is grounded, in some way, in his or her third-generation inheritance.[25]

At the time, it was easy to be lulled into the sense that all of my fellow 3G writers who were writing fiction had taken primarily "historical" approaches in which the grandchild as character and/or narrator might be relegated to an epilogue or a single story. But about a year after my *Fiction Writers Review* essay was published, I discovered the work of another grandchild-writer whose style more closely resembled that of *Our Holocaust*, featuring a first-person grandchild-narrator.

Guatemalan-born Eduardo Halfon had been writing for several years in his native Spanish; it was not until 2012 that I learned of *The Polish Boxer*, a compilation of stories (marketed as a novel) that was the work of Halfon's collaboration with a number of translators. (*El boxeador polaco* had appeared already in 2008.)

Again, more or less from the outset, the personal/familial history behind the fiction was made explicit in extra-narrative materials. Here, however, I was advised as well to the narrative's quality as resembling more the approach of Amir Gutfreund than Julie Orringer. Noting that Halfon's protagonist was, like the author, "a Guatemalan writer and literature professor, with the same name and biography," *Publishers Weekly* advised in a pre-publication review that "we're in the murky half-light where fiction meets memoir meets memory and the impossibility thereof."[26]

Indeed, in an interview published shortly after *The Polish Boxer*'s British and American releases, Halfon (who immigrated to the United States as a child and speaks English fluently) was asked to explain its "origins" and replied: "A number on my grandfather's forearm was the beginning of *The Polish Boxer*: this one image in my head of growing up as a kid in Guatemala [Halfon was born in 1971], and looking at my grandfather's forearm, and him telling me it was his phone number."

The interviewer pressed on: "And how did you go from image to story?"

Halfon: "I guess that that image—of a Holocaust tattoo as his phone number—later became a conversation. One rainy afternoon, I was drinking whiskey with my grandfather when he told me the true story behind that number, behind those five green digits. A very brief story that had to do with Auschwitz, and a twenty-dollar gold coin, and a boxer, and the saving power of words. He spoke for hours that afternoon, about many things that had happened to him. But that story about a boxer instantly crept under my skin."[27]

Not all of the book's ten segments (I will continue to refer to them as "stories") relate to the titular Polish Boxer (whose importance, we learn, stems from his role in helping "Eduardo Halfon's" grandfather survive Auschwitz). Nor do they, in fact, relate directly to the grandfather himself. But even in stories that ostensibly focus elsewhere, the grandfather and his Holocaust history hover.

Attentive readers will catch one line in the story titled "Twaining," for example, when the professor-narrator considers the Polish origins of another participant whom he meets at a Mark Twain conference in North Carolina: "I thought of my grandfather and the bottle of whiskey we'd drunk together while he told me about Sachsenhausen and Auschwitz and the Polish boxer."[28] And in "White Smoke," set in a Guatemala bar, Narrator Halfon meets a couple of young Israelis, one of whom shares a surname with his mother, compelling the narrator to muse: "I started to think about the remote possibility that we were related, and I imagined a novel about two Polish siblings who thought their entire family had been exterminated but who all of a sudden find each other after sixty years apart, thanks to the grandchildren, a Guatemalan writer and an Israeli hippie, who meet by chance in a Scottish bar that isn't even Scottish in Antigua, Guatemala."[29]

Halfon (the Author) is quick to admit the centrality of the title story in the larger work: "That story is the centerpiece of the book. The Polish boxer himself—the character—is a figure that is barely present, or not present at all. Yet he is. He's like a specter, or like a breath that permeates the book. Something that you can't point to, that you can't really see, but that you can feel. And that's what my grandfather's story was to me. It was this huge story that was barely present."[30]

Or, as one critic has phrased it, "Halfon's curiosity about his grandfather's experience in a concentration camp burns through every chapter from the most subtle level to deep investigation. Halfon only knows that it was a Polish boxer who saved his grandfather, Oitze, in Auschwitz, but the details remain a mystery. Oitze only shows Halfon the most gruesome yet blurriest mental slides of Auschwitz. 'The claustrophobic image of the dark, damp, crowded cell stuffed with whispers' sets the tone for most of the novel. To Halfon, the idea of a boxer saving Oitze is a relic, like a phoenix rising from the ashes, and he holds tightly to the hopes that something or someone will come along to save him too."[31]

Maybe. It's not clear to me the extent to which Halfon (Author or Narrator) requires saving, the degree to which his childhood, like mine or that of the fictional Levis' granddaughter, included Holocaust-inspired nightmares. Asked in another interview whether writing this book was "freeing" for him, Halfon replied, "It wasn't an emotional trip for me. None of my books are. For me, they are not releases, or ways of coming to terms with things, or of understanding the world, or of feeling better about a situation. I never feel better after writing a book. I never feel as though I've come to understand something. I just keep writing. And writing, for me, is never an ending. I don't arrive. I keep going. I have to keep going."[32]

THE VIEW FROM HERE

And five years later—five years after the publication of *Quiet Americans* and my *Fiction Writers Review* essay—I find myself, in a sense, back where I started with that London conference paper. Writing about Holocaust fiction and the third generation. But I am also in a very different place. Books by Amir Gutfreund and Julie Orringer and Eduardo Halfon and so many others fill my shelves. I am "friends"—on Facebook and in real-life ("IRL," as the latter is abbreviated in discourse within the former)—with other 3G writers.

I am no longer alone.

There's so much more to say. In "big picture" issues, I've barely scratched the proverbial surface of "3G fiction," and said absolutely nothing about other ways in which grandchild-writers have turned to nonfiction, poetry, and documentary film in addressing their grandparents' experiences and/or their own navigation of that history. And as I've made clear, my ability to read only in English and French has also restricted my scope.

I've shared only a couple of examples and explanations of the connections between my own family history and my fiction. And I've surely neglected some writers and writings that others might have included. On the other hand, I can end this chapter alerting you to the work of two writers you are not likely to know just yet.

While I was working on this chapter, I received some very welcome news from my friend Rachel Hall: *Heirlooms*, her collection of linked short stories, had been selected by Marge Piercy as the latest manuscript to win G. S. Sharat Chandra Prize for Short Fiction; as such, the manuscript will be published by BkMk Press in the fall of 2016. I have had the privilege of reading this forthcoming collection, so I can predict with confidence that it augurs most favorably for anyone interested in fictional narratives about World War II and the Holocaust as rendered by descendants of those who endured it.

Like Amir Gutfreund, Rachel Hall might be more properly "categorized" as a part of the "second-and-a-half generation"; her Jewish mother was a French toddler when the Germans invaded France. But again, so many of the stories in *Heirlooms* train a narrative lens so intensely on the experiences of "the grandparents"—characters modeled on Hall's biological and adoptive grandparents—that I find it impossible not to consider her part of the 3G cohort.

Stylistically, the approach of *Heirlooms*, particularly in the book's first several stories, is Orringer-esque, with Hall painting a vivid historical portrait based on family history, research, and sheer artistry. Noting that her maternal family history of flight and loss has left her with few tangible "heirlooms," this author believes that in their absence, she "was given stories. In order to turn those stories into *Heirlooms*, I imagined and invented the missing pieces, filled in parts that had been omitted out of shame or modesty, or simply forgotten in the attempt to forge a new life. These stories are my way of remembering a past I didn't live through and an attempt to recover what was lost."[33]

And there are still others in this unusual but ever-widening circle whom you should know about, such as my friend Suzanne Reisman. When her novel manuscript, *This Eden Called Warsaw*, was longlisted for a literary award, she explained the work's genesis in her own graduate studies in creative writing, when she wrote about her grandfather, "a man with a mysterious past [whom] I loved dearly. He was the only person in his large religious family who survived the Holocaust, but he never spoke about them or his life before the war. I wanted to know who they (and he)—were."

To this end, Reisman "researched his community in the 1930s. I integrated this with the few genealogical details that were available, and filled in the blanks with my imagination. I will never know how close I am to their true lives. It is my deepest wish that I have honoured those who were lost—including my grandfather—with this novel."[34]

I can't be certain that Hall or Reisman speak here for all—or even most—of us whose grandparents' lives were so profoundly affected by Nazism and the Holocaust, and who have recorded, transmitted, and/or transformed this history in fiction. But I know this much: In their statements about their work, they are definitely not alone.

Equally, they make this 3G writer continue to feel less so.

NOTES

1. "Admiral Stockdale—1992 VP Debate—'Who Am I? Why Am I Here?,'" YouTube video, 1:17, posted by Educational Video Group, June 19, 2012, https://www.youtube.com/watch?v=T1w3FgB0Ohc.

2. Some might argue that I still don't quite "fit" the definition of a "grandchild of Holocaust survivors." As Melvin Jules Bukiet observed early in his 2002 anthology, the word "survivors" is "complicated": "We live in an age in which victimization carries a special weight and is therefore deliberately adopted. So who is a survivor? Obviously, anyone who spent any time in a German extermination, concentration, or labor camp qualifies. Also obviously, anyone in hiding for their lives in the woods in Poland or in an attic in Amsterdam qualifies. But what if you fled eastward, into Russia? Is there a line on the map at, say, the Volga River that, when crossed makes you a refugee rather than a survivor? I believe so." Bukiet acknowledges that "this leads to awkward distinctions," but ultimately decides, "for clarity, and solely for the purposes of this book . . . to include only writers with at least one surviving ancestor who spent at least one day between September 1, 1939, and May 8, 1945, under the flag of the twisted cross." I am sensitive to such thinking—and by nature scrupulous about accuracy. Therefore, I do not typically refer to my paternal grandparents as "Holocaust survivors"; I prefer the term "refugees from Nazism," which I feel more accurately describes their experience; I take a more capacious view of the entire "3G" concept than others might, believing that there are bonds and similarities—as well as differences—among grandchildren of those who fled from, survived, or were murdered during the Nazi era in Europe. See Bukiet, "A Note on Method and Category" for *Nothing Makes You Free: Writings by Descendants of Jewish Holocaust Survivors* (New York: W. W. Norton, 2002), 27–28.

3. Johannes Dieter-Steinert to H-Museum, August 8, 2011, http://bit.ly/1R9vhxi.

4. Erika Dreifus, "Ever After? History, Healing, and 'Holocaust Fiction' in the Third Generation," in *Beyond Camps and Forced Labour: Current International Research on Survivors of Nazi Persecution,* edited by Johannes-Dieter Steiner and Inge Weber-Newth (Osnabrück: Secolo Verlag, 2005), 524–30. ISBN 3–929979–73-X. (Revised version of paper presented at "Beyond Camps and Forced Labour" conference at the Imperial War Museum, London, 29–31 January 2003.)

5. Dreifus, 524. See also Erika Dreifus, "Lebensraum," in *Quiet Americans: Stories* (Boston: Last Light Studio, 2011), 61–80. "*Lebensraum*" is the only story of the seven in the *Quiet Americans* collection that I had begun to write prior to my grandmother's death. For what turned out to be her final Hanukkah, I sent her a large-print version of the first draft. My normally stoic grandmother telephoned me in tears after reading it: "You've been listening to me!" she said. Also, as I'd suspected she might, she appreciated that, in fiction, I'd done something she was unable to do in life. For in reality, my infant father had been named for my grandfather's late father (who, as mentioned in the story, had indeed "died of diabetes"). But because my grandparents could not agree on the second name—my grandfather wanted to honor his supervising officer; my grandmother wished to use the name of her favorite uncle, who had been killed at Dachau—they'd compromised by choosing something else entirely, a name that frankly did not mean much to either of them. The fictional baby, however, was also named for his mother's father, who had "died of Dachau." My grandmother indeed caught it. Through still more tears, she said, "And you named the baby for Uncle Michael!"

6. Dreifus, "Ever After?" 525.

7. Dreifus, "Ever After?" 525–26.

8. Astute readers may realize that April 2002 brought the publication of Jonathan Safran Foer's *Everything Is Illuminated*. I was slow to perceive/approach the book—and then, frankly, put off by its opening pages. For months as I worked on this essay, I renewed and re-renewed a

library copy of the novel, determined to plow through it at long last. But, as my deadline grew ever-nearer, the book remained unread. I realize that this is a significant omission, and I do hope to remedy it someday.

9. I cannot write another word without noting that it was during the months I was drafting this essay that I began work at my desk one morning only to discover the terribly sad news from Israel that Amir Gutfreund had passed away. It may sound melodramatic to say that I gasped and whispered, "Oh, no," as I discovered the information online. He was fifty-two years old. As for the review-essay, its citation is as follows: Erika Dreifus, "From Generation to Generation: Writings by Holocaust Survivors and Their Descendents [sic]," *The Chattahoochee Review* 26.4 (Fall 2006): 134–40.

10. Dreifus, "From Generation to Generation," 138.

11. Amir Gutfreund, afterword to *Our Holocaust*, trans. Jessica Cohen (New Milford, CT: The Toby Press, 2006), 406.

12. Amir Gutfreund, *Our Holocaust*, trans. Jessica Cohen (New Milford, CT: The Toby Press, 2006), 49.

13. Gutfreund, *Our Holocaust*, 49–50.

14. Gutfreund, *Our Holocaust*, 21.

15. Gutfreund, *Our Holocaust*, 32.

16. Gutfreund, *Our Holocaust*, 48.

17. Gutfreund, *Our Holocaust*, 94.

18. Erika Dreifus, "Looking Backward: Third-Generation Fiction Writers and the Holocaust," *Fiction Writers Review*, April 28, 2011, accessed February 6, 2016, http://fictionwritersreview.com/essay/looking-backward-third-generation-fiction-writers-and-the-holocaust/.

19. "People of the Book: Interview with Julie Orringer," Momentmag.com, accessed February 6, 2016, http://www.momentmag.com/people-of-the-book-interview-with-julie-orringer/.

20. An example: As much as "Homecomings," one of the stories in *Quiet Americans*, relies on information about my grandparents' 1972 European trip as shared with me in later years, including their very real refusal to stay more than a few daylight hours in Germany and my grandmother's uncharacteristically emotional reaction upon seeing her family's apartment building again, their trip did not coincide with the terrorist attack on Israeli athletes at the Munich Olympics; that is something that, as a fiction writer, I was able to bring into the story. In my view, as an historian-writer, and as a Jew, what happened at Munich is at least as essential to the story—and obviously just as true—as the real-life snippets from my grandparents' trip. See "Homecomings," in Dreifus, *Quiet Americans*, 81–97.

21. Orringer, quoted in "People of the Book."

22. Mark Shechner, Victoria Aarons, and Thane Rosenbaum, "The New Jewish Literature," *Zeek*, April 1, 2011, accessed February 6, 2016, http://zeek.forward.com/articles/117238/.

23. Erika Dreifus, "Passport from the Past," *Boston Sunday Globe*, August 24, 1997: D1+. For a similar account from another 3G, see Michal Lemberger, "German Again," Slate.com, March 6, 2012, accessed February 10, 2016, http://www.slate.com/articles/news_and_politics/jurisprudence/2012/03/an_american_jew_becomes_a_german_citizen_.html.

24. Julie Orringer, *The Invisible Bridge* (New York: Knopf, 2010), 756–57.

25. It seems worth noting here another observation from the essay by Shechner, Aarons, and Rosenbaum: "[E]ven though so many of [the new] writers still can't seem to break free of the gravitational pull of the Shoah, the fictional characters they create live in a post-Shoah world, seek to examine the legacy, but don't present the same kind of damage that we saw" in the characters who populated earlier fiction.

26. "The Polish Boxer," *Publishers Weekly*, accessed February 6, 2016, http://www.publishersweekly.com/978-1-934137-53-6.

27. "Origin Stories: Dwyer Murphy interviews Eduardo Halfon," *Guernica*, April 15, 2013, accessed February 6, 2016, https://www.guernicamag.com/interviews/origin-stories/.

28. Eduardo Halfon, *The Polish Boxer*, trans. Daniel Hahn et al. (London: Pushkin Press, 2012), 43.

29. Halfon, *The Polish Boxer*, 71–72.

30. Joshua Barnes, "No Borders: An Interview with Eduardo Halfon," *Sampsonia Way*, December 10, 2012, accessed February 6, 2016, http://www.sampsoniaway.org/literary-voices/2012/12/10/no-borders-an-interview-with-eduardo-halfon/.

31. Julie Morse, "'The Polish Boxer,' by Eduardo Halfon," *The Rumpus*, October 11, 2012, accessed February 6, 2016, http://therumpus.net/2012/10/the-polish-boxer-by-eduardo-halfon/.

32. Halfon, quoted in Barnes. A postscript: Where the struggle seems to have been personal for Halfon, so far as I can discern, is in the storytelling process itself. We get hints about this in *The Polish Boxer*'s penultimate story, "A Speech at Póvoa," in which the narrator essentially distills a number of nagging issues about literature and reality, fact and fiction, to their core.

33. Rachel Hall, e-mail message to author, November 22, 2015.

34. Suzanne Reisman, "On Being Longlisted," BathNovelAward.co.uk, accessed February 6, 2015, http://bathnovelaward.co.uk/2015/06/16/on-being-longlisted-by-tanya-atapattu-suzanne-reisman/.

Chapter Two

Memory's Afterimage

Post-Holocaust Writing and the Third Generation

Victoria Aarons

In *Futurity: Contemporary Literature and the Quest for the Past*, Amir Eshel describes "the predicament of our age" as "a time overshadowed by a sense that the future, that reliable horizon, might be forever lost."[1] Such anxiety about a possible future predicated on the past is a response to the events and terrors of our age: persecution, tyranny, subjugation, war, genocide, and environmental catastrophe. The patterns of predation and victimization that have come to characterize late-modernity would seem to limit the open destiny of life promised by liberal democracy and its possibilities for a future not mortgaged to the devastations and pathologies of the past. As Eshel suggests, ours is a history that threatens to eclipse the future, an impermeable condition rather than a promise of new prospects. Late-modernity is thus burdened by the pathologies of the past, and we find ourselves faced with, as Andreas Huyssen suggests, in *Present Pasts: Urban Palimpsests and the Politics of Memory*, "a fundamental crisis in our imagination of alternative futures."[2] The weight of the past constricts our understanding of our world, the dimensions of the future reduced to a reiterative playing out of and subjugation to the defining events of our time. As a character in one of Thane Rosenbaum's novels cautions, "Some . . . histories are so big, the future can't overshadow the past."[3]

The anxieties of our present condition are a result of a persistent apprehension not only that history will repeat itself by being denied or forgotten, but that the brutalities of the past will frame and suspend the future. The defining shape of the past constricts not only forward movement, but also the opportunity to envision a future untarnished and un-delimited by the history from which we have, exhaustively and apprehensively, emerged. The effect is a collectively psychic one. Our world, Eshel suggests, becomes reduced by fear and by an oppressive sense of inevitability, a prevailing sense of dread that the future can only repeat the savagery of the past. Thus, like Lot's wife, we cannot help but look back, both drawn to and arrested by the influence of that which we most desire to flee. The way in which the sculpting events of our time "function in our collective consciousness," Eshel suggests, is analogous to "the working of trauma in the psyche of individuals," creating a kind of collective anxiety that shapes the conditions of our lives.[4] We perceive the world in which we live as shadowed by an afterimage of memory, an image of an event or a series of events that continue to appear in our vision long after their initial occurrence. The future threatens to become a return to the same history. The disposition of history might be thought of as a metaphorical anaphora, literally a "carrying back" to those axial moments of traumatic origin. It is this restrictive burden of history, Eshel explains, "the sense of a world deprived of a future," that much contemporary literature, in its elastic reimagining of the past, hopes to resist.[5] We find such an impulse in the literature—fiction as well as memoirs—of third-generation Holocaust writers who approach the subject of the Holocaust from a position of looking to the past as a means of constructing a future that is not bound to that defining history.

Writing against the constraining influence of the past, contemporary writers, in navigating a consciousness of past trauma, contest not the reality of those historical events themselves, but the destined inevitability of arrested momentum, of a future demarcated and forever fixed by such traumatizing events. In writing in defiance of the atrocities of the past, contemporary literature opens up possibilities for hope—if not optimism, then faith in the making of alternate futures. This is not to say that history's failures—a very real history of catastrophe—should be dismissed, but rather that the defining events of history might be navigated and engaged in such a way as to serve as cautionary road maps crossing into, adjudicating, and arbitrating, a future. In other words, as Eshel proposes, "As contemporary literature engages modernity's man-made catastrophes, it also moves toward the future," and thus resists the pernicious pull of the past.[6] This forward movement—"futurity"—the opening of possibilities, the resistance to a claustrophobic shrinking of present conditions and a strangulation of a future overshadowed by the past, Eshel argues, is made possible in certain literary narratives "by expanding our vocabularies, by probing the human ability to act, and by prompting reflection and debate," by refiguring the language and thus the landscape, not only of past events, but of discourse about them.[7] No longer a harbinger of the future, memory's afterimage, the haunting images of our time, exists parallel to our collective consciousness as we reconstruct a future. Futurity is thus, by necessity and for reasons of accountability, "tied to questions of liability and responsibility, to attentiveness to one's own lingering pains and to the sorrows and agonies of others. Futurity marks literature's ability to raise, via engagement with the past, political and ethical dilemmas crucial for the human future. . . . By engaging such circumstances, they point to what may prevent our world from closing in on us."[8]

Rather than running in fear from the past, such literary narratives take on history, that is, arbitrate, reckon with, and pass judgment on that history, all the while holding on to what is valuable and cautionary in its memory. Writing against adversity thus opens up possibilities for hope. As novelist David Grossman puts it, in writing "we feel the world in flux, elastic, full of possibilities—unfrozen. . . . I feel the many possibilities that exist in every human situation, and I feel my capacity to choose among them."[9] Here, the ability to choose leads not to a revisionist retelling of history, but an act of defiance against the very language that defines that story and that hems in our thinking about it. As Svetlana Boym proposes, in *The Future of Nostalgia*, an imaginative return to the past "can be retrospective but also prospective."[10] That is, a creative reimagining of past events can both look ahead and propose alternative possibilities for a future, a future in which one is held accountable to the past and can also be freed to move beyond it.

Such efforts to negotiate and reevaluate past events are not merely compensatory, for there is no imagined recompense for the legislated barbarity of our times. Rather, futurity—the potential for openness and realignment—requires a kind of dual vision: one that looks back as it moves forward. The questions raised by such claims of futurity, of course, are complicated: How can literature—narratives that look back to the events of the past—move us into a more open, fluid, unconstrained, and hopeful future without erasure, that is, without denial and a deliberate abandonment of the memory of those who suffered? How, in other words, can narratives that hope to return to, reinvent, and redefine such events for a contemporary era remain vigilant and faithful to the realities of the past? How might a conscious remembering of events, a matter of, as Eshel suggests, "revisiting some of the darkest moments of modernity," propel us forward and "make us aware of our own role in the writing of our lives," all the while not betraying those whose lives were forever eroded and destroyed by those past events that threaten to overshadow future lives?[11] How might the remembrance of suffering and the obligation to pass on the memory of the past to future generations create the conditions for openness, for imagined worlds that do not "close in . . . not grow smaller," but rather open up, enlarge, and create opportunities for alternate scenarios?[12] Futurity requires us to participate, not only in a reckoning of the past, but also in our responsibility to the future. The ethical acts suggested by the concept of futurity become, in this way of thinking, a matter of "making sense of what has occurred while imagining whom we may become."[13]

Such attempts to revisit, to re-describe, and thus reframe those "darkest moments of modernity," I would propose, characterize the literature of third-generation Holocaust writers, whose attempts both to memorialize and to fight against the debilitating specter of the past shapes their writing, especially those novels, short stories, quasi-historical fictions, and memoirs that return to the sites—both physical and psychic—of the Nazi genocide. In resisting but also engaging responsibly in a reinvention and reckoning of the events of the Holocaust, contemporary writers resist the pull of closure, of remaining encased in the stranglehold of history, all the while paying homage to the past in ways that invite the participation of the reader, as Grossman has described, "in the direction of what is open, future, possible."[14] The current literature of the third generation—the grandchildren of Holocaust survivors as well as those who engage in a third-generation perspective—is deeply invested in a return to the past, in preserving the memory of the Shoah, all the while opening future possibilities, writing in opposition to the Shoah existing as the singular marker of Jewish history and identity and thus of a future forfeited, forever mortgaged to such loss. Such writers invoke loss, all the while reimagining—reasserting, re-inserting—that which was eradicated. Writers such as Daniel Mendelsohn, Nicole Krauss, Julie Orringer, Jonathan Safran Foer, Margot Singer, Erica Dreifus, Joseph Skibell, and other contemporary writers attempt to navigate and midrashically fill in the gaps of the fragmented narratives of the Holocaust. These third-generation writers create out of absence a deeply felt presence. It is, indeed, in such literature that, as Grossman suggests, "both the thing and the loss of it can co-exist."[15]

Third-generation literary attempts to represent the Holocaust emerge in narratives of return—both literal and fictional—stories that reconceive and reimagine, both spatially and temporally the places and times of the events of the Holocaust. Contemporary writers—those writing in the late twentieth-early twenty-first centuries—who carry the memory of the Holocaust into the present create a kind of contemporary midrash that extends the memory of the Shoah—the text of the experience of extreme suffering and loss as well as survival—without claiming authority over the experience or the memory of it. As Monica Osborne suggests, third-generation narratives are "about rescue and recovery—especially when things seem irretrievable."[16] Such writers traverse the past as a way of navigating the future. This is a generation for whom the Holocaust has "arrived" in many ways belatedly, a generation for whom memory comes mediated not only through the defended recollections of those remaining survivors but also through the interpreted and guarded "translations" of the second generation, the children of survivors, who grew up with those who experienced the events directly. While such transmission from direct witnessing to a generation once removed—"nonwitnesses," as Gary Weissman proposes—is not without its mediated intrusions, those who write from and "experience" such memories from a third-generation, all-the-more-distanced perspective, must negotiate and make coherent the fragments of stories—often competing or incomplete—from the interstices of memory.[17] Osborne puts it this way: "For third-generation writers . . . it is less about imagining that one knows or remembers what happened during the Holocaust than it is about struggling to piece together bits of information through exposure to documents and narrative fragments."[18] That is, third-generation Holocaust writers must negotiate a plethora of information stored in popular and cultural sites of memory all the while contending with aborted and truncated narratives, stories cut short, stories, as memoirist Daniel Mendelsohn fears, "lost."[19] Such memories are lost in large part, as Mendelsohn concedes, because of the failure to have asked questions of survivors before such knowledge is "gone forever," "information that people you once knew always had to give you, if only you'd asked. But by the time you think to ask, it's too late."[20] As Gerd Bayer suggests, "As time moves away from World War II, memory takes on a different quality as it becomes transformed from direct witnessing and the resulting testimonials to archival and mediated forms of remembering that carry the responsibility of firmly embedding the Holocaust in the cultural memory of later generations."[21] Memory, in this increasingly distanced context, becomes a matter of containing and making sense of the flashing series of images from a variety of sources and navigating increasing levels of abstraction: receding memories of survivors; documents, archival, and ancillary materials; faceless computations of numbers, dates, and places; a roll-call of names lost; an absence. Absence is a recurring trope in the contemporary literature that returns by way of reimagined memory to the events of the Holocaust. But for the third generation, the trope of absence exists alongside the trope of recovery, the struggle through the figures, textures, and imagined shapes and weight of language—albeit a wanting substitute for memory's acuity—to make coherent the fleeting events of the past.

The transformation of memory and the ways memory is received and processed—those "forms of remembering"—takes on newly shaped patterns of expression in third-generation narratives. A contemporary generation of writers who engage the Holocaust in the imagination move the experience of bearing the legacy of the Shoah well into the twenty-first century. I would propose that this body of literature does not constitute a new genre, but rather might be considered part of the evolving expression and memory of such events. Third-generation representation extends and broadens survivor and second-generation attempts at representation. While survivor writing might certainly be considered the more authentic—perhaps the only legitimate—form of witnessing, all are genuine expressions of remembered memory and testimony—if only in the imagination—of bearing witness and carrying the legacy, if not the direct memory, of the events of the Holocaust. They take their place in the line-up, the lineage, of writers whose attempts at ethical representation occupy a rightful place in the canon of Holocaust literature. Such attempts at "rescue and recovery" call upon the increasingly mediated stories, as third-generation scholar Hilene Flanzbaum proposes, of a merging of "memory with imagination to form a coherent narrative" of the past.[22] The task of third-generation writers, Flanzbaum argues, is to "explore places they have never been, recover what they can and re-create what time has rendered irretrievable."[23] Here imagination becomes a substitute, a placeholder, for memory. The facts of the past—the events as they occurred in history—take root in the developing consciousness of those who follow, recovered and reanimated through the imagination, not unlike the murdered band of Klezmer players in Joann Sfar's graphic novel *Klezmer: Tales of the Wild East*, who reemerge in the dream of the only surviving member of the troupe. Their persistent ghostly presence lingers long after their deaths: "as long as we don't know where to go . . . we're staying in your head."[24] Such an afterimage similarly is grafted upon the third-generation adolescent narrator's developing consciousness in Julie Orringer's novel *The Invisible Bridge*, fragments of narratives overheard and taking root as "strands of darker stories . . . absorbed through her skin, like medicine or poison. Even when she wasn't thinking about those half stories, they did their work in her mind."[25] The "presence" of the memory of the Holocaust, the presence, that is, of all that has been lost, creates the conditions for a reevaluation of and imaginative reinvestment in the ongoing representation of the Holocaust, creating luminal moments that blur boundaries between periods of time and thus extend a "text" that finally can't be completed.

For the second generation—the children of Holocaust survivors—memories were often conveyed directly from firsthand witnesses, though never entirely unmediated or uncensored. The children of survivors may have received secondhand accounts of the events their parents and other survivors endured, but they *lived with* or *among* the direct witnesses and thus were made privy—either directly or implicitly—to their experiences. Here the point of origin is the trauma of the Holocaust transferred, grafted upon the generation that followed in the direct aftermath of the war. As second-generation writer Melvin Bukiet acknowledges, for the children of survivors, "In the beginning was Auschwitz," an origin myth hideously distorted, inverted—obliteration rather than creation.[26] As such, the point of entry into the past is positioned differently for those generations who navigate the stories of their parents and those survivors who shaped their lives. The accounts received and iterated are shaped by a reverse trajectory not unlike the stories of Margot Singer's character in the short story "Deir Yassin," who "prefers to look to the past, not the future: his stories run like memory, from back to front, the answers written at the beginning, not the end."[27] Here the beginning, the point of traumatic rupture, outlines the future. The points of departure and points of arrival remain static, reminiscent of the stage for survivor Charlotte Delbo's prose poem "Street for Arrivals, Street for Departures," in which "a station where those arriving are the same as those leaving / a station at which those arriving have never arrived, to which those leaving / have never returned."[28] Time and space are arrested at the moment of traumatic rupture, the world closing in, frozen. Second-generation narratives suggest this rupturing of time, as we find, for example, in Art Spiegelman's first volume of *MAUS*, the graphic novelistic account of his father's experience in Auschwitz. Here the gutters, the spaces around the illustrated frames suggest the separation and fragmentation of images that represent Holocaust memory and the incursion of past events in the present consciousness of the son of survivors.

For a generation approaching the Holocaust from a significantly more distanced position, however, the investment in the stories of the traumatic past may be just as determined, though transferred with less immediacy, less direct guidance and intervention, "silent clues," as Flanzbaum suggests of her own experience.[29] Here the point of origin is the present, present conditions that bring the third generation back to the past. In distinguishing between the two perspectives—the direct, immediate descendants of survivors and those in successive generations—it is useful to consider the shift in perspective as suggested by Marianne Hirsch's discussion of "postmemory," a form of memory "mediated not through recollection but through an imaginative investment and creation," and Eva Hoffman's focus on the shape of memory "after such knowledge," a condition characterized by anxious belatedness in approaching narratives of the past.[30] Cathy Caruth, in locating the difference in direction and focus, suggests that the second generation, a generation marked by Hirsch's definition of "postmemory," "defines itself through a sense of belatedness that puts the zero degree of memory at the moment of the trauma," while the "after" in "'after such knowledge' . . . holds on to the present and looks for a place of memory within the everyday life. The memory of trauma after such knowledge thus places the past alongside other aspects of life . . . in order to guarantee its place in the cultural memory."[31] It is thus through this particular "prism of time and memory," to borrow a phrase from novelist David Grossman, that the third generation unsteadily and with fractured knowledge and lost narratives proceeds into the legacy of the Holocaust.[32] If not "an heir to the Holocaust," then "heir to a great storyteller," as Daniel Mendelsohn puts it, to one whose stories help breech the gap in time and experience.[33] Thus, as Grossman suggests, these are stories "which have to be told again and again because that is the only way to assemble the traces of identity and fuse the fragments of a crumbled world."[34]

Such stories become the catalyst for self-invention and a reckoning of past events and the place of the present and the future in the continuing legacy of the past. Such stories—imagined or told—become an essential part of the fabric of third-generation identity and place. Fantasized reinvention through figurative structures of articulation, then, in some ways might hope to resolve history by reimagining it. Thus third-generation narratives—literature as well as film—as Bayer proposes, attempt "to bridge the gap to the present, thereby making traumatic events of the past relevant for the present; they at the same time emphasize the ethical component in such art."[35] But how, for a third generation, are such stories navigated alongside other intervening and competing narratives? How are such stories articulated ethically? What is passed on to subsequent generations? Such hermeneutics, as Eshel rightly suggests, involve "a set of choices . . . opting to combine a reading of a work's display of trauma with its possible gestures toward new beginnings."[36] How, then, might the past be linked to the present in productive ways that move us forward into a future? How might contemporary literature that bears witness to the Holocaust, that approximates the trauma of such a defining rupture in time and consciousness, erect the scaffolding to bridge the gap between the irresistible disposition of the present and the pressing specter of the past? As one of novelist Gwen Edelman's characters, who escaped the Warsaw Ghetto in 1942 and now years later encouraged by his wife to return, admonishes, "Another lifetime. You won't find your way back."[37] Finding one's way back, however, is the project of the third generation, return narratives that revisit the sites of their relatives' lives prior to and during the Shoah.

Bridging the generational chasm between past and present involves traversing temporal, spatial, and experiential distances, understood here both literally and metaphorically. The third generation, as suggested in the title of Julie Orringer's 2010 novel *The Invisible Bridge*, is linked to stories of the past by an "invisible bridge" that brings us back to the enduring consciousness and legacy of the Holocaust. The metaphorical bridge in Orringer's epic novel of the fate of Hungary's Jews under Nazi occupation connects past events to the present in ways that suggest the intergenerational extension of narratives that define one's place in a consciousness of shared suffering and survival. Narrated—like the author herself—as we come to discover, by the granddaughter of Hungarian Jews who fortuitously survived the erosion of their lives and the lives of their families and communities, the return to the past, characteristic of third-generation narratives, moves us toward a more hopeful, more open future, one that is not solely determined by the events of the past.

Orringer's novel begins in 1937 with the departure to Paris of the young Andras Lévi, a promising Hungarian-Jewish student on route to begin studies at the École Spéciale d'Architecture. Against the backdrop of Andras' story, his ill-fated plans to proceed with his education and his impassioned love affair with Klara Morganstern, the enigmatic woman who will become his wife, exists a landscape of fascism and tyranny, an anti-Semitism that, as

Orringer makes very clear, has twisted and insidious roots in Europe. As the apprehensive Andras, traveling amidst "the growing dread that radiated across Europe," recognizes, "the seeds were there" for the persecution that will unfold.[38] *The Invisible Bridge* presents a portrait of an era, a period of escalating fear and persecution, collapsing time and giving a shape to suffering. In doing so, Orringer imaginatively invokes the cumulative and systematically expanding encroachment of restrictions placed upon Europe's Jews, the prohibitions, laws, and measures governing their lives and restricting movement. In this detailed account, Orringer shows the world closing in, getting smaller for Europe's Jews for whom there is no escape.

Andras, in the novel's opening sections, is poised, "holding his breath," in anticipation of the impending disaster that he and others are powerless to prevent.[39] *The Invisible Bridge*, at its center, posits a world "growing smaller, growing narrower, every day."[40] Orringer reveals the maze of terror for Europe's Jews as they are hunted and, literally, caged in. Andras, on route to Paris to begin his studies that will soon be derailed, stops at a café near the train station only to find "a small sign, hand-lettered in Gothic characters, that read *Jews Not Wanted*. . . . From the platform of every small-town German station, Nazi flags fluttered in the slipstream of the train. The red flag spilled from the topmost story of buildings, decorated the awnings of houses, appeared in miniature in the hands of a group of children marching in the courtyard of a school beside the tracks."[41] It is against this backdrop of increasing unease and instability that Orringer recreates the tightening noose of Nazi control, from vague rumors of vandalism and prohibitions, to anti-Semitic propaganda, to quotas, and to proscribed anti-Jewish legislation: "One by one they read that Jews must be removed from positions of influence . . . and that they should cease to exercise authority . . . that Jewish organizations . . . must be dissolved . . . that the rights of . . . citizenship must be taken away from all Jews, who must henceforth be regarded as foreigners . . . and that all Jewish goods and belongings should become the property of the state."[42] Orringer reenacts the systematic persecution of Europe's Jews, the closing in, reducing, and collapsing of their worlds until, one by one, countries fall, succumbing to widening Nazi tyranny. As Grossman puts it, "when your predator closes in on you, your world does get smaller. So does the language that describes it."[43] Orringer's language is a language of loss, a language that mimics the unraveling of lives of those so brutally persecuted. Through the entwined narratives of her characters, Orringer shows palpably the shrinking world of Andras and Klara Lévi, their families, and the communities that are shattered by such loss, individual lives increasingly circumscribed against the backdrop of countries preparing for and enacting war: "People . . . starved and crowded to death in ghettoes. People . . . shot by the thousands," people rounded up and deported to hard labor and to death camps.[44]

But this is also a novel of fortuitous and determined survival, of lives rescued and reclaimed, transferred to other landscapes and other generations, moving beyond the sites of devastation. Previously "tied to a continent intent upon erasing its Jews from the earth," Andras and Klara at the end of the war flee Europe for America, a passage unlike Andras' opening journey into the center of the Nazi stranglehold.[45] This time, "they could cross an ocean and live in a city . . . without the sense of tragedy that seemed to hang in the air like the brown dust of bituminous coal."[46] It is in America that the grandchild of these survivors, at the novel's close, will take us back to a time prior to the telling of her grandparents' story, to the point of her own conscious embrace of a past she has yet to comprehend. All this adolescent narrator knows is that she "wanted to hear the whole story. . . . [S]he would ask. . . . She was old enough now to know."[47] Here the title's metaphorical impact is made transparent. The "invisible bridge" allows the grandchild of survivors to traverse the gap, the literal gulf made by time and place, but also the metaphorical link to memory transferred, transported from generation to generation. Orringer's invisible bridge, like the desk that is passed along from one person to another in third-generation writer Nicole Krauss' novel *Great House*, "moves between owners and across generations. It both carries and conceals memory."[48] The bridge takes this third-generation granddaughter of Holocaust survivors back to the place of the catastrophic rupture of their lives and the lives of their families and communities, and even farther back to lives of imagined possibility. The bridge, here, like other artifacts in the literature of the third generation functions midrashically; it becomes an extension, bringing the past into the present, filling the gap. The bridge linking the generations and past to future, is, as Orringer poses "invisible" since it exists only in fantasy, but its scaffolding is firm, indelible, guiding those who were not present back to the sites of traumatic origin. But such representational "homecomings," a longing to return, are predicated upon, as suggested by Svetlana Boym's work on nostalgia, "a romance with one's own fantasy," a compelling fantasy that one can return, in this case, not only to the past, but to a past and a place that one never lived.[49]

What does it mean to participate in the extended memory of those who suffered such tremendous loss? This is a generation of Jews who have grown up with the collective admonition not to forget, to preserve the memory of the Holocaust. But, as one of novelist Rachel Kadish's characters fears, there is a kind of sterility, a routinized flatness in such repetitive refrains: "I dredge lessons learned in Hebrew school: *We will remember the six million, we will preserve the memories, in our hearts we keep them alive.* I shake my head with confusion. How pallid, how insulting these phrases seem. *Always remember, never forget*, the Hebrew school teachers urged us. I want to ask them, What can that possibly mean?"[50] What does it mean to remember? What are the obligations inherent in remembrance? How is memory enacted?

The granddaughter of survivors in *The Invisible Bridge*, like others in the literature of the third generation, desires a kind of knowledge that takes her beyond the platitudes of remembrance and perfunctory memorialization of the past. But what are the consequences of playing out the fantasy of return? Finding and occupying a "place" among those who experienced the traumatic events of the past involves both a conscious caution, a reminder, that, finally, one cannot know, if knowing means experiencing firsthand the events as they occurred. At the same time, such fantasies of knowing may create an embrace, conscious or not, of the trauma of others. Orringer's grandchild of survivors in *The Invisible Bridge* awakens one night from disturbing dreams in which her identification with her grandparents' experiences becomes a projection of her own fears:

> A few weeks ago she'd had a dream from which she'd woken shouting in fright. She and her parents had been standing in a cold black-walled room, wearing pajamas made of flour sacks. In a corner her grandmother knelt on the concrete floor, weeping. Her grandfather stood before them, too thin, unshaven. A German guard came out of the shadows and made him climb onto a raised conveyor belt. . . . The guard put cuffs around his ankles and wrists, then stepped to a wooden lever beside the conveyor belt and pushed it forward. A meshing of gears, a grinding of iron teeth. The belt began to move. Her grandfather rounded a corner and disappeared into a rectangle of light, from beyond which came a deafening clap that meant he was dead. . . . That was when she'd shouted herself awake.[51]

Here Orringer's third-generation, internally focalized character absorbs the trauma and unconsciously participates in its "memory." However fantasized, the dream is an unconscious attempt to resolve some of her deeply held fears and anxieties about a history that is and is not her own.

Despite the amount and range of information available as well as the ease of access—printed and electronic media, film, museums, research facilities, memorials—the third generation's grasp of the particulars that come, to borrow Eva Hoffman's referent, "after such knowledge," continues to be elusive. This is a generation that requires more than catalogued dates, places, and registers of names that lack individual stories, that is, the stories of members of their own extended, if unknown, families. Orringer's granddaughter in *The Invisible Bridge* lacks the surety of how such narratives made their way into her consciousness: "she didn't know how she'd heard them. . . . Something about labor camps. Something about being made to eat newspapers. Something about a disease that came from lice . . . half stories."[52] Despite the plethora of information available for the third generation coming of age in the material culture of the twenty-first century, these writers are still caught between knowing and not knowing. For this grandchild of survivors, this third-generation witness to history who comes only belatedly to such a calculation of loss, such understanding not only involves an acknowledgment of the remote facts of history—"she'd learned about that war in school"[53]—but, even more crucially, an awareness of the immediacy of that history, the imprint and scope of her family's loss on her own, as yet unformed and uninformed, life. The desire to participate in the ongoing, collective continuum of memory protracted and embraced opens itself up to the transference of loss and suggests the ways in which the traumatic rupture of the Holocaust does not conclude with those who survived the events, nor with the children of survivors born in the direct aftermath of the war, but rather spills over into subsequent generations, carrying the weight of history into the future as well as the present. As Andreas Huyssen interestingly suggests, we think of "memory as a mode of re-presentation and as belonging ever more to the present. After all, the act of remembering is always in and of the present, while its referent is of the past and thus absent."[54] And moreover, as Huyssen concludes, this way of thinking about memory has "consequences for the past," as it does, I would suggest, for the present as well as the future.[55]

What, in the case of the Holocaust, is passed down to the descendants of survivors? What, other than the *facts* of genocide—who did what to whom, when, and where?—is available to the third generation and how is such information received? How do we measure the appropriate response to such a legacy? And how does such knowledge inform and shape the lives, the consciousness, of those who, unprepared, uneasily follow?

There is a telling moment in Art Spiegelman's collected volume of comic strips *Breakdowns: Portrait of the Artist as a Young %@&*!* in which the autobiographical character of Art, the child of Holocaust survivors for whom the Holocaust has been both an obsession and the frame for his life (as we see especially in the first volume of *MAUS*), offers to his child—the grandson of survivors—their shared birthright. "Look at what Papa has for you!" Art eagerly announces to his son Dash, as he hands him a treasure chest, a box imagined by the delighted child to contain untold riches. This "present"—a treasured heirloom that has "been in the family for years!"—turns out to be a box of horrors. The artifact, an inheritance passed along from generation to generation—as Art tells his son, "My dad gave it to me when I was a little boy . . . And now I'm giving it to *you*!"—once opened cannot be contained. Holding the key in his hand, the unsuspecting child opens the treasure chest to discover the inheritance he has been gifted. From the magical box emerges a monster, a dragon with the head of Hitler extending from its cavernous, fanged mid-section, a hideous creature that expands, increasing in size and ferocity—flames shooting from its mouth—as the young son, the grandchild of the original bearer of the treasure chest, attempts to flee.

However, once freed from its container, once set in motion, the trauma of the past cannot be reversed. The maniacal, fire-breathing, taloned monster can be shut back in its box, but the memory of what has been exposed cannot be undone. The forked-tongue of Hitler protrudes from the fiery dragon as the young boy attempts to flee its fearsome and lethal attack. The monster will be, at least temporarily, shut back in the box by Art, who, undeterred, bestows upon his son the gift of generations and the tacitly understood obligation that he, too, will "someday . . . be able to pass it on to *your* son!" But the passing on of his birthright leaves the young boy ravaged, singed by his all-too-close exposure to a raging legacy that imperils him. In the final frame Dash is shown to have been aged by the experience; he is hunched in a corner, scorched by the fire, clothes torn. His eyes are closed, covered by his blackened arms, because he cannot bear to see what is both behind and before him. He ineffectively tries in retrospect to shield himself from the past that now belongs to him. This brief sketch (constituting only seven frames) is prefaced by an illustrated panel in which an eerie, monstrous, and grisly hand emerges out of a grave, on whose stone is inscribed with the epitaph, "A Father's Guiding Hand." Appearing out of the dead, the hand will guide the third-generation descendant back in time to the specter of past horrors, and he will receive it not with willing embrace, but with resigned and defeated acknowledgment that he has no control over the life bequeathed to him. There is, we are to understand, no way to hide from the past.

It is significant that this strip is drawn by the child of survivors. Here the legacy is handed down fervently—fanatically, even—but accepted fearfully, its horrific truth disempowering. In the literature of the third generation, however, such moments of reckoning and discovery are made voluntarily and willingly; in some instances silences surrounding the past must be deliberately breached. As Daniel Mendelsohn says of his quest to uncover the fate of his grandfather's brother and family, "For a long time I had thirsted after specifics, after details . . . the concrete thing that would make the story come alive."[56] Often such efforts are thwarted by memories that remain sealed, memories and thus lives, as Mendelsohn puts it, "vanished not only from the world but . . . from my grandfather's stories."[57] As Miranda Richmond Mouillot, in her memoir, *A Fifty-Year Silence*, suggests of her grandfather who survived the war,

> He did his remembering in silence. He never said anything about what had happened to his parents [who perished in Auschwitz], and I never dared to ask him. I knew a little from hints and slips of stories I'd picked up from other people in the family, but broaching the topic with him seemed as foolhardy as exposing pure sodium to air, as if it could spark a grief strong enough to deafen and blink us, a white-hot sadness that would stun and burn us beyond remedy.[58]

Rather than stories bequeathed to them with feverish embrace, the third generation must actively seek out memories of the past, of family members lost, those who perished but also those who survived to tell the tales, in order to make sense of the significance to the present and future of past trauma.

Rather than hiding in fear of the past, Mendelsohn, like others of his generation, actively revisits the past in an attempt to fulfill "an impossible wish, a wish that nothing will be left behind, that we will carry the imprint of what is over and done with into the present and future."[59] For many of the second generation, as we see in Spiegelman's illustrated frames, "the concrete thing that would make the story come alive" is still very much alive. The legacy passed along generationally contains within it a living, breathing threat. In Spiegelman's imagined terror, this legacy of destruction still has claws, has the capability to destroy lives. The shape of dread that is the Shoah defines both the past and the present, and the implication—the imperative—that this history will be passed on to future generations—"Just think!" the fictionalized Art tells his son, Dash, "Someday you'll be able to pass it on to your son!"—suggests with the bitterest of irony a future beholden to, indeed mortgaged to, this defining moment in history. The future, in fact, is frozen. We find a similar pattern of stasis in the second-generation narratives of Thane Rosenbaum, whose recurring character Adam Posner, the son of Holocaust survivors, finds himself, in the story aptly titled "Cattle Car Complex," entrapped in an elevator as he departs his office building late one night. The experience of entrapment catalyzes the terrified Posner's phobic reaction: "What had once become a reliably sharp and precise lawyer's mind rapidly became undone, replaced by something from another world, from another time, the imprinting of his legacy."[60] The shrinking confines of the elevator transport Posner into his parents' past: he is imprisoned in a cattle car, a conveyance of sure death, on route to a concentration camp. Time and space reverse themselves in the psychic unraveling of Posner's frayed consciousness.

Rosenbaum makes emphatic this fraught condition of feared imprisonment through the recurring character of Adam Posner, who reappears throughout the interlocking collection of stories in *Elijah Visible*. In each story, the Posner's age, profession, environment, and position in relation to other characters changes. But these differences are, as Rosenbaum makes uncomfortably evident, only thin guises, transparent and insignificant markers of personhood. For Adam Posner has only one defining identity: the child of survivors. He, as others of his generation, "had inherited their perceptions of space."[61] And thus the very terrain upon which he gingerly navigates, for this grown son of Holocaust survivors, like the elevator in which Posner is encased, is perpetually and tragically "growing smaller, a shrinking enclosure, miniaturizing with each breath."[62] The world of the second generation characteristically collapses past, present, and future, inviting the conditions for a traumatic replay of the events of the past, lives forever held captive by the stranglehold of history. The past here is depicted as paralyzing, as eclipsing all possibility for a future unfettered by the defining rupture of the past. For so many of the characters who appear in the literature of the second generation, the world is reduced, delineated to the ghostly shape of the past, mirroring Grossman's concern with a future "growing smaller, growing narrower."[63] For these characters, children of survivors, children for whom, as Rosenbaum's Adam Posner fears, "Parental reminiscences had become the genetic material that was to be passed on," there is only one way to see the world in which they live.[64]

For the third generation, however, the Holocaust does not overshadow present conditions; nor is it the defining condition of personhood, of identity. Rather, the two worlds—past and present—exist in a kind of parallel relation. For this generation, the trauma of the past does not inhibit or prevent an open future. Rather it exists as a cautionary framework against which we might re-envision our lives, assuming a posture of looking ahead. Futurity, in this sense, as Eshel suggests, creates the conditions for negotiating past atrocities, "not as the depiction of a given, unchangeable state of things but rather as a warning, as a disruption to our way of thinking and acting. . . . We need not succumb to the idea of human history as a recurring set of storms."[65] Instead, "By *re*ordering and *re*presenting a certain historical event through innovative modes of emplotment, fictional narrative can cause us to view the past differently and allow us to *re*shape how we conceive ourselves in relation to the past. And such narratives may furthermore enable us to take advantage of this new relation to the past to remake ourselves."[66] Such reshaping of modes of representation that reckon with history, that hold accountable those who committed such atrocities, all the while looking toward a future that is open, possible, and not simply a replay of the past is, I believe, at the center of the literature of third-generation Holocaust writers.

The difference between second- and third-generation Holocaust expression may locate itself primarily, as Mendelsohn suggests, in negotiating the tension between distance and proximity. For the second generation, there has not been distance—temporal and emotional—standing between the events of the Holocaust and the generation born of survivors, a generation who came of age as the direct recipients of not only the memories but the psychic aftershock and attempts to reconstruct the lives of those who directly experienced the events. For the third generation, increased distance—temporal, spatial, perceptual, emotional—and abundant mediated influences and interruptions have intervened. Thus the third generation must attempt to navigate the tenacious yet tenuous space between what Mendelsohn refers to as the poles of "proximity" and "distance."[67] The waning years since the Nazi genocide and, even farther back, to a time before the events were set in motion to annihilate Europe's and, indeed, the world's Jews, become, as time proceeds, increasingly unreachable. Yet, "distance and proximity . . . become confounded."[68] As Mendelsohn puts it in his memoir *The Lost*,

> A unique problem faces my generation ... a problem that will face no other generation in history. We are just close enough to those who were there that we feel an obligation to the facts as we know them; but we are also just far enough away ... to worry about our own role in the transmission of those facts, now that the people to whom those facts happened have mostly slipped away.[69]

Thus third-generation narratives expose the anxious and precarious condition of being at once *just* close enough and, at the same time, *not* close enough to those whose memories and stories might help frame and guide their perceptions of the past. As Bayer rightly suggests, these narratives self-reflexively "comment on the difficulty of representation while simultaneously insisting on its necessity."[70]

Finally, there may be no way to bridge the gap between distance and proximity, since, as Mendelsohn says, "If you get the small details wrong, the big picture will be wrong, too."[71] However these narratives struggle against time's insistent intrusions by returning to the physical sites of displacement and catastrophe as if "standing in a place ... that for a long time you thought was hypothetical, a place of which you might say *the place where it happened* and think, it was in a field, it was in a house, it was in a gas chamber, against a wall or on the street," might bridge the epistemological distance.[72] Thus Daniel Mendelsohn, in *The Lost*, will return to Bolechow, in the steps of his grandfather's brother and the family who perished; Julie Orringer's novel *The Invisible Bridge* will revisit France and Hungary to retrace the memory of the grandparents who survived; Andrea Simon's memoir *Bashert: A Granddaughter's Holocaust Quest* will return to Belarus in an attempt to reconstruct her grandmother's life; Johanna Adorján, in *An Exclusive Love*, will travel to Mauthausen, the concentration camp where her grandfather was incarcerated; Jonathan Safran Foer's novel *Everything Is Illuminated* will take the American-born narrator to the unknown territory of Ukraine to unearth and thus complete his grandfather's story; Joseph Skibell's fabulist novel *A Blessing on the Moon* takes us back to the Polish shtetl in which the murder of the narrator who tells the story posthumously and his fellow Jews is replayed; and Miranda Richmond Mouillot, in the memoir *A Fifty-Year Silence*, will journey to France to uncover her grandparents' war experiences so that she might "break a silence that is not [her] own."[73] So, too, a host of other third-generation writers attempt to bridge the distance to the past, complicated as such a project is by the hypotheticals, the approximation, and the disturbances and interruptions of, as Mendelsohn suggests, this "business of living."[74] And even when, as the title of third-generation graphic novelist Jérémie Dres's *We Won't See Auschwitz* would have it, these writers do not set foot on the site of the actual, physical locus of deportation, incarceration, or death, they return imaginatively to the past, to, in Mendelsohn's words, "the beginning of things," in order to fill in the gaps and attempt to make sense of and bridge familial continuity.[75] After all, "once you know a thing you cannot unknow it."[76] Yet, such writers are, in large part, fabulists; through acts of reconnaissance, they attempt to recreate a presence *in place of* absence. We find this impulse, say, in Joseph Skibell's novel *A Blessing on the Moon*, in which his narrator, though dead at the novel's opening, will not die; instead he is wounded again and again, a metonymy for the suffering of many. Here the narrator, dead but reanimated, goes on a quest, a return journey to his appropriated home but also to the site of his death. We are asked to suspend belief and we, all too willingly, are seduced by that narrative voice, by that provisionally imagined history that reanimates the dead.

"Place" in these texts is thus both literal and metaphorical: the actual site of the events as they unraveled for those who perished in the Holocaust and those who survived. But "place" also suggests *room for*, a place made for another generation to bear witness to the Holocaust. So, too, "place" might here be thought of as the imaginative space for carrying the legacy of the past, "untangling the thread of . . . memory."[77] The third generation, through the conscious choice to identify with but not limit their lives to the memory of the Shoah, hope to close the gap between proximity and distance by creating the conditions for felt connection and a measured calculation of loss, one that invites the reader to participate in a transference of memory through narrative. For a generation who come to the Holocaust, in large part, by way of mass media's commercialization of and bartering in suffering, these contemporary writers set the stage not only for past trauma but also, and centrally, for the value in and of survival, a newly framed ethical calculation. In other words, these contemporary, third-generation narratives—memoirs and novels—are primarily interested in locating and shaping an appropriate response to living in a post-Holocaust world, living, that is, among others in a world we know. As Cathy Caruth proposes, "What the next step might well turn out to be is a move towards placing Holocaust memory in a sphere outside the commodification of mass media and simultaneously situating it in a space of emotional proximity that allows and even demands ethical responses."[78]

In creating return narratives, the third generation midrashically performs the conditions leading up to as well as the fitting response to loss. From the "calculated silence in all things associated with the past . . . a conscious avoidance of bringing together those who knew, who had been there, with those of the next generation" that we find among some of Rosenbaum's second-generation fraught characters, here we find the carefully salvaged weight of words extended into the future.[79] This is a literature that attempts, through an array of narrative constructions, to impose order on both a morally fraught series of catastrophic events and the fragments of memories and artifacts that remain in its aftermath. Such narratives assign accountability. For example, Skibell's character Ola, the infirm daughter of the Poles who appropriated the murdered Chaim's home in *A Blessing on the Moon*, says, very simply, "So this is what we've done."[80] While her family and the other Poles in the community are indifferent to and, in fact, participate in the suffering of others, she alone can witness Chaim's murdered ghost because she recognizes suffering when she sees it. For Skibell, as for others, the reanimation of the dead, whether in memory or in fantasy, resists historical closure in order to defy genocide. Third-generation Holocaust literature attempts to contain and redirect the memory of this potentially deafening and overwhelming historical trauma. We thus find attempts to order the chaotic events of the past through their continuing transmission. Mendelsohn, for instance, suggests that writing his memoir was motivated by "the desire both to know and to order what I knew," so to make coherent the muddied and competing fragments of memory, "to impose order on a chaos of facts by assembling them into a story that has a beginning, a middle, and an end."[81] Such attempts to revisit and rewrite the past are done so, not to alter the truth of its circumstances, but rather to understand them and contain them in an ethical response. The past here thus becomes a frame of reference for both living in the present and fashioning a future.

Such structures of return and modes of un-covering, however, run the risk of nostalgic reinvention and fantasy, imagined worlds that reveal only the fantasized desires of the storyteller in search of the past. As Sarah Wildman, in *Paper Love*, the story of her journey through Eastern Europe to uncover her grandfather's history, admits, the narrative she tangentially pieces together "speaks to what we want to believe as much as what we do believe."[82] We find a similar impulse in the wished-for antidote to the circumstances of Jewish resistance and retaliation during the Nazi occupation of Europe in Daniel Torday's 2015 novel *The Last Flight of Poxl West*. Here the third-generation narrator drawn to his "uncle" Poxl's fabricated stories of his heroic efforts during the war, finds in this grandfather-surrogate a possible construction of heroic Jewish identity set against alleged passivity. Poxl's professed Jewish heroism provides for this third-generation Jew, coming-of-age in the twenty-first century, a kind of reprieve, an historical revision, an alternative to the events that he has been raised to accept as true, as the orthodox reading of history. Poxl's largely fictionalized account provides an alternative, ameliorative version of the events. The weight of the stories of the Shoah, the set-in-stone, "authorized" version is contested by Poxl's chronicle of Jewish aggression and opposition, and thus is deeply seductive to the young narrator. As the narrator explains of lessons inculcated in Hebrew school, "our aging teachers would ply us with tales of woe, melancholy stories of the survivors of death camps and ghettoization. . . . I can see even now my young brain being tattooed with anxiety and pensive fear. . . . It compounded my sense then that history was some untrammeled force acting upon us. Leveling any hope of heroism like some insuperable glacier flattening mountains to plains."[83] The narrator, whose grandfather survived the war only to die before he knew him, desires an antidote to the refrain of "*It will happen again. Beware. Be always aware,*" but also to "the inevitable bearing down of history," and "victimhood" that would define Jewish identity.[84] What this young narrator wants is the story of a Jew, like Poxl, who "had not only survived the Nazi threat but had combated it, literally," one who "had sought the fight when others fled . . . the master of his own narrative."[85] What the narrator, in retrospect, comes to know, however, is that Poxl's "emotional sleight of hand" allowed him, at least temporarily, to fill the "absence" and to conjure a narrative of, as he says, "hope."[86] But he comes to recognize that even Poxl's noble stories, finally, "didn't undo his [uncle's] parents' deaths, the morbid facts I was attempting to sidestep."[87] No amount of revision or rewriting of the narrative can, in fact, outrun the reality of history. As the narrator admits, "We can't undo the past."[88]

Nostalgia, the fantasized return to an unrecoverable place and time might be a gesture toward, as Boym cautions, the unrecognized desire "to obliterate history and turn it into private or collective mythology."[89] To be sure, the return to the past in the fictional representations and memoirs of third-generation Holocaust writers cannot entirely avoid such nostalgic, wishful impulses to recreate a coherent narrative out of absence, a story that connects the generations through a kind of mythic or fabled unfolding of familial lineage and collective memory. The romantic, nostalgic view is always at the back of the quest, fantasy worlds reimagined. Indeed, as the narrator of Edelman's novel *The Train to Warsaw* cautions, it is deceptively wishful thinking to believe one can "step out into a [place] that is no more."[90] The collective structures of memory cannot adequately bridge the gap between self and other. And fantasy is always, in part, an act of self-protection and wish-fulfillment. As Huyssen suggests, "Inevitably, every act of memory," especially imagined, "borrowed" memory, "carries with it a dimension of betrayal, forgetting, and absence."[91] Is the fantasy, in this case, that a lost, reimagined world might be reclaimed or that one can participate in the past from a secure present? But here the fantasy is routinely measured against reality. Skibell's Chaim, for example, who "climbed out of the grave" and, joined by his comrade-in arms, the deceased rabbi fantastically transformed into a black crow, together will enact stratagems of revenge, but, nonetheless, such wishful reinvention only provisionally, for the space of the fantasized narrative, creates the fictionalized conditions for retaliation, adjudication, and adjustment.[92] What is very clear in the literature of the third generation is that there is no singular paradigmatic, orthodox narrative that sets the standard for exactitude or accuracy in the representation of the Shoah. There are neither talismanic touchstones nor redemptive returns in the quest for the stories of the unfolding events of the Shoah as they played out and extend over time. If there were one it might be this: that the imaginative return to the past provides only partial knowledge of the lives of those whose experiences one can only empathetically infer; but such a quest tells us a great deal more about ourselves, our own recovered motives and desires to be other than what we are. Ultimately defenseless against history, third-generation narratives, in navigating the interstices between present and past, knowing and not knowing, familiarity and unfamiliarity, presence and absence, hope to apprehend both individual and collective loss as they look ahead to an unimpeded if grateful future that continues to participate in the unraveling calculation of the past.

NOTES

1. Amir Eshel, *Futurity: Contemporary Literature and the Quest for the Past* (Chicago: The University of Chicago Press, 2013), 1.
2. Andreas Huyssen, *Present Pasts: Urban Palimpsests and the Politics of Memory* (Stanford, CA: Stanford University Press, 2003), 2.
3. Thane Rosenbaum, *The Golems of Gotham* (New York: HarperCollins, 2002), 42.
4. Eshel, *Futurity*, 2.
5. Eshel, *Futurity*, 3.
6. Eshel, *Futurity*, 4.
7. Eshel, *Futurity*, 4.
8. Eshel, *Futurity*, 5.
9. David Grossman, *Writing in the Dark: Essays on Literature and Politics*, trans. Jessica Cohen (New York: Farrar, Straus and Giroux, 2008), 64–65.
10. Svetlana Boym, *The Future of Nostalgia* (New York: Basic Bks., 2001), xvi.
11. Eshel, *Futurity*, 5.
12. Grossman, *Writing in the Dark*, 65.
13. Eshel, *Futurity*, 5.
14. Grossman, *Writing in the Dark*, 65.
15. Grossman, *Writing in the Dark*, 13.
16. Monica Osborne, "Holocaust in Third-Generation American Jewish Writers" in *The Edinburgh Companion to Modern Jewish Fiction*, ed. David Brauner and Axel Stähler (Edinburgh: Edinburgh University Press, 2015), 160.
17. Gary Weissman, *Fantasies of Witnessing: Postwar Efforts to Experience the Holocaust* (Ithaca, NY: Cornell University Press, 2004), 20.
18. Osborne, "Holocaust in Third-Generation American Jewish Writers," 152.
19. Daniel Mendelsohn, *The Lost: A Search for Six of Six Million* (New York: HarperCollins, 2006), 15.
20. Mendelsohn, *The Lost*, 73.
21. Gerd Bayer "After Postmemory: Holocaust Cinema and the Third Generation," *Shofar* 28.4 (Summer 2010): 116.
22. Hilene Flanzbaum, "The Trace of Trauma: Third-Generation Holocaust Survivors," *Phi Kappa Phi Forum* (Spring 2012): 13. https://www.questia.com/magazine/1G1–298057492/the-trace-of-trauma-third-generation-holocaust-survivors.
23. Flanzbaum, "The Trace of Trauma," 14.
24. Joann Sfar, *Klezmer. Book One: Tales of the Wild East*, trans. Alexis Siegel (New York & London: First Second Books, 2006), 19.
25. Julie Orringer, *The Invisible Bridge* (New York: Knopf, 2010), 596.

26. Melvin Jules Bukiet, *Nothing Makes You Free: Writings By Descendants of Jewish Holocaust Survivors* (New York: W. W. Norton & Co., 2002), 13.
27. Margot Singer, "Deir Yassin," in *The Pale of Settlement* (Athens, GA: The University of Georgia Press, 2007), 91.
28. Charlotte Delbo, "Street for Arrivals, Street for Departures," in *Truth and Lamentation: Stories and Poems on the Holocaust*, ed. Milton Teichman and Sharon Leder (Urbana and Chicago: University of Illinois Press, 1994), 218.
29. Flanzbaum, "The Trace of Trauma," 13.
30. Marianne Hirsch, *Family Frames: Photography, Narrative and Postmemory* (Cambridge: Harvard University Press, 1997), 22.
31. Cathy Caruth, *Unclaimed Experience: Trauma, Narrative, and History* (Baltimore: Johns Hopkins University Press, 1996), 132.
32. Grossman, *Writing in the Dark*, 69.
33. Elaine Kalman Naves, "Six from Six Million: Daniel Mendelsohn Interviewed," *Queen's Quarterly* 115:1 (2008), accessed September 20, 2013, http://www.elainekalmannaves.com/interview1.
34. Grossman, *Writing in the Dark*, 13.
35. Bayer, "After Postmemory," 120.
36. Eshel, *Futurity*, 254.
37. Gwen Edelman, *The Train to Warsaw* (New York: Grove Press, 2014), 13.
38. Orringer, *The Invisible Bridge*, 18–20.
39. Orringer, *The Invisible Bridge*, 21.
40. Grossman, *Writing in the Dark*, 59.
41. Orringer, *The Invisible Bridge*, 20–21.
42. Orringer, *The Invisible Bridge*, 99.
43. Grossman, *Writing in the Dark*, 61.
44. Orringer, *The Invisible Bridge*, 427.
45. Orringer, *The Invisible Bridge*, 511.
46. Orringer, *The Invisible Bridge*, 593.
47. Orringer, *The Invisible Bridge*, 597.
48. Osborne, "Holocaust in Third-Generation American Jewish Writers," 152.
49. Boym, *The Future of Nostalgia*, xiii.
50. Rachel Kadish, *From a Sealed Room* (New York: Houghton Mifflin, 1998), 236.
51. Orringer, *The Invisible Bridge*, 596.
52. Orringer, *The Invisible Bridge*, 596.
53. Orringer, *The Invisible Bridge*, 596.
54. Huyssen, *Present Pasts*, 3–4.
55. Huyssen, *Present Pasts*, 4.
56. Mendelsohn, *The Lost*, 502.
57. Mendelsohn, *The Lost*, 15.
58. Miranda Richmond Mouillot, *A Fifty-Year Silence: Love, War, and a Ruined House in France* (New York: Crown/Random House, 2015), 30.
59. Mendelsohn, *The Lost*, 503.
60. Thane Rosenbaum, "Cattle Car Complex," in *Elijah Visible: Stories* (New York: St. Martin's Griffin, 1996), 6.
61. Rosenbaum, "Cattle Car Complex," 5.
62. Rosenbaum, "Cattle Car Complex," 5.
63. Grossman, *Writing in the Dark*, 59.
64. Rosenbaum, "Cattle Car Complex," 5.
65. Eshel, *Futurity*, 258.
66. Eshel, *Futurity*, 8.
67. Mendelsohn, *The Lost*, 88.
68. Mendelsohn, *The Lost*, 88.
69. Mendelsohn, *The Lost*, 433.
70. Bayer, "After Postmemory," 120.
71. Mendelsohn, *The Lost*, 17.

72. Mendelsohn, *The Lost*, 501.
73. Mouillot, *A Fifty-Year Silence*, xiii.
74. Mendelsohn, *The Lost*, 73.
75. Jérémie Dres, *We Won't See Auschwitz*, trans. Edward Gauvin (London: SelfMadeHero, 2012), 35.
76. Mendelsohn, *The Lost*, 58.
77. Mouillot, *A Fifty-Year Silence*, 256.
78. Caruth, *Unclaimed Experience*, 131.
79. Thane Rosenbaum, "Elijah Visible," in *Elijah Visible: Stories* (New York: St. Martin's Griffin, 1996), 95.
80. Joseph Skibell, *A Blessing on the Moon* (New York: Berkley Books, 1999), 33.
81. Mendelsohn, *The Lost*, 37–38.
82. Sarah Wildman, *Paper Love: Searching for the Girl My Grandfather Left Behind* (New York: Riverhead/Penguin, 2014), 363.
83. Daniel Torday, *The Last Flight of Poxl West* (New York: St. Martin's Press, 2015), 4.
84. Torday, *The Last Flight of Poxl West*, 4, 139.
85. Torday, *The Last Flight of Poxl West*, 67, 69.
86. Torday, *The Last Flight of Poxl West*, 143, 140, 4.
87. Torday, *The Last Flight of Poxl West*, 144.
88. Torday, *The Last Flight of Poxl West*, 144.
89. Boym, *The Future of Nostalgia*, xv.
90. Edelman, *The Train to Warsaw*, 44.
91. Huyssen, *Present Pasts*, 4.
92. Skibell, *A Blessing on the Moon*, 4.

Chapter Three

A Visible Bridge

Contemporary Jewish Fiction and Literary Memorials to the Shoah

Avinoam Patt

Published in 1961, Edward Lewis Wallant's *The Pawnbroker* is often described as one of the first American novels to examine the trauma of the survivor in the aftermath of the Holocaust. Set in a dark and foreboding Harlem with a survivor detached from his surroundings, his emotional self, and his past, Wallant's novel anticipated a preoccupation with the Holocaust that would only continue to gather force in American Jewish writing fifty years later. When Wallant wrote *The Pawnbroker*, he imagined Sol's suffering during the war without the aid of historical studies of the Holocaust based on archival research and with limited access to survivor testimony. *The Pawnbroker* juxtaposed the suffering of the two "wretched worlds" Sol Nazerman inhabited: the Nazi concentration camp universe and the underworld of 1950s Harlem in a figurative setting rife with symbolic comparisons to Sol's wartime experiences.[1] In the twenty-first century, with seemingly limitless stacks of research on the Holocaust and thousands of survivor testimonies available for use, writers continue to return to the subject of the Holocaust—now armed with ample contextual material to situate their characters within the historical context of World War II. How does the availability of such source material affect the ways in which writers grapple with the tension in representing the Shoah, balancing a focus on individual experiences with fiction based in an overwhelming framework of historical facts? This chapter will examine the growing concern with the legacies of the Holocaust in American Jewish fiction among several recent winners and finalists for the Wallant Award, writers who might be considered the "third generation" (perhaps but not necessarily the grandchildren of survivors) who have made the Holocaust a focal point of their storytelling.[2] Included in this examination here are writers like Julie Orringer (*The Invisible Bridge*), Sara Houghteling (*Pictures at an Exhibition*), and Molly Antopol (*The UnAmericans*), who construct fictional narratives of survival within a framework of historical fact, along with writers Boris Fishman (*A Replacement Life*) and Daniel Torday (*The Last Flight of Poxl West*) who re-examine the tensions between fact and fiction in Holocaust literature. For these new, young Jewish writers, past Jewish experience—defined in a variety of ways—shows itself to be the starting point for an exploration of personal identity, often in the shape of family history that has been transmitted from one generation to the next, or is desperately sought through a personal journey of discovery and recovery across generations. At the same time, the Holocaust serves as a figurative vehicle to explore the power of storytelling and love to grapple with loneliness, grief, mourning, and fear of nonexistence. Whether intentional or not, contemporary writers of the third generation create literary memorials to the Holocaust that help readers understand and appreciate the lives of those who preceded them.

GENERATIONS OF HOLOCAUST LITERATURE

The current cohort of young writers in the first decades of the twenty-first century who engage with the Holocaust must be distinguished from those writers who examined the continuing impact of the Shoah on the "second generation." Thus, among the children of survivors, like Thane Rosenbaum (1996 Wallant winner), Melvin Bukiet (1992 Wallant winner), and even Art Spiegelman, their work often examines the intergenerational transmission of trauma. In Rosenbaum's work, for example, the Holocaust seemed to induce genetic mutations passed from parent to child:

> Adam's parents had been in the camps, transported there by rail, cattle cars, in fact. That was a long time ago, another country, another time, another people. An old, trite subject—unfit for dinnertime discussion, not in front of the children, not the way to win friends among the Gentiles. The Holocaust fades like a painting exposed to too much sun. A gradual diminishing of interest—once the rallying cry of the modern Diaspora; now like a freak accident of history, locked away in the attic, a hideous Anne Frank, trotted out only occasionally, as a metaphorical mirror, reminding those of what was once done under the black eye of indifference.
>
> Adam himself knew a little something about tight, confining spaces. It was unavoidable. The legacy that flowed through his veins. Parental reminiscences had become the genetic material that was to be passed on by survivors to their children. . . . Their own terrible visions from a haunted past became his.[3]

For some among the second generation, like Melvin Bukiet, there is a tendency to assert primacy for writer-descendants of "true" survivors:

> To be shabbily proprietary, we own it. Our parents owned it, and they gave it to us. [. . .] I'd like to tell everyone from the Bellows and the Ozicks to the Styrons and the Wilkomirskis, "Bug off. Find your own bad news," but no one can legislate artistic temperament, and perhaps no one should.[4]

In their recent volume *Holocaust Literature*, David Roskies and Naomi Diamant categorize this post-1985 Holocaust Literature as *Authorized Memory* and define the second generation as "Haunted Children." As they ask of Spiegelman: "[C]ould a child become the repository of his parents' suppressed and unknowable past? Could their experience be imagined, reenacted, and transfigured?" In most cases this is the goal of such literature, which in the cases of writers like "Spiegelman and [David] Grossman (*See Under: Love*), not just the manner and the generational perspective but the very sound of the narration changed—in a shift from the languages in which the Holocaust was lived to the languages in which it was relived."[5]

Writers like Rosenbaum and Bukiet, who represent this second-generation mentality, show us how contemporary consciousness may be shadowed by the Shoah. Even so, as Ruth Franklin persuasively argues, being related to a Holocaust survivor is not an essential criterion to write Holocaust literature. Franklin, in *A Thousand Darknesses: Lies and Truth in Holocaust Fiction*, is critical of what she sees as the second generation's co-optation of ownership, that is, writers like "Bukiet and Rosenbaum have been at the forefront of what is surely one of the most disturbing trends in contemporary Jewish literature . . . driven by ambition, guilt, envy, or sheer narcissism, a number of children of survivors—commonly referred to as the "second generation"—have constructed elaborate literary fictions in which they identify so strongly with the sufferings of their parents as to assert themselves as witnesses to the Holocaust."[6] She attacks what she sees as "the most pernicious aspect of the second generation phenomenon: the virtual displacement of the survivors by their own descendants through the appropriation of Holocaust narratives."[7]

While the appropriation of Holocaust narratives by their descendants might seem to be a case of identity theft, for contemporary writers approaching the subject of the Shoah, Adorno's dictum (*To write a poem after Auschwitz is barbaric*) lurks in the background, as do the concerns of commentators like Lawrence Langer that "the aesthetic stylization of the Holocaust experience, especially the condensed expression of verse, [which] might violate the inner (and outer) *incoherence* of the event, casting it into a mold too pleasing or too formal."[8] How do early twenty-first-century writers approach the subject of the Holocaust without allowing readers to gain "illicit pleasure" from an aesthetic experience inspired by the Holocaust?[9] Ruth Franklin suggests that

> [T]his is precisely what the newest generation of writers has been trying to do, to return art to the realm of aesthetics. (I hesitate to call them "Holocaust writers," because although their works do touch on the subject, tangentially or more directly, it is never their main focus. Indeed this is part of their literary liberation.) The generation to which my contemporaries and I belong is the last generation privileged to learn about the Holocaust from survivors—either from our own family members or from the strangers who were once fixtures at school assemblies or synagogue functions. But we also learn about it from books. As the writers of this generation begin to tell these stories from their own vantage, they have turned Jewish literary tradition inside out. And in doing so, they demonstrate that the stories of the Holocaust remain tellable.[10]

And despite such concerns about whether or not the second generation can or should represent the sufferings of their parents' generation in literary form, what we continue to see even more in the most recent "third" generation of writers (often not necessarily related to a survivor), that the emotional remove from the subject matter enables writers to make the Holocaust a basis for a literary examination that is not too emotionally raw but also grapples with questions that concern Jewish Americans at the beginning of the twenty-first century. In fact, it would seem that more Jewish fiction grapples with the Shoah now than ever before. I can speculate on several reasons why this might be the case: the passing of the survivor generation, the post-1993 resurgence of Holocaust awareness, the role of the children of survivors in the rise of Holocaust consciousness, the continuing difficulty of explaining why this happened, and the realization that we have still not fully understood the impact of an event of such terrible and catastrophic proportions on contemporary Jewish life, and more. One might even ask why this current generation of writers seems to be drawn to stories that focus on the Holocaust rather than 9/11, a traumatic event which occurred in their lifetimes, not one seventy years earlier.

As Josh Lambert has argued in *Tablet Magazine*, historical novels that draw from extensive archival research, documented chronicles, and recorded interviews in reconstructing a world that has been lost have become even more common in recent years.[11] While such choices "might reflect the feeling among young American Jews that there is nothing poignant about their lives," Lambert also suggests something else might be at play here: that "the specifically archival character of these most recent prize-winners suggests another vector of influence: the positioning of creative writers within the university and on academic payrolls. . . . A literary novel is much more likely to be a credential for tenure these days than a popular entertainment, and some of our novelists—whether formally employed by universities or just having been educated by them—increasingly resemble our academic scholars."[12] Even so, the influence of survivor testimony on such works must also be appreciated. As narratives of survivors have become more widely available over the past twenty years, thanks to the work of such institutions as the Shoah Foundation Visual History Archive (and its over 53,000 Holocaust Survivor testimonies), the United States Holocaust Memorial Museum (opened in 1993) and the Fortunoff Video Archive at Yale University (which began recording testimonies in 1979) the predominant role of the survivor in shaping collective memory of the Holocaust has influenced both the fields of Holocaust history and the place of the Holocaust in popular culture.[13]

At the same time, these works are often deeply personal for these writers, who feel compelled to *tell a story that remains untold*, a story that is more likely than not rooted in family history that has been fictionalized. (It is worth noting that for most of the writers discussed here, the work is a debut novel, and that their first painstaking foray into the world of the novel engages either directly or indirectly with some aspect of family history.) For Jewish writers, the Holocaust functions both as a great mine of untold, almost unbelievable stories (better than fiction) and a place to explore the basis of one's Jewishness in the twentieth and twenty-first centuries. These works have also become a means of exploring the role of the writer in transmitting narratives of survival to a broader audience, while continuing a long tradition of situating works of fiction against a background of historical fact.[14]

In the background of this examination is a question raised by data from the recent Pew Study which asks us to take into consideration the place of "Remembering the Holocaust" in contemporary Jewish identity; 73 percent of respondents to the Pew Survey identified it as an essential part of what being Jewish means to them.[15] This of course raises the central question: how do we remember something we never personally experienced? While there is no single way in which these authors use the Holocaust as a source of literary material, what we can also see in most recent literature is a willingness on the part of the newest generation of writers to approach the Holocaust anew—not to examine the emotional baggage passed down in the literature of Rosenbaum, Bukiet, or Spiegelman, but to mine it for untold stories and to use the tools of fiction to recreate for an audience two generations removed an experience they would not otherwise "remember." Holocaust novels thus function as imaginary memorials for lives that may have been lived by loved ones or remarkable stories of survival that can be proven plausible through historical research. While these are not works of history, writers often conduct meticulous research in order to construct a historical framework that is accurate and a context in which their characters live that is plausible, while the thoughts and emotions of their characters are imagined, enabling the reader to feel empathy and understanding for the lived experience of a character who may or may not have existed.

If novels function as literary memorials (related but still distinct from *yizker bikher*), how do these books ask readers to reflect on the emotional impact of history? They are not dispassionate historical texts, but instead ask us to consider the impact of the Holocaust on the individual, familial, or communal level. *Yizkor* books, which were created by *landsmannschaftn* to function as "textual gravestones for those who perished in mass graves and gas chambers"[16] provided detailed necrologies of those who perished and included sections on life before the war, fulfilling a memorial function for descendants of those from the town; as such, they generally enjoyed limited print runs and readership that did not extend beyond those who could trace their roots back to the destroyed community. These novels, however, seem to function as collective memorials for an entire people, but usually focused through the prism of an individual or one family's experiences. Jonathan Safran Foer's *Everything is Illuminated* is perhaps the most obvious example of a novel constructed as a *Yizkor* book to the destroyed community of Trachimbrod, although as Heidi Bollinger suggests, the book "both exemplifies and problematizes the descendant's attempt to compose a Jewish memorial book."[17] While the magical realism of Foer (and Nicole Krauss in *The History of Love*) suggests that historical reconstruction is ultimately impossible in their novels, which do not attempt to remain faithful to the historical record, the more recent works detailed below, gesture at the possibility of creating a workable relationship between history, memory, and literature.

LITERARY MEMORIALS TO THE HOLOCAUST

Two recent Wallant Award winners, Sara Houghteling (2009) and Julie Orringer (2010), have created great works of fiction that are literary memorials to the Holocaust and WWII history. Both novels, *Pictures at an Exhibition* and *The Invisible Bridge*, are fictionalized narratives of survival, historical fiction based in survivor testimony and extensive archival research. At the same time, they situate individual histories of survival within the much broader sweep of World War II, paying careful attention to the historical framework within which their characters live and survive.

A Museum of the Mind

Sara Houghteling's *Pictures at an Exhibition*, set in Paris both before and after the Shoah, looks at the Nazi looting of museums and private art collections during the war. The novel tells the story of the Berenzon family and the painful lessons of loss learned by the young protagonist Max, who is gradually forced to appreciate that what has been plundered can never be fully recovered. Houghteling shapes the novel as a memoir of sorts, told from the perspective of Max, and it is a reflection on the power of memory to recover that which has been lost:

> In the twilight of my life, I began to question if my childhood was a time of almost absurd languor, or if the violence that would strike us later had lurked there all along. I revisited certain of these memories, determined to find the hidden vein of savagery within them.[18]

Even before the war, Daniel Berenzon unknowingly prepares his son, Max, who despairs over every painting sold by the family of collectors, to deal with loss and the plunder that is to come, cautioning him to remember that "The object's absence or presence is irrelevant. They're all up here"—he tapped his head.... "You'll have a museum of the mind."[19] After the war Max is still obsessed with recovering his father's lost paintings, a personal loss that pales in comparison to the monumental losses of the war, losses which are never explicitly detailed, but form a gaping chronological hole in the center of the novel. Max and his father gradually become aware of the atrocities in the East, together with Houghteling's readers:

> We staggered into and out of a newsreel in which we saw the horror of the extermination centers of the East. There was open weeping in the theater, and also a few men who called out "propaganda," "lies," and "unbelievable." Then, posted on a wall near the Metro, printed on broadsheets of newspaper, were pictures of bulldozers pushing heaps of bodies.[20]

While the atrocities of the war and the details of the Final Solution reach Max through rumors, hearsay, and "unbelievable" newsreels, Houghteling rooted her novel in painstaking historical research on Nazi looting of art during the war and based her central female character Rose Clément, on the real life Rose Valland, who secretly recorded as much as possible of the more than 20,000 pieces of art brought to the Jeu de Paume Museum; as the character Rose Clément notes in the novel:

> I took note of each painting's departure, hoping to coordinate it with what I knew of its arrival. Then I gave copies of Alexandre's orders to the rail workers in the Resistance. Thus they knew which boxcars contained paintings, and I knew which paintings were on board the train. The Resistance, in turn, told General de Gaulle in London which trains should not be bombed and even which parts of a train should be spared. We were piecing together clues for the day when the Germans were defeated and reassembling could begin.[21]

In interviews, Houghteling detailed the level of research involved in constructing a work of fiction so rooted in the historical record, basing her research on looted art on *The Rape of Europa* by Lynn Nicolas, interviewing art dealers and collectors, and conducting archival research at the Centre de

Documentation Juive Contemporaine and the Bibliothèque Nationale de France.[22] At the same time, Houghteling noted the influence of family history (including her father's and grandmother's memories of postwar Paris) and the remarkable story of Rose Valland, a story she feared would never be told. The novel becomes a vehicle for Houghteling to make Valland's heroism known, while also chronicling the lost world of French Jewish art and art collectors like Paul Rosenberg.[23] Max's "museum of the mind" becomes a memorial for the irretrievable and unrecoverable pillaging of the war.

A Visible Bridge

Julie Orringer's novel *The Invisible Bridge* painstakingly examines the Nazi occupation of Hungary and the fate of Hungarian Jews. (Like Houghteling, Orringer also spent eight years writing this book.) Here Orringer shows the intersection of History—the war against the Jews—and personal histories through the confluence of exhaustive research and the penetrating radar of her own keen imagination. For Orringer, the granddaughter of Hungarian Jews, the process of writing the novel, which began as a book about her grandfather, "a young man who moved to Paris who tries to study architecture and loses his scholarship," helped her to understand her own family history in a way she never had before. As Orringer noted in interviews, bits and pieces of family history intrigued her, but "she didn't know much about what happened to Hungarian Jews during the war" before she began working on the novel.[24]

While inspired by her grandfather's experiences before the war as an architecture student in Paris, the fictional love affair between Andras Levi and Klara Morgenstern and their fates (and those of their families) hang in the balance unfolding against a backdrop of impending doom and growing uncertainty in Europe rooted in this cold realities of history. Like Houghteling, Orringer deftly weaves together personal history and European history.

The Invisible Bridge follows the fate of the brothers Lévi, Andras and Tibor and Matyas, from the individual, middle-class aspirations of their prewar existences into the collective desperation of wartime, as Jewish men are forced to work in the labor gangs behind the front lines in Hungary, the *Munkaszolgálat*, where conditions are as lethal as those at the front. The novel becomes a memorial to those who died and to the untold stories of the Shoah in Hungary. Orringer's research process, which included archival research, interviews, use of videotaped testimonies at the Shoah Foundation's Visual History Archive, and uncovering underground journals published by the men of the Hungarian labor battalions, indicates a dedication to hew as closely as possible to the historical record in her fiction. In a striking moment at the novel's close when those Hungarian Jews who survived the war fill the synagogue searching for names of families and friends, Orringer recreates the devastation and enormity of loss that Hungary's Jews experienced in the long recitation of names of the dead: "An alphabet of loss, a catalogue of grief. Almost every time they went, they witnessed someone learning that a person they loved had died. . . . [A]fter a while it seemed they were just looking, trying to memorize a new Kaddish composed entirely of names."[25] The "catalogue of grief" and a "new Kaddish" speaks to the almost unimaginable numbers murdered. In this way, *The Invisible Bridge* is a contemporary *Yizkor* book, a chronicle of remembrance.[26]

For Orringer, the novel is also a means of reflecting on her role in the process of transmitting history, both personal family histories. In her epilogue, Orringer writes of the Lévis' granddaughter who heard about the war "every now and then [as] it drifted into their speech":

> There were strands of darker stories. She didn't know how she'd heard them; she thought she must have absorbed them through her skin, like medicine or poison. . . . Even when she wasn't thinking about those half stories, they did their work in her mind.[27]

Orringer, describing herself, the literary granddaughter, continues: "Maybe that was the problem: She hadn't asked. Or maybe even now they didn't want to talk about it. But she would ask, next time she went to visit. It seemed right that they should tell her, now that she was thirteen. She wasn't a child anymore. She was old enough now to know."[28]

Even though the novel became a fictional account of Hungarian Jews swept up by the war, the process of writing the novel was still incredibly personal for Orringer, as she has detailed in interviews:

> What happened, though, was that my family's experiences became real to me in a way they hadn't before. Part of what I found so difficult was not only sorrow for the characters I had created—in the end they are just figments of my imagination—but much more importantly, I experienced the real misery of understanding, finally, what happened to my grandparents and that whole side of my family. It's one thing to hear bits and pieces but it's another thing to be living the life of the characters for a couple of years and begin to see those lives break down. You really start to see that it wasn't just this large scale tragedy, but an infinite series of tiny tragedies that added up to something completely beyond our imagining.[29]

Both Orringer and Houghteling, as representatives of the "third generation," note the influence of stories told by grandparents, survivors, and historical figures who preceded them as motivations to tell untold stories of the war. The process of writing fiction and imagining the suffering of loved ones in the past became a vehicle to memorialize the Holocaust. And yet, in the case of both historical novels, they include a disclaimer: "This is a work of fiction. Names, characters, places, and incidents either are the product of the author's imagination or are used fictitiously. Any resemblance to actual persons, living or dead, events, or locales is purely coincidental."[30] In these cases, however, resemblance to actual persons, living or dead, seems like something more than a coincidence.

Writers of fiction, perhaps with such disclaimers in mind, have in turn grappled with the tension between testimony and fiction, narratives of survival and narratives of fiction. Several recent works have directly interrogated the defining role played by a reliance on survivor testimony, both real and imagined, as the stories of grandparents related to the grandchildren who have now become the storytellers.

Telling Stories

Molly Antopol in "My Grandmother Tells Me This Story" (recipient of the O. Henry Prize for Best Short Fiction 2015) relates the story of a young heroine who has escaped through the sewers to join a group of partisans in Belarus. The story is told entirely in the voice of the survivor, the listener's fictional grandmother:

> *Some say the story begins in Europe*, and your mother would no doubt interrupt and say it begins in New York, but that's just because she can't imagine the world before she entered it. And yes, I know you think it begins specifically in Belarus, because that's what your grandfather tells you.[31]

Retelling her story, the grandmother emerges as a heroic figure, who joins the Yiddish Underground, a partisan group in the forests of Belarus, where she meets the listener's grandfather. The literary technique is quite effective, allowing Antopol to deliver a fictional survivor's testimony as if retold to her grandchild in the form of a dramatic revelation:

> Your grandfather was running around, stopping at every station. It seemed obvious he was the leader, which I learned for certain that night at dinner, when five new boys arrived at the campfire.
> They were young, your grandfather's age, and had just come back from a mission. Your grandfather crouched beside me and explained. Everyone here was part of a brigade, he said, called the Yiddish Underground. He'd started it back with his youth group, doing combat training in basements around the city. In the beginning, they'd slipped into nearby villages and robbed peasants for food and tools and weapons. But every day the war seemed to be getting worse, he said, and now the brigade was traveling farther to carry out attacks. They torched cottages and stole guns. When they ran out of bullets, they sneaked into cities with empty shotguns and long, straight branches, which, from a distance, could pass as rifles. They chopped down telephone poles, attacked supply depots, burned bridges to disrupt military routes—and that night, the five boys at the campfire had just returned from dislodging two hundred meters of rail line.

And? your grandfather said then, turning to one of the boys.

And the conductor stopped the train, the boy said, spearing a sausage from the fire. And I walked right on and shot four soldiers in the dining car. They didn't even have time to put down their forks.

Your grandfather clapped the boy's shoulder like a proud parent, and I just sat there swallowing. . . .[32]

The grandmother's testimony is interspersed with references to her granddaughter's life, told with an awareness of the role of her audience in receiving the story and the subjective nature of how the listener might hear her story, as she tries to imagine a world before she existed. The story's climax focuses on the grandmother's morally ambiguous role in a partisan raid on the town of Haradziec in Belarus and a guerilla attack on a train line. The grandmother, suddenly tired of telling her story, clues the granddaughter into what can be learned through historical research, and which details can only be learned by listening closely to the stories of a survivor, even as she questions why her granddaughter would even be interested in listening to her in the first place:

And no, I won't tell you the rest. You can guess. You can go to the library and read about the sixty-four soldiers killed that night in Haradziec, in a train explosion engineered by an unknown anarchist group. You can waste full days in the research room, ruining your eyes scrolling through microfilm. . . . I don't understand you. All your life you've been like this, pulling someone into a corner at every family party, asking so many questions it's no wonder you've always had a difficult time making friends. It's a beautiful day. Your grandfather's on the patio grilling hamburgers, your mother's new boyfriend is already loud off beer, she's hooked up the speakers and is playing her terrible records. Why don't you go out in the sun and enjoy yourself for once, rather than sitting inside, scratching at ugly things that have nothing to do with you? These horrible things that happened before you were born.[33]

For Antopol, "My Grandmother Tells Me This Story" was inspired by curiosity about "the one place I never heard about was Antopol, the Belarusian village, virtually destroyed in World War II, where my family originated." An encounter with an elderly woman from Antopol living in Israel led her to the Antopol *Yizkor* book, and "the moment I finished reading it, I began working on this story." Even so, Antopol the writer wrestled with two tensions in telling this story: how to convey the partisan experience in the forests of Belarus as accurately as possible, and how to answer the question of why she was so interested in this story to begin with.[34] In an article in the *New Yorker* published in advance of the publication of *The UnAmericans*, Antopol shared a story detailing the genesis for "My Grandmother Tells Me a Story." Inspired by the survivor testimonies included within the Antopol *Yizkor* book, Molly Antopol notes that "perhaps what fascinated me most were accounts of the village's partisan fighters, teen-agers who escaped the ghettos during the Second World War and joined underground resistance movements in the forests surrounding Antopol." As is the case with so many of these *Yizkor* books, however, which are repositories of individual memory that become collectivized, Antopol pointed to the internal inconsistencies that invariably emerge from such a collective project as another source of inspiration and the role of the writer to distill the emotional truths that lie within each testimony:

> The Antopol book was so enormous, so detailed, containing such a variety of voices that I had wanted to believe it was a pillar of fact. But the more I read other books, the more my doubts grew: these books were flush with inconsistencies. A dozen memoirs and biographies on partisan life near Antopol and, still, I had questions. [. . .]
>
> I've never believed it's a fiction writer's job to create an exact replica of the past, a diorama the reader can step right into. But it *is* my responsibility to learn everything of the world I'm writing about, to become an expert in the politics and history that formed my characters' identities. But certain details refuse to add up, and despite intensive research I remain uncertain as to where the truth actually resides. I still don't know how I'll ever glean facts about a village where there's no one left to answer my questions. [. . .] Rather, I imagine that by writing these books (or allowing biographers to write about them) they were attempting to make sense out of a harrowing history, trying to shape and control it through language. It *is* important to focus on the blackberries. But where those facts don't jibe, I try to get at deep, emotional truths of my characters. Whether they ate blackberries or turnips, carried pistols, rifles, or sticks, they were living, hunted, in a freezing forest with no anchor to the lives they had once known. What must that have *felt* like? What must that *do* to a person—both there, in the forest, and, for the lucky ones, when they trudged out, filthy, bone thin, and exhausted?[35]

Antopol therefore recreated the experience of a Jewish female partisan in Belarus as a conversation between a grandmother and a granddaughter—a story that is mediated by the listening of the granddaughter and the role the author plays in retelling it to us. Like a *Yizkor* book therefore, Jewish fiction can play an important role in re-telling the stories of Holocaust survivors, as they *might* have been. Antopol notes the vagaries of memory in recreating and retelling a story to oneself and to one's audience, and then through meticulous research, imagines for herself and her audience what the experience may have been like for the Jewish female partisan who escaped from a ghetto to survive in hiding in the woods of Belarus. This tension between reconstructing the history of the Holocaust and the emotional experience of survivors in such literary memorials and the role of the writers in their construction have been the focus of two recent novels that directly engage with the question of truth and fiction in narratives of the Holocaust.

Surviving in America

In Boris Fishman's *A Replacement Life* (finalist for Wallant Award in 2014) Slava Gelman, the grandson of Soviet Jews now living in Brooklyn, fictionalizes narratives of survival in order to secure reparations payments for Jews from the former Soviet Union who suffered during the war, just not according to the categories of survival recognized by the Claims Conference. At the novel's beginning, however, Slava, born in Minsk (like Fishman) is desperate to leave his immigrant roots behind in order to succeed as a writer in America:[36]

> If Slava wished to become an American, to strip from his writing the pollution that repossessed it every time he returned to the swamp broth of Soviet Brooklyn, if Slava Gelman—immigrant, baby barbarian, the forking road spread-eagled before him—wished to write for *Century*, he would have to get away.[37]

Slava struggles to find success in New York and ultimately finds his voice as a writer narrating the stories of old Soviet Jews in Brooklyn, including those of his grandparents. Looking to break away from his Soviet Jewish past, Slava is torn between a desire to forge his own path and narrate his own immigrant tale in America and an awareness that there is a hole in his memory that needs to be filled, an awareness that his grandmother had experienced horrible things in World War II that he would never know about:

> Grandmother had been in the Holocaust—*in* the Holocaust? As in the army, the circus? The grammar seemed wrong. *At* the Holocaust? Of it, with it, from it, until it? The English preposition, stunned by the assignment, came up short—though she said no more than that, and no one disturbed her on the subject. This Slava couldn't fathom, even at ten years old. Already by then he had been visited by the American understanding that to know was better than not to know. She would go one day, and then no one would know. However, he didn't dare ask. He imagined. Barking dogs, coils of barbed wire, an always gray sky.[38]

Never learning his grandmother's story, Slava imagines what might have been, while forging false narratives of survival for other "old Russian Jews" who had suffered during the war, just not in ghettos, camps, or hiding in the forests. In one final scene, Slava visits his grandmother's grave, Grandmother who did in fact survive in the ghettos and forests of Eastern Europe only to never receive reparations. Standing before her gravestone, a simple memorial to the life she lived, Slava is forced to only imagine a conversation with her through his writer's notebook but "it isn't her, because she never spoke like this. But she is no longer around to answer for herself. And so she will have to live on in the adulterated form in which he must imagine her. He cannot strip himself out of the imagining. If she is to live, she will live as

Slava+Grandmother, one person at last."[39] Slava, the writer, is able to give Jews new lives, "what the Nazis took away, Slava restored."[40] Slava becomes an American Jewish writer by narrating stories of Holocaust survival, giving voice to the unknown stories from the past that will function as more poignant memorials to the generations that preceded him, keeping his grandmother's memory alive.

Made-up stories

Finally, Daniel Torday's *The Last Flight of Poxl West* (St. Martin's Press, 2015) is the most recent meditation on the uses and abuses of fact and fiction to narrate stories of heroism and survival in World War II. Torday, although inspired by his own family's experiences to write about the war—his father was born in Hungary two years after World War II ended and his grandparents were Hungarian Jewish survivors who only admitted they were Jews long after arriving in America—wrote his novel as counter-history, a response to the un-heroic stories of survival in concentration camps he remembered hearing as a young man. As Torday suggested in an interview:

> I don't know if I exactly want to validate that experience of being 15 and wanting a hero instead of a victim, but that definitely was the experience of hearing these stories over and over and over again. I don't feel that now in my late 30s, but there's a way in which there's only so many Elie Wiesels or so many Primo Levis you can read before you start to say, "So was somebody fighting back?" That is just the knee-jerk reaction that I think I wouldn't want to validate. But at the same time . . . there's this experience where maybe putting the big, capital "H" Holocaust word on top of the experience can keep us from seeing all the various stories. [. . .]
>
> I think ultimately for me, trying to seek those stories and then finding them was a particular kind of validation. There were tons of stories of Jews who ended up fighting either for Canada, for the United States and Britain, for the war apparatus in lots of ways. There were multiple Eastern European wings in the Royal Air Force; there were some Jewish pilots amongst them. So the idea that there were these other stories, and they may not have been the central story, that kind of perked my ears up and felt like ripe emotional territory.[41]

Eli Goldstein, Poxl's "nephew," after discovering that elements of Poxl West's best-selling memoir have been fictionalized, is despondent to learn that Uncle Poxl is a "fraud." For Torday, however, the novel is also a reflection on our powerful need to believe in stories, even if they are fictional. Eli's Hebrew School teacher, Rabbi Ben, tries to comfort Eli, explaining to him that even the Zohar, "the main book of the Kabbalah," was fictionalized. Even though Moses de Leon claimed to have discovered an ancient text that explained the tenets of Jewish mysticism, Rabbi Ben explains,

[T]here was no ancient Aramaic text called the Zohar. There was a book that Moses de Leon wanted to write. A book based on how he saw Adonai, Ha-Shem, the unspeakable represented by the Tetragrammaton, the God he wanted us to reach. And people wouldn't listen to it from him, so he said he was translating some ancient text—and then he just went ahead and made up his story. *That's what people do when they write. They make up stories, details to fit the stories they need to tell.* [my italics] And people are still reading—worshipping—that book, almost seven hundred years later.[42]

We believe what we need to believe, even in the case of the Holocaust, Torday seems to suggest.

CONCLUSION

This brief summary of the recent literary preoccupation with the Holocaust in contemporary Jewish literature bring us back to the question: what do these authors seek to find in the Holocaust? Could it be that they are searching for a contemporary Jewish identity rooted in the past, in the stories of their grandparents' generation? How do contemporary writers narrate stories of survival seventy years after the war? And do they suggest a means of "remembering the Holocaust" when the last living survivors of the war are no longer here? There is in fact something very Jewish about this process of "remembering survival" without the survivors. If we think about the verb Zakhor—which Yosef Hayim Yerushalmi pointed out appears 169 times in the Hebrew Bible—Judaism is a religion of remembering and implicitly of not forgetting.[43] According to Yerushalmi, one might argue that the commandment to remember has been central to the survival of the Jews in dispersion over thousands of years. But how does one remember what one never experienced? As E. M. Forster has suggested in *Aspects of the Novel*, fiction enables readers to know characters completely in a way that is even impossible in daily life, "But people in a novel can be understood completely by the reader, if the novelist wishes; their inner as well as their outer life can be exposed. We cannot understand each other, except in a rough and ready way; we cannot reveal ourselves, even when we want to; what we call intimacy is only makeshift; perfect knowledge is an illusion. But in the novel we can know people perfectly."[44] Fiction enables the writer to create empathy for a survivor of the Holocaust in a way that is impossible in daily life, allowing us to glimpse the inner lives and feelings of the victims and survivors of the Shoah. How then do we remember something we never experienced? Fiction can offer a lens to view inner experiences we never personally endured.

In a time when we are indeed observing the secularization of Jewish identity, the memory of a historical event has come to replace memory of the covenant, memory of the Sabbath, or the memory of Creation. Thus, the fascination with the lasting legacy of the Holocaust has taken on or replaced that which is deemed essential to what it means to be Jewish. So—if 73 percent of Pew respondents say "remembering the Holocaust" is an essential part of what being Jewish means to them, then there is certainly an audience for these books. And as long as the audience continues to consume, the writers will continue to be consumed by the subject, creating literary memorials that ensure the Holocaust is not forgotten.

NOTES

1. See D. G. Myers, "The Pawnbroker at Fifty," *Commentary Magazine*, June 9, 2011, http://www.commentarymagazine.com/2011/09/06/pawnbroker-at-fifty/, accessed July 2, 2015. For example, Raul Hilberg's *Destruction of European Jewry* was first published in 1961.

2. I hesitate to use the term "third generation" without qualification for several reasons: first, I do not think it explains much aside from identifying an individual as the grandchild of survivors. There is so much variance between survivor families: How do we define survival? Did one grandparent, two grandparents, four grandparents survive? Did they share their stories? When? How much? What is the difference between the grandchild of survivors and a Jewish writer whose grandparents did not survive but who has taken an active interest in the history of the Holocaust? Not included in this list of recent Wallant Award winners whose works engage with the Holocaust either directly or indirectly are Edith Pearlman (*Binocular Vision*) and Kenneth Bonert (*The Lion Seeker*), primarily for reasons of space.

3. Thane Rosenbaum, "Cattle Car Complex," in *Elijah Visible: Stories* (New York: St. Martin's Griffin, 1996), 5. Scientific research has in fact documented elevated stress hormone levels among children of survivors. See http://www.scientificamerican.com/article/descendants-of-holocaust-survivors-have-altered-stress-hormones/.

4. See Melvin Jules Bukiet, *Nothing Makes You Free: Writings by Descendants of Jewish Holocaust Survivors* (New York: W. W. Norton, 2002), 16–17.

5. David Roskies and Naomi Diamant, *Holocaust Literature: A History and Guide* (Lebanon, NH: Brandeis University Press, 2012), 168.

6. Ruth Franklin, *A Thousand Darknesses: Lies and Truth in Holocaust Fiction* (New York: Oxford University Press, 2011), 216.

7. Franklin, *A Thousand Darknesses*, 216. Franklin is especially critical of Bukiet in this regard (220).

8. Lawrence Langer, *Art from the Ashes: A Holocaust Anthology* (New York: Oxford University Press, 1995), 555.

9. Irving Howe, "Writing and the Holocaust." First published in *The New Republic*, October 27, 1986.

10. Franklin, *A Thousand Darknesses*, 237–38.

11. Josh Lambert, "Archive Fever," *Tablet Magazine*, May 31, 2011, http://www.tabletmag.com/jewish-arts-and-culture/books/68568/archive-fever.

12. Lambert, "Archive Fever."

13. In the field of Holocaust Studies, Christopher Browning has made a compelling argument for the validity of survivor testimony in historical research. In his recent study, *Remembering Survival: Inside a Nazi Slave Labor Camp* (New York: W. W. Norton and Company, 2010), Browning demonstrates that it is possible to write the history of an unexamined phenomenon, the slave labor camp, on the basis solely of survivor testimony, as a type of "history from below," not from the perspective of the perpetrators, whether in Berlin or on the ground in Poland, or even from the perspective of the Jewish leadership on the Jewish councils, but through the eyes of individual Jewish survivors. Even survivors, however, were aware during and after the war that not only did their stories need to be told and their memories shared, they also needed to be told well. Ruth Franklin quotes Jorge Semprun (*Literature or Life*) in her introduction, detailing an awareness among survivors in the immediate aftermath that their

story had to be told but as Semprun suggests: "Telling a story well, that means: so as to be understood. You can't manage it without a bit of artifice. Enough artifice to make it art!" (Franklin, *A Thousand Darknesses*, 14). One survivor tells Semprun "novels . . . will let you imagine, even if they can't let you see." (Franklin, *A Thousand Darknesses*, 15).

14. As James Young has argued in "Holocaust Documentary Fiction: The Novelist as Eyewitness," in *Writing and the Holocaust*, ed. Berel Lang (New York: Holmes and Meier, 1988), 200–15, by mixing together actual events and fictional characters in documentary fiction, "the writer simultaneously relieves himself of an obligation to historical accuracy (invoking poetic license) even as he imbues his fiction with the historical authority of real events." For an examination of this phenomenon in very early post-Holocaust fiction, see Nancy Sinkoff's analysis of John Hersey's *The Wall* in "Fiction's Archive: Authenticity, Ethnography, and Philosemitism in John Hersey's *The Wall*," *Jewish Social Studies: History, Culture, Society* 17, no. 2 (Winter 2011): 48–79.

15. See Pew Research Center, "A Portrait of Jewish Americans," 14, http://www.pewforum.org/files/2013/10/jewish-american-full-report-for-web.pdf (accessed July 7, 2015).

16. See as described by Daniel Magilow and Lisa Silverman, *Holocaust Representations in History: An Introduction* (New York: Bloomsbury Press, 2015), 37. Kugelmass and Boyarin's *From a Ruined Garden* (Bloomington: Indiana University Press, 1993) is still the standard text on *Yizkor* books.

17. Heidi Bollinger, "The Persnicketiness of Memory": Jonathan Safran Foer's Audaciously Imaginative Jewish Memorial Book," *Genre* 45, no. 3 (Fall 2012): 443–69.

18. Sara Houghteling, *Pictures at an Exhibition* (New York: Vintage, 2010), 3.

19. Houghteling, *Pictures at an Exhibition*, 82.

20. Houghteling, *Pictures at an Exhibition*, 81.

21. Houghteling, *Pictures at an Exhibition*, 158.

22. From: "Art and Arms," *Guernica Magazine*, September 1, 2009, https://www.guernicamag.com/interviews/sara_houghteling/ (accessed June 25, 2015).

23. From: http://flavorwire.com/14542/exclusive-sara-houghteling-schools-us-on-art-history (accessed July 1, 2015). Houghteling: And then really when I discovered Rose Valland, who the character in my novel Rose Clément is based on . . . and just realizing that this was an extraordinary woman who had acted very bravely, who had seen something that no one else had seen. Her autobiography had gone out of print and it's not translated into English. In some ways that was almost part of her personal plan, because during the war she tried to make herself unassuming so that she could carry out this work. She's become sort of overlooked by history, in part because she kept reminding members of the French establishment of a past that they, for various reasons, wanted to put behind them. So I had the story of Rose Valland, and also the story of Paul Rosenberg, and this huge role that Jewish art dealers had played before the war in fostering the changes that occurred in modern art. Then this group of people completely disappeared after the war, and the artwork changed so drastically. The big three [roots of the book] would be my family history, Dr. Tanay, and reading Rose Valland's autobiography.

24. See Symi Rom-Rymer, "People of the Book: Interview with Julie Orringer," February 11, 2011, https://momentmagazine.wordpress.com/2011/02/11/people-of-the-book-interview-with-julie-orringer/ (accessed July 1, 2015).

25. Orringer, *The Invisible Bridge*, 582.

26. Kenneth Bonert also concludes *The Lion Seeker* (winner of the 2013 Wallant Award) by inserting historical documentation at the end of the novel, creating a list of those who perished similar to the necrology sections included in *Yizker bikher*; in the novel's epilogue, Bonert quotes directly from the Jaeger Report, which details the murder of 137,346 Jews by the Einsatzgruppen in Lithuania (556–57).

27. Orringer, *The Invisible Bridge*, 596.

28. Orringer, *The Invisible Bridge*, 597.

29. Rom-Rymer, "People of the Book."

30. Special thanks to Maya Patt for this suggestion. LOC categorization usually includes World War, 1939–1945—Fiction. As Nancy Sinkoff points out, in Hersey's *The Wall*, the

author included a disclaimer indicating that the historical detail upon which the novel had been constructed, an archive resembling the Oyneg Shabbes archive and historical characters resembling Emanuel Ringelblum, Rachel Auerbach, Mordecai Anielewicz, and others, had been contrived: "This is a work of fiction. Broadly it deals with history, but in detail it is invented. Its 'archive' is a hoax. Its characters, even those who use functions with actual precedent—such as the chairmanship of the Judenrat, for example—possess names, faces, traits, and lives altogether imaginary" (Sinkoff, "Fiction's Archive," 53).

31. Molly Antopol, "My Grandmother Tells Me This Story," in *The UnAmericans* (New York: W. W. Norton, 2014), 59.

32. Antopol, "My Grandmother Tells Me This Story," 65–66.

33. Antopol, "My Grandmother Tells Me This Story," 83–84.

34. As Antopol noted in an interview: "[I]t ended up taking me almost two years to get the story where I wanted it to be. I read every memoir and biography of partisan life near Antopol that I could get my hands on, spent months in different archives, and traveled to Eastern Europe to visit partisan bases and conduct interviews. But it was only when I realized, after more than a year of wrestling with the story, that the tension in the piece was as much about why the granddaughter was so obsessed with these dark periods of history (a question I've been struggling to answer about myself for years) as it was about the war that the story really cracked open for me." http://lithub.com/o-henry-prize-winner-molly-antopols-my-grandmother-tells-me-this-story/.

35. Molly Antopol, "The Book of Antopol (or, Can We Ever Know the Past)," *New Yorker*, January 28, 2014, http://www.newyorker.com/books/page-turner/the-book-of-antopol-or-can-we-ever-know-the-past.

36. Boris Fishman also recalled being drafted "[i]n the 1990s, though I was only a teenager, to write my (real-life) grandmother's Holocaust-restitution paperwork—she was a survivor of the Minsk ghetto—was given to me because I had the best English in the family. (We immigrated from the former Soviet Union in 1988.) I was struck by the application's low burden of proof—if you could tell a persuasive story, you were in, so to speak. That got me thinking." http://current.nyfa.org/post/95387071263/meet-a-nyfa-artist-boris-fishman.

37. Boris Fishman, *A Replacement Life* (New York: Harper Row, 2014), 11.

38. Fishman, *A Replacement Life*, 4.

39. Fishman, *A Replacement Life*, 315.

40. Fishman, *A Replacement Life*, 90.

41. http://www.npr.org/2015/03/17/393468478/wwii-novel-memoir-explores-the-blurry-line-between-fact-and-fiction.

42. Daniel Torday, *The Last Flight of Poxl West* (New York: St. Martin's Press, 2015), 231.

43. Yosef Hayim Yerushalmi, *Zakhor: Jewish History and Jewish Memory* (Seattle: University of Washington Press, 1982), 5.

44. E. M. Forster, *Aspects of the Novel* (New York: Rosetta Books, 2012), 98; see also: http://www.storyinsight.com/techniques/media/forster.html.

Chapter Four

Storytelling, Photography, and Mourning in Daniel Mendelsohn's *The Lost*

Paule Lévy

Daniel Mendelsohn's *The Lost*, the author's second autobiographical publication,[1] is a hybrid, multilayered piece of work, whose title expresses both a haunting absence ("The Lost") and an urgent need to retrieve a singularity annihilated by mass extermination (the book's subtitle is "A Search for Six of Six Million"). Both the story of a quest and the quest for a story, the book relates the efforts of a third-generation writer to fill in the gaps in his family history by discovering the exact circumstances of the death of his greatuncle, Shmiel Jager, and his children, who were killed by the Nazis during World War II. For the better part of five years Mendelsohn traveled all over the world, across oceans and continents, in search of testimonies from the few scattered survivors of Bolechow, the once Austrian, then Polish, then German, then Russian, and at present Ukrainian town where his ancestors used to live.

Written at the intersection of psychoanalysis, philosophical speculation, and the epic, at once a fascinating textual construction and a cryptic family album, *The Lost* resists all attempts at generic categorization. In its disorienting structure and far-reaching implications it constitutes an essential contribution to the literature of "postmemory": that of generations already removed from, yet still haunted by the Shoah, bearing "the scar without the wound,"[2] "a phantom pain where amnesia functions as a site of memory."[3] According to Henri Raczymow, postgenerations are unwitting inheritors of a memory which is indirect, dispersed, and lacunary, "shot through with holes": "a parenthesis was formed by the before and after [. . .] it was a frame in whose center lay silence."[4] As Marianne Hirsch explains:

The "post" in "postmemory" signals more than a temporal delay and more than a location in an aftermath. It is not a concession simply to linear temporality or sequential logic. [It implies] both a critical distance and a profound interrelation [. . .] layering and [. . .] belatedness [. . .], an uneasy oscillation between continuity and rupture. I see it rather as as a structure of inter- and transgenerational return of traumatic knowledge and embodied experience [. . .] a consequence of traumatic recall [. . .] at a generational remove.[5]

In her essay entitled *After Such Knowledge*, Eva Hoffman, another daughter of survivors, expresses the paradox as follows: "The facts seemed to be such an inescapable part of my inner world as to belong to me, to my own experience. But of course they didn't; and in that elision, that caesura, much of the postgeneration's problematic can be found."[6] Hoffman also points out that the burden of the Shoah still reverberates onto the members of the third generation, though they be at a further remove from the oft-repressed stories that have shaped them.[7]

How is this paradox expressed by Daniel Mendelsohn? What is the nature of the quest it determines? What lesson can be drawn from this experience and its constitutive aporias? Beyond amnesia or obsession what type of poetics or rhetoric may allow third-generation writers to mourn over people and over a world they have never known and to come to terms with a loss which, to them, has no concrete shape or face? These are the questions I will address in this article, while devoting special attention to the complex interweaving of text and image in *The Lost*: two modes of expression which keep competing with, paralleling and doubling each other, in an eager effort to circumscribe an ever-receding truth.

BEREICHIT: "THE FORMLESS VOID"[8]

At the very start of his memoir, Mendelsohn recalls a bewildering and oft-repeated scene from his childhood, one already mentioned in *The Elusive Embrace*, and which in retrospect he views as having triggered his entire project. As a little boy, he would cause the elderly members of his family to burst into tears whenever they saw him:

> they would look at me and [. . .] would put both twisted hands [. . .] to their dry cheeks and say with a stagy little indrawn breath: "*Oy, er zett oys zeyer eynlikh tzu Schmiel!*"
> "Oh, he looks so much like Shmiel!"
> And then they would start crying, or exclaiming softly and rocking back and forth [. . .] and there would then begin a good deal of rapid-fire Yiddish from which I was, then, excluded.[9]

Mendelsohn depicts with tender irony the disarray these outbursts would plunge him in. In *The Elusive Embrace* he even sees them as somewhat constitutive of his identity: "These cries of recognition gave me the first clear sense of who I was."[10] The boy is all the more puzzled since he has never met this great-uncle he resembles so much, yet about whom nobody seems to have anything to say apart from this elliptic statement which in fact obliterates all possibilities of representation: "Uncle Shmiel, killed by the Nazis." The pictures of Shmiel have been stored away ("carefully inside a plastic baggie inside a box inside a carton in my mother's basement,")[11] and even Daniel's garrulous grandfather, an indefatigable storyteller and guardian of the family lore, keeps eluding all questions on the subject. He even seems to have forgotten how many children his brother had as well as their names: "to me [they] seemed not so much dead as lost, vanished, not only from the world but—even more terribly to me from my grandfather's stories."[12]

Daniel, who after his grandfather's suicide (for "which pain"? he wonders)[13] has discovered the imploring letters Shmiel would send from Poland in 1939 ("*get me out of this* Gehenim." *Gehenim* in Hebrew means "hell."),[14] begins to suspect dark layers of remorse and guilt in his family's memory. Why didn't they help Shmiel, their only relative still in Bolechow to escape in time? What was the exact nature of the grandfather's relation to his brother, the favorite child in the family ("he was a prince [. . .] he looked like a movie star").[15] For some obscure reasons Shmiel's entreaties strike a chord with his grandson: "it is difficult [. . .] not to feel implicated [. . .] vaguely responsible."[16] Daniel, from then on, is determined to lift the veil of denial and silence, and to solve the mystery surrounding his dead relatives: "Killed by the Nazis [. . .] Where? When? What? With guns? In the gas chambers"?[17]

This leads him to even more troubling questions: "Who am I if I am him? If I am a reincarnation of my great-uncle, who am I? My whole book is an attempt to fill in this blank so I can finally be myself and not just a reminder of him. If you were doing a psychoanalytical reading of this book, that would be one way to go."[18] Who is/are "the lost," after all? One is tempted to read the title *The Lost* as a sort of *mise en abyme* referring to the author himself—and possibly including the disoriented reader whose quest for meaning parallels that depicted in the book.

Mendelsohn feels devoured by a sort of "archive fever."[19] For years and years he assails his eldest relatives with questions and letters; he explores his genealogy and consults all available sources on the larger context of the Holocaust in Eastern Europe. To no avail: as regards Shmiel and his family, "there were no facts to pencil on the index cards, no dates to enter in the genealogy software, no anecdotes or stories to tell."[20] A vague and elliptic scenario emerges: supposedly, Shmiel's daughters were raped; at some point the whole family found refuge in a castle (the detail is important); the two elder daughters joined the Polish partisans; eventually all were denounced. Around the age of forty, Mendelsohn is about to let the dead sink into oblivion when unexpected encounters and letters "like the unexpected touch of a cold hand," "tantalizing us that the dead were not so much lost as waiting," act as reminders, prompting him to embark upon his crazy quest.[21]

"TO FRAME ELABORATELY A QUESTION":[22] CHINESE BOXES AND PHOTOGRAPHS

At once monumental and kaleidoscopic, the narrative of this quest, which the author had initially projected as a mere magazine article,[23] is based on a strategy which, curiously enough, is both concentric and systematically decentered. This can be felt in the book's micro-structure: that of the paragraphs, or of the sentences themselves, at times dry and factual ("Uncle Shmiel killed by the Nazis"), at times almost Proustian,[24] in their endless digressions and circumvolutions ("coiled in an infinite and intricate loop,").[25] It also affects the book's macro-structure. Mendelsohn resorts to a skillful juxtaposition of styles and to a complex interweaving of narrative layers which, entering in a dialogic relation with one another, ceaselessly open new vistas of knowledge and experience. First comes an account of the journey itself: frustrating episodes, troubling coincidences as well as illuminating encounters with survivors or bystanders whose testimonies are carefully recorded. This storyline, however, is constantly interrupted by the insertion of the few artifacts of the past Daniel still has in his possession (old letters and photographs) and of the historical sources he keeps pondering upon. This in turn leads to moments of purely abstract speculation as the narrator draws parallels between the history of the Bolechow Jews and various episodes of the Bible. Evoked in italics, these function as subtext and hermeneutic frame ("certain of its stories were allegories for the way the world is").[26] Mendelsohn borrows the title of his five chapters from various *parachot* of the Torah. Thus the first section, *Bereichit*, evokes his growing fascination for Shmiel and the early stages of his quest. The tensions in his family as well as the strong antagonism between Jews, Poles, and Ukrainians in Eastern Europe ("It was like a big family")[27] are then related to the conflict between Cain and Abel ("the Urtext of brothers, not getting along"). In the third chapter, his journey across the world is compared to Abraham's departure from Ur: "*Lech Lecha* or *Go forth!*"[28] In the fourth, *Noah* or *Total Annihilation*, the Shoah is seen as a reenactment of the Flood or of the destruction of Sodom and Gomorrah. The last chapter, *Vayeira* or *The Tree in the Garden*, has to do with the place where Shmiel was killed while it also recalls the author's family tree posted at the outset of the book.

The biblical text, whose omissions and obscurities are systematically underscored, is by no means proposed as a final explanation or justification. What fascinates Mendelsohn, instead, is its plasticity, its remarkable compression yet infinite potential for deployment, as well as its rapid alternation of foci: "from the universe to the earth to humankind to specific lands and peoples to a single family. And yet [. . .] the wider cosmic concerns [. . .] provid[e] the rich substratum of meaning that gives depth to that family's history."[29] Pointing out semantic and linguistic subtleties, Mendelsohn ceaselessly confronts various rabbinic interpretations while often proposing his own. All in all, his memoir appears as a fascinating *midrash*, not only of the book of Genesis but also of the whole history of the destruction of the Jews of Europe. This is permeated with subtle irony, for Mendelsohn, a distinguished classicist,[30] admits he prefers Ulysses to Abraham and often refers to Homer or Virgil, thus adding new layers to his fascinating palimpsest.[31] He chooses to write his story "precisely how the Greeks told their stories," turning digression into progression and proceeding, just as his own grandfather used to do:

> [i]n vast circling loops, so that each incident, each character [. . .] had its own mini-story, a story within a story, a narrative inside a narrative, so that the story [. . .] was not [. . .] like dominoes, one thing happening just after the other, but instead like a set of Chinese boxes or Russian dolls, so that each event turned out to contain another, which contained another and so forth.[32]

As he telescopes the individual and the collective, anecdote and archetype, history and imagination, proximity and distance, as he opts for an indirect, oblique approach to the Shoah, Mendelsohn attempts to "frame elaborately a question [. . .] in a way that didn't seem inappropriate."[33] He devises a form apt to express both the entire scope of the tragedy and its strictly subjective and personal dimension. His aim is to wrench the dead from the anonymity and oblivion of the mass graves and crematoria, to restore their contours and identity, to give a voice to silence and a face to absence.

A series of photographs is meant to supplement the narrative. These photographs are of two kinds. There are those of the dead, found in the family archives, and those (strangely framed in black) taken by Daniel's brother, Matt, a professional photographer who accompanies him and takes pictures of the witnesses they meet (and, at times, of the places they visit). The book is to some extent a tale of two artists, a tale of two brothers[34] whose relationship, as we will see, evolves in the course of their joint venture.

The photographs, are dim, black and white (as if to recall "the black, white and gray world of the past,"[35] small-sized, and often truncated. They are inserted in the very body of the text, which they illustrate but also periodically puncture, creating visual gaps, blank margins upon the page. Most of the time, this also occasions ruptures in logic and chronology. Indeed, the pictures tend to be deliberately separated from the passages they relate to—whether they precede them or follow at a distance, thereby obscuring and destabilizing meaning, "anarchiving" the archive.[36] This is particularly striking at the beginning of the memoir. Page 7, for example, shows two mysterious pairs of eyes juxtaposed horizontally, meant to attest to the resemblance between Daniel and Shmiel. The reader immediately recognizes the pair on the left as a detail of the portrait of Mendelsohn the child, posted on the first page of the book. The origin of the second pair of eyes is disclosed only on page 10, which shows a full-length picture of Shmiel. A similar effect is created several pages later[37] by the insertion of two other fragments of the same pictures, this time it is the characters' mouths. Likewise, a picture of Shmiel,[38] posing as a prosperous businessman in front of his trucks between two strangers (his employees?), is commented upon only several pages later.[39] No need to say that the photographs bear no captions in *The Lost*. On the rare occasions when a caption appears, it designates pictures that we do not get to see: for example, the picture of Shmiel, together with his wife, Esther, and their youngest daughter, Bronia, dated June 1939, which bears on its back the mention "*Zur Errinerung*" ("as a remembrance of,")[40] is shown long after we have read the caption.[41]

The gap between past and present, object and representation is thus made palpable on the very grain of the page and the reader finds himself in a position akin to that of the author himself, scrutinizing messages he cannot refer to a sender, and pictures he can decipher only in retrospect, if at all.[42] As for the placid pictures of the survivors, they create an even eerier effect: their flat two-dimensionality and ordinary domestic backgrounds point, with cruel irony, to the incommensurability of a tragedy they reveal nothing about.

Placed at strategic moments in the text, the photographs do not only create dramatic effects: in their sparse economy[43] and harrowing immediacy they wound, prick, and shock, literally electrocuting the viewer at times. Placed right under the intriguing title of the first chapter in capital letters, "THE FORMLESS VOID," the portrait of Mendelsohn, a pensive little boy, with hair neatly combed, white shirt and black tie, creates a ghastly and puzzling impression. Similar effects are produced by the brutal insertion of the beaming, dimpled, and chubby face of Ruchele, Shmiel's third daughter just after an account of the 1941 mass shootings in Bolechow[44]; or by the fragile figure of Bronia, who was too much of a child, it seems, to have left a lasting impression on anyone.[45] Or, to mention one last example, by the moving sight of Dizya, a survivor, a benevolent old lady in a polka dot nightgown, gently smiling at the camera on her hospital bed[46]: her picture[47] follows a long transcription of her testimony[48] and the brutal mention of her death.[49] Photographs of places can be just as unsettling: vacant Jewish cemeteries in Austria[50] and Eastern Europe,[51] a gang of cute, blond, boisterous Ukrainian kids playing on abandoned Jewish tombs in Ukraine.[52]

In *Camera Lucida* (*La Chambre claire*), Roland Barthes opposes what he calls the *studium* of a picture (its intellectual content, whatever can be deciphered through the lens of culture) to what he calls the *punctum*, that is to say what has to do strictly with affect: "this element which rises from the scene, shoots out of it like an arrow and pierces me. [. . .] [S]ting, speck, cut, little hole [. . .], that accident which [. . .] bruises me, is poignant to me."[53] In *The Lost* it is as if some of the photographs functioned as *punctum* in and by themselves. In their sweet gravity, silent eloquence, and disarming simplicity they forcefully *advene* (as Barthes would say, playing on the dual register of *advenience* and *adventure*),[54] plunging narrator and reader in shared sideration.

As Barthes later remarks, a *punctum* common to all photographs is the "lacerating emphasis" of time,[55] their capacity to suggest both presence and absence, life and death. Though inevitably subjective (determined by angle, light, and frame) every photograph seems to be "literally an emanation of the referent," it bears undeniable testimony to the "this has been"[56]; in this respect, "[it] has something to do with resurrection."[57] However, a photograph is also a harbinger of death: "I observe with horror an anterior future of which death is the stake."[58] This "madness of photography"[59] is particularly harrowing in the context of Holocaust photographs. Susan Sontag evokes the "posthumous irony" of Roman Vishniac's photographs of Polish ghettoes in 1938: "photographs state the innocence, the vulnerability of lives heading toward their own destruction"; "the contingency of photographs confirms that everything is perishable."[60] In *The Lost*, even the photographs of the survivors, stubborn affirmations of life, shed light on their extreme old age and fragility. For example, which grim future is this tiny old man ("the last Jew of Striy," "*the Last of the Mohicans*")[61] heading to, as we see him, from the back and against the light, slowing descending a stairway. . . .[62] Is he not clearly on the way out?

Because they are fetish objects, pure simulacrum,[63] photographs merely deepen the sense of loss. Despite their deceptive transparency, they remain impenetrable, yielding no disclosure of the subject's essence: "I could scrutinize Shmiel's face and maybe as I looked at it [. . .] it would occur to me how easy it is for someone to become lost, forever unknown."[64] Though they trigger reminiscence, photographs may, in their immutable and hypnotic fixity, eventually block the flow of memory and even act as "counter-memory."[65] "How casually we rely on photographs really," muses Mendelsohn, "how lazy we have become because of them. What does your mother look like? [. . .] and you'll say, Wait, I'll show you and run to an album or a drawer."[66] As Barthes contemplates pictures of his recently deceased mother, he comes to the realization that nothing in a photograph can help transform grief into mourning: "it is a denatured theater where death cannot 'be contemplated,' reflected and interiorized."[67] Open windows into the past, photographs do have a powerful capacity to move the viewer. They are also irresistible invitations to reverie. Yet, they show nothing, heal nothing. In *The Lost* there is nothing to expect from their sealed lips[68] and vacant eyes.[69]

Mendelsohn's quest is in fact an attempt to animate "the mute photographs"[70] of the living and the dead, to retrieve the missing captions. Yet text and pictures merely point to their respective lacks. They interlace in a Moebius strip of interrogations.

THE "ELUSIVE EMBRACE"

After years of archival endeavor, the narrator has reassessed his vision of what life was like in Galician *shtetle* at the turn of the century—a world which his grandfather, as well as Jewish authors like Singer, had so nostalgically embellished.[71] He has studied in detail the history of European Jews. Yet he realizes that the knowledge he is searching for is not to be found in books, websites, or databases. Even his visits to the sites of Jewish life in pre–World War II Europe prove disappointing, revealing either emptiness or—which, to him, is worse—"over-exposure."[72] In Auschwitz for example he sees nothing but trivialization, cheap sentimentalism, not to say an obscene type of voyeurism:

> All of this has been reproduced, photographed, filmed, broadcast and published so often that [. . .] you find yourself looking for [. . .] "the attractions," for the displays of the artificial limbs or glasses or hair, more or less as you'd look for the newly reconstructed apatosaurus as the Natural History Museum [. . .]
>
> As if [. . .] one could understand significantly better the experience of those who came to this place not in air-conditioned tour vans but in cattle cars.[73]

To museum exhibits, to hackneyed clichés or dry generalizations, to the charts, lists, and statistics of the historians, Mendelsohn prefers the emotion that overwhelms him in Bolechow upon encountering former acquaintances of Shmiel's: "It was the sudden and vertiginous sense of proximity to them [. . .] that made my sister and me start crying [. . .] the sixty years and the millions of dead didn't seem bigger than the three feet that separated me from the fat arm of the old woman [. . .].[74] The traumatic memories of the interviewed fuse with similar intensity. Thus they instinctively lower their voice to disclose innocuous secrets of times long past: during the war,

Shmiel, who was a butcher, would sell non-kosher meat [75]; as for his daughter Frydka, she dated a Goy. . . .

Part of the puzzle is reconstructed: Shmiel's wife and three of his daughters were killed during the "Holocaust by Bullets." What happened to the other members of the family, however? Why would this version be more authentic than the one proposed in America? Mendelsohn is fully aware of the subjectivity of his informers, of their potential lies, omissions, or extrapolations ("embellishments or even fabrications" [76]), be they conscious or not. Memory can play tricks, of course, and trauma, by definition, precludes full registration or cognition. [77] Moreover everyone speaks from his own limited perspective, and some may prefer to keep embarrassing details undisclosed: "Nobody has ever told me a story without having some kind of agenda." [78] Last but not least, all testimonies of the Shoah are necessarily indirect. *"Niemand / Zeugt für den / Zeugen,"* wrote Paul Celan. [79] No one bears witness for the witness. Nobody has ever returned from a gas chamber. "[T]he thing [. . .] was never witnessed and is therefore unknowable." [80] The testimonies gathered along the quest contradict each other and fail to fit in a coherent whole. The necessity for Mendelsohn to rely on translators from Yiddish, Polish, or Ukrainian makes access to meaning even more problematic. [81]

Mendelsohn begins to perceive the limits of his own approach: of his naivity, awkwardness, or downright self-centeredness. Wasn't it crazy, he wonders, to embark his brothers and sisters on an ill-prepared first trip to Bolechow ("almost a cliche of family unity" [82])? Wasn't he just trying not to bear alone the family guilt? He also becomes more sensitive to his informers' reactions. Isn't it heartless, after all, to show them pictures he himself is used to, yet whose emotional charge might be too strong for them? [83] "[S]*unt lacrimae rerum*," he reflects, quoting Virgil. "There are tears in things; but we all cry for different reasons." [84] Mendelsohn also fears his questions themselves might be inappropriate: "If someone asked me now to describe certain of the neighbors who'd lived across the street from me forty years ago, I'm not sure I'd have much to say except 'He was an engineer, they were very nice.'" [85]

Little by little, the quester modifies the very nature of his quest. His relatives' lives, the very texture and color of their everyday existence may matter more, after all, than the circumstances of their death. Mendelsohn now resolves to perceive them as ordinary people "instead of sepia icons." [86] Could it be, he wonders, that his own quest partook of the very museography he dislikes so much, objectifying people and turning their stories into archival material? The point is expressed by one of his informers, Meg Grossbart: "'I don't want my life in your book,' she told me. [. . .] She knew that the minute she allowed me to start telling her stories, they would become my stories." [87]

Moreover, there might be something just as predatory, acquisitive, or manipulative about Matt's photographs. Indeed, as Susan Sontag remarks, "There is an aggression implicit in every use of the camera"; "To photograph is to appropriate the thing photographed."[88] Nowhere is the witnesses' reluctance to testify better expressed than in the picture of Meg Grossbart.[89] Within its black frame, it shows a close shot of her face, almost entirely covered by a black rectangle. She is holding in front of her mouth, yet slightly decentered, a small black and white photograph of Shmiel's daughter, Lorka, about whom—this is made very clear—the essential facts will remain undisclosed. The photograph as such appears in its very composition as a fascinating *mise en abyme* of the book itself.

From then on the stress is on the personality of "the Lost," on the telling details, the amusing or poignant anecdotes that might bring them back to life. Shmiel was a self-assured man with hearing problems. He used to love strawberries. His wife Esther was a distinguished woman with pretty legs. Ruchele was a blonde, placid girl with long beautiful hair which she wore plaited. She had a brown spot in one of her green eyes.[90] As for Frydka, she was a strong-willed young woman of uncommon courage. She had fought together with the Polish partisans and was pregnant at the time of her death.

Mendelsohn now shows his informers as much respect, attention, and tact as a psychoanalyst, showing empathy and refraining from judgment. A minute observer, he draws textual portraits[91] which are just as suggestive as his brother's photographs—beautifying their subjects and endowing them with amazing dignity. Indeed, "To photograph is to confer importance."[92] The picture of Mrs Begley, so dear to Daniel,[93] is a case in point. In the mundane setting half-enveloped in darkness, the witty-eyed old lady, sitting straight up on the edge of her bed, her cane behind her, seems to emanate tranquil courage, humor, and pathos.[94]

CAMERA OBSCURA: BLACK HOLES AND SECOND GLANCES

As he patiently confronts historical sources and oral testimonies Mendelsohn eventually reaches a clear vision of the various stages of mass extermination in Bolechow: "The first *Aktion*. The second *Aktion*. The *Lager*. The *Fassfabrik*. The final liquidation in 43."[95] At this point he hopes a second trip to Bolechow will bring his quest to a conclusion. He is then able to identify his grandfather's house as well as the old movie house where the Jews had been gathered before they were taken to the forest and shot in 1941. Photographs now abound in the memoir as if they might concur to delineate "the whole picture."[96] Giving free rein to his imagination, Mendelsohn is more and more tempted to elaborate on the missing parts. Yet "fantasies so intense" never take precedence over ethical concerns.[97] For beyond stupor or terror, "even if (say) a photograph of the town existed today that had been taken on October 28 1941," how could one possibly imagine what Esther, Ruchele, or Lorka had in mind as they walked to their death?[98] How could one conceive of the horror of the mass graves, the stench of the cattle cars, the shrieks of the dying? How could one render the effacement of all traces, a last outrage to the dead on the part of the Germans? "It's like a black hole."[99]

It is no coincidence, then, that Mendelsohn's quest should end (or so he thinks) precisely in a black hole ("steeped in a profound inky black"[100]): the pitch dark hiding place located in the basement of the house of two Ukrainian schoolteachers where Shmiel and his eldest daughter, Frydka, had found refuge before they were denounced. As he goes down there, Daniel seized by claustrophobia feels as if he were in a box . . . a *kestle* in Yiddish! The truth occurs to him in a sort of epiphany as he suddenly realizes that his grandfather had in fact mistaken the Yiddish word *Kestle* for the word "castle" in English. As in psychoanalysis, meaning is approached through a subtle shift in signifiers. The truth had been there, all the time. Mendelsohn depicts with humor his discomfiture:

> Oh my God, I was so stupid. [. . .] All those years I [. . .] had heard what I'd wanted to hear, a story like a fairy tale, a tragic drama, complete with a nobleman and a castle. It had [. . .] required that I [. . .] see the place with my own eyes before the fact, the material reality, allowed me to understand the words at last.[101]

Here, one is of course reminded of the author's peculiar Chinese box technique. It is as if his amazing talent for storytelling had made possible the improbable coincidence between the signifier and the signified, between fable and reality, between erasure and memory. As if he had at last circumscribed, made literally palpable

> the gaping, vertiginous black hole of the unsayable years in which an impossible romance of one's own origins was being engulfed [. . .] the compact void of impossible speech.[102]

Mendelsohn takes a picture of the hole, thinking he has touched the rockbottom of things: "it had been *there.* I had always wanted specifics. Now I had found them."[103] Yet, on second glance, there is something purely tautological about this finding. "The hole was just that: a hole."[104] The photograph of the open trap in the two Ukrainians' livingroom is surprisingly undramatic.[105] As for the picture taken inside the hole itself, it is not even inserted in the book. The turn of the screw has proved ineffectual.

Significantly *The Lost* does not end there. Unexpected twists of events eventually lead Mendelsohn to the very place where Shmiel and Frydka were shot and where, according to the Jewish custom, he leaves a few pebbles as sign of his passage. The quester is then able to leave the place of origins with a *certain* sense of accomplishment. As his car drives away from Bolechow, he even forgets to cast a last glance backward: "we had travelled too far, and Bolochow had slipped out of sight."[106]

The book proposes, however, no Aristotelian denouement or totalizing picture. The archive cannot be closed; the list of the dead will never be complete as shown by the abundant "paratext" proposed at the end of the volume.[107] When it comes to the Shoah, meaning, it would seem, exceeds all frames of reference. Ceaselessly deferred, deported, it remains beyond the realm of representation.

Nevertheless Mendelsohn has come to terms with the traumas "encrypted"[108] in the family's memory and passed on from one generation to the next. That of the Shoah, of course, and of the family guilt, but also, this should be added, the constant rift between siblings which "runs through [his] family as surely as do certain genes."[109] Indeed the grandfather's troubled relation to Shmiel ("the sin between brothers,"[110] which Daniel relates to the Abel and Cain motif), is itself a reflection of that which had tied Abraham Jager to his own uncle, whom he had held responsible for his sister's death: in exchange for the price of their passage to America, the uncle had forced his own sister (Abraham's mother, then a destitute widow with seven children) to give him the hand of her eldest daughter for his son (an ugly hunchback). The girl (of whom we get to see a moving picture in her wedding dress)[111] had died a few weeks after the wedding. As he listens to these stories, Daniel is reminded of "the obscure but ferocious competitiveness,"[112] which had long opposed him to his own brother Matt (a cute little boy[113] and "a hero in high school"[114]) and which once led him to break the boy's arm in a fit of rage. One trauma reverberates onto the other: as he tries to imagine the screams of the martyred Jews of Bolechow, Mendelsohn recalls his younger brother's screaming on this occasion.[115] In the course of their adventures, Daniel gets closer and closer to Matt ("a brother whom I'd never really known before, a deep-feeling and soft-hearted man, an artist who says little and sees much"[116]); and he makes him, so to speak, the co-author of the volume. While also developing strong ties of friendship to the survivors, the author feels as if he had constructed a new and larger family for himself: "it is difficult not to think of them as such."[117]

All in all, the quest has been an opening to the Other, within and without. It has led Mendelsohn, the classicist, to return to his Jewish roots and to explore a part of his biography which had remained undisclosed in *The Elusive Embrace*. In all probability the experience has also been cathartic for his informers to whom Mendelsohn has offered the salutary relief of words, the possibility to work through their trauma. In any case, he has endowed their story of dispossession and victimization with epic dignity. To the dead, to those left unburied ("nothing more than the earth and weather in some

Ukrainian pasture"),[118] Mendelohn has offered a grave, made of words and pictures, a magnificent *Kaddish*. The grip of obsession and melancholia has been released. A work of mourning has taken place at last. What had been lost in translation, lost in transcription, will not be forever lost in transmission.

NOTES

1. His first memoir, entitled *The Elusive Embrace: Desire and the Riddle of Identity* (New York: Vintage Books, [1999] 2000), was published in 1999.
2. Efraim Sicher, "The Burden of Memory: The Writings of the Post-Holocaust Generation," in *Breaking Crystal: Writing and Memory after Auschwitz*, ed. Efraim Sicher (Urbana: University of Illinois Press, 1998), 27.
3. Nadine Fresco, "La diaspora des cendres," *Nouvelle Revue de Psychanlyse* 24 (1981): 212. Translation mine.
4. Henri Raczymow and Alan Astro, "Memory Shot Through With Holes," *Yale French Studies* 85, *Discourses of Jewish Identity in Twentieth-Century France* (1994): 102.
5. Marianne Hirsch, *The Generation of Postmemory: Writing and Visual Culture After the Holocaust* (New York: Columbia University Press, 2012), 5–6. For a reading of *The Lost* focused on the notion of trauma, see Marc Amfreville's illuminating article (Marc Amfreville, "Family Archive Fever in Mendelsohn's *The Lost*," in *Contemporary Trauma Narratives*, ed. J. M. Ganteau and Susana Onega [New York: Routledge, 2014]: 241–66). He perceives the book as a "trauma-text" whose very structure mimics the functioning of trauma (255).
6. Eva Hoffman, *After Such Knowledge* (New York: Vintage, 2004), 6.
7. Hoffman, *After Such Knowledge*, 185.
8. Daniel Mendelsohn, *The Lost: A Search for Six of Six Million* (New York: HarperCollins, 2006), 3.
9. Mendelsohn, *The Lost*, 6.
10. Mendelsohn, *The Elusive Embrace*, 132.
11. Mendelsohn, *The Lost*, 7.
12. Mendelsohn, *The Lost*, 15.
13. Mendelsohn, *The Lost*, 58.
14. Mendelsohn, *The Lost*, 24.
15. Mendelsohn, *The Lost*, 69.
16. Mendelsohn, *The Lost*, 98.
17. Mendelsohn, *The Lost*, 8.
18. Daniel Mendelsohn, Interview: *Queen's Quarterly: A Canadian Review* (Spring 2008): 68. According to Nadine Fresco, postgenerations are doomed to live "in a sort of exile, not from any present or future location, but from some bygone time which might be that of identity itself" (211, translation mine).
19. Jacques Derrida and Eric Prenowitz, "Archive Fever: A Freudian Impression," *Diacritics* 25, no. 2 (Summer 1995): 9–63. Derrida describes this "fever" (*mal d'archive*) as follows: "It is to burn with a passion. It is never to rest, interminably, from searching for the archive, right where it slips away. It is to run after the archive, even if there's too much of it, right where something in it anarchives itself. It is to have a compulsive, repetitive, and nostalgic desire for the archive, an irrepressible desire to return to the origin, a homesickness, a nostalgia for the return to the most archaic place of absolute commencement" (57). Interestingly, Derrida recalls the dual etymology of the term "archive": *arkhe* means both commencement and commandment (9). He also points out that "archive fever" is a symptom of the disappearance of "either memory or anamnesis as spontaneous, alive and internal experience" (9).
20. Mendelsohn, *The Lost*, 42.
21. Mendelsohn, *The Lost*, 44, 43.

22. Mendelsohn, *The Lost*, 22. This phrase is precisely the title of Richard Pedot's article: Richard Pedot, "To frame, elaborately, a question: *The Lost* (D. Mendelsohn) ou le récit malaise," *L'Atelier* 14, no. 1 (2012): 2–11.

23. Mendelsohn, *Queen's Quarterly*, 64.

24. See Mendelsohn: "Obviously there are many examples of Proustian references and recollections and verbal echoes [. . .] I go about telling my Jewish-Polish-Shtetl story through the lens of Proust" (*Queen's Quarterly*, 61–62). The epigraph of the book is borrowed from Proust.

25. Mendelsohn, *The Lost*, 156.

26. Mendelsohn, *The Lost*, 6.

27. Mendelsohn, *The Lost*, 121.

28. Mendelsohn, *The Lost*, 263.

29. Mendelsohn, *The Lost*, 18.

30. He wrote, for example, an outstanding doctoral dissertation on *Gender and the City in Euripides' Political Plays*, published by Oxford University Press in 2002, and in paperback edition in 2005.

31. Mendelsohn, *The Lost*, 167.

32. Mendelsohn, *The Lost*, 33.

33. Mendelsohn, *The Lost*, 22.

34. "I the writer [. . .] the one with his words to write and inscriptions to decipher, and the other [. . .] with his photographs to pose and to print, the two of us, two brothers, traveling to Australia and Prague and Vienna and Tel Aviv [. . .]" (Mendelsohn, *The Lost*, 72).

35. Mendelsohn, *The Lost*, 45.

36. Derrida and Prenowitz, "Archive Fever," 57.

37. Mendelsohn, *The Lost*, 17.

38. Mendelsohn, *The Lost*, 21.

39. Mendelsohn, *The Lost*, 24.

40. Mendelsohn, *The Lost*, 23. As if Shmiel, aware of his imminent death, intended to prick his brother's conscience. The point is repeated even more forcefully on the back of another picture: *Zur Errinerung an dein Bruder*: To remember your brother "in his 44th year" (25).

41. Mendelsohn, *The Lost*, 184.

42. Mendelsohn himself recalls that it took him years to identify the mysterious young man posing next to Shmiel in an Austrian army uniform (*The Lost*, 75) as "Herman the Barber," someone whom he himself had known (and systematically avoided) all his childhood, thus overlooking a most precious source of information (72–73). Likewise, he realizes only upon aggrandizing the picture, that a tombstone he had photographed in Ukraine is precisely that of his great-aunt Taube (133).

43. Such scarcity has to do, of course, with what little remains of the past. Yet Daniel and Matt have selected only a few of the "many hundreds of photographs of [their] trips" (*The Lost*, 96).

44. Mendelsohn, *The Lost*, 213.

45. Mendelsohn, *The Lost*, 297.

46. Mendelsohn, *The Lost*, 360.

47. Mendelsohn, *The Lost*, 360.

48. Mendelsohn, *The Lost*, 354–59.

49. Mendelsohn, *The Lost*, 359.

50. Mendelsohn, *The Lost*, 135.

51. Mendelsohn, *The Lost*, 292.

52. Mendelsohn, *The Lost*, 134.

53. Roland Barthes, *Camera Lucida: Reflections on Photography*, trans. Richard Howard, http://monoskop.org/images/c/c5/Barthes_Roland_Camera_Lucida_Reflections_on _Photography.pdf, 26.

54. Barthes, *Camera Lucida*, 19.

55. Barthes, *Camera Lucida*, 96.

56. "*Le ça a été.*" Barthes, *Camera Lucida*, 96.

57. Barthes, *Camera Lucida*, 82.

58. Barthes, *Camera Lucida*, 96.
59. Barthes, *Camera Lucida*, 13. On this paradox, see also Maurice Blanchot: "Les deux versions de l'imaginaire" ("The two versions of the imaginary" [translation mine]), in *L'espace littéraire* (Paris: Gallimard, 1955), 341–57. Georges Didi-Huberman prefers to speak of *l'image déchirure*, of the image as breach (Georges Didi-Huberman, *Ce que nous voyons, ce qui nous regarde* [Paris: Minuit, 1992], 192).
60. Susan Sontag, *On Photography* (New York: Penguin, 1977), 70, 80.
61. Mendelsohn, *The Lost*, 141, 142.
62. Mendelsohn, *The Lost*, 143.
63. All the more so since in *The Lost* all photographs are posed. Most pictures of the dead are studio shots. As for those of the living, they are artfully composed. At one point for example, Matt takes his subjects to the beach, so that he might take "a picture that says 'Australia'" (Mendelsohn, *The Lost*, 257). We can observe him at work, waiting till the evening light is adequate, making several pictures of the same scene, and eventually asking a surfer to pose in the background. The picture (259) is given depth and local color at once. The outcome is amazingly beautiful and moving.
64. Mendelsohn, *The Lost*, 71.
65. Barthes, *Camera Lucida*, 91.
66. Mendelsohn, *The Lost*, 182.
67. Barthes, *Camera Lucida*, 10.
68. Mendelsohn, *The Lost*, 17.
69. Mendelsohn, *The Lost*, 7.
70. Mendelsohn, *The Lost*, 7.
71. Mendelsohn, *The Lost*, 48.
72. Mendelsohn, *The Lost*, 112.
73. Mendelsohn, *The Lost*, 113.
74. Mendelsohn, *The Lost*, 123.
75. Mendelsohn, *The Lost*, 309.
76. Mendelsohn, *The Lost*, 103.
77. See for example Dori Laub (in Cathy Caruth, ed., *Trauma: Explorations in Memory* [Baltimore: Johns Hopkins, 2003], 6): "it is a record that has yet to be made."
78. Mendelsohn, *The Lost*, 118. Thus one of the survivors, Meg, fears she might be led to reveal that her husband used to work for the Jewish militia which collaborated with the Germans. As for those who were bystanders of the crime, the Ukrainians, in particular, they might also have quite a few things to conceal. The slaughter of East European Jews was effected with the active participation of the local populations.
79. Paul Celan, "Aschenglorie," *Choix de poèmes réunis par l'auteur* (Paris: Gallimard, [1952] 1998), 264.
80. Mendelsohn, *The Lost*, 205.
81. On this respect, see Yves-Charles Grandjeat's study of heteroglossia and translation in *The Lost*: Yves-Charles Grandjeat, "Translation, Heteroglossia and Othering in Daniel Mendelsohn's *The Lost*," in *(Se) construire dans l'interlangue: Perspectives transatlantiques sur le multilinguisme*, ed. F Bonnet-Falandry, S. Durrans, and M. Jones (Villeneuve d'Ascq: Presses Universitaires du Septentrion, 2015), 165–75.
82. Mendelsohn, *The Lost*, 81.
83. Mendelsohn, *The Lost*, 182.
84. Mendelsohn, *The Lost*, 183.
85. Mendelsohn, *The Lost*, 199.
86. Mendelsohn, *The Lost*, 191.
87. Mendelsohn, *The Lost*, 253.
88. Sontag, *On Photography*, 7, 4.
89. Mendelsohn, *The Lost*, 262.
90. Mendelsohn, *The Lost*, 200.
91. See, for example: "When she answered the door, a slightly pear-shaped woman with a tentative, pretty face and the delicate complexion and faintly ginger hair of someone who avoids the sun, she was wearing a sleeveless white blouse and a narrow gray skirt that reached

the tops of her knees. As with my grandmothers, the heavy flesh on her upper arms was both plump and sleek, like a dough that has been kneaded for a long time" (Mendelsohn, *The Lost*, 293).
92. Sontag, *On Photography*, 28.
93. The book is in part dedicated to her.
94. Mendelsohn, *The Lost*, 445.
95. Mendelsohn, *The Lost*, 336.
96. Mendelsohn, *The Lost*, 17.
97. Mendelsohn, *The Lost*, 67.
98. Mendelsohn, *The Lost*, 205.
99. Mendelsohn, *The Lost*, 388.
100. Mendelsohn, *The Lost*, 482.
101. Mendelsohn, *The Lost*, 482.
102. Nadine Fresco, "La diaspora des cendres" ("The diaspora of the ashes"), *Nouvelle Revue de Psychanalyse* 24 (1981): 206, 208. Translation mine.
103. Mendelsohn, *The Lost*, 483.
104. Mendelsohn, *The Lost*, 483.
105. Mendelsohn, *The Lost*, 482.
106. Mendelsohn, *The Lost*, 503.
107. Mendelsohn, *The Lost*, 505–16. A list *in memoriam* of the deceased witnesses (505), a postscript evoking the circumstances of Bronia's death, an author's note, as well as a series of acknowledgments.
108. The term is here used in the strong sense ascribed by Abraham and Maria Torok in *L'écorce et la noyau* (Paris: Flammarion, 1987). See in particular chapter IV, "The crypt within the self" (translation mine).
109. Mendelsohn, *The Lost*, 96.
110. Mendelsohn, *The Lost*, 79.
111. Mendelsohn, *The Lost*, 97.
112. Mendelsohn, *The Lost*, 44.
113. Mendelsohn, *The Lost*, 32.
114. Mendelsohn, *The Lost*, 111.
115. Mendelsohn, *The Lost*, 205.
116. Mendelsohn, *The Lost*, 430.
117. Mendelsohn, *The Lost*, 513.
118. Mendelsohn, *The Lost*, 25.

Chapter Five

Life After Death

A Third-Generation Journey in Jérémie Dres's We Won't See Auschwitz

Alan L. Berger

Assessing the impact of the Shoah on family legacy, Eva Hoffman attests that it continues unto the third generation. "The grandchildren of survivors," she writes, "are still deeply affected by their elders' experiences, memories, accounts."[1] Moreover, she contends that "for the aging survivors, relationships with the third generation can be deeply solacing and liberating."[2] But third-generation post-Holocaust Jewish identity is a complex and multifaceted phenomenon forged on the anvil of Auschwitz and in the crucible of postmodernity; genealogical research supplants theological attestations. The search for roots is widespread and gives prominence to the role of agency in choosing how and if the Shoah is represented in an individual's consciousness. In addition, third-generation literary responses appear in a variety of genres: films, memoirs, novels, poetry, and short stories. Collectively, these responses reveal a fuller understanding of their authors' identities while seeking to assemble the missing pieces of a vanished Jewish world. Furthermore, third-generation literature is a paradigm shift in literary representation of the Shoah for two basic reasons: it appears near the era of "after testimony," and it concerns itself with intergenerational transmission of a story that is both chronologically remote yet deeply personal.

Third-generation accounts exhibit two points on a continuum. On the one hand, there is a concern for working through the burden of their inheritance. This, in turn, requires an unblinking confrontation with the facts of history as revealed in works such as Johanna Adorján's *An Exclusive Love*, Daniel Mendelsohn's *The Lost: A Search for Six of Six Million*, Julie Orringer's *The*

Invisible Bridge, and Andrea Simon's *Bashert: A Granddaughter's Holocaust Quest*, to name but a few. The third generation seeks to discover as much as they can about relatives victimized in the Shoah. They visit "sites of memory," including, and especially, death camps and sites of massacres, as well as grandparents' birthplaces. They also interview both Jews and non-Jews, relatives and strangers, and engage in archival research seeking to discover more about the Shoah and their own post-Auschwitz Jewish space. On the other hand, there is an emerging—and highly controversial—Israeli phenomenon of grandchildren tattooing their grandparents' Holocaust numbers on their own flesh. This practice is intended to honor the grandparents and perpetuate Holocaust memory. Several tattooed third-generation members were interviewed for a 2012 *New York Times* article. Each responded that "they wanted to live the mantra 'Never forget' with something that would constantly provoke questions and conversation."[3] Nevertheless, this borders on kitsch and runs the risk of trivializing the Shoah.

THIRD-GENERATION RETURN NARRATIVES

Third-generation return narratives are fraught. Their authors experience the uncanny phenomenon of returning to a place they have never physically been. They are, in Victoria Aarons's words, "less going back than they are setting forth, an incongruous forward march into the past."[4] Return instantiates a prominent feature of the third generation: a pilgrimage to the sites of a survivor's pre-Shoah existence, and extensive research into the past. It is significant to recall that the word pilgrimage has a specific intent: a life-changing journey to a "special or unusual place" that assumes aspects of ritual. A pilgrim's goal is to deepen, enhance, and otherwise alter his or her self-understanding and her or his relationship to a particular community. Consequently, return narratives comprise both historical and psychic components, affective and cognitive modes of learning.

Jérémie Dres's *We Won't See Auschwitz* broadens our understanding of the third-generation return narrative by undertaking a path which offers a distinctively different point of view.[5] The author, a Parisian Jew, has written a graphic novel, his first book, which won the 2012 prize *France Info* in the category of News and Reporting Comic Strip. This genre-bending work—memoir, sociological inquiry, history lesson, and political primer interspersed with humor—is divided into thirty-one topics, and contains interviews with fourteen individuals. Dres uses Poland as a living laboratory in which he will investigate and come to a more complete understanding of his Jewish roots. The volume combines the author's personal quest with the question of how his odyssey relates to the Jewish people. While acknowledging the enormity of the Shoah, he chooses to focus on his Jewish roots by pursuing instead the deuteronomic call to choose life over death, seeking to uncover more fully the way of life of a vanished world. This quest brings to mind Yaffa Eliach's iconic "Tower of Life," a display of approximately 1,500 photographs, at the United States Holocaust Memorial Museum. Eliach's focus is on the Jews of the Polish shtetl of Eishyshok, her birthplace. Her goal is to show the *life* of the pre-Shoah Jewish community and to underscore the *vitality* of Judaism. Dres frames his quest succinctly. He writes, "Auschwitz: five years of devastation for more than a thousand years of Jewish life and history . . . a trauma still so present as to overshadow the rest. But the rest was what I'd gone looking for in Poland."[6]

Dres's book problematizes the issue of third-generation response by emphasizing a break between the sorrow of the survivor generation and the proximity of the second generation to their survivor parents. Jean-Yves Potel, in his preface to the volume, observes: "This third [French] generation has put some distance behind them, which isn't the same thing as forgetting." Rather, he continues, this generation "can shoulder [the Shoah] differently . . . [they] are no longer obliged to perpetuate family sorrow."[7] Potel, continues, observing that, by intentionally avoiding Auschwitz or any other death camp, Dres's concern is to "reconstruct the life from before, share the little every day joys and sorrows from a time gone by, a vanished world, a distant culture" in order to "better appreciate what our grandmothers or grandfathers have passed down. We go to the old country to find them again."[8]

Dres and his older brother Martin spend a week in Poland seeking to trace the life of their beloved Polish-born Grandmother Thérèse, Tema Dres, née Barab, who survived occupied Paris by hiding in a closet. Furthermore, Jérémie Dres's return to the old country is *not only an exploration of his grandmother's pre-Shoah existence*. It is as well a *way of mourning* Tema, who died in 2009, while simultaneously filling in the considerable lacunae in his knowledge of Polish Judaism both past and contemporary. Like the American third-generation writer Jonathan Safran Foer in *Everything is Illuminated*, Jérémie also seeks to shed light on his identity. Unlike the hero in that novel who returns, uninformed, to Ukraine searching for the person who allegedly saved his grandfather's life during the Shoah, Dres succeeds in his efforts. But these efforts would not have come to fruition without his going to Poland. The country serves as a laboratory for him to explore third-generation post-Shoah Jewish identity. His journey is given impetus by two events: one very personal and the other intellectual.

Jérémie attests that his grandmother has become his confidante over the last few years. In a touching series of eight panels, which reinforces Hoffman's observation concerning the relationship between survivor grandparents and their grandchildren, he draws himself visiting Tema. They sit at her kitchen table, drinking coffee while she pats his hand, offering solace to her grandson who has just broken up with a girlfriend. Assuring him that he will find someone else, she reverts to Yiddish, exclaiming: "*Kain ein horeh* [against the evil eye]. You'll find another, a nice one."[9] Tema's face exudes compassion and warmth; Jérémie's visage has a bemused look. The balloon reads, "My grandma is a droplet of pure water from a spring over there that has since vanished. Seventy years of French life have done nothing to change her Yiddish accent."[10] Interrupted by his ringing cell phone, he leaves the room to take the call. Returning, he discovers that his grandmother has died. Later, he draws himself in front of a Warsaw apartment house, where he muses "If I'm here, it's partly to find her again."[11] Jérémie dedicates his book to Tema.

Dres is also motivated by an article in *Le Monde Magazine*, "The Revival of Polish Jewry," by Olivier Guez, a writer and journalist. The article explodes familiar stereotypes about the complete disappearance of Jews from Polish soil. Prior to reading the article, Dres—along with many in the Jewish community—believed two things about Poland: that it was a country comprised solely of anti-Semitic killers, and that the Jewish community in Poland consisted only of archival photos. Consequently, he contacts various Jewish Poles quoted in Guez's article in order to explore the past, present, and future of Polish Jewry. Moreover, he begins to believe that his personal mission will have a universal dimension. He draws two panels whose dominant images are the top of his head—emphasizing the cerebral element—and his computer's keyboard. The balloon over the first panel contains the words, "So the journey wouldn't just be a personal one. It'd bear witness to the future of an entire people."[12] He continues this line of thinking in the second image, writing "to life before and after, over the course of my research into my family."[13]

A VARIANT OF POSTMEMORY

Marianne Hirsch has advanced the theory of postmemory in describing how survivor memory is inherited, so to speak, by their children. Her theory seeks to clarify the intimate relationship between memory and collective identity in the process of transmitting survivor history to the second generation. Postmemory, asserts Hirsch, is "distinguished from memory by generational distance and from history by deep personal connection."[14] Moreover, it names "the experience of those who grow up dominated by narratives that preceded their birth, (and) whose own belated stories are evacuated by the stories of the previous generation shaped by traumatic events that can be neither understood nor recreated."[15] Although her primary focus is on the second generation and specifically treats the issue of intergenerational trauma transmission, Hirsch does extend her theory to the third generation and beyond in speaking about both *affiliative* and *familial* postmemory. Her rubric contains elements which are applicable to the third generation.

Tema's memory, conveyed through her endless tales of pre-Shoah Jewish existence in Poland, is etched in the minds of the Dres brothers. As noted, Jérémie's journey to Poland is in part his attempt to find his grandmother again which is also in a manner of speaking his way of continuing their relationship. In a moving postscript to Jérémie's book, titled "Her Name Was Tema," Martin stresses the fact that their grandmother was "a link across several generations. A link between the war and today."[16] She communicated two types of experience. On the one hand, "she knew how to re-create the fear she experienced in occupied Paris where she survived by hiding in a closet." On the other hand, Tema "recounted her Warsaw childhood so well that after more than a hundred years, *we seem to remember it ourselves*."[17] Furthermore, their Polish sojourn also reunited the brothers, not unlike the journey undertaken by Daniel Mendelsohn and his siblings in *The Lost*. Martin writes: "In a way our grandmother, from her distant, eternal abode, guided our steps to reunite far away in time and space, in Poland, the land of her birth."[18]

IN POLAND: SHATTERING STEREOTYPES AND DISCOVERING JEWISH ROOTS

The brothers' pilgrimage is "a journey in three stages."[19] Initially, they travel to Warsaw, retracing the life of Tema and her parents. They then go to the village of Żelechów, seeking traces of their paternal grandfather. Krawkow, site of the biggest European festival of Jewish culture, is their final stop before returning to Paris. Each of these sites, two big cities and one village, bears distinctive witness both to the Jewish past and present. Jérémie's familial response to his Polish journey reveals the extent to which many members of the second and third generation cling to the stereotype of Poland as a nation of murderers of the Jewish people. One travels there only to see death camps. Furthermore, there is a pervasive Dres family taboo about Poland. The author draws his computer screen on which appears a message from his father: "Hello Jérémie. If you're going to Poland, above all watch out for Polacks. Hugs, Dad."[20] His cousin and aunt reply in kind, sending him text messages on his cell phone. He draws himself, puzzled look on his face, reading those texts. His cousin texts, "I would have loved to come with you. I mean, not to see those dirty Polacks!" Dres's aunt writes "Oh really? You are going to see Auschwitz?"[21] Drawing the interior of his Paris apartment, in which a framed photo of his grandmother occupies pride of place, Dres remembers that she always said "Marry whoever you want but not a Polack or a Kraut." This admonition was followed by her concern for his physical well-being: "And have a banana, you're so thin."[22]

JEWISH ROOTS AND THE TROPE OF POSTMODERN IDENTITY

Jérémie and Martin's experience in Warsaw, by far the volume's largest section, constitutes an intense immersion in visual pre-Shoah history of the Jews in Poland which, in turn, yields important information and some surprises. As an aside, it is significant to note that both France and Poland were, for many decades following the Second World War, in denial both about the particularity of the Jewish experience and the respective national role in the fate of the Jews during the Catastrophe thereby constituting an assault on memory and identity. Both countries have more recently begun to come to terms with the legacy of the Holocaust. To return to the discussion, in contemporary Poland Dres interviews a variety of figures, among them his contemporaries, rabbis (both from America and from Israel), agency officials both Jewish and non-Jewish, bureaucrats, and the director of the Warsaw cemetery.

To his surprise Dres learns that the search for Jewish roots is widespread. A non-observant Jew, the author emerges from his Polish pilgrimage more connected to Jewish history and to the milieu in which his grandmother had lived. This connection reveals three important facts: First, it expands our knowledge of the variety of third-generation identity, especially in Europe where, as Diana Pinto contends, all contemporary European Jews are "voluntary Jews," who choose their own form of Jewish identity.[23] Furthermore, this quest for Jewish roots occurs among what is termed an "unexpected generation" of Polish Jews. These are Jews whose grandparents were Jewish and who were given to non-Jewish Poles during the Shoah in order to save their lives. In the third place, it emphasizes the issue of agency stressing that the postmodern quest for roots supplants halakhaic (normative) theological attestations. Post-Shoah and postmodern identity frequently becomes a cultural phenomenon as grandchildren explore their grandparents' lives seeking to connect to their own Jewishness and to better understand both their ancestors and themselves in a Jewish context. Agency and intersectionality become part of the Jewish roots phenomenon.

Jérémie's quest includes long discussions with Jewish Poles who shed light on the country's tortured historical response to its Jewish citizens. In the section titled "Young, Jewish, and Polish," he meets Jan and Danka, two of his contemporaries. Jérémie confesses his astonishment that Jews still live in Poland and asks Jan why he remains in the country. Jan's response helps clarify the nature of post-Shoah Polish/Jewish identity. Those who left Poland after the war, he reports, were Orthodox or poor. Everyone who felt more Jewish than Polish left for Israel, America, or France. Moreover, the Soviets effaced Jewish history by not rebuilding the ghetto because it "didn't hold much interest."[24] Jan contends that Polish Jews today are highly visible in public life. However they are not halakhic Jews. Furthermore, in a stinging critique of orthodoxy, he reports that the devout "have learned nothing here. They welcome only Halakhic Jews, whereas most of us aren't."[25] Jan illustrates his point by referencing his own family, many of whom belong to the elite but rarely go to synagogue. Consequently, Dres learns that Poland—which consists of a very small Jewish community—is not immune from the economic and social fissures that exist in every Jewish community.

The discussion turns to the issue of the Jewish future. Illustrating their discussion, Jérémie portrays Jan, Danka, and himself sitting in an outdoor café. Jan expansively contends "If you start digging, everyone in Warsaw's Jewish."[26] However, he also attests that there is no future for Polish Jews. Furthermore, the two males agree that marrying endogamously is important, although not for religious reasons. Jérémie attests that his grandmother wanted him to marry a Jewish girl. "Old traditions," he exclaims. Jan also speaks of marrying Jewishly "Out of duty to my grandparents."[27] As if to illustrate the secular nature of this discussion, Dres draws a group of nearby fans enthusiastically cheering while watching the World Cup quarter finals.

Drawing himself speaking with Jan, Dres has a perplexed and worried look as he confesses his fear of telling Polish people too much of his story. He opines that "it's not a memory they want stirred up. They much prefer tourists, not people like us, carrying around a tragic history that involves them."[28] Jan responds by saying that while anti-Semitism still exists, "it's ok in the big cities," but admonishes Jérémie to be careful about people in small towns.[29] He reports that Danka and he edit a small circulation magazine called *Zoom*. The current edition has a cover story titled "8 Stories That Haven't Changed the World" dealing with accounts of Holocaust survivors who, notes Jan, were "asked about their childhood—nothing about the war." Consequently, the Shoah which is a central part of the Polish historical experience is not a topic directly engaged by Dres's Polish/Jewish contemporaries.

In the section "The Words of the Elders" Jérémie visits TSK, a sociocultural organization of Jews founded in 1950 by the Soviets. Seeking some perspective, he interviews Edward Odiner, TSK's director and his iconoclastic colleague Janek (Jan). Both men appear to be in their late sixties. The author learns that Poland experienced turbulent times in 1968. In order to calm things down the government played the anti-Semitic card. Following Israel's victory in the 1967 War, Polish Jews were accused of helping Israel, and of being "enemies on the inside, a fifth column." Odiner's face portrays a reflective mood. Jérémie learns two important things: a country does not need Jews to have anti-Semitic attitudes and policies, and that "throw them the Jews" is a time-tested method for dictators to employ.

Jewish identity is presented as an inherited phenomenon having little or nothing to do with religious observance. Jérémie asks the two if they attend synagogue. Neither does. Edward exclaims, "We're Jewish because our parents and grandparents were Jewish, that's all." This prompts Jan to exclaim "An accident of birth!"[30] Both Edward and Jan had lived abroad, America and Sweden respectively, but returned to the land of their birth: Edward because his wife, a judge, would have had to start all over, Jan returned because he did not know where to go. He refers to himself as a "Luftmensch," literally an "air man," one who has his head in the clouds. Odiner, drawn with a somewhat dismissive look on his face, tells Jérémie that "mostly old people" come to TSK. The so-called "New Jews"—the young people—go to the synagogue next door. Having discovered their Jewishness "a bit late" or "only one member of their family was Jewish," he contends, "They want to feel Jewish so badly that they go to the synagogue."[31] He and Jan do not need to go to synagogue to prove they are Jewish.

If Jérémie was hoping to get a clear response to the question of anti-Semitism in contemporary Poland, he is mistaken. Edward Odiner problematizes the question of whether Poland is anti-Semitic. He soliloquizes before the author, who draws his own visage in rapt attention. On the one hand, observes Odiner, "Jews have been in Poland for more than a century. So it's hard to say Poland is anti-Semitic." Yet, "On the other, a century is a long time. They've had enough and want us to leave."[32] Jérémie is perplexed. Poland appears to have the hallmarks of a structured Jewish community. The country has a chief rabbi, the American-born Michael Schudrich. Moreover, there are two other rabbis who play a significant role in the life of Poland's small Jewish community: Pinchas Zarcynski, an Israeli Chabad rabbi, and Burt Schuman, a Galician-born American who leads *Beit Warszawa*, a progressive movement founded in Poland in the early part of the twenty-first century.

Both rabbis speak of a Jewish renewal movement in Poland. Zarcynski identifies one strand of contemporary Jewish identity in attesting that some Jews feel Jewish "only because their parents survived the camps."[33] Moreover, for a Jew, he states, a trip to Poland is an incredible thing, it's a way for the non-practicing "to find religion."[34] He tells Jérémie that people come to Poland from all over. "The synagogue," he says, "is their first port of call." Rabbi Zarcynski, responding to Jérémie's query, makes three distinctions concerning contemporary Polish anti-Semitism: it is not part of the governmental position, some people are anti-Semitic and, supporting Jan's claim, "the old country folk" tend to be anti-Semites. The rabbi speaks regularly in local schools about Jewish history, culture, and religion. Invited by Zarcynski to stay for the minyan (daily prayer service), the brothers claim prior appointments. The final panel of this section shows the brothers in their room, relieved that they had dodged the prayer service. Jérémie observes, "Bit of a proselytizer, wasn't he?" Martin responds, "I thought he'd never let us leave."[35]

Rabbi Schuman is referred to in the text as "Super-Rabbi." He states that the Jewish origins of his movement's 200 members is unclear. "There are," he reports, "lots of psychological wounds. People are still traumatized by the Shoah and the years of Communism."[36] Like his rabbinic colleague, Schuman is a teacher who seeks to translate Judaism into the Polish milieu. Moreover, he hosts lectures for adults and programs for children. In addition, he contends that an increasing number of towns are "building relations with survivors and their children." We are, he stresses, "reaching a new stage."[37] Schuman speaks of a revival of Yiddish theater, Yiddish culture, the Jewish Historical Institute, and the Museum of the History of the Polish Jews as contributing to the revival of Jewish life.[38] Schuman encourages the brothers to visit his movement's synagogues in Israel and Paris, also providing them with pamphlets containing the movement's principles.

The response of Jérémie and Martin to Rabbi Schuman's overtures reveals three major points relevant to third-generation identity. In the first place, there is a difference in the third-generation attitude itself. Jérémie draws the two brother's faces. His is full of wonderment. The words in the balloon read, "Amazing how dedicated he is!"[39] Martin's face is, however, different, displaying relief at leaving the rabbi's house. The balloon above his head reads "Enough with the rabbis now, or they'll wind up noticing we're not practicing Jews at all, and force us to have a bar mitzvah."[40] Next, it is neither Jewish texts nor teachings that motivate the brothers to explore their Jewish identity. Rather, it is the stories told by their grandmother. Third, the role of agency is crucial. The brothers will choose which feature(s) of Judaism address their existential needs. It is significant that whenever the talk with rabbis turns to formal religious observance, Jérémie and Martin get uncomfortable, utter an apology, and leave. This compels readers to reflect on the essential component of a religion-less Judaism.

Visiting their maternal great-grandparents' graves in the Warsaw cemetery—this section is subtitled "The Jungle of the Forgotten"—Martin observes, "anchored our journey in a concrete and objective reality.[41] The brothers have only a vague sense of Jewish ritual. Jérémie wonders if it is necessary to wear a kippa in the cemetery. Martin has no idea and is, moreover, ready to leave after waiting only a short period of time to speak with the cemetery director. Jérémie draws the brothers sitting on a bench. Impatient and not as invested in the journey as Jérémie, Martin walks toward the cemetery gate. The words in the balloon over his head read "Clearly they don't give a damn."[42]

Mr. Isroel Szpilman, director of the Warsaw cemetery, provides the brothers additional information that helps them understand both the complexity of Poland's history during the Shoah and Jewish legends about the cemetery itself. Dres draws Szpilman, himself, and Martin walking through rows of graves. Szpilman reveals that his predecessor was a self-hating Jew who collaborates with one of Poland's biggest anti-Semites. Jérémie's face is absorbed and inquisitive. While some tombstones are overturned, including that of his great-grandfather, the director assures the brothers that "Poland is changing. A lot."[43] Jérémie's experience moves from the particular—seeing the family grave sites—to the universal. He draws himself and Martin searching for stones so that they may honor the Jewish tradition of placing them on the grave to "mark our passing."[44] Moreover, in response to his question about whether people come looking for graves a lot, Szpilman attests, "Every day."[45] In addition, the director tells them two further pieces of information which shed further light on traditional Jewish beliefs: the cemetery plots are good "forever," and "In Jewish tradition, when you die you're buried. Period."[46] Although Dres makes no reference to the fact, the Jewish cemetery in Warsaw is the burial place of many illustrious rabbis, thinkers, and scholars. Among the graves is that of L. L. Zamenhof, inventor of Esperanto, the universal language, who was fascinated by the idea of a world without war.

In a sequence titled "Once upon a time in Warsaw," Jérémie recalls Tema—whose voice is a constant, if invisible companion on their Polish sojourn—telling him about her own father. Jérémie draws an image of himself and Tema seated at her kitchen table. Séance-like, the face of Tema's father takes shape in the steam emanating from a cup of tea. I will return to the role of the non-rational in Jérémie's experience shortly. Jérémie draws his own face rapt in attention, Tema's visage is reflective. Appropriately, the face of Jérémie's great-grandfather appears ethereal. In an eight-page sequence, the reader learns that Tema's father was a talented builder who, after paying his workers, regularly bought them a round of vodka and snacks. Tema's father died of peritonitis during the First World War. Everything fell apart following his death. The children all left Poland one by one. Jérémie draws his grandmother's angry and bitter face as she relates her story.

In a revealing section titled "Being Jewish: A User's Guide," Jérémie portrays the brothers' visit to Warsaw's Jewish Historical Centre's Genealogical Learning Centre. Jérémie draws himself interviewing Ms. Anna Przybyszewska Drozd, an associate of Yale Reisner, who founded the centre in the mid-nineties. Her facial expression is straightforward. Jérémie's visage is alert and intense. He learns the centre receives from 50 to 100 requests per month, and that "initially they all came from abroad, but now more and more Polish people come to see us. Often, they've accidentally discovered evidence of their Jewish roots."[47] She shares the story of a Polish man who left the centre office bitterly disappointed when he discovered that he was not Jewish. Drozd pinpoints the question of third-generation Polish Jewish identity. She observes, "the [Jewish] tradition was interrupted, for various reasons: war, communism, the Holocaust. Two generations fallen into neglect." She correctly attests that the real question is: "What does it mean to be Jewish?"[48]

Here the central postmodern identity issue is that of agency. Postmodern and post-Holocaust identity is fragmented and seeking cohesion. Drozd articulates a central feature of Dres's quest in observing, "I think we each create our own definition with our conscience and the choices we make."[49] She then outlines five identity choices. To be Orthodox one must convert or have a Jewish grandmother. The Reform welcome everyone. To be officially recognized, one needs to join the community. The two remaining options are the ones that appeal to the brothers. "If you want to talk about it," writes Drozd, "all you have to do is visit us." "Or," she concludes, "you can simply rejoice in having discovered your roots."[50] This last option is, however, more complex for the third generation. What does it mean to rejoice when the Shoah forms part of your Jewish root system? As Jérémie reflects near the end of the book, "So, we never went (to Auschwitz). What did it matter? We would only have perpetuated the nightmare haunting all of us."[51] Jérémie's narrative of return, while avoiding Auschwitz, clearly does not eliminate it from his consciousness.

"Cold Sweat in Żelechów" portrays the brothers' insecurity about their Jewish identity. Seeking to discover remnants from their grandfather's life, Jérémie and Martin travel to this rural village sixty miles from Warsaw. In route they decide not to tell anyone they are Jewish. Instead, they will say they're searching on behalf of a "dumb friend who is Jewish." Employing a negative stereotype of Jews, Martin suggests they say that their Jewish friend paid them to take pictures, "Cos he's rich."[52] Jérémie draws the two of them walking in Żelechów's town square, where they are recipients of suspicious glances from local residents. Jérémie, eager to pursue their quest, attributes Martin's nervousness—for the second time in the volume—to the presence of a dybbuk (the soul of a deceased individual who inhabits the living).

Ultimately, they discover the Jewish cemetery which is overgrown with weeds. Accentuating the forlornness of the place, Jérémie draws some of the tombstones in a ghost-like shape. While Martin waits anxiously in the car, Jérémie feels that he has been given "a divine mission" to photograph the graves while there is still time.[53] His visit to the cemetery upends his previous impressions of Polish tolerance and Jewish revival. These feelings, he confides, are replaced by those of absence and indignation. Metaphorically, this suggests that the return narrative—no matter its existential and Jewish importance—can never recreate a world that has vanished forever. Jérémie states that the headstones with their Hebrew inscriptions "look like the remains of some classic civilization."[54] In a certain sense, he does not need to see Auschwitz to understand the magnitude of Jewish loss. Following their cemetery visit the brothers go to the town hall to do some research about their grandfather. However, they are afraid to provide the clerk their family name which would have revealed their Jewish identity. They leave without accomplishing their goal. It symbolically important that Dres chooses the brothers' visit to the Żelechów cemetery for the volume's cover art.

On the final day of their stay in Poland the brothers interview a variety of cultural leaders including Stanislas Krajewski, Director of the Polish Council for Jewish-Christian Relations, and a Jewish activist, who emphasizes the progress made in Jewish life in Poland. "Whoever thought twenty years ago," he exclaims, "Jewish life would flower in Poland again, and be facing classic questions of identity."[55] The brothers attend a performance of the Bester Quartet at Krakow's Jewish festival. The performance takes place in a synagogue. Jérémie draws himself in what he terms "sacred space." He writes of "spirals of sound," which wrapped him up and carried him delicately away.[56] He draws himself on a cloud which functions as a type of magic carpet. As he is transported out of the synagogue, the scene is framed by the Hebrew letters *yod heh vav heh*, the name of God.[57] He asks his guide where they are going. The guide tells him to get off. "This is your home," he continues, "You'll find the answers to your questions."[58] Jérémie drops from the cloud onto a pre-Shoah Polish village. He asks, in letters vertically arranged "But whyyyyyy?" His guide responds, "Because what you see no longer exists."[59] The author then draws himself back in the synagogue, a groggy, perplexed look on his face. This quasi-mystical and dream experience reminds one of Julie Orringer's novel *The Invisible Bridge*, which, as Aarons observes, also employs a dream-state transmission of transgenerational trauma.

Jérémie returns to Paris, his Polish sojourn results in new information about family history. He does, however, want to discover more about the lives of Jan and Edward of the TSK. He calls their friend, Anna Rabcynska, a Polish ex-patriot living in Paris. She is Jewish and the daughter of "enlightened Jews" who were completely assimilated. Her mother, a physician, was in the Warsaw ghetto. Anna's father, a diplomat, saved his wife by trading two packs of cigarettes. The couple was hidden by farmers. Anna's mother saved the life of a Polish partisan. Anna, like the French filmmaker Pierre Sauvage, only discovers that she is a Jew at age 18. Politically astute, she flees Poland after the 1967 Arab/Israeli War. She views Poland as a "massive cemetery." Jérémie draws the two of them sitting at an outdoor café. He says: "today Poland has changed, hasn't it?" The balloon above Anna's head contains the words, "Not for me. They're still just as anti-Semitic."[60] Anna returns to Poland once a year to visit childhood friends and for her research. But she believes that what Jérémie saw in Poland is "a Disneyland financed by the Americans, to enlighten the little Poles about the Jews who lived among them."[61] Anna believes that the word "Jew" has two negative implications: it is an insult, or it refers to statuettes, Jewish caricatures, sold in souvenir shops. She concludes by correctly claiming that Jérémie's voyage will change him.

CONCLUSION

We Won't See Auschwitz is a significant contribution to the emerging third-generation literature. Dres is a new writer, he is European, and his book bends genres. The fact that he concludes his narrative with six pages of actual family photographs heightens the drama of Jewish discovery. Jérémie's narrative of return opens up new historical and sociological vistas for him. Furthermore, while he eschews synagogue attendance and is definitely not religious in the formal sense of that term, he discovers his own sensitivity to holiness through his visit to the Krawkow synagogue. He also has a quasi-mystic experience that transports him back to a Polish shtetl. His dream-state experience reveals that while he may know more than before about his Polish/Jewish heritage, he will never be able to live in this vanished world. This realization is a shared feature of the third generation. He also learns, as Potel notes, that "The Jews have returned (or emerged in Poland) in the form of questions."[62] Dres ends his volume in a manner similar to Art Spiegelman's *Maus*. He draws himself standing before his grandmother's grave in Paris. Placing stones on Tema's tombstone, he muses "Perhaps this story will help put things back in order."[63]

Dres's quest narrative does, however, raise questions. While Dres's account shares certain similarities with other third-generation narratives of return, on the one hand, he writes: "today we are no longer the children of those lucky enough to survive the death camps. We are worthy heirs to the Jewish legacy, and its rich, complex history on Polish soil. That broken, hidden part of our identity—we've found it again, at last."[64] On the other hand, he departs from them in a significant way. His narrative seeks to wrap up all "loose Jewish ends," so to speak. What does "putting things in order" mean after Auschwitz? It could imply a *tikkun olam* (repair or restoration of the world). Is this possible and, if so, to what extent? More likely it suggests a *tikkun atzmi* (repair or restoration of the self). Part of this third-generation self-repair involves immersion in Jewish and ancestral history. Moreover, Jérémie is familiar with certain Jewish symbols and rituals. He exemplifies Orringer's "invisible bridge" phenomenon: while non-observant he clearly is still attached to certain key markers of Jewish identity. In the final analysis his grandmother's stories—not classical texts—open the gates for Dres to enter more fully into his Jewish identity. It remains to be seen what the fourth generation will do.

NOTES

1. Eva Hoffman, *After Such Knowledge: Memory, History, and the Legacy of the Holocaust* (New York: Public Affairs, 2004), 185.
2. Hoffman, *After Such Knowledge*, 185.
3. J. Rudoren, "Proudly Bearing Elders' Scars, Their Skin Says 'Never Forget,'" *New York Times*, September 30, 2012. Accessed March 3, 2016.
4. Victoria Aarons and Alan L. Berger, *Third-Generation Holocaust Representation: Trauma, History, and Memory* (Evanston, IL: Northwestern University Press, 2017). Chapter 1. Forthcoming.
5. Jérémie Dres, *We Won't See Auschwitz*, translated by Edward Gauvin (London: SelfMadeHero, 2012). Page references in the text are to this edition.
6. Dres, *We Won't See Auschwitz*, 10–11.
7. Jean-Yves Potel, preface to Jérémie Dres, *We Won't See Auschwitz*, v.
8. Jean-Yves Potel, preface to Jérémie Dres, *We Won't See Auschwitz*, v.
9. Dres, *We Won't See Auschwitz*, 4.
10. Dres, *We Won't See Auschwitz*, 4.
11. Dres, *We Won't See Auschwitz*, 5.
12. Dres, *We Won't See Auschwitz*, 12.
13. Dres, *We Won't See Auschwitz*, 12.
14. Marianne Hirsch, *Family Frames: Photography, Narrative and Postmemory* (Cambridge: Harvard University Press, 1997), 22.
15. Hirsch, *Family Frames*, 22.
16. Dres, *We Won't See Auschwitz*, 190.
17. Dres, *We Won't See Auschwitz*, 190, emphasis added.
18. Dres, *We Won't See Auschwitz*, 191.
19. Dres, *We Won't See Auschwitz*, 12.
20. Dres, *We Won't See Auschwitz*, 8.
21. Dres, *We Won't See Auschwitz*, 10.
22. Dres, *We Won't See Auschwitz*, 9.
23. Cited in Katka Reszke, *Return of the Jew: Identity Narratives of the Third Post-Holocaust Generation of Jews in Poland* (Brighton, MA: Academic Studies Press, 2013), 185. The history of Polish/Jewish relations is complex. Resident in the country for one thousand years, the fate of non-Jewish and Jewish Poles is inextricably intertwined. On the one hand, Poland's prewar Jewish population of three and a half million was almost completely obliterated during the Shoah. Frequently, Poles willingly aided Nazis in their gruesome task as demonstrated by Professor Jan T. Gross in his carefully researched book *Neighbors: The Destruction of the Jewish Community in Jedwabne, Poland* (Princeton, NJ: Princeton University Press, 2001). Moreover, there was widespread denunciation and betrayal of Jews by Polish people. In addition, Professor Nechama Tec, herself a hidden child who passed as a Christian in Poland during the Shoah, writes of what she terms the country's "diffuse cultural antisemitism." (*When Light Pierced the Darkness: Christian Rescue of Jews in Nazi Occupied Poland* [New York: Oxford University Press, 1986]).

On the other hand, Poland was the only country under Nazi occupation which had a national resistance movement devoted to assisting Jews. Established by Polish leaders in exile, the "Council for aid to Jews"—code-named Zegota—operated from 1942 to 1945 issuing false identification papers and providing hiding places. The Council's actions saved thousands of Jewish lives. In addition, Yad Vashem, Israel's national Holocaust monument and archival research center, has planted over six thousand trees honoring the *Hasidei Umot ha-olam* (Righteous Among the Nations). This number far exceeds that of any other nation. Neither of these two sets of facts cancels the other. The tension between them underscores the complicated nature of Jewish/Polish relations.

24. Dres, *We Won't See Auschwitz*, 16.
25. Dres, *We Won't See Auschwitz*, 20.
26. Dres, *We Won't See Auschwitz*, 23.
27. Dres, *We Won't See Auschwitz*, 23.
28. Dres, *We Won't See Auschwitz*, 17.
29. Dres, *We Won't See Auschwitz*, 17.
30. Dres, *We Won't See Auschwitz*, 42.
31. Dres, *We Won't See Auschwitz*, 43.
32. Dres, *We Won't See Auschwitz*, 35.
33. Dres, *We Won't See Auschwitz*, 66.
34. Dres, *We Won't See Auschwitz*, 67.
35. Dres, *We Won't See Auschwitz*, 72.
36. Dres, *We Won't See Auschwitz*, 77.
37. Dres, *We Won't See Auschwitz*, 79.
38. Dres, *We Won't See Auschwitz*, 81.
39. Dres, *We Won't See Auschwitz*, 83.
40. Dres, *We Won't See Auschwitz*, 83.
41. Dres, *We Won't See Auschwitz*, 190.
42. Dres, *We Won't See Auschwitz*, 89.
43. Dres, *We Won't See Auschwitz*, 99.
44. Dres, *We Won't See Auschwitz*, 97.
45. Dres, *We Won't See Auschwitz*, 93.
46. Dres, *We Won't See Auschwitz*, 93.
47. Dres, *We Won't See Auschwitz*, 116.
48. Dres, *We Won't See Auschwitz*, 117.
49. Dres, *We Won't See Auschwitz*, 117.
50. Dres, *We Won't See Auschwitz*, 117.
51. Dres, *We Won't See Auschwitz*, 173.
52. Dres, *We Won't See Auschwitz*, 121.
53. Dres, *We Won't See Auschwitz*, 130.
54. Dres, *We Won't See Auschwitz*, 131.
55. Dres, *We Won't See Auschwitz*, 152.
56. Dres, *We Won't See Auschwitz*, 165.
57. Dres, *We Won't See Auschwitz*, 166.
58. Dres, *We Won't See Auschwitz*, 166.
59. Dres, *We Won't See Auschwitz*, 167.
60. Dres, *We Won't See Auschwitz*, 180.
61. Dres, *We Won't See Auschwitz*, 181.
62. Dres, *We Won't See Auschwitz*, vi.
63. Dres, *We Won't See Auschwitz*, 186.
64. Dres, *We Won't See Auschwitz*, 173.

Chapter Six

The "Generation without Grandparents"

Witnesses and Companions to an Unfinished Search

Malena Chinski

This chapter is inspired by a casual remark I found in a work by the Uruguayan Jewish historian Graciela Ben-Dror on the topic of the Argentine Catholic Church in the times of the Third Reich. Although the book does not focus on the problematic of generations, the author's personal link to the subject of Nazism is presented in the foreword:

> The Holocaust was not alien to me. As the daughter of those who had the fortune of emigrating from catholic Poland to liberal and democratic Uruguay before the tragedy, I belong, like many of my contemporaries, to a "generation without grandparents," as these had been exterminated by the Nazis in Poland.[1]

The expression "generation without grandparents" involves a definition of third generation as the one made up of the grandchildren of victims of the Shoah. The particularity of such a generation would be thus the entire or partial absence of grandparents, since birth, as a consequence of the Shoah.

But examining Ben-Dror's expression more carefully, two simultaneous meanings can be distinguished. On one hand, it points to an inter-familial condition: the grandchildren of victims within a family. On the other hand, the same expression has a cultural implication, referring to all those people without a family connection but who share the condition of being grandchildren of victims. The present paper will deal with both meanings.

Finally, a geographical element delimits a more specific subject of study. Motivated by the case of Ben-Dror, whose parents had emigrated from Europe to Uruguay before the war, this paper will focus on the experiences of the third generation, in the terms defined above, born to and raised in families that had immigrated to Argentina. Thousands of Jews living in Argentina in the times of the Shoah were not native Argentines but had settled throughout the interwar years, and had formed families in the new home. (The same profile also characterizes many Uruguayan Jewish families.)

Data provided by the Fourth General Census of the city of Buenos Aires carried out in 1936 indicate that more than sixty thousand Eastern European Jews resided in the city then, a figure that made up around 80 percent of the foreign Jewish population (completed by a lower number of Jews from Central Europe, and from Asian and African countries). This amount was even higher than the number of native Argentinean Jews living in the same city that year (approximately forty-six thousand).[2] In addition, the foreign Jewish population kept increasing up until 1945 due to the arrival of refugees escaping from Central and Eastern Europe after Hitler's rise to power (approximately thirty-nine thousand, most of whom entered Argentina illegally by reason of restrictive immigration policies applied).[3]

The borrowed category of "generation without grandparents" refers thus to a particular group of Argentinean Jews, children of Jewish immigrants, who lived through the Shoah at a distance during childhood or were born after the end of the war, and had to deal with a situation of family mourning, as most of their parents' parents and other relatives had been murdered in the Shoah. The age range of this generation today is approximately between sixty and eighty-five years old.[4]

But can they be considered a collective? The term "generation," when applied to the Shoah, is generally used to refer to descendants of the survivors (the so-called "children of the Holocaust"), who for a few decades now have recognized themselves as bearers of a shared condition.[5] Children of survivors in Argentina have founded the organization "Generaciones de la Shoá" (Generations of the Shoah), which has gradually incorporated survivors' grandchildren to a certain extent.[6] As opposed to that, grandchildren of victims have not so far constituted a self-recognized collective group in Argentina or anywhere else.[7]

The above represents a difficulty insofar as few members of the "generation without grandparents" in South America have given voice to their personal experiences in this respect. In addition, while survivor testimonies have been largely collected by various institutions throughout the world (such as the USC Shoah Foundation, which collected more than seven hundred testimonies in Argentina alone to be included in the Visual History Archive), descendants of the victims have not as often been object of social science research.

In what senses did the Shoah affect the childhood of a generation of Jews born in a country distant from Europe and not directly involved in the war conflict? As a preliminary hypothesis, I propose that grandchildren of the victims of the Shoah became witnesses and companions to their parents' search for survivor relatives and to their long process of mourning the deceased. The following three sections will explore various aspects of the experiences of the third generation on the basis of different sources, mainly an oral testimony, materials from the Jewish press, a photograph, and a novel. These will require a multidisciplinary approach, appealing to concepts from historiography and social science.

THE CONSEQUENCES OF THE SHOAH FROM THE PERSPECTIVE OF THE THIRD GENERATION

In March 1945 the Argentinean Yiddish daily newspaper *Di Yidishe Tsaytung* warned its readers: "If we were able to reflect deeply on and understand the meaning of the scope of our national catastrophe, desperation and madness would take hold of more than one Jewish mind."[8] Even though the paper was explicitly pointing to the "national" dimension of catastrophe, it was possibly implying as well the superlative dimension of family loss suffered by thousands of Jews in Argentina as a consequence of the Shoah. This section will focus on this dimension from the perspective of the third generation, through the analysis of an oral testimony, which sheds light on the experiences of others.

My interviewee, Teresa, was born in Buenos Aires in 1931 to a working-class family of Polish origin. Her parents had arrived from Lublin a few years before her birth, while their families had remained in Poland. Teresa indicated that the interruption of overseas family correspondence during the war was an early manifestation of the events unfolding against the Jews in Europe: "At the beginning of the war my mother still received some correspondence. Later, of course, it broke off, and when the war was over *you can imagine the atmosphere here, as everyone had most of their families there.*"[9]

The word "everyone" in Teresa's statement should not be understood literally, since only families belonging to the immigration wave of the interwar years had most of their relatives in Europe. But as oral historian Alessandro Portelli points out: "Subjectivity is as much the business of history as are the more visible 'facts.' What informants believe is indeed a historical *fact* (that is, the fact that they believe it), as much as what really happened."[10] Following Portelli, Teresa's use of the word "everyone" reveals the interviewee's perspective. Precisely, the narrator was referring to the social circle of her childhood; according to the way she saw it then, "everyone" was undergoing the same situation. This belief was probably the result of the "atmosphere" she perceived, consisting in a sense of uncertainty and preoccupation that transcended the private realm of her family and affected many other Jews around her (in her case, Polish Jews).

Teresa's testimony also provides a clue helping to grasp her perspective on family loss and survival. Her account became ostensibly fragmentary, as she intended to summarize the itineraries of her parents' relatives:

> So all the brothers, the nephews . . . [were killed]. One niece of my mother's was saved because she went to Palestine to work as a stonecutter. One of my father's siblings was saved by going to Palestine with his son. [. . .] And from my father's side, a few were saved because they went to Paris before the war, two sisters and a brother. The brother was deported, when the Nazis arrived he was denounced and sent back [to Poland] with his wife and daughter. His son escaped to the south of France and is now 91 years old. This one survived. The others, all of them [were killed]. You can imagine that if they were thirteen siblings of my both parents, each one married and with large families, *they were a lot of people.*[11]

This narrative reveals a crucial aspect of the experience of having lived through the Shoah at a distance, which remains valid for many Jewish families in Argentina: in the assessment of death and survival, it resulted easier to determine the limited number of survivors than the large number of family members murdered. The reason was that the scope of family loss was so extensive that it became almost impossible to elaborate an exhaustive list.

In the case of my interviewee, such a list included her parents' parents (Teresa's four grandparents), ten of their siblings among a total of thirteen, and an undetermined number of nephews, nieces, brothers- and sisters-in-law, and cousins. Teresa's concluding statement ("they were a lot of people") is eloquent not only because of its power of synthesis, but also because it connotes the distant perspective of a member of the third generation, who never met any of the numerous relatives murdered in Poland, deemed as "a lot" and impossible to be enumerated fully.

Finally, Teresa talked about the postwar time and her mother's frustrated hope of finding survivor relatives:

> The anguish was immense. I remember that my parents used to receive the newspaper *Di Prese* every day, and when the war was over lists started to appear, of people who had survived and who knew they had relatives here and were seeking them. Every day, buying the newspaper meant in the first place the anguish of searching for a relative who might be looking for us. But unfortunately there was never even one looking for us. I remember my mother weeping. Women are weepy, we express the pain. And this lasted years.[12]

At this point the testimony led me to the topic of the search for survivors after the war. According to Teresa's account, her parents did not assume the death of their entire families until a period of waiting and searching had elapsed. Consequently, Teresa became a daily witness to her parents' anxious search and to her mother's lasting process of mourning as well.

She related that lists of names used to appear on the Yiddish daily *Di Prese*. In fact, archival research evinces that all main Jewish periodicals of Buenos Aires, in Yiddish, Spanish, and German, used to publish lists of this type after the liberation of the camps and even before then, while liberation was advancing in Europe in the last stages of the war.

Already beginning 1945, the German Jewish weekly *Jüdische Wochenschau* would publish lists of names of Jewish survivors, as well as announcements regarding the arrival of new lists to be consulted at Jewish institutions in Buenos Aires. For example, on January 9 it published on the same page: (1) a list of Jews liberated from Lublin, (2) the announcement of the arrival of lists of survivors from Belsen at the local office of World Jewish Congress, (3) a list of persons who had been deported to Terezin, and (4) an enumeration of survivors from Poland provided by the Polish Israelite Central Union (located in Buenos Aires).[13]

The publication of lists intensified in the early postwar months. Between May and July 1945 *Di Yidishe Tsaytung* published, on different dates, partial lists of Jewish survivors from Buchenwald submitted by the correspondent of the Jewish Telegraphic Agency.[14] That same newspaper published other lists classified according to the city of origin of the survivors.[15] While a few full lists could be found in the press, the length and number of circulating lists made it necessary to make specific spaces at certain Jewish institutions available for consultation in person.

These examples can convey the complexity of the activity of searching for survivor relatives in Europe from afar, without mentioning the effort and high costs entailed in the process of bringing over a survivor to Buenos Aires, in those rare cases when one was left alive. Moreover, in the following months the number of circulating lists of multiple types increased, and the classification categories became more specific, to such an extent that in October 1945 *Di Yidishe Tsaytung* published a list of lists, which outlined thirty-seven different types of lists that had arrived, to be consulted in the South American branch of the World Jewish Congress. As an example, the first five items are quoted below:

1. List of Jews of diverse nationalities in Flak-Kaserne, Munich, liberated from Landsberg. They had earlier been in the Dachau concentration camp.
2. Polish Jewish women and men liberated from the concentration camp of Kaunetz, 73 Kreis Wiedenbrueck, Germany.
3. List of Polish Jews from various concentration camps, liberated and currently living in Hamburg and Frankfurt.
4. List of Polish Jews liberated from Bergen-Belsen.

5. List of Polish Jews in Bardowick.[16]

Through these various examples I wish to indicate the representativity of Teresa's testimony (being at the same time unique), in regard to the search for survivor relatives in postwar Jewish Buenos Aires. The extremely long and heterogeneous lists of names made available to Argentinean Jewish families are not only evidence of the dramatic loneliness of the survivors after liberation, who were looking for a relative and a home anywhere in the world, but they are also indirect evidence of the active demand for such lists in Argentina.

As was the case of Teresa's parents, Jewish immigrants and Polish Jews in particular mostly acknowledged the death of their families after a period of searching (except when this information had arrived through other channels, such as letters or witness accounts). However, Teresa's testimony leaves the impression that the generation of the children did not perceive this search as its own, since the relatives sought after were unknown, distant in time and space, and too numerous to be apprehended. However, in the coming section I will argue that children also became involved, to a limited extent, in the task of searching.

THE THIRD GENERATION AS A COMPANION TO THE SEARCH FOR SURVIVORS

The present section is an attempt to carry out a visual analysis of a photograph, with the aim of adding new clues on the perspectives of the third generation. The picture belongs to the institutional collection of the Society for the Protection of Jewish Immigrants (usually referred to with the acronym of Soprotimis). Founded in 1922, Soprotimis was specifically dedicated to issues related to Jewish immigration to Argentina, such as the candidates' mode of travel and entrance into the country, and their general orientation upon arrival. It coordinated its work with the international Jewish immigration society HICEM (created through an agreement of the Hebrew Immigrant Aid Society [HIAS], the Jewish Colonization Association [JCA], and Emigdirect).[17]

After the Second World War, Soprotimis provided services to Argentinean Jewish families who intended to bring over survivor relatives to Argentina, in coordination with the HIAS.[18] The picture I will analyze seems to have been taken with the purpose of documenting the daily work of Soprotimis in the early postwar period (figure 6.1).

At first sight, the picture is a conventional depiction of a working environment. Thirteen men are posing, six of them sitting at the front, each one looking down and holding an open folder, and the other seven standing at the

Figure 6.1. Headquarters of Soprotimis (Society for the Protection of Jewish Immigrants) in Buenos Aires. Undated. Photograph from the IWO Foundation's Historical Archive, Soprotimis Collection, Box 5. Courtesy of IWO.

back while looking at the camera. The wide horizontal frame emphasizes the relation between the individuals posing and the setting, which looks like a former hall transformed into a workspace.[19]

The small sign located on the upper left side of the picture, next to the open door, reveals the function of this room. The half-visible three handwritten lines in Spanish allow a likely reconstruction of the text as follows: "CONSULTE las LISTAS de SOBREVIVIENTES de EUROPA en esta PUERTA" ("CONSULT the LISTS of SURVIVORS from EUROPE at this DOOR"). The sign indicates that the picture was probably taken during the second half of 1945 at the earliest, when such lists were already available in large numbers.

Moreover, the handwriting suggests that the sign was also elaborated in view of Soprotimis's new postwar function and that the room may have been turned into an "improvised" new office by institutional leaders, in order to provide visitors with a space to sit comfortably while reviewing the lists. In addition, the fact that the poster was written in Spanish (instead of Yiddish or German) insinuates that visitors expected to come were either born Argentine Jews, or immigrants having spent enough time in the country to be able to understand the words. The bureaucratic formulation of the sign is almost shocking in hindsight, in virtue of the contrast between its apparent banality and its dramatic meaning.

Looking closely at the different attitudes of the two groups of posing men, we may well guess that those standing at the back may have been Soprotimis employees (with the exception of the intriguing man wearing a strapped suit and a cap, who seems to be a newly arrived Polish Jew), while the men sitting may have been visitors. Rather, the photographer seemed to have had the intention of presenting such two groups through a distinct pose.

The open folder held by the man seated at the center shows that it contained lists. The man standing and smiling behind the desk seems to be someone whose task it was to provide visitors with the folders. On the picture, he is raising a folder and twisting it in direction to the camera. The folder is labeled "Wroclaw," a city in Western Poland. Not only does this label indicate that lists available at Soprotimis were organized by cities (either referring to Jews liberated in those cities or to the city of origin of the survivors), but also that the picture must have been taken after the Potsdam Conference (July 17 to August 2, 1945), when the Polish name of that city (formerly known as Breslau) became official.

The smiling employee contributes to the conventional depiction of a normal working day, conveying at the same time the idea of smooth functioning and efficacy. However, there is one element in the picture that stands out and does not fit in the scene: the presence of a child. Somehow, the child sitting on the right side of the room is pointing to a state of exceptionality, since nobody would have expected to find a child in a workspace directly dealing with the consequences of genocide.

He appears to be between eight and twelve years old, in contrast with the homogeneous higher age range of the adults present there. The child and the man seated to his left look notably similar, so we may assume they were father and son. In such a way, the photograph reveals the involvement of a member of a younger generation accompanying a parent in the search for survivor relatives.

The child, holding a folder himself, apparently labeled "Varsovia" (Warsaw), is looking down at it, while pursing his lips in a serious air. If his presence might go unnoticed at first sight, it is precisely because he is integrated into the same activity of checking the lists. Even presuming that the people in the picture were just posing, we still must acknowledge the photographer's likely choice to ask the child to sit and look seriously at the folder, along with everyone else. The suggestion is that the child was checking the lists as well. How aware might he have been of the meaning of this apparently simple and playful task of finding names on a list? His demeanor suggests that he did not take the activity as a game.

The child present at Soprotimis is not only immersed (involuntarily perhaps) in a world of adults, but also in an exclusively masculine environment. No woman was visiting Soprotimis office to search the lists on the day the picture was taken, and we may guess that probably few did, generally speaking. Why so? In this respect, Teresa's testimony quoted in the former section should be recalled, regarding women and the expression of feelings ("I remember my mother weeping. Women are weepy, we express the pain"). As opposed to women, who were legitimately able to express their emotions, men were socially expected to "behave" (and to some extent they still are expected so today). In fact, none of the men in the picture are expressing any visible emotion, aside from the child pursing his lips. The task of checking the lists of survivors may have seemed more suitable for men and the young boy seemed to be doing his best to meet the adults' expectations.

As a final remark to this section, if we assume that the picture was taken in the second half of 1945 and that the child, whose name remains unknown, was then between eight and twelve years of age, we must conclude that he might be the only person still alive today, and if so, he would be approximately between seventy-nine and eighty-three years old. Might he keep any memories of his visit to Soprotimis with his father that day? This picture is likely to be the only vestige of his incursion into the search for missing relatives.

THE THIRD GENERATION AND THE SEARCH FOR THE MISSING GRANDPARENTS WITHIN THE REALM OF IMAGINATION

In this section I will turn to the realm of narrative to seek the memories of the "generation without grandparents." A paradigmatic example of a narrative by a member of this third generation (understood as the grandchildren of Shoah victims) was produced in France. The book by historian Ivan Jablonka, *Histoire des grand-parents que je n'ai pas eus* (History of the grandparents I did not have), was the result of the author's efforts to trace the itineraries of his relatives murdered in the Shoah, drawing from a varied spectrum of historiographical sources, such as letters, interviews, and archival documents. A comparable project had already been undertaken by the journalist Daniel Mendelsohn in the United States, with the aim of tracking the story of his "lost" great-uncle and his descendants in this case, resulting in the popular book entitled *The Lost: A Search for Six of Six Million*.[20]

In contrast with such works, based mostly on archival research and oral history, as far as I know, no parallel research by someone belonging to the same third generation has been produced in Latin America so far.[21] One of the most representative narratives by the "generation without grandparents" produced in this region is the autobiographical novel *Lenta biografía* (Slow biography) by Sergio Chejfec, in which the search for missing relatives occurs within the realm of imagination of the narrator, rather than through actual research.[22]

As opposed to my interviewee Teresa and to the child we have seen in the Soprotimis picture, Chejfec was born more than a decade after the end of the Second World War (1956). His book *Lenta biografía*, published in 1990, consists of a stream of childhood memories, without any chapter divisions and deprived from any plot. Mostly, it contains descriptions of the weekly Sunday gatherings at the narrator's home when he was a child. In such venues, Chejfec's father—an immigrant from Poland and maybe the novel's main character—and his friends from the old country recounted and collected different versions about the last days of a man's life, referred to as "the pursued," before he got killed in occupied Europe.

As the title of the book anticipates, the narrative is slow. It is also abstruse and purposely repetitive, resulting in the creation of an oppressive atmosphere. Between various accounts about "the pursued," the narrator speaks of his childhood obsession with his father's past, of which he knew almost nothing. But what mostly unveiled to him was the fact that he had not met his grandparents and uncles. Since the father persisted in keeping silent in this respect, the narrator tried to recreate the image of his missing relatives, observing his father and appealing to his own imagination to transpose his father's features into the missing ones. For example, every Saturday night after dinner, when they played chess, he took advantage of the occasion to carry out this strange exercise:

> In those moments playing the game, we had the possibility of thoroughly, frontally, directly, observing my father's face for a considerable period of time. In the midst of voices and laughter—sounds of voices and laughing, exaggerated bursts of laughter and screams—I also concentrated on imagining possible faces—features, gestures—and the voices my uncles or my grandparents may have had.[23]

As opposed to Daniel Mendelsohn's search for his great-uncle, of whom he had a photograph that is a central element within the narrative, the narrator of *Lenta biografía* possessed no remaining picture as a possible means to construct a consistent image of his missing relatives. He had to rely on his imagination.[24] Chejfec reiterates the same type of exercise many times in various ways along the book, subtly blaming his father for the lack of transmission, and affirming his need to fill the gap:

> From the beginning—I don't remember when it was—I knew that there was a dimension of things that was frankly irretrievable for me, but at the same time irretrievability was some kind of condition for me to try to discover them. That dimension bore upon the fatal and tragic episodes of my father's past: the

death of his siblings and parents; as perhaps I wrote long ago, *their status as dead, as non-existent, as people who will never show, so to speak, their faces and bodies to the air and to the light.* This was the circumstance that allowed me to engage in a sort of exercise of the imagination: guessing my uncles' and grandparents' faces. I used to imagine them very much like my father's, as if they had been slight variations on his face.[25]

In the narrator's fruitless effort to recreate his unknown relatives' faces, gestures, and voices as a substitute for the lack of information, I find a transformation of the concept of "search"—as treated in the former sections, which consisted in the concrete seeking for survivor relatives—into a symbolic search within the narrator's inner self, an effort to fill his relatives' non-existence. The universal resonance of Chejfec's work is this struggle to deal with absence in solitude.[26]

CONCLUSIONS

Rather than focusing on survivors and their descendants, as is usually the case when the topic of generations is addressed in respect to the Shoah, in this essay I chose to blur the limits between "direct" survivors of the Shoah and the Jewish communities that lived through the Shoah at a distance and experienced the murder of their families from afar. I aimed at discussing other generational perspectives on family loss, incorporating, precisely, the aspect of geographical distance.

The expression "generation without grandparents," which I came upon in Ben-Dror's book, has proved to be a productive means of reflecting on a particular group of people who still bear the consequences of the Shoah: the grandchildren of the victims. In the South American context, so far, they have not been approached as a collective group, nor have they constructed a self-identity based on their particular familial losses. In this respect, we may well argue that the existence of a "generation without grandparents" remains an "accidental" effect of Nazism, still awaiting further investigation. Therefore, my conclusions do not pretend to be exhaustive but a preliminary reflection, based on the limited sources available.

The three sections above have aimed at contributing to the understanding of how members of the third generation witnessed their parents' loss and grief, and to a certain extent became companions to their search. Firstly, Teresa's testimony enabled me to trace her perspectives on her parents' daily seeking of survivor relatives and her mother's mourning process. This aspect also stressed the representativeness of Teresa's case in the early postwar years.

Secondly, the visual analysis of a photograph from the archival collection of Soprotimis permitted me to discuss the actual involvement of a member of the third generation in the search for missing relatives. Again, the singular case under discussion was presented as potentially representative of other families.

Finally, I analyzed Chejfec's autobiographical novel as the psychological whereabouts of an Argentinean Jew who suffered, throughout his childhood, his father's silent state of mourning, and persistently longed for his "nonexistent" grandparents and uncles, recreating them in his imagination.

As a few voices of the "generation without grandparents" have emerged in Latin America, they might be considered an unacknowledged potential "invisible community."[27] In order for the grandchildren of victims to become a community, a sense of a shared common family history, in cultural terms, would need to arise. This transformation would entail a move away from the position of witnesses, of "accidental" bearers of their parents' fate, in order to become protagonists.

Precisely, I suspect that a sense of otherness is still characteristic of members of this generation, regarding the history of the grandparents they never had, and the aforementioned transformation will probably not occur in most cases. As I look around in my native Buenos Aires, I keep discovering people who would fit into my definition of third generation, but who probably never thought of themselves in such terms. I have the impression that they have naturalized family loss, the fact that they never met their grandparents, uncles, aunts, and many other relatives murdered in the Shoah. Actually, naturalization seems to remain the rule.

If children of survivors were, in Helen Epstein's words, "possessed by a history that they have never lived," grandchildren of Shoah victims could be described as *dispossessed* of the history of their murdered relatives.[28] In this regard, Chejfec's relatively recent work represents a turning point, since he was capable of enunciating these two words together, "*my* grandparents," in spite of the lack of traces to relate to. This use of the possessive pronoun has made of Chejfec an isolated voice of the third generation. Even though collective self-identification cannot be anticipated, a few more might still add their voices.

NOTES

1. Graciela Ben-Dror, *Católicos, nazis y judíos: La Iglesia argentina en los tiempos del Tercer Reich* [Catholics, Nazis and Jews: The Argentinean Church in the times of the Third Reich] (Buenos Aires: Lumiere, 2003), 17 (my translation from Spanish).

2. Víctor Mirelman, *En búsqueda de una identidad: los inmigrantes judíos en Buenos Aires 1890–1930*, trans. Natalio Mazar (Buenos Aires: Milá, 1988), 16.

3. Haim Avni, *Argentina y la historia de la inmigración judía 1810–1950* [Argentina and the history of Jewish immigration 1810–1950] (Buenos Aires: Editorial Universitaria Magnes, 1983), 542–45. The subject of Argentina and the arrival of Jewish refugees from Nazi Europe has been thoroughly researched by Leonardo Senkman in *Argentina, la Segunda Guerra Mundial y los refugiados indeseables, 1933–1945* [Argentina, the Second World War and the

undesirable refugees, 1933–1945] (Buenos Aires: Grupo Editor Latinoamericano, 1991). In part as a result of all these waves of migration, Buenos Aires had become by 1945 the largest and most important Jewish cultural center in Latin America. Seventy percent of the Argentine Jewish population—some 273,400 individuals, as estimated by demographers Schmelz and DellaPergola—resided by then in Buenos Aires, where central Argentine Jewish institutions had their headquarters. Data extracted from Raanan Rein, *Argentina, Israel y los judíos: Encuentros y desencuentros, mitos y realidades* [Argentina, Israel and the Jews: Understanding and misunderstandings, myths and realities] (Buenos Aires: Lumiere, 2001), 27; and Susana Bianchi, *Historia de las religiones en la Argentina: Las minorías religiosas* [History of religions in Argentina: The religious minorities] (Buenos Aires: Editorial Sudamericana, 2004), 183.

4. As a matter of fact, in many cases two generations of Argentinean Jews have lost their grandparents in the Shoah. Indeed, many people who emigrated from Europe in the interwar years had left both their parents and living grandparents behind, all of whom were murdered by the Nazis. This immigrant generation consists of the parents of those who constitute the subject of this work. It also should be noted that in some cases young adults had left Europe with their children, who would also make part of the "generation without grandparents" treated here, with this one difference, that they were born in Europe and usually had met their grandparents. For the purpose of this paper, I focused on the children born in the land of emigration; therefore I will not discuss such cases, even though they are relevant too.

5. See for example Helen Epstein, *Children of the Holocaust: Conversations with Sons and Daughters of Survivors* (New York: Penguin Books, 1979); and Dina Wardi, *Memorial Candles: Children of the Holocaust*, trans. Naomi Goldblum (New York: Routledge, 2013 [1992]).

6. Founded by psychotherapist Diana Wang in 2001, Generaciones de la Shoá works in partnership with the local survivors' institution, Sheerit Hapleitá. For further information, please visit http://www.generaciones-shoa.org.ar/english/index.htm.

7. As a counterpoint to the above, grandchildren of the victims of the Franco regime have recently become active memory entrepreneurs, demanding the exhumation of their relatives from clandestine pits. This topic has been the subject of a documentary film directed by Marie-Paule Jeunehomme, *Los Nietos* (The Grandchildren). Please see Marie-Paule Jeunehomme, "Au sujet de Los Nietos, un film de Marie-Paule Jeunehomme" [About Los Nietos, a film by Marie-Paule Jeunehomme], *Cultures & Conflicts* 72 (Winter 2008), http://conflits.revues.org/14203. In Argentina, many babies who had been kidnapped by the military and given up for adoption illegally in the last dictatorship (1976–1983) were found as young adults by their grandmothers (in most cases). Such individuals have gained a collective identity as "the recovered grandchildren," and many of them became active participants in human rights movements. The most paradigmatic example is the case of Guido Montoya Carlotto, the grandson of the founder of the organization Abuelas de Plaza de Mayo (Grandmothers of Plaza de Mayo, created in 1977), Estela Carlotto. He discovered his original identity in 2014 at the age of thirty-six. Even though the murdered relatives are in such cases the parents of the kidnapped children, they recognize themselves as "grandchildren," since they recovered their identity thanks to their grandmothers' decades-long search. Please see the history of Abuelas de Plaza de Mayo in Rita Arditti, *Searching For Life: The Grandmothers of the Plaza de Mayo and the Disappeared Children of Argentina* (Berkeley, CA: University of California Press, 1999).

8. "Lomir nisht fargesn, mir zenen in der shive-vokh!" [Let's not forget, we are in the week of mourning!], *Di Yidishe Tsaytung*, March 11, 1945, 8 (my translation from Yiddish).

9. Teresa, in discussion with the author, February 2014 (my translation from Spanish, emphasis mine).

10. Alessandro Portelli, "What makes oral history different," in *The Oral History Reader*, ed. Robert Perks and Alistair Thomson (London and New York: Routledge, 2003), 67.

11. Teresa, in discussion with the author, February 2014 (my translation from Spanish, emphasis mine).

12. Teresa, in discussion with the author, February 2014.

13. "Fluechtlinge suchen ihre Angehoerigen" [Refugees seek their relatives]. *Jüdische Wochenschau*, January 9, 1945, 5.

14. *Di Yidishe Tsaytung*, May 25, 1945, 11; June 1, 1945, 5; June 6, 1945, 6; June 8, 1945, 5; July 4, 1945, 7; July 5, 1945, 7; July 8, 1945, 7. The publication of lists continued throughout the whole year but became less frequent by the end of the second semester.

15. See for example a list of survivors from Riga in *Di Yidishe Tsaytung*, May 1, 1945, 9, and list of survivors from Kovno in *Di Yidishe Tsaytung*, May 10, 1945, 7.

16. "Naye reshimes zenen ongekumen in zid-amerikan. byuro fun Yid. Velt-Kongres [New lists have arrived in the South American office of the World Jewish Congress], *Di Yidishe Tsaytung*, October 10 1945, 6 (my translation from Yiddish). Note the over-representation of Polish Jews in the first five items quoted (80 percent).

17. Avni, *Argentina y la historia de la inmigración judía*, 346–52.

18. The process of bringing over survivors to Argentina was studied by Leonardo Senkman in "Los sobrevivientes de la Shoa en Argentina: su imagen y memoria en la sociedad general y judía: 1945–50" [Shoah survivors in Argentina: their image and memory in general and Jewish society: 1945–1950], *Arquivo Maaravi: Revista Digital de Estudos Judaicos da UFMG* 1, no. 1 (October 2007), http://www.periodicos.letras.ufmg.br/index.php/maaravi/article/viewFile/973/1084. The work of the HIAS oriented toward Jewish settlement in Latin America after the war and its quantitative results can be consulted in Mark Wishnitzer, *Visas to Freedom: The History of HIAS* (Cleveland, OH: The World Publishing Company, 1956), 228–30.

19. Visual analysis is based on the concepts and guidelines proposed by Martine Joly in *La imagen fija* [The still image], trans. Marina Malfé (Buenos Aires: La marca editora, 2009).

20. Ivan Jablonka, *Histoire des grands-parents que je n'ai pas eus* [A history of the grandparents I did not have] (Paris: Éditions du Seuil, 2012); Daniel Mendelsohn, *The Lost: A Search for Six of Six Million* (New York: Harper Perennial, 2006).

21. However, my shared work with Elizabeth Jelin, based on Jelin's private family archive, goes in a comparable direction. Please see Malena Chinski and Elizabeth Jelin, "La carta familiar: información, sentimientos y vínculos mantenidos en el tiempo y en el espacio" [The family letter: information, feelings and bonds across time and space], *Políticas de la memoria* 15 (Summer 2014/2015): 47–52.

22. Sergio Chejfec, *Lenta biografía* [Slow biography] (Buenos Aires: Puntosur, 1990). It must be pointed out that Diana Wang, founder of the aforementioned organization Generaciones de la Shoá, wrote a memoir that is also interesting to grasp the perspectives of the third generation in the sense defined here. However, as Wang's parents were Shoah survivors and Wang was not born in Argentina, I have privileged Chejfec's work. In addition, Wang's book primarily adopts the point of view of the second generation of Shoah survivors, as the title indicates; see *Hijos de la guerra: La segunda generación de sobrevivientes de la Shoá* [Children of the war: The second generation of survivors of the Shoah] (Buenos Aires: Marea Editorial, 2007). Actually, experiences of the children of survivors have points in common with those of the "generation without grandparents," precisely because in many cases the latter category overlaps with that of children of the survivors.

23. Chejfec, *Lenta biografía*, 60 (my translation from Spanish).

24. In an autobiographical novel, Uruguayan writer Mauricio Rosencof associates his unknown grandparents with photographs stored in his house: "My mama has a whole bunch of pictures inside a shoebox. Boxes are for keeping things in. They put all kinds of stuff in boxes. And the shoebox is where Mama keeps her sisters, and her *mamele,* that's her mama, Mama's, I mean." *The Letters that Never Came*, trans. Louise B. Popkin (Albuquerque: University of New Mexico Press, 2004), 10.

25. Chejfec, *Lenta biografía*, 119 (my translation from Spanish, emphasis mine).

26. The question about the universal resonance of the third generation's writings has been borrowed from Alan L. Berger, "Unclaimed Experience: Trauma and Identity in Third Generation Writing about the Holocaust," *Shofar: An Interdisciplinary Journal of Jewish Studies* 28, no. 3 (2010): 151.

27. This expression was used by Helen Epstein to refer to the children of survivors; *Children of the Holocaust: Conversations with Sons and Daughters of Survivors* (New York: Putnam, 1979), 15.

28. Epstein, *Children of the Holocaust*, 14.

Chapter Seven

Avatars of Third-Generation Holocaust Narrative in French and Spanish

Alan Astro

NARRATIVES IN FRENCH

What constitutes a third-generation Holocaust narrative? The answer requires going over other questions. Who is a survivor? Someone who went through the camps? Does it include those who spent the war fighting in the resistance? Those not active but who remained hidden? Jewish POWs (insofar as the Nazis partially respected the Geneva Convention)? And what of people who survived openly as Jews in countries under the Nazis or allied with them, obvious Jews who because of officials' variable zeal in collaborating with the Germans—or the vagaries of bureaucracy—were never arrested?

These issues are particularly relevant in the case of France, where a quarter of the Jews met their deaths at the hands of the Nazis and with the aid of French collaborators.[1] Twenty-five percent is a low percentage, and the three quarters who survived included residents of Paris wearing yellow stars at the time of the city's liberation; they simply, as it were, had not yet been arrested.[2]

There is debate among historians as to the causes of this French particularity,[3] which flies in the face of the reputation of France as having extremely collaborationist—compared to the relatively good press enjoyed by the Netherlands, despite the fact that upwards of 70 percent of the Jews there were killed. Indeed, even in the more popular French arena, there is some awareness of how the Gaullist myth of a France largely united behind the resistance has given way to an equally untrue construct, according to which most French were enthusiastic collaborationists.[4]

Given the relative sparing of Jews in France—relative, but real—a portion of post-Holocaust writing in France concerns not only the losses but also the continued Jewish life on French soil, something quite different from post-Holocaust writing in countries of immigration such as the United States or Israel (in both places, the survivors come to start a new life), or of nearly total destruction of the Jewish population, such as Poland.

Lest I be accused of edulcorating the picture, I shall cite an early source on the difference between immediate postwar Jewish reality in France and that in the Netherlands. Georges Wormser, president of the Jewish Consistory of Paris, wrote in 1946 of what followed his shock at seeing the remnants of Jewish life in Amsterdam:

> I found joy in the fact that, in comparison, Judaism in France—despite so many painful losses—could continue with a significant population. Our communities live on; our synagogues, with some exceptions, are in a usable state. Our former organizations have been reborn; new ones are being created.[5]

Yet it should be noted that the survival rate for ancestrally French Jews was much higher (43 percent) than that for recent immigrant population (17 percent), a statistic that reflects the particularly xenophobic thrust of French anti-Semitism and the fact that those with a shorter history in France had fewer connections to and less knowledge of non-Jewish milieus into which to escape.[6]

The concept of a third-generation Holocaust narrative, like that of survivor, is fraught with ambiguity. *Stricto sensu* it might seem to designate an account grappling with the Holocaust by a child of second-generation parents, who (equally *stricto sensu*) would themselves have been born to survivors after the war. But in France, given networks of solidarity both Jewish and non-Jewish, many Jewish children were placed into safety. Non-French habitus—including, frequently, a Yiddish accent—made adult foreign Jews "visible even when hidden"[7]; their children, less conspicuous as Jews, often survived but were left orphaned. Thus France has a significant "1.5 generation," to use the term suggested by Susan Suleiman: "child survivors of the Holocaust, too young to have had an adult understanding of what was happening to them, but old enough to have been there during the Nazi persecution of Jews."[8] The 1.5 generation is so numerous in France[9] that the organization Nazi hunter Serge Klarsfeld formed for those with parents murdered—Fils et Filles des Déportés Juifs de France [Sons and Daughters of Jewish Deportees from France]—has been one of the most influential in determining the course of Holocaust memory in France. To the 1.5 generation writers belongs French writer Georges Perec, whose 1975 *W or the Memory of Childhood* has become a classic.[10] And the children of child survivors of the Holocaust—whom Suleiman suggests calling, though she admits the arithmetic seems a stretch, the "2.5 generation"—frequently present a different profile from that of the second or third generation.[11] A distinction exists also between child survivors of the Shoah who did not lose their parents, and those who lost one or both; it is the children of the latter category who appear to be the 2.5-generation writers.

Something else clouding the idea of a third-generation writer as the scion of a second-generation parent *stricto sensu* is a work that is often cited as the very example of third-generation production: Daniel Mendelsohn's *The Lost*.[12] Mendelsohn's parents and grandparents spent the war in the United States; his work explores six members of his grandparents' generation who were left behind in Europe and murdered. Accordingly, a third-generation narrative *lato sensu* would concern members of two generations before who bore the brunt of the Holocaust. But would that include writers of the second generation who focus not only on what their parents went through but also on their grandparents? And what of those in the 1.5 generation who deal with their grandparents? Often forgotten in analyses of Perec's *W* is what we learn about his father's mother. He recounts that during the occupation she pretended to be mute lest her Yiddish accent give her away; at the war's end, she left for the land of Israel.

For such reasons, I prefer to speak of *avatars* of third-generation narrative. Indeed, in the French case, generations merge; perhaps not only the disruption but even the superimposition of generations can be seen as a common result of the Holocaust. One very clear example is that of Marcel Cohen, son and grandson of Turkish Jews who had immigrated to France. A child at the time of the occupation, Cohen owed his life to mere circumstance: the maid had taken him out for a walk shortly before his father and pregnant mother were arrested. Hidden during the war with the maid's family in Brittany, Cohen grew up afterwards in close proximity to his maternal grandparents, who had survived, unlike his father's parents. This configuration, as son more than grandson of his grandparents, made Cohen, for his generation, an unusually able speaker and writer of Ladino. Though the bulk of his work is in French, one of his most moving texts is a lengthy letter in Ladino to the Spanish painter Antonio Saura, which he published in 1997 both in that language and in a French version he produced himself.[13]

A 2013 book by Cohen—*Sur la scène intérieure* [On the inner scene (or stage)][14]—focuses on photos of family members who were killed; this pictorial analysis, used in *The Lost*, may well have as its first instance the procedure used by Perec in *W*. Cohen adopts another strategy employed by Perec: an alternation of passages in roman characters and those in italics. Perec switched between chapters in ordinary typeface (in which he attempts to reconstruct his childhood during the occupation) and others in italics (where Nazi concentration camps are allegorized into an inhuman Olympic village in Tierra del Fuego)[15]; Cohen employs italics to indicate what he actually remembers (these could be considered 1.5-generation memories) as opposed to passages in roman characters that present the reconstructions based on conversations with surviving members of his family and his own research. Such careful perusal of sources may seem more characteristic of a third-generation narrative. As Nathalie Skowronek, one of the writers to be discussed here, puts it: "It is said, in a kind of shorthand, that the third generation is the one that digs up secrets."[16]

The phenomenon of the second-generation child as a Yahrzeit candle, a replacement for a child murdered, has been documented[17]; but Cohen describes a different experience, as the 1.5-generation child who for his grandparents is a memento mori of his parents. He at once compensates for the loss of their own children and yet reminds them *too much* of those they lost. His place in the generational chain is troubled by excessive closeness and distance. When Cohen asked his grandparents about their daughter Marie—his mother—this was their reaction:

> They repeated to me a hundred times that nobody, nothing, could resist Marie. When I tried to find out more, the selfsame adjectives would come and tell me nothing: she was "funny," "beautiful," "affectionate," "intelligent."
> Anything further, and my grandparents were on the verge of tears. If I persisted in questioning them, my obstinacy seemed a lack of consideration; I was not respecting their pain. Their faces quickly froze: "I beg of you, stop!" The closer I got to Marie, the more her image was clouded by tears. In my teenage years, my pique increased in equal measure to the displeasure caused by my curiosity. It was as if Marie had remained the daughter of her parents without becoming the mother of her son.[18]

Only from sources other than his grandparents could Cohen find out more about his mother, "including her relationship with her parents."[19] (A somewhat similar confusion of generational structure can be found in the writings of Henri Raczymow, one of the best-known literary writers on the Holocaust in France; see the introduction to "Simon and Mania," the text on his grandparents that I have translated for this volume.)

I would like now to consider a recent narrative by a member of the 2.5 generation: historian Ivan Jablonka's 2012 *Histoire des grands-parents que je n'ai pas eus*. Given the two meanings of the French word *histoire*—and this is key—the title can be translated either as the "Story" or "History of the Grandparents I Did Not Have": "I am going to write a book about their story, or rather a history book about them."[20] The choice of the verb in "the grandparents I did not have" (as opposed to "the grandparents I did not *know*") bespeaks the peculiar absence of grandparents engulfed in the Holocaust.

Son of a father born to Polish Jews on the eve of the war in Paris, Jablonka applies his sharp tools as historian to investigating the fate of his paternal grandparents arrested in France and murdered at Auschwitz. Indeed,

Jablonka is a particularly able chronicler; we see this in his continuing critic Éric Marty's debunking of the myth of Jean Genet, who despite his own praise of evil and of the Nazis has been elevated to the position of Third-Worldist saint in his support of Black Panthers and the Palestinians.[21] Jablonka's work on the author of *The Maids* and *The Balcony*[22] shows how Sartre's explanation, nay defense, of Genet's thievery—his supposed mistreatment at the hands of typically uncaring foster parents—is belied by state social-service archives recording benevolent treatment by those who took him in.

Jablonka's book on his paternal grandparents starts with the trope of replacement. He begins by quoting at length a letter he wrote at age seven-and-a-half to his mother's parents, Jews who like some others (as we have seen) managed to stay alive in France throughout the war: not only unhidden but wearing a yellow star. Jablonka wrote to these grandparents, drawing hearts at the end of each line:

> You can be sure that when you have died, I shall think sadly of you all my life. Even when my life is over, my children will have known you. Even their children will know you when I am in my grave. For me, you will be my gods, the gods I worship and who will watch over me, just over me. I shall think: My gods are protecting me, I can remain in hell or paradise.[23]

We may well see a future historian in this passage, but this troublingly maudlin declaration of love beyond the grave to grandparents still alive suggests they stand in for archetypal ancestors, "who are dead and have always been so."[24] Jablonka states he had never been told "the terrible truth" that his paternal grandparents were killed; he just knew it. "There are family truths as there are family secrets."[25] Their death was part of the backdrop; perhaps this may be called "prememory," along the lines of Marianne Hirsch's "postmemory," the assumption or exploration of memory of an earlier generation.[26]

Jablonka's over four hundred pages reconstructing his grandparents' lives and deaths are well documented yet by no means tedious. His account is loving and respectful but not maudlin; that is a sentiment he obviously got out of his system early on. The pathos is more historical than mnemonic. Some of the most intimate moments occur when he realizes the continuity between the drama undergone by his grandparents and his own life; these are examples of the persistence of French Jewry *in situ* despite the Shoah. Residing not far from where these forbears did, Jablonka discovers that his daughters' school is located in the very block where his grandparents were arrested. Having been the target of identity theft (already something eerie in the case of a descendant of Holocaust victims), Jablonka is coincidentally asked to file a report in the police precinct where his grandparents had been taken; but he does not ask to be shown the holding tank where they were doubtless jailed as they awaited transfer to a camp.

Jablonka's research leads him to a conclusion particularly troubling (insofar as anything can be particularly so in the case of the Holocaust): though his grandmother was gassed on arrival to Auschwitz, his grandfather was apparently assigned to the Sonderkommando and perhaps even disposed of his own wife's body. This brings him to question a notion developed by one of the most eminent witnesses: Primo Levi's idea of a gray zone between perpetrator and victim. Jablonka recounts that after some hesitation he rejects outright even the mildest condemnation of his grandfather: "Matès did not take part in evil; he was destroyed by it."[27] Given agreement in dates he comes across, Jablonka wonders whether his grandfather took part in a revolt by Sonderkommando members: "It is possible that I am a grandson of one of the heroes of the twentieth century . . . but the border between feasibility and fantasy is blurry."[28]

Jablonka recounts a previous generation's ambivalence toward such inquiry. For a long time his father had avoided these matters. For example, in the 1980s he declined to meet someone who had seen *his* father in the camp: "No, I am not interested."[29] Yet Jablonka's father belonged at the time to Klarsfeld's organization of French children of Holocaust victims, the previously mentioned Fils et Filles des Déportés Juifs de France. As a young boy, Jablonka was amused by its French acronym, FFJDF, and would say to his father that another letter has come from the "FFFJJJ" or the "FJFJFJ." "My father smiles."[30]

In his search, Jablonka asks his father to help find out about the Courtoux, the couple who took him and his sister into their rural home and saw to their safety during the war:

> My father is reticent, comes up with arguments to show it would serve no purpose, no one would answer, etc. I insist, he writes letters halfheartedly but I believe he is secretly happy to set off on the discovery of his own story.[31]

In fact, when Madame Courtoux's niece surfaces, his father is "enthusiastic" about calling her.[32] He starts regretting missed opportunities to have learned more about his past from those surviving: "He's sick over it, because in the 1970s he could simply have visited Moïse, Madame Erpst or the Odryzinskis, and asked them."[33] Thus Jablonka's book is an example of a quest that the previous generation could not embark upon.

Another author whose father's parents were killed, Marianne Rubinstein, quotes a survivor's daughter who recounts her experience reading Holocaust testimony: "The tears, the suffering are not mine. They belong to my parents. I cry because they could not."[34] As generous as this idea seems, it is also an instance of not necessarily felicitous generational merging. Rubinstein quotes her father who, in a telling moment, confuses himself (and his generation) with his daughter (and her generation): "You see how pretty *your* mother was," he says, showing a picture of *his* murdered mother, i.e., not her mother but her *grandmother*.[35]

Rubinstein has devoted two works to what she terms the third generation, the children of Holocaust orphans. The first, appearing in 2002, was *Tout le monde n'a pas la chance d'être orphelin* [*Not Everyone Is Lucky Enough to Be an Orphan*]. The second, which came out in 2009, is titled *C'est maintenant du passé* [*It's Now Part of the Past*], in which one can hear clearly as well the contrary idea "now is part of the past" (i.e., the past is and is not present). In somewhat Perecian mode, the first book alternates chapters (in roman characters) that present narratives by different children of Holocaust orphans, and others (in italics) that contain her own reflections. We see in many cases the confusion of generations wrought by the Holocaust: "Remaining first and foremost orphans, they sometimes placed us into the role of their deceased parents"; "I was my mother's substitute father," "he called his relationship with his parents a 'child-to-child relationship.'"[36] One woman expressed a similar feeling in terms reminiscent of the Yahrzeit candle phenomenon: it was if she had "been conceived in homage to [her] grandparents."[37] The title quotes the bitter remark the author's father made, "in quasi-systematic manner," when she began as an adolescent to complain about him and her mother: "Not everyone is lucky enough to be an orphan."[38] The expression may seem to hark back to the words of Sholem-Aleichem's character Motl Peyse: "Mir iz gut, ikh bin a yosem" ("Lucky me, I'm an orphan"[39]); however, if it arrives in the mouth of this rather de-Judaized orphan, the sole mode of transmission of that expression would be via the unconscious. Rubinstein's father seems to hold it against her that she has parents; the remonstrance takes an even stranger form in the life of another child of a Holocaust orphan, who had "the impression that my father reproached me for his parents' death at the hands of the Nazis."[40]

It's Now Part of the Past presents what Rubinstein calls her "frenzied research" into the traces of her grandparents' lives and circumstances of their murders.[41] Yet she is unable to produce the kind of gripping tableau that Jablonka would come up with, even as he gave due attention to the fragmentary nature of much of what he finds. Rubinstein writes:

> Here I am at the end of my book and have not written the slightest line of the saga I had dreamt of: five hundred pages filled with unexpected events, characters seemingly off the pages of a novel, stories of love and hatred, voyages and wanderings, narrating the destruction of the Jews of Europe and inserting it into the passage of time and the chain of generations.[42]

Instead, she privileges what is incomplete:

> As my search progressed, I came to love the fragments, not only because of what they revealed to me of my family's history, but also due to their very fragility, their incompleteness, which bear witness to the violent annihilation, to the will that nothing should remain of them, and to what had subsisted despite everything.[43]

Another difference between Jablonka's and her narratives concerns their fathers' attitudes. Rubinstein's father's ambivalence is greater and sometimes borders on hostility, as we have seen in his comment on her not being an orphan. Though he himself, in the 1980s, had questioned, even "interviewed," people who might have known his parents and had three letters from them translated from Polish,[44] he objects to his daughter's quest: "All this stirs up a past that is as painful as ever, and it is not by chance I have let it lie sleeping"; "the work you're doing is opening up trapdoors" (the author "notes mentally: 'not doors, trapdoors'"); "I did not have parents,"[45] he exclaims, roundly reducing her search to nothing. Rubinstein, in turn, is quite ambivalent about her father. She retorts, "Yes, you had parents. . . . They left too soon, but you had parents," thereby "insinuating how much they had loved *him*" and how deficient his love for her had been.[46] In a calmer moment, she comes to feel "disgust at herself" for this attitude worthy of a "spoiled child" in the face of the enormity of the experience of her father and grandparents.[47] Yet the search does offer some kind of reparation: though her challenge to her father's denial "I had no parents" is aggressive, she helps him lift another refusal to acknowledge something obvious. She quotes his comments about his mother's fate:

> I was never able to think that she had been gassed; no one ever told me that. It was as if she had flown off somewhere high. I understood only by reading Marianne's book [*Not Everyone Is Lucky Enough to Be an Orphan*].[48]

Marianne had demanded from him "a father's normal attitude, loving and tender, toward a daughter"[49]; he had hoped that their relationship "could be made peaceful" and seems content that the search was being made with her "hand in hand"—words she repeats in the acknowledgments at the end of *It's Now Part of the Past*.[50] Yet she still chose to begin that book by stating that her father refused to let her quote much of a letter his father had managed to write from a camp, a missive he could not bring himself to read: "Why do you want to publish my parents' letters? Something troubles me about it; I don't know what."[51]

The question of the appropriateness of such inquiry by descendants is posed by the Belgian Nathalie Skowronek. She is the author of three more "classical" third-generation narratives (insofar as she is the granddaughter of a survivor): *Karen et moi* ([*Karen and I*], 2011),[52] *Max, en apparence* ([*Max, Seemingly*], 2013),[53] and *La Shoah de monsieur Durand* ([*Monsieur Durand's Shoah], 2015). While there was a greater percentage of Jews murdered in Belgium than in France (estimates are around 45 percent), there is continuity, often unsuspected, between life before and after the Holocaust. Just as Jablonka was surprised to learn his daughters attend school in the street where his grandparents had been arrested, Skowronek discovers that the Liège citadel, a medieval structure around which her mother would play as a child, was used to detain one third of the city's prewar Jewish population before deportation to Auschwitz.[54] To that camp was also shipped Skowronek's maternal grandfather, Max, a Polish Jew who had settled in Liège; after a few postwar years in that city, Max divorced her grandmother and moved to Berlin. An enigmatic character, he enriched himself in the German capital through the questionable transfer of merchandise between the east and west sectors. Wondering about the surprising choice of residence, Skowronek becomes convinced that he sought in Berlin "people like him, people who want to live and forget.... Numerous were those in Germany who wished not to look back, either out of self-interest or necessity."[55]

After much digging into her family's past, Skowronek begins to wonder. What if this search were precisely a failure to respect her grandfather's legacy: a wish to forget? She writes,

> Therein lies the paradox: whereas the grandparents strove to spare their children, to blur traces, not to remain "stuck" in that place, not to imprison therein their families, grandchildren go back over it, again and again, until they can't stand it anymore.[56]

Yet she notes, "the past cannot be erased so quickly. The number 70807 is there, tattooed on his forearm."[57] Indeed, the tattooed number may partially explain Max's choice to live in Berlin and prosper there in the margins of legality. If Germans should ask what he is up to, "he just has to let them glimpse his number and they fall silent. Their discomfort is a license to do as he likes.... He savors his revenge."[58]

The tattooed number is the indelible cipher of memory—or not. Another writer whom I shall consider, the Guatemalan-American Eduardo Halfon, retells what his grandfather would say when asked about the digits on his arm: it was his telephone number.[59] That response is also given to a child by an elderly Jew in a French film short from 1997, *Madame Jacques sur la Croisette* [*Madame Jacques on the Cannes Promenade*]: he was so forgetful that he needed to have his phone number imprinted on his arm.[60] However, evoking the concentration camp number as a mnemonic aid precisely implies the possibility of forgetting.

Indeed, after Max has died, Skowronek discovers that she cannot remember the numbers in his tattoo. Likewise, she meets a woman in Tel Aviv who refused to take note of the digits on her mother's arm, so that "at the death of her mother the number disappeared with her."[61] Our author becomes fascinated by what seems to be ubiquitous tattoos of all kinds on cool Tel Aviv youth—markings "which had quite a lot to do with my need to go back to Max's story."[62] Indeed, another important male presence in her childhood was tattooed: a non-Jewish employee of her family of whom she was particularly fond had emblazoned on four fingers the letters L O V E.[63] She wonders if she should have herself tattooed, but gives up the idea after discovering her grandfather's number, a "palindromic" 70807, in a diary entry she had made decades before.[64] Likewise, one of Rubinstein's third-generation interviewees describes his adolescent fantasies thus: "If I saw an old man with a tattoo on his arm, I thought it looked nice. I would have liked to be in his place, to be an object of admiration."[65]

To tattoo or not to tattoo: Skowronek comments on a strange though thankfully limited fad among young Israelis who have their grandparents' concentration camp numbers tattooed on their own arms.[66] And she wonders whether Holocaust narrative has itself become a similar kind of farcical, or at least trivial, rewriting of the repetitive, assembly-line, tragic process of marking that one's forebears had undergone. She speaks of how third-generation authors have become "legion": "In the publishing world they speak of a 'generational phenomenon,'" of "the grandchildren of survivors also arriving at the time of testimony."[67] Editors complain "with some embarrassment about saturation" of the market ("luckily for me," adds Skowronek with some humor, "my publisher was not one of them"[68]). These writers are not only "guided by the pioneers of the 'second generation'" such as Patrick Modiano[69] and Georges Perec[70]; they often enough explicitly mention them. For example, *W* is evoked by Jablonka,[71] Rubinstein,[72] and Skowronek.[73] They also refer to third-generation writers, including each other. Besides Rubinstein's and Skowronek's predictable invocation of Mendelsohn,[74] Skowronek mentions Jablonka (his name means "appletree" in Polish as hers signifies "lark" in the same language)[75]; Jablonka included a piece by Rubinstein in a volume he edited on "the Shoah child" (*L'enfant-Shoah*).[76] Third-generation writers thus form a cohort in the strictest sociological sense of the word[77]—with an *enfant terrible* (or *petit-enfant*—grandchild—*terrible*) among them. That would be Skowronek, who wryly remarks they might as well say to each other, "Begin a sentence and I'll finish it for you."[78] (Though she does not point it out, the ability to go back and forth, to answer the question before it is asked, seems an uncanny reflection of her grandfather's palindromic tattoo 70807.)

Of course, Skowronek is not the first to speak of Holocaust fatigue; interviewed on French Jewish philosopher Alain Finkielkraut's radio program *Répliques*,[79] she refers to Tova Reich's *My Holocaust*,[80] a book far more corrosive than any of the three she has written—though the title of her last one, *Monsieur Durand's Shoah*, is ironic enough. The joke behind it is worth telling here; the reader must keep in mind that Durand, like Dupont, are archetypal French surnames, the equivalent of Smith or Jones in the English-speaking world.

It is the story about Maurice Dupont who goes to the civil registry and asks that his name be changed to Maurice Durand. The employee says he does not understand; he could see why last year he had his name changed from Maurice Shmulewicz to Maurice Dupont, but now, he asks, "Why do you wish to be called Maurice Durand?"

The answer is simple, Dupont replies with a Yiddish accent. When he says his name is Maurice Dupont, people ask him what his name was before, and he has to say Maurice Shmulewicz; if he were to become Maurice Durand, he could say that his last name used to be Dupont.[81]

The would-be Monsieur Durand wishes to forget but cannot; the Yiddish accent remains, even harder to remove than the tattooed number. But *Monsieur Durand's Shoah* can also refer to the bandying-about of the Shoah, its not always felicitous universalization whereby any significant tragedy is equated to some aspect of the Holocaust, which must "never again" be allowed to occur. Thus the Danish government's requirement that Syrian refugees with means hand over assets in order to finance their absorption raises the outcry: This is what was done to the Jews.[82] Little does it matter that in the earlier case destitution was part of a long-range program of eliminating a settled population, whereas now the assets serve to help a group integrate. The idea of "never again" can signify two different things. In Europe the meaning is often enough: *never again* shall anything occur that could marginalize any ethnic group in any way; whereas Amos Oz quotes his father as saying the following on the night the UN vote on the partition of Palestine made the State of Israel possible: "From now on, from the moment we have our own state, you will never be bullied just because you are a Jew and because Jews are so-and-sos. Not that. Never again."[83]

A prime example of the overly general "never again"—the universalization of the Holocaust whereby its specifically Jewish import is dismissed—is a book I would argue is an avatar of third-generation narrative: a rather successful novel from 2007, translated into English as *Brodeck*, by the non-Jewish Frenchman Philippe Claudel, born in 1962.[84] This work enjoyed a significant following among young readers—three to four generations after the Holocaust—and won a major literary prize awarded yearly by a jury of lycée students. Hailed on the French Ministry of Education website as a "political allegory on the monstrosity of the Shoah,"[85] it is the story of a man from a town in Germany (or perhaps Alsace, since the narrative is in French, with Germanic toponyms and words in faux Germanic dialect), a town apparently populated solely by Christians. The churchgoing eponymous narrator, Brodeck, has returned from a concentration camp to which he has been sent for no apparent reason. Scenes from the book read like a pastiche of Franz

Kafka and Primo Levi; as in the first writer's oeuvre but differently from the second's, the word Jew is never spoken. Only the vaguest hints suggest anything in that vein. One of the inmates is named Moshe; another has a noticeable proboscis ("the nose is what gives them away," says a camp guard), and the main character, adopted after his parents were killed in a fire at the start of the *First* World War, mentions "a bit of flesh missing between my thighs."[86] Though the author was surely guided by the purest intentions, *Brodeck* shows how universal Holocaust education can lead to nearly total erasure of the Jewish specificity of the Holocaust.

I would like to end this section on third-generation narrative in French by discussing a work at the antipodes of the best-selling *Brodeck*: a little-noticed volume titled *Waiting for Godot: From the Absurd to History*.[87] This work begins with a conversation between a grandfather and grandson. The forbear is a retired history teacher named Valentin Temkine, husband of well-known theater critic Raymonde Temkine and a passionate theatergoer himself; the grandson is Pierre Temkine, a philosophy professor specializing in Spinoza. The rest of the volume is made up of reactions by scholars to their dialogue.

Valentin Temkine wishes to *de-universalize* a major work of the twentieth century. He argues that *Waiting for Godot* does not portray the absurdity of the human condition but rather the particular situation of Jews and resistance fighters in occupied France. Thus the eternally-not-yet-arriving eponymous character would be the *passeur* hired to smuggle Vladimir and Estragon over to the marginally safer southeastern Vichy zone. (It is interesting that while the original interview is available in French on the Internet, the book of essays appears in book form only in German translation; this reflects no doubt the encounter between a peculiar German passion for Beckett, who often aided in production of his plays in Germany, and German attempts at *Vergangenheitsbewältigung*, the "coming to terms with the past," real though imperfect as it may be.)

Temkine's most convincing evidence for his thesis of the Jewish import of *Waiting for Godot* is the name given to Estragon in early manuscripts: Lévy. But there are other factors. Though an Irishman, Beckett joined the French resistance. His explanation: "I was so outraged by the Nazis, particularly by their treatment of the Jews, that I could not remain inactive."[88] Beckett's network having been uncovered, it became necessary for him to hide out in a locality in the Vichy zone, where he supported himself by picking grapes for a farmer (the name of the town and his employer figure in the French original of the play but disappear in Beckett's own English version). A dialogue between Vladimir and Estragon, little dwelt upon by critics, clearly alludes to the Holocaust. In that scene, the "pseudo-couple"[89] contemplates what up to then had loomed as a setting empty except for a tree:

VLADIMIR: Where are all these corpses from?

ESTRAGON: These skeletons?

VLADIMIR: Tell me that.

ESTRAGON: True.

VLADIMIR: We must have thought a little.

ESTRAGON: At the very beginning.

VLADIMIR: A charnel-house! A charnel-house!

ESTRAGON: You don't have to look.

VLADIMIR: You can't help looking.

ESTRAGON: True.[90]

I can personally attest to Beckett's sympathy for Jews; when I was so privileged as to interview him for my doctoral thesis, he understandably showed far less interest in my overwrought graduate-student questions than in the simple story of my mother's birth in the small Jewish community of Dublin.[91]
A 2013 Yiddish version of *Waiting for Godot* staged in New York—with English and Russian supertitles—is, as I write this piece, possibly being brought to Paris.[92] As an insightful blogger wrote,

> Merely by speaking Beckett's lines in Yiddish, with only the faintest hint otherwise that the "action," so to speak, is being played out in a specific post-Holocaust landscape (concentration camp stripes poke out from the undergarments of one character; another seemingly is wearing camp pants), the play takes on entirely new resonance.[93]

However, there are problems with interpretation of the play that would de-universalize and re-Judaize *Godot*. Temkine argues that Vladimir's regret at no longer being allowed to go up the Eiffel Tower symbolizes prohibitions on Jewish activity in occupied France; but as his grandson Pierre admits, it turns out that the Germans closed the famed attraction to the general public. Likewise, Valentin Temkine claims that the school on the rue de la Roquette in Paris, where the two characters as children viewed biblical maps, would have to be a Talmud Torah on that street where a major Sephardic synagogue still operates. However, this contention disregards important facts: the English version of the play speaks of their reading not just the Bible but "the Gospels,"[94] and colored maps of the Holy Land are more characteristic of Protestant bibles than Hebrew Tanachs. Finally, it is clear that Beckett himself chose to subdue any Jewish aspect of the play: he *renames* Lévy Estragon; he removes the reference to his own hideout under Vichy in his English version; he claimed he did not know who Godot is.

As often happens with correctives, this one goes too far, but a Jewish dimension of the play *is* there. The title given to the texts on and by the Temkines, "From the Absurd to History," summarizes the lesson. Post–World War II malaise—variations on the existentialists' absurd sense of life—is partially rooted in the camps, as an assault on the "human race" (as the title of Robert Antelme's masterpiece has it[95]), but precise history must be remembered. The Holocaust was a program targeting *Jews*.

NARRATIVES IN SPANISH

Critic Edna Aizenberg starts her recent *On the Edge of the Holocaust: The Shoah in Latin American Literature and Culture*[96] by citing the knee-jerk reaction to her inquiry: "Didn't all the Nazis go to Argentina?"[97] Her conclusion: "The Nazis may have gone to Argentina, but the anti-Nazis were there, then and now."[98] Thus she argues that were it not for a certain "Euro-U.S.-centrism" on the part of Shoah scholars, Jorge Luis Borges would be commonly known as one of the first writers of "Holocaust fiction."[99] It was in 1944 that the Argentine master published his tale "The Secret Miracle" on a Czech Jewish writer facing a Nazi firing squad: the miracle consists in God's stopping the world for a year to allow the playwright to finish, in his mind, the work that he has been composing.[100] Likewise, 1946 saw the appearance of Borges's "Deutsches Requiem," which dissected the perversity of the Nazi mind.[101] This was sixty years before Jonathan Littell's supposedly innovative *The Kindly Ones* came out in its original French.[102]

Among the Latin American writings on the Shoah that Aizenberg has studied is an excellent second-generation novel by the Argentinean Sergio Chejfec, *Lenta biografía* [*Slow Biography*] that originally appeared in 1990.[103] The slowness refers to the protracted rate at which the author finds out anything about the life of his father, who survived. The book is less about transmission of his forbear's story than about the lack of transmission; it is not so much narrative as it is metanarrative, commentary not only on the not-said but also on its non-saying. This is how he reacts when he learns his father had been a shoemaker in the old country:

> That information, far from eliciting my enthusiasm, disappointed me without my knowing why. Much later I realized that the unease arose not because I had found out what my father's trade had been during his brief existence in Poland (this was rather the subject I needed to reconstruct), but because each discovery—or each evasive confession of his—ended up corroborating and irremediably increasing the distance between his past and our present.[104]

Though Chejfec does not remark upon this fact, I would argue that the gap between his father's past and his present is figured in the Polish orthography of his surname. In this regard, his case is similar to that of Georges Perec; though the surname is pronounced in French as *Perek*, in Polish C denotes the sound *ts*; Perec's relationship to the Yiddish writer Y. L. Peretz, supposedly his great-great-uncle, is thus obscured. Likewise, Chejfec becomes a practically unpronounceable *Chekhfek* in Spanish, whereas it should be pronounced *Heifetz* (as in the name of the famed violinist), a Hebrew word paradoxically meaning both "desire" and "object." In this nearly inaccessible meaning of the name as it passes from the Holocaust survivor to his son, we may read the problematic *desire* to know a slippery *object*: the past so difficult for oneself to retell and for others to grasp. Aizenberg remarks that "the narrator rewrites in Spanish the Yiddish autobiography"[105] that his father claimed he wanted to write. "Not for a moment did I believe" in the existence of such a desire on his father's part, says our author.[106] The father does not have enough Spanish to recount what happened and barely wants to do so; the son is not only ignorant of Yiddish but describes it as hardly being speech. Innumerable times he calls it a language "similar to chewing"[107]—a mastication we indeed hear in the consonantal clusters of the Spanish pronunciation of his name. (Malena Chinski, in her piece written for this volume, discusses the third-generation elements of Chejfec's book.)

As we move from such a second- to third-generation narrative in Latin America, a pattern emerges similar to the one we saw operating in France. Like Western Europe, countries to the south became a destination of choice for Jewish immigration after the United States closed its doors in 1924; thus Latin American Jews have often enough a chronologically closer familial relationship to Europe and the Holocaust than do their American counterparts. It stands to reason that Jewish children born in the 1930s to immigrants to Latin America might well have had more immediate awareness of grandparents who stayed in Europe and met a terrible fate. We see such a consciousness in a successful book from 2000 by Uruguayan former political prisoner Mauricio Rosencof, translated into English as *The Letters that Never Came*.[108] Born in 1933 in Uruguay to Polish Jewish immigrants, Rosencof was interned and tortured for leftist activity by the military régime between 1973 and 1985. *The Letters That Never Came* offers episodes from his Uruguayan childhood, from his own time in jail, and from the little he knows about relatives left behind in Poland. The title refers to imaginary epistles his father's brother Leon (or Leibu) could have sent from the ghetto and Treblinka.

Most interesting for our subject is the merging of the generations. Rosencof's Polish-born older brother, also named Leon/Leibu, died as a teenager in Uruguay. As the name he had in common with his uncle might suggest, he seems from an earlier generation than the author, even though only a few years separated them. Leon/Leibu spoke and read Yiddish, a language that Mauricio understands little and does not decipher at all; its cursive alphabet in a letter his father writes to Poland looks to him like "a bunch of little sticks."[109] His brother explains that "they're not sticks, that up on the top those sticks say 'Mamele,' and that means 'Mama.' Papa has a mama he calls 'Mamele.'" Still unsure, Mauricio asks his brother, looking at the picture of the lady in question: "Is she your mamele?" Leon responds:

> No, stupid, Mama's my mamele, and Papa's mama is my *bubele*—you understand now?—and Bubele is your bubele too, so you have two bubeles, same as I do, Papa's mamele and Mama's mamele.[110]

Little Mauricio's reaction: "So now I know. Bubeles are mameles who get their pictures taken."[111] This childhood incomprehension reflects the feeling suggested in Jablonka's title: grandparents who died in the Holocaust are not grandparents one has never known but rather grandparents one has never *had*. In a variation of the Yahrzeit candle phenomenon—wherein a postwar child stands in for a murdered one—it is only following the birth of a daughter he names Esther (after his grandmother) that Rosencof can say, "This way, I always know I had (or once had) a grandmother, a bubele, named Esther."[112]

Another instance of the Yahrzeit candle phenomenon emerges when not a birth but Leon/Leibu's premature *death* allows him to represent those murdered; however, they figure not as murdered victims but as people still alive and able to remember the boy from when they all were in Poland. Thus Rosencof describes what he thought of upon visiting the ghetto monument in Warsaw:

> What came back to me, Papa, is how when we'd go to the cemetery to visit Leon . . . you and Mama would start mumbling in Yiddish, listing the names of everyone who could have come by there and would have stopped to remember . . . saying that Leon was in their memories too; you and Mama knew they were the only ones who could have remembered.[113]

In keeping with the motif of unsent letters, Rosencof describes the extreme strictures placed on the rare correspondence he was allowed to write in prison. Yet despite evident similarities in the experience of incarceration, he never drives home an analogy between what he went through as a tortured Latin American political prisoner and the fate of his relatives murdered in the Holocaust.

The parallel is made more explicit in the account by another former political prisoner, *Daughter of Silence* (1999) by the Argentinean Manuela Fingueret, whose mother survived Terezin but whose grandmother succumbed.[114] But do we have any right to say that Fingueret engaged in undue metaphoric extension of the Holocaust in screaming to her tormentors that they were "fucking Nazis"?[115] At less traumatic moments, she shows some hesitation regarding such analogies: "Linking my grandmother, my mother and myself: Rebellion. Conviction. Fate?"[116] A Peronist, Fingueret wonders (ironically?) about the parallels she draws: "What do they [her mother and grandmother] have in common with Evita? What do I have in common with Evita?"[117] And while she can be so ideologically sectarian as to declare Perón as the man who restored "honor" to an Argentina destroyed by "Nazi-capitalism" (just compare this to the charge that Perón saved Nazis), she half-declares, half-asks, "Here I am walled in and still spouting those rigid speeches I invented?"[118] She exonerates such rhetoric, "There is no other way to lead the struggle,"[119] and then compares herself to a Warsaw ghetto leader: "What must Mordechai Anielewicz have been like? . . . He was able to do it, and I accomplished something."[120] Those last words, however, allow us to hear her consciousness of the gap between even her radical combat and that of Holocaust resisters.

"Nuestra Shoá" [our Shoah]: this is how Argentine-Israeli critic Amalia Ran has termed the metaphor used by many Latin American writers to describe the imprisonment, torture, murders perpetrated by Latin American dictatorships of the 1980s.[121] Florinda F. Goldberg, also an Argentine-Israeli scholar, has argued that the analogy is best seen not as history but as myth in its most positive sense.[122] However, the parallel is reinforced by a historical fact: the number of Argentine political prisoners included Jews in higher numbers than their proportion in the general population, no doubt due to their greater involvement in leftist causes; and once arrested, Jews were often singled out for particularly harsh treatment.[123]

Now I shall focus on a more recent writer, a "classical" case of a third-generation author: Eduardo Halfon, who lived in Guatemala to the age of ten, then immigrated to the United States with his family. He returned to Spanish when he started writing. Three of Halfon's grandparents were Jews from Lebanon, but one grandfather was a Polish survivor of Auschwitz who settled among the infinitesimal Jewish community of the Central American republic: "a hundred families, as they usually say," in what was apparently a ritual invocation of the group's tininess.[124]

Halfon is an excellent storyteller; one of his non-Holocaust-related works is a 2004 novel that suggests, rather convincingly, what could happen when a researcher discovers documents that indicate Cervantes had traveled to the New World.[125] As a character in another book by Halfon puts it, "You Jews are born with a novel under your arm."[126] But Halfon's usual genre is the short story, written in the first person—tales he recombines in different ways in various editions of his works in diverse languages. (He claims this as a legacy from Julio Cortázar's novel *Hopscotch*, whose chapters can be read in two diverse sequences.[127])

The eponymous tale in his collection *The Polish Boxer* recounts how his grandfather, newly interned at Auschwitz, is saved by a fellow Jew—a boxer—who spends a whole night telling him what to say in a Nazi kangaroo court. Halfon draws a parallel between the boxer speaking all night and Scheherazade; are we to understand that Jews tell stories of the Holocaust in order to survive? Unlike Scheherazade, the storyteller himself, the boxer, apparently did not make it out alive. However, the metaphor from *The Thousand and One Nights* suggests that the Holocaust story can be told in infinite variations, a felicitous version of Skowronek's decrying the "self-generating" third-generation narrative [128]—with the additional difference, of course, that she keeps to testimony where he is writing fiction, even if it is largely autobiographical.

Holocaust fiction itself is a self-conscious trope of Halfon's. For example, on meeting an Israeli woman doing a typical post-army-service tour of Latin America, he discovers that her last name, Tenenbaum, is the same as his mother's:

> I imagined a novel about two Polish siblings who thought their entire families had been exterminated but who all of a sudden find each other after sixty years apart, thanks to the grandchildren, a Guatemalan writer and an Israeli hippie, who meet by chance in a Scottish bar that isn't even Scottish in Antigua, Guatemala. [129]

We have already seen something else Skowronek's and Halfon's oeuvre have in common: meditation on the numbers tattooed on their grandfathers' arms. Let me cite at length Halfon's introduction of the number in the incipit to the eponymous short story in the volume *The Polish Boxer*:

> 69752. That it was his phone number. That he had it tattooed there, on his arm, so he wouldn't forget it. That's what my grandfather told me. And that's what I grew up believing. In the 1970s, telephone numbers in Guatemala were five digits long. [130]

That number "hypnotized" Halfon as a child; adoring this grandfather (a different sentiment than toward the rest of the family, as we shall see), he "liked that number"[131] and in flights of novelistic fantasy he would imagine different scenarios wherein that tattoo was imprinted. Here is one such moment of fancy chosen from three in the story, another example of Holocaust fiction as trope:

> my grandfather, sitting on a wooden bench in front of a semicircle of Germans in white coats and white gloves, with white lights fastened around their heads, like miners, when suddenly one of the Germans stammered out a number and a clown rode in on a unicycle and all the lights shone their white light on my grandfather while the clown—with a big green marker, in ink that could never

be erased—wrote that number on his forearm, and all the German scientists applauded.[132]

In a more austere passage, Halfon reminds us of other variations on the tattooed number: writer Rena Kornreich had it surgically removed but kept the piece of skin in formaldehyde (she was tired of people asking if it was her phone number), Primo Levi not only kept it but instructed that it be engraved on his tombstone, along with his name.[133] We can add the case of Ka-Tzetnik 135663, who made his number part of his pseudonym.

How Halfon defines his Jewish identity is hardly the best part of his writing. The other authors studied here generally assume their Jewishness as a matter of fact. For example, Jablonka asks whether someone so nonobservant as he should be considered "a non-Jewish Jew."[134] Rubinstein, child of a mixed marriage, ponders the paradox whereby the scion of a Jewish mother and a non-Jewish father is Jewish according to Orthodox law yet might carry a recognizably gentile surname; whereas she is non-Jewish halakhically but very Jewish onomastically.[135]

Halfon seems a bit sophomoric in his attitude toward Jewishness, writing for example that his recurring narrator is "not Jewish anymore"[136] or is Jewish "sometimes."[137] Less pleasantly, we are treated to a parallel with the Nazi definition of a Jew. This occurs when Halfon's alter ego contemplates a group of Haredim with his brother: "Whether you like it or not, he said, whether you accept it or not, you're as Jewish as all of them. That's the way it is. That's your heritage. It's in your blood."[138] Rather disingenuously interpreting such a comment about Jewish "blood" as being literal, Halfon writes, "the discourse about Judaism being in the blood, the discourse about Judaism not being a religion but something genetic, sounded the same as the discourse used by Hitler."[139]

Almost needless to say, his comments about Israel are equally peremptory. For example, the Jewish state's security barrier is analogized to the walls around the Warsaw ghetto.[140] A comparison with another writer seems apposite: Manuela Fingueret—who, unlike Halfon with his P.C. *opinions*, was jailed and tortured for her leftist *activity*—is far less trenchant and actually mocks her own anti-Israel discourse. This is similar to how she questioned the parallels she herself drew between her own persecution as political prisoner and that of her mother and grandmother at the hands of the Nazis:

> My father's stories preserve the warmth of a tradition that unites me with my people. Even with Israel, to which my father is devoted, and in another time I had embraced with passion but today define as the "capitalist-ogre-aggressor-of-the-Middle-East." But I can't completely banish it from my affections. It hurts him to hear that from me. And I must confess it pains me not to share with him those things that brought us together, but between betraying the Israel of my father and betraying the Israel of the cause I have no choice.[141]

By "the Israel of the cause," Fingueret may mean the ideal Promised Land—certainly not the State of Israel—to be created by the Leftist Cause. Or else she cannot bring herself to "betray" the Cause's definition of Israel as the "capitalist-ogre-aggressor." In either case, her convictions are far from mine, but I see her feelings as more nuanced than Halfon's jejune reflections on Jewishness and Israel. Indeed, his insistent use of the term *discourse* in making a parallel between Jewish "blood" discourse and "the discourse used by Hitler" can well be a marker of prepackaged ideology (though to be fair to Halfon, I have just used the word with respect to Fingueret—but to point to her self-irony). Again, in contrast to Halfon's ambivalence about Jewishness, Fingueret has only disdain for revolutionary comrades, as Jewish as she, but who say something "as stupid as: 'I'm of Jewish *origin*,'" i.e., they are not actually Jews themselves.[142]

Finally, I would like to consider a writer whose political stance (like Fingueret's and unlike Halfon's) demands courage: the Cuban Eduardo Padura, whose detective novels include rather critical remarks on the régime. He is tolerated on the island, but his books are not widely available there despite their success elsewhere in the Spanish-speaking world. He is appreciated even in Hollywood, where a contract for a movie about his Sherlock Holmes character, named Mario Conde, is in the offing; it would star the inevitable Antonio Banderas.[143] Not Jewish, Padura has penned an extensive third-generation novel (translated so far into French, though others of his books are available in English) titled *Herejes* [*Heretics*], which came out in 2013.[144]

Heretics begins with the second (or 1.5) generation, as the story of Daniel Kaminsky, a teenage boy who before World War II has been brought to Havana by his immigrant uncle. His parents (the first generation) and sister, arriving later, wait to disembark from an ill-fated vessel docked in the harbor: the *St. Louis*, whose Jewish refugee passengers are refused entry both to the United States and Cuba. They are returned to Germany and murdered in the camps.

Padura's hero Daniel ultimately marries the daughter of Spaniards, for whose sake he becomes Catholic; they later emigrate to Miami, where he is re-Judaized and she takes on the Jewish religion. Their son Elías—the third generation—is a painter who returns to Havana to search for the most surprising element of the plot: a portrait of a Semitic-looking Jesus by Rembrandt or a Jewish student of his, which had been in the family since the Sabbatean heresy. In vain the fleeing German Jewish family had hoped to exchange the artwork for permits to enter Cuba; instead, it was confiscated by a corrupt government official.

The twists and turns of the grandson's attempts to recover the painting, as well as numerous subplots, are worthy of a somewhat postmodern detective novel that leaves many ends untied but still provides old-fashioned narratological satisfaction. One of the questions left unanswered is posed by the very existence of the book: what does it mean that a non-Jewish Cuban writer should delve into three generations of the Holocaust? Padura avoids recuperation of the catastrophe; while he is critical of the régime there is no suggestion that Cubans have suffered anything like a genocide at Castro's hands. (Incidentally, the government conflates incommensurate events in the opposite direction, by proclaiming that the U.S. blockade is "the longest genocide in history"—as seen on a billboard I photographed in Havana in December 2015 [figure 7.1]).

Unlike Philippe Claudel's *Brodeck*, Padura universalizes the Holocaust *without* de-Judaizing it; rather, he Judaizes Cuban memory by bringing attention to the *St. Louis* catastrophe that linked the island to the Holocaust. (So great is the general ignorance regarding that incident in Cuba that historian Adriana Sosa was wary lest young generations who read about it in Padura's novel presume that it is a fictional construct.[145]) Moreover, exploiting the trope of the 1492 expulsion from Spain as a prefiguration of the Holocaust, Padura weaves a tale wherein Rembrandt's student—a member of the re-Judaized community of Amsterdam descended from marranos—carries

Figure 7.1. "Blockade: The Longest Genocide in History": sign facing the Juan Marinello Institute in Havana. Photo by Alan Astro, December 17, 2015.

along the painting of the Jewish-looking Jesus when he sets out for Poland to join followers of Shabbetai Tsvi. This circumstance explains how the artwork could show up centuries later as an heirloom among Polish Jewish refugees from Germany.

The handing-down of the painting that straddles Jewish and Christian iconography functions as a cipher for the transmission of the Holocaust to generations of mixed Jewish and Christian parentage. The heretics in Padura's title are Sephardim such as the Abrabanel family, Uriel Dacosta and, obviously, Baruch Spinoza, who are both inside and outside Judaism. Daniel Kaminsky, about to be baptized in Havana to appease his fiancée's family, remembers the story of Judah Abrabanel that his father Isaías—a doctor from Cracow who settled in Berlin—would tell him and that he in turn would tell his son Elías (the third generation) "in the steamy Miami Beach nights."[146]

This "real or fictitious" Judah Abrabanel, forced to convert, seems to be a composite of several members of the illustrious family. Dr. Isaías imagines him thus:

> Perhaps Judah Abrabanel . . . in the moment he felt the holy water fall upon his head, had thought he was immersing himself in the Jordan before setting off to the rebuilt Temple of Solomon and prostrating himself before the Ark of the Covenant.[147]

Daniel, son of a Holocaust victim, inspired by this apochryphal Abrabanel, thus manages to Judaize his very break from Judaism in a way located at the antipodes of the notion of Christianity as the "completion" of Judaism. As the book ends, grandson Elías—a painter, like his forbear who studied under Rembrandt—is attempting to recover the finally located painting and donate it to a Jewish museum.

In the notion of "multidirectional memory" touted by the academy, the Holocaust becomes a *means* for remembering slavery or colonialism, which necessarily entails replacement, or displacement, of the Holocaust by other historical traumas.[148] Contrarily, Padura *coordinates* Jewish and Hispano-Cuban memory. The very distance implicit in the third-generation structure can allow for constructed—or perhaps even contrived—memory that is an appropriation but not a recuperation/expropriation. This is an aspect of the Holocaust as useable past, wherein we move not beyond mourning but outside of it.

In some of these works—to use I. A. Richards's terminology[149]—the Holocaust is the metaphorical *vehicle* for talking about something else (for example, the Argentine dictatorship). However, I shall end my study by referring to a work in which the Holocaust serves as the *tenor* of the metaphor, wherein something else is spoken of in order to evoke the Holocaust. This takes place in 2013 work of "journalit": *Los crímenes de Moisés Ville* [*The Crimes of Moisés Ville*][150] by Javier Sinay, prize-winning writer for the Argentine edition of *Rolling Stone*.[151] Sinay interviews his grandparents and their contemporaries on events reported by his great-grandfather, one of the first Yiddish journalists in Argentina. He focuses on an article his ancestor published quite late in life, in 1947, on a forgotten episode of Argentinean Jewish history from some fifty years before: the bloody murders of Jewish farmers by gauchos on the pampas.[152] Why had his grandfather waited so long to write about them? Sinay comes to realize that the piece constituted a way of talking indirectly about the then Jewish "present that had been made totally dark by mass murder. My great-grandfather's article seemed to arrive at its proper time."[153] His forbear thus grappled with what was not yet called the unrepresentability of the Holocaust.

It seems fitting that an article on avatars of third-generation narrative should end on an evocation of Sinay's fourth-generation text. Narratives of *toldot ha-Shoah*—generations of the Holocaust—may continue *le-olam va-ed*, for whatever eternity the world may know. They may be tedious and counterproductive, as Skowronek warns and *Brodeck* shows; or creative and enriching, as exemplified by Jablonka's or Padura's works—or even by Skowronek's cautionary writing against the surfeit of memory.

NOTES

1. Estimates of the percentage of Jews murdered in different countries vary, but the *relative* proportions I mention regarding figures for France, the Netherlands, and Belgium (25 percent, 70 percent, 45 percent, respectively) seem constant. For one source, see this page on the website of the Los Angeles Museum of Tolerance: http://www.museumoftolerance.com/site/c.tmL6KfNVLtH/b.5052465/k.ED04/36_Questions_About_the_Holocaust.htm#5 (accessed February 21, 2016).

2. Simone Veil, "Réflexions d'un témoin," *Annales* 48 (1993): 693.

3. On the question of how the majority of Jews in France escaped being sent to camps, see Jacques Semelin, *Persécutions et entraides dans la France occupée: comment 75% des Juifs en France ont échappé à la mort* (Paris: Seuil, 2013).

4. The major work problematizing views on the Vichy period is Henry Rousso, *The Vichy Syndrome: History and Memory in France Since 1944*, trans. Arthur Goldhammer (Cambridge, MA: Harvard University Press, 1994).

5. Georges Wormser, quoted by Annette Wieviorka, *Déportation et génocide: entre la mémoire et l'oubli* (Paris: Plon, 1992), 338. All translations here are mine, unless otherwise noted.

6. Ivan Jablonka, *Histoire des grands-parents que je n'ai pas eus* (Paris: Seuil, 2012), 272. Further references to this work will be noted as *Histoire*.

7. Jablonka, *Histoire*, 272.

8. Susan Suleiman, "The 1.5 Generation: Thinking About Child Survivors and the Holocaust," *American Imago* 59, no. 3 (2002): 277.

9. Suleiman (quoting Debórah Dwork) reminds us that only 11 percent of prewar Jewish children in all countries under Nazi rule or allied with the Nazis were alive in 1945 (278). In France, 84 percent survived. The latter statistic (11,000 children murdered, compared to a prewar child population of 70,000) is derived from Marianne Rubinstein, *Tout le monde n'a*

pas la chance d'être orphelin (Paris: Seuil, 2002), 7. Further references to the latter work will be noted as *Tout le monde*.

10. Georges Perec, *W or the Memory of Childhood*, trans. David Bellos (Boston: Godine, 1988).

11. Suleiman, "The 1.5 Generation," 292.

12. Daniel Mendelsohn, *The Lost: A Search for Six of Six Million* (New York: HarperCollins, 2006).

13. Marcel Cohen, *In Search of a Lost Ladino: Letter to Antonio Saura*, trans. Raphael Rubinstein (Jerusalem: Ibis, 2006).

14. Marcel Cohen, *Sur la scène intérieure* (Paris: Gallimard, 2013).

15. See my "Allegory in Georges Perec's *W ou le souvenir d'enfance*," *MLN* 102 (1987): 867–76.

16. Nathalie Skowronek, *La Shoah de Monsieur Durand* (Paris: Gallimard, 2015), 32. Further references to this work will be noted as *Durand*.

17. Dina Wardi, *Memorial Candles: Children of the Holocaust*, trans. Naomi Goldblum (New York: Routledge, 2013 [1992]).

18. Cohen, *Sur la scène intérieure*, 30.

19. Cohen, *Sur la scène intérieure*, 30.

20. Jablonka, *Histoire*, 95.

21. Jablonka, *Les vérités inavouables de Jean Genet* (Paris: Seuil, 2004); Éric Marty, "Jean Genet's Anxiety in the Face of the Good," in *Radical French Thought and the Return of the Jewish Question*, trans. Alan Astro (Bloomington: Indiana University Press, 2015), 1–52.

22. Jean Genet, *The Maids; Death Watch; Two Plays*, trans. Bernard Frechtman (New York: Grove, 1954); *The Balcony*, trans. Bernard Frechtman (New York: Grove, 1966).

23. Jablonka, *Histoire*, 9.

24. Jablonka, *Histoire*, 10.

25. Jablonka, *Histoire*, 10.

26. Marianne Hirsch, *Family Frames: Photography, Narrative and Postmemory* (Cambridge, MA: Harvard University Press, 1997). Marianne Rubinstein also speaks of grandchildren who "have always known" their grandparents were murdered by the Nazis (*Tout le monde n'a pas la chance d'être orphelin* (Paris: Seuil, 2002), 82, 87).

27. Jablonka, *Histoire*, 354.

28. Jablonka, *Histoire*, 362–63.

29. Jablonka, *Histoire*, 331.

30. Jablonka, *Histoire*, 294.

31. Jablonka, *Histoire*, 304.

32. Jablonka, *Histoire*, 304.

33. Jablonka, *Histoire*, 281.

34. Rubinstein, *C'est maintenant du passé* (Paris: Gallimard, 2009), 115. In a review in the *Forward* (24 May 2010), "Marianne Rubinstein: Grandchild of the Shoah," Benjamin Ivry translates the title as "That's All Over With" (http://forward.com/the-assimilator/128270/marianne-rubinstein-grandchild-of-the-shoah/ [accessed 24 Feb. 2016]); I point out later here that the phrase is more ambiguous regarding the passage of time. Further references to this work will be noted as *C'est maintenant*.

35. Rubinstein, *C'est maintenant*, 127, emphasis added.

36. Rubinstein, *Tout le monde*, 123, 10, 88.

37. Rubinstein, *Tout le monde*, 10, 23.

38. Rubinstein, *Tout le monde*, 42.

39. Sholem-Aleichem, *The Letters of Menakhem-Mendl and Sheyne-Sheyndl and, Motl, the Cantor's Son*, trans. Hillel Halkin (New Haven, CT: Yale University Press, 2000), xx.

40. Rubinstein, *Tout le monde*, 36.

41. Rubinstein, *C'est maintenant*, 29.

42. Rubinstein, *C'est maintenant*, 151.

43. Rubinstein, *C'est maintenant*, 40.

44. Rubinstein, *C'est maintenant*, 74, 61.

45. Rubinstein, *C'est maintenant*, 30–31, 67, 128.

46. Rubinstein, *C'est maintenant*, 128–29.
47. Rubinstein, *C'est maintenant*, 129.
48. Rubinstein, *C'est maintenant*, 108.
49. Rubinstein, *C'est maintenant*, 104.
50. Rubinstein, *C'est maintenant*, 129, 163.
51. Rubinstein, *C'est maintenant*, 14.
52. Nathalie Skowronek, *Karen et moi* (Paris: Arléa, 2011). Further references to this work will be noted as *Karen*.
53. Nathalie Skowronek, *Max, en apparence* (Paris: Arléa, 2013). Further references to this work will be noted as *Max*.
54. Skowronek, *Max*, 70.
55. Skowronek, *Max*, 213.
56. Skowronek, *Durand*, 32.
57. Skowronek, *Max*, 213.
58. Skowronek, *Max*, 215.
59. Eduardo Halfon, *The Polish Boxer*, trans. Daniel Hahn et al. (New York: Bellevue Literary Press, 2012), 78. Further references to this work will be noted as *Boxer*.
60. Emmanuel Finkiel, dir., *Madame Jacques sur la Croisette*, prod. Films du Poisson, 1997.
61. Skowronek, *Max*, 21.
62. Skowronek, *Max*, 22.
63. Skowronek, *Karen*, 57; *Max*, 13, 67, 116.
64. Skowronek, *Max*, 234–35, 166–67.
65. Rubinstein, *Tout le monde*, 102.
66. Skowronek, *Durand*, 55. Cf. Jodi Rudoren, "Proudly Bearing Elders' Scars, Their Skin Says 'Never Forget,'" *New York Times*, September 30, 2012, http://www.nytimes.com/2012/10/01/world/middleeast/with-tattoos-young-israelis-bear-holocaust-scars-of-relatives.html (accessed February 19, 2016).
67. Skowronek, *Durand*, 33–34.
68. Skowronek, *Durand*, 34.
69. Many novels by French author Patrick Modiano, winner of the 2014 Nobel Prize for Literature, chronicle and rework in fictional form his Jewish father's somewhat questionable activities under the occupation.
70. Skowronek, *Durand*, 34.
71. Jablonka, *Histoire*, 242–43.
72. Rubinstein, *C'est maintenant*, 100.
73. Skowronek, *Durand*, 34.
74. Ruberstein, *C'est maintenant*, 28, 96; Skowronek, *Max*, 137; Skowronek, *Durand*, 34.
75. Skowronek, *Max*, 165; Skowronek, *Karen*, 97.
76. Marianne Rubinstein, "Restaurer la colonne vertébrale de nos familles," in *L'enfant-Shoah*, ed. Ivan Jablonka (Paris: Presses Universitaires de France, 2014), 237–45.
77. One of Rubinstein's third-generation interviewees is a statistician whose thesis was a "study, from a statistical point of view, of the population made up of grandchildren of concentration-camp victims" (Rubinstein, *Tout le monde*, 91).
78. Skowronek, *Durand*, 47.
79. Alain Finkielkraut, interview with Michel Marian and Nathalie Skowronek, "Un génocide fait-il une identité?" *Répliques*, France Culture, June 20, 2015, http://www.franceculture.fr/emissions/repliques/un-genocide-fait-il-une-identite (accessed February 19, 2016).
80. Tova Reich, *My Holocaust* (New York: HarperCollins, 2007). Skowronek refers in Finkielkraut's interview also to a similarly titled work: Noam Chayut's *The Girl Who Stole My Holocaust*, trans. Tal Haran (London: Verso, 2013). The book totes the post-Zionist "Israeli occupation = Holocaust" line.
81. Skowronek, *Durand*, 26–27.
82. Patrick Kingsley, "Denmark to Force Refugees to Give Up Valuables Under Proposed Asylum Law," *The Guardian*, January 12, 2016, http://www.theguardian.com/world/2016/jan/

12/denmark-to-force-refugees-to-give-up-valuables-under-proposed-asylum-law (accessed February 21, 2016).

83. Amos Oz, *A Tale of Love and Darkness*, trans. Nicholas de Lange (New York: Harcourt, 2003), 359.

84. Philippe Claudel, *Brodeck*, trans. John Cullen (New York: Anchor, 2010).

85. Xavier Darcos, "Le rapport de *Brodeck* de Philippe Claudel, Prix Goncourt des lycéens 2007," http://www.education.gouv.fr/cid20341/-le-rapport-de-brodeck-de-philippe-claudel-prix-goncourt-des-lyceens-2007.html (accessed February 18, 2016).

86. Claudel, *Brodeck*, 54–55, 16, 133, 186.

87. The work appears in book form in German translation: Pierre Temkine et al., *"Warten auf Godot": Das Absurde und die Geschichte*, trans. Tim Trzaskalik (Berlin: Mattes & Seitz, 1st ed. 2008, 2d ed. 2009). The original French is available only in the internet journal *Texto* 13, no. 1 (2008), http://www.revue-texto.net/docannexe/file/88/dossier_godot_maj.pdf (accessed February 18, 2016).

88. Deirdre Bair, *Samuel Beckett: A Bibliography* (New York: Harcourt Brace Jovanovich, 1978), 308.

89. Samuel Beckett, *The Unnamable* in *Three Novels* (New York: Grove, 1965), 297.

90. Samuel Beckett, *Waiting for Godot* (New York: Grove, 1954), 41.

91. Personal interview with Samuel Beckett, Paris, June 23, 1983.

92. Samuel Beckett, *Vartn af Godot*, trans. Shane Baker. See the review by Ezra Glinter, "The 'Godot' We've All Been Waiting for," *Forward*, October 3, 2013, http://forward.com/culture/184917/the-godot-weve-all-been-waiting-for/ (accessed February 24, 2016).

93. Seth Rogovoy, "'Waiting for Godot' in Yiddish," http://rogovoyreport.com/2013/09/30/waiting-for-godot-new-yiddish-rep-2/ (accessed Febraury 21, 2016).

94. Beckett, *Waiting for Godot*, 8.

95. Robert Antelme, *The Human Race*, trans. Jeffrey Haight and Annie Mahler (Marlboro, VT: Marlboro, 1992).

96. Edna Aizenberg, *On the Edge of the Holocaust: The Shoah in Latin American Literature and Culture* (Waltham, MA: Brandeis University Press, 2016).

97. Aizenberg, *On the Edge of the Holocaust*, ix.

98. Aizenberg, *On the Edge of the Holocaust*, 163.

99. Edna Aizenberg, *Books and Bombs in Buenos Aires: Borges, Gerchunoff, and Argentine Jewish Writing* (Hanover, NH: University Press of New England, 2002), 130, 135.

100. Jorge Luis Borges, "The Secret Miracle," in *Collected Fictions*, trans. Andrew Hurley (New York: Viking, 1998), 157–62.

101. Jorge Luis Borges, "Deutsches Requiem," in *Collected Fictions*, trans. Andrew Hurley (New York: Viking, 1998), 229–34.

102. Jonathan Littell, *The Kindly Ones*, trans. Charlotte Mandell (New York: HarperCollins, 2009).

103. Edna Aizenberg, "*Lenta biografía*: Chejfec's Post-Holocaust, Postcolonial *Had Gadya*" in *The Jewish Diaspora in Latin America: New Studies on History and Literature*, ed. David Sheinin and Lois Baer Barr (New York: Garland, 1996), 53–60; Sergio Chejfec, *Lenta biografía* (Buenos Aires: Alfaguara, 2007 [1990]).

104. Sergio Chejfec, *Lenta biografía* (Buenos Aires: Alfaguara, [1990] 2007), 17.

105. Aizenberg, "*Lenta biografía*: Chejfec's Post-Holocaust, Postcolonial *Had Gadya*," 57.

106. Chejfec, *Lenta biografía*, 10.

107. Chejfec, *Lenta biografía*, 31, 37, et passim.

108. Mauricio Rosencof, *The Letters that Never Came*, trans. Louise B. Popkin (Albuquerque: University of New Mexico Press, 2004). Further references to this work will be noted as *Letters*.

109. Rosencof, *Letters*, 16.

110. Rosencof, *Letters*, 17.

111. Rosencof, *Letters*, 17.

112. Rosencof, *Letters*, 43.

113. Rosencof, *Letters*, 57–58, translation modified as per the original: Rosencof, *Las cartas que no llegaron* (Mexico City: Alfaguara, 2010 [2000]), 100.

114. Manuela Fingueret, *Daughter of Silence*, trans. Darrell B. Lockhart (Lubbock, TX: Texas Tech University Press, 2012). Further references to this work will be noted as *Daughter*. Since the translator, in his introduction, notes that he adapted the text extensively (a strategy justified by Fingueret's fragmented style), I have on occasion chosen to render into English passages from the original: Manuela Fingueret, *Hija de silencio* (Buenos Aires: Planeta, 1999). Further references to that work will be noted as *Hija*.

115. Fingueret, *Daughter*, 74.
116. Fingueret, *Hija*, 149.
117. Fingueret, *Hija*, 149.
118. Fingueret, *Daughter*, 102.
119. Fingueret, *Daughter*, 102.
120. Fingueret, *Hija*, 145.
121. Amalia Ran, "Nuestra Shoá: Dictadura, Holocausto y represión en tres novelas judeoreoplatenses," *Spanish Language and Literature*, paper 48, Modern Languages Commons, http://digitalcommons.unl.edu/modlangspanish/48 (accessed February 20, 2016). Originally published in *Letras hispanas* 6, no. 1 (2009): 17–28.
122. Florinda F. Goldberg, "'Judíos del Sur': El modelo judío en la narrativa de la catástrofe argentina," *EIAL: Estudios Interdisciplinarios de América Latina* 12, no. 2 (2002), http://eial.tau.ac.il/index.php/eial/article/view/983/1018 (accessed February 20, 2016).
123. Guillermo Lipis, *Zikarón—Memoria: Judíos y militares bajo el terror del Plan Cóndor* (Buenos Aires: Del Nuevo Extremo, 2010), 36, 44.
124. Halfon, *Boxer*, 180.
125. Halfon, *De cabo roto* (Barcelona: Littera, 2003).
126. Halfon, *El ángel literario* (Barcelona: Anagrama, 2004), 49.
127. Mauro Libertella, "Una boda judía y otras historias," *Clarín*, May 26, 2015, http://www.revistaenie.clarin.com/literatura/Eduardo-Halfon-boda-judia-historias_0_1362463765.html (accessed February 24, 2016); Julio Cortázar, *Hopscotch*, trans. Gregory Rabassa (New York: Pantheon, 1966).
128. Skowronek, *Durand*, 34.
129. Halfon, *Boxer*, 73–74.
130. Halfon, *Boxer*, 78.
131. Halfon, *Boxer*, 79, 78.
132. Halfon, *Boxer*, 79.
133. Halfon, *Boxer*, 183.
134. Jablonka, *Histoire*, 365.
135. Rubinstein, *C'est maintenant*, 50.
136. Halfon, *Boxer*, 72. The assertion is repeated in a slightly different version of the same story, "White Smoke," included in Eduardo Halfon, *The Monastery*, trans. Daniel Hahn et al. (New York: Bellevue Literary Press, 2014), 105. Further references to the latter work will be noted as *Monastery*.
137. Halfon, *Monastery*, 23.
138. Halfon, *Monastery*, 45.
139. Halfon, *Monastery*, 45.
140. Halfon, *Monastery*, 136.
141. Fingueret, *Hija*, 92; cf. *Daughter*, 63–64.
142. Fingueret, *Daughter*, 134, emphasis added.
143. Elizabeth Wagmeister, "Antonio Banderas to Star in Detective Drama 'Havana Quartet' for Starz," http://variety.com/2015/tv/news/antonio-banderas-havana-quartet-starz-series-1201554271/ (accessed February 20, 2016).
144. Eduardo Padura, *Herejes* (Barcelona: Tusquets, 2013).
145. Adriana Sosa, "Análisis discursivo del periódico *Alerta* en relación con los sucesos del St. Louis," paper read at the Instituto Cubano de Investigación Cultural Juan Marinello, Havana, Cuba, December 17, 2015.
146. Padura, *Herejes*, 90.
147. Padura, *Herejes*, 90.

148. See Michael Rothberg, *Multidirectional Memory: Remembering the Holocaust in the Age of Decolonization* (Stanford: Stanford University Press, 2009); and Rothberg et al., eds., *Noeuds de mémoire: Multidirectional Memory in Postwar French and Francophone Culture*, Yale French Studies 118/119 (2010). For a trenchant critique of the concept of multidirectional memory, see chapter 3, "Dangerous Parallels: The Holocaust, the Colonial Turn and the New Antisemitism" in Bruno Chaouat's *Is Theory Good for the Jews?* (Liverpool: Liverpool University Press, forthcoming).

149. I. A. Richards, *The Philosophy of Rhetoric* (New York: Oxford University Press, 1936), 96–101.

150. Janvier Sinay, *Los crímenes de Moisés Ville: Una historia de gauchos y judíos* (Buenos Aires: Tusquets, 2013). An excerpt of the book has appeared on the Internet in English: *The Crimes of Moisés Ville: A Story of Gauchos and Jews*, trans. Matthew Fishbane, http://www.tabletmag.com/jewish-arts-and-culture/books/181601/moisesville (accessed February 20, 2016).

151. For his coverage of an episode of Buenos Aires street crime, Sinay won the 2015 García Márquez Prize for Journalism, the Latin American equivalent of the Pulitzer Prize.

152. Such gaucho hostility flies in the face of the legendary symbiosis between Argentine cowboys and Jewish farmers, a storyline that served as apologetics for Jewish immigration to the South American republic. The prime instance of that narrative is Alberto Gerchunoff's 1910 *Los gauchos judíos* [*The Jewish Gauchos*]; see the translation of that book and its deconstruction by Edna Aizenberg, *Parricide on the Pampa?: A New Study and Translation of Alberto Gerchunoff's* Los gauchos judíos (Madrid: Iberoamericana, 2000).

153. Sinay, *Los crímenes de Moisés Ville*, 259.

Chapter Eight

Measure for Measure

Narrative and Numbers in Holocaust Textual Memorials

Jessica Lang

In Cynthia Ozick's novella "A Mercenary," the protagonist, a Polish-born Jew and Holocaust survivor named Stanislav Lushinski, urges his mistress Lulu to read books about the Holocaust: "There were easy books and there were hard books. The easier ones were stories; these she brought home herself. But they made him angry. 'No stories, no tales,' he said. 'Sources. Documents only. . . . There are no holy men of stories,' he said, 'there are only holy men of data.'" Lulu weeps over the easy books, including one entitled *Night*, pleading an inability to separate "the stories from the sources." Lushinski responds: "'Imagination is romance. Romance blurs. Instead count the numbers of freight trains.'"[1]

Ozick's well-documented trepidation about writing stories of the Holocaust often centers around the numbers that historical data reveal and the absence of such data in Holocaust stories. The "easy books" that Lulu willingly engages in, such as *Night*, about the history of a single person, in the mind of Lushinski fail to capture adequately not only the scale of destruction ("Destruction" being the name of the huge tome that Lushinski tosses to Lulu to read) connected to the Holocaust but also the need to read materials devoid of the pleasure that is often connected with reading. In "A Mercenary" Ozick manages to reenact precisely her trouble with Holocaust representation, advocating for the absolute need for historical data, on the one hand, and the unquenchable desire to create a narrative, one that is organized, readable, and so in some way cathartic, on the other.

Ozick draws a sharp line between data and stories, between the numbers that reveal the magnitude and enormity of loss and the story that enlivens a single life. In fact, however, a range of what I shall call here "textual memorials" involving the Holocaust bring these two aspects together quite deliberately. Textual memorials adhere to the oldest of Jewish memorials, recorded language, and center on legibility and textuality as among their core elements.[2] Memorials remembering those who perished in the Holocaust face innumerable challenges, none more prominent than that characterized by Paul Celan in his poem "Todesfuge," the necessity and difficulty of marking, in ways both publicly and personally resonant, "a grave in the air."[3] What Celan captures in this phrase is the catastrophe of embodiment and disembodiment—the need, on the one hand, for the living to remember, honor, and mark the dead, and the impossibility of providing a resting place for a body—singular and collective—that not only no longer exists but which through the death camp crematoria have wholly disappeared. Importantly, the living are characterized by Celan with the first person plural: "we." "Black milk of daybreak we drink it at evening / we drink it at midday and morning we drink it at night / we drink and we drink / we shovel a grave in the air there you won't lie too cramped." Those who are gone (to call them "the dead" lends them a physicality not present in Celan's language) are marked by the singular and by the indirect article: "a." It is this ever-so-small gesture of Celan's that looms large in many Holocaust memorials, presenting a contrast between plurality and singularity, the definite and the indefinite, which one more often observes as the reverse, with the singular attached to the remember and the many attached to the perished.

A significant subset of Holocaust memorials derive their symbolic and literal meaning through an invocation of numbers and counting, which typically serves as a means of both representing the many and the individual—an illustration of the relationship between, on the one hand, the vast sense of loss and destruction associated with the Holocaust, and, on the other, the meaning found in investigating and remembering a single life. In certain ways this discussion invokes a more familiar dichotomy between two competing views of the Holocaust as a historical event, namely, the divide between understanding it as universal or as particular. To understand the Holocaust in universal terms is to believe that since it happened once, there exists the possibility of its equivalent happening again or of comparable events having occurred previously. Yehuda Bauer states this view succinctly in the opening of his book *Rethinking the Holocaust*: "[The planned total murder of a people] happened because it could happen; if it could not have happened, it would not have done so. And because it happened once, it can happen again. Any historical event is a possibility before it becomes a fact, but when it becomes a fact, it also serves as a possible precedent. And although no event will ever be repeated exactly, it will, if it is followed by similar events, become the first in a line of analogous happenings."[4] Universalists strive to position the Holocaust in global terms, attempting to derive universal lessons from it, such as the struggle against all forms of racism. Religion scholar

Alan Berger understands universalism in relation to the Holocaust as a striving toward *tikkun olam*, the repairing of the world's fractures.[5] At odds with this understanding is the particularist point of view, one which understands the Holocaust as a unique event comprised of a set of particular actions and reactions, involving specific victims and perpetrators.

In his work *Post-Holocaust*, philosopher Berel Lang admits the possibility for the two claims both to be right, recognizing from the outset that, when viewed one way, they are contradictory and yet, viewed another, "they require or entail each other, with each of the two claims plausible in its own separate terms. The two representations, then, turn out to be at once contradictory and necessary."[6] Lang, instead of attempting to reconcile these conflicting positions, recognizes that each is "valid in its own terms." This acknowledgment is useful, especially in light of the many Holocaust memorials that try to bring together symbolically precisely these contradictory qualities in a single construct. I do not attempt here to resolve the differences between these two competing views. To the contrary, I suggest that the representation of the relationship between the universal and the particular is, at least in part, sustained by the relationship between counting and countlessness found in textual memorials that were created before or shortly after the war ended. This relationship becomes increasingly complicated—and co-exists far less easily—in contemporary textual memorials, indicating a shift in the ways memory and symbolism interact with each other and in how the reading or understanding of numbers impacts sites of memory. Here I address Holocaust memorials that not only use specificity and particularity in combination with countlessness but, in addition, Holocaust memorials that center on language and reading as among their core elements. These include, among earlier textual memorials, the *Oyneg Shabes* archives and *Yizkor* books; contemporary textual memorials include the work *And Every Single One Was Someone* and the *Stolpersteine* Art Project. I wish to uncover and define the relationship between reading and counting, and the relationship and influence of earlier textual memorials on more recent ones.

Holocaust memorials are typically not divided up into the generational assignments that accompany Holocaust literature: first, second, or third. In contrast to authors, many fewer artists or sculptors identify themselves (or are identified by others) as bearing a direct inheritance to the Holocaust. One reason behind my wish to examine textual memorials is because their hybridity bridges the gap between Holocaust literature and Holocaust memorial. By considering textual memorials produced over the course of seven decades, we are able to see a series of gestures and movements that correlate roughly with literature written by Holocaust survivors and that written by the third generation. There are differences, of course. While literature can and is identified generationally in terms of the passage of time, with approximately every twenty years marking a new beginning of sorts, the very different nature of memorials to temporality—their (at times unrealistic) assignation as timeless; their objectification, a presence that works as an exhibit; their physicality, enjoined, in the case of textual memorials, with literary and rhetorical components—affects our relation to and understanding of them. In light of this understanding, I have resisted calling textual memorials first, second, or third generation and instead have opted to identify them, somewhat clumsily, as those produced during or shortly after the war and those that are contemporary, i.e., produced in the past two decades.

Any memorial that relies on counting, and in relation to the Holocaust there exist thousands of memorials that hold numeric symbolism at their core, creates an uneasy relationship between the three entities crucial to sites of memory: the viewer, the object that comprises the memorial, and the act of remembering. This uneasiness stems in part from the artificial connection between the act of counting and what is being counted. The former requires the participation of the viewer or audience, while the latter refers to a symbol of remembering. A relationship between the rememberer and the remembered is at the heart of most, if not all, memorials. And yet contemporary memorials that engage in numerical symbolism, because they center on and are often completed by the rememberer, increasingly risk marginalizing the event and the victims they memorialize, thus obfuscating the object with the subject. As such, for some contemporary memorials the act of memorialization dramatically changes the nature of a given site of memory in large part because it conflates and confuses particularism and universalism. The impulse to count characterizes or influences, in one way or another, many of the memorials that relate to the Holocaust, including those created or recorded during the war years and, although in a range of different forms, continuing into the present. Understanding the relationship between the act of counting and numbering as it takes place in a textual memorial in contrast to the act of counting by readers and viewers, in which their participation is, indeed, counted upon, complicates and even disrupts the nature of numeric symbolism in its more originary form.

Earlier textual memorials, those produced during and shortly after the war, have a different and less explicit relationship to the monumental than later ones, where the tangible heft of objectivity is central to the memorial's meaning. This distinction relies on the definition of memorials formulated by James Young, namely that all sites of memory are memorials; the "plastic objects within these sites" are monuments. And while a memorial need not be itself, as a whole or in part, a monument, all monuments are memorials.[7] Young notes that memorials "provide the sites where groups of people gather to create a common past for themselves, places where they tell the constitutive narratives, their 'shared' stories of the past."[8] Memorials, then, have become places that do not simply mark the process of a historical event, but also function as an experience of remembering and, beyond that, of remembering remembering. For all their physicality, Young notes, memorials manage to keep their "own past a tightly held secret, gesturing away from [their] own history to the events and meanings we bring to it in our visits."[9] The aim of memorials more generally is to locate a specific past, a move that both includes the memorial and points beyond it, rendering it in many ways invisible.[10] The invisible exists because of the impossibility of granting memory true physical form. For most of those murdered in the Holocaust, the absence of even a grave, the earliest of monuments, lends special meaning to the accessibility and inaccessibility of memory-sites. The memorials I consider here are deeply textual, taking the form of archives, memorial books, and engravings. The numbers articulated in these memorials are essential to the experience of remembering that they are intended to evoke, although whether they succeed is another question.

One early and poignant example of numeric symbolism within a textual memorial can be found in the *Oyneg Shabes* archive, the collection of a wide range of documents—testimonies, journals, essays, articles, poems, stories, and more—that were gathered under the direction of historian Emanuel Ringelblum to document life in the Warsaw Ghetto during the German occupation. Buried in tin boxes and metal milk canisters (figure 8.1), which themselves have come to serve as a monument to those who lived and died in the Warsaw Ghetto, one part of the archive, namely ten tin boxes, was located and unearthed with the help of several of its contributors in 1946. Several of the milk cans were discovered by Polish construction workers in 1950. Other parts of the archive have not been recovered. The papers are preserved at the Jewish Historical Institute in Warsaw; one of the three milk cans in which the papers were stored is currently on exhibit at the United States Holocaust Memorial Museum. Disinterred from the wreckage of the former Warsaw Ghetto in a symbolic unearthing that could never take place for those who perished, the *Oyneg Shabes* archive presents a unique site of memory both in narrative, place, and object. As Samuel Kassow documents in his book *Who Will Write Our History?* Ringelblum "insisted that the archive tabulate the statistics for reports that would avoid pathos and excess emotions. The numbers would speak for themselves."[11] Gustawa Jarecka, a contributor of many of the statistics to the archive, notes: "Written accounts can only provide some additional details about events and specific incidents. But basically nothing is more expressive than statistics!"[12]

Acquiring statistics, however, was only one of Ringelblum's ambitious goals for the *Oyneg Shabes* archives. Ringelblum was intent on researching even minute details about the ghetto, sending out contributors to interview numerous individuals as well as to investigate a range of broader subjects that became the topics for essays, recorded in notebooks distributed specifically for this purpose. These included subjects as varied as the search for

Figure 8.1. One of the three milk cans used by Warsaw Ghetto historian Emanuel Ringelblum to store and preserve the secret "Oneg Shabbat" ghetto archives. Courtesy of Zydowski Instytut Historyczny imienia Emanuela Ringelbluma.

employment, soup kitchens, and examples of resistance. The archive also served as a collection point for testimony, with contributors soliciting descriptions from individuals asking them to record their feelings in the wake of the death of family members, on witnessing the destruction of their homes and communities, on being forced to take flight. In short, the archive is a remarkable collection because of its sheer size and diversity—the ultimate collecting memorial, it contains poetry, letters, last wills and testaments, stories, essays, diaries, songs, drawings, photographs, leaflets, invitations, study notes, recipes, candy wrappers, and more. Taken as a whole, the archive serves as "a collective story composed of hundreds of smaller narratives, accounts of everyday horrors from different individual perspectives, yet illuminated by moments of reprieve, of dignity and courage."[13] Part of this collective endeavor includes professional analyses and data, including, for example, German documents that list the daily numbers of deportees and, in another example, the numbers of those shot in the streets.[14] Another part of the archive brings together a wealth of material from individuals, written in their hand, conveying their voices, their names, their stories—and then placing these in the company of detailed information, statistics, and data about the Warsaw Ghetto and, even more broadly, Polish and (in part) eastern European Jewry. What transforms the *Oyneg Shabes* archive into a memorial as distinct from a collection of catalogued materials like many other archives, was the collective realization at the time of its gathering that its contents would serve as a marker of a life lived for most of its contributors who—accurately—predicted their own deaths. The *Oyneg Shabes* became for many an opportunity to record for future generations not only ideas and images but the bare fact of their authors' existence in the face of imminent death and the wish for this existence to be remembered. It is a site of memory that recognizes that the symbolism in recording a single voice, and that conveyed by larger studies, do not necessarily interfere or cancel each other out. This is not so much a case of breaking down larger numbers into smaller numbers and making the two sides of the equation meet. Rather, each number in the *Oyneg Shabes* archive, each single voice, each piece of data denoting groups of Jews, bears a quality comprised of both numerical and figurative value, this latter conveying a meaning that goes beyond the number in and of itself.

The *Oyneg Shabes* archive as a memorial entity invokes both numbers and number symbolism; many of the papers that involve narrative accounts—testimonies, stories, autobiographical essays—contain these same qualities. The designers of the archive themselves recruited a number of historians, journalists, and writers to interview recent arrivals to the ghetto and to record their stories. One example of such a narrative was composed by Rachel Auerbach, whom Ringelblum requested in the fall of 1942 to record the testimony of a few recent arrivals to the Warsaw Ghetto who had managed to escape from Treblinka, an extermination camp located to the northeast of Warsaw that was in operation from July 1942 to October 1943. One of these interviews (when compiled and typed it was close to a hundred pages long) was with a Jew from Danzig named Abraham Jacob Krzepicki, who escaped Treblinka after spending eighteen days there and successfully made his way to Warsaw. In Krzepicki's harrowing testimony, which manages to capture both irony and horror, he makes a concerted effort to provide specific details about his ordeal, possibly urged on by his interviewer. Forced to dispose of the bodies of people who had died while in transit on their way to Treblinka, Krzepicki notes that when he first surveyed the scene "we beheld a horrible sight. Countless dead bodies lay there, piled upon each other. I think that perhaps 10,000 bodies were there. . . . We, the new arrivals, were terror-stricken. We looked at each other to confirm that what we were seeing was real. But we were afraid to look around too much, because the guards could start shooting any minute. I still did not want to believe my eyes. I still thought that it was just a dream."[15] Krzepicki's testimony gestures in two different directions: "Countless dead bodies lay there," he recalls, and then he clarifies in the following sentence: "I think that perhaps ten thousand bodies were there." On the one hand, Krzepicki's testimony registers the enormity of the crime, its horrible implications. The "countless bodies" that he refers to resists the effort to count the dead, to enumerate or quantify the atrocity. And yet the wish to document, coming from himself and perhaps urged on by his interviewer, aware of his role as one of the first eyewitnesses of Treblinka to contribute to the *Oyneg Shabes* archives, requires him to use referents that readers, both contemporary and postwar, might be able to grasp.

This use of numbers in Krzepicki's testimony happens multiple times. Having been ordered to unload boxcars from a new transport that has just arrived, he notes that, looking into the cars, he is "stunned by what I saw there. The cars contained only corpses. They had all suffocated on the journey from lack of air. The cars were jam-packed and the corpses lay piled one on top of the other. It is not possible to imagine the impact of the sight of these cars full of dead bodies. I inquired where the transport had come from and I found out that it had come from Międzyrzec (Mezrich). About 6,000 souls, men, women and children."[16] Later that day, Krzepicki records that he was forced to pull bodies out of a well located next to the watchtower. "Many corpses had accumulated in this well, and we had to pull them out that day. A Pole from Penal Camp Treblinka No. 1 was working with us. He stepped into a bucket which was attached to the well's chain, and we lowered him into the well. He would tie the corpses to the bucket, one by one, and we would turn the crank and pull the bodies up. I counted a total of 35 corpses."[17] In trying to summarize the devastation around him, he writes: "There were corpses all over the place, corpses by the tens, hundreds, and thousands. Corpses of men, women and children of all ages, in various postures and facial expressions, as if they had been frozen immediately after they had taken their last breath. Heaven, earth, and corpses! A gigantic enterprise which manufactured corpses."[18]

Krzepicki's testimony engages in both the act of counting while at the same time maintaining the countlessness of the tragic horror he has witnessed. By combining numerical specificity with descriptive language expressing magnitude, Krzepicki's testimony moves in two directions, one particularist—this is his story and the story of Polish and, by implication, eastern European Jewry—and one universalist: "Heaven, earth and corpses!" This genocide is not only of this moment, but one that is predictive of future possibility. Krzepicki presents an account of genocide that is dream-like, divorced from the real world, with a sense of capacity and even transferability that make it possible to exist in other settings and times. Future genocide would involve a different cast of victims and perpetrators and the specific numbers would vary as well. But the sense of countlessness would remain even when such vast and wide-ranging devastation targeted a specific population. The particularity and universality of Krzepicki's account (and even of the *Oyneg Shabes* archives more generally) both diverge and reinforce one another: the numbers themselves connect the world he sees to the world he knows, bringing together experience and mindfulness. And yet the narrative of vast destruction promotes a sensibility about the numbers, investing them with universal qualities of feeling, morality, and being. In short, as Krzepicki surveys these vast numbers of bodies, almost all of them anonymous, his narrative urgently tries to account for them as the individuals he recognizes they are, while aware at the same time that they will all be turned to "scrap." His combination of numeric specificity with the language of magnitude establishes an important series of relationships: between himself and a past he knows can never be reclaimed or understood in the same terms it once was; between himself and the victims he sees, people he recognizes could just as easily be himself; between himself and his anticipated readers, for whom this landscape is utterly improbable. By combining actual numbers with words describing vastness, Krzepicki implies that either description by itself would be insufficient, further demonstrated by the fact that even taken together, the meaning of what he has witnessed defies description—it can neither be counted nor not be counted. Instead Krzepicki struggles to process the scene before him, a struggle encapsulated by his seeming self-correction that moves from "countless bodies" to "ten thousand bodies, "a shift that implies a resistance to thinking of numbers as "things," i.e., "bodies," and instead suggests a desire to acknowledge their humanity, their individuality. Mirroring Krzepicki, the reader of his testimony will be limited in combining the meaning of two numerical and opposing values conveyed in the competing sense of value and valuelessness that Krzepicki identifies.

Krzepicki's description of magnitude and enormity are not, at first, the numbers that become the source of data and statistics. They are words of description and feeling: "countless"; "jam-packed"; "many"; "all ages"; "heaven, earth, and corpses." The implicit contrast that comes with his words lies in his own presence, a solitary being in a landscape that is drowning in death. The words allude to genocide and even as Krzepicki directs them toward the murder of his fellow Jews, the description bears the qualities and properties of the more universal understanding of genocide. The words of narration are followed by actual numbers: 10,000; 6,000; 35. Krzepicki counts, sometimes one by one, as with the bodies extracted from the well, at other times as he only estimates the numbers of bodies. His ability to count, the actual act of his counting, is an act of witnessing, one that illuminates his role among the living. The numbers themselves symbolize lives lost. Their accumulation is the most pressing fact that urges him to attempt to free himself from being counted among Treblinka's dead.

Much of the power of the *Oyneg Shabes* archive as a site of memory stems from its origination: those contributing to it did so with the knowledge of their own impending deaths. They understood that the archive would be one way—probably the only way—for their names and histories to be remembered. ("*Remember, my name is Nahum Grzywacz,*" enjoins one of the authors at the end of his testament, emphasizing this final line.[19]) Clearly other sites of memory, particularly those initiated after World War II, take on a dramatically different aspect, often differentiating themselves from earlier memorials by reworking the relationship between counting and countlessness, between remembering the event as universal and remembering a single individual whose life profoundly changed as a result of the event. *Yizkor* (memorial) books, which were produced by small associations populated by survivors, provide moving eyewitness accounts of murder and loss that are notable for their specificity, providing names and even brief family histories of those who died, and, at the same time, speak to the destruction of an entire way of life. Selections from *Yizkor* books reveal a gradual shift in memorial counting and the way in which numbers are read and interpreted, a shift fueled by the predominantly postwar perspective of their contributors.

Designed to cover the history of a particular town and its residents before, during, and after World War II, *Yizkor* books bring together essays, newspaper articles, maps, photographs, and other documents that collectively recall the lives and inhabitants of a specific community. In her thoughtful exploration of the history of *Yizkor* books, Rosemary Horowitz speculates that contributors, in spite of the fact that they were not professional writers or historians, felt a "basic responsibility for writing the history of the destroyed town" from their particular perspective.[20] "The object of the memorial book," write the publishers of the Korczyner *Yizkor* book, "is not to create a literary or historical masterpiece but to create a memorial, a tombstone in the memory of our fathers, our mothers, our brothers, our sisters and our children from Korczyn that were innocently killed by the Germans."[21] The editors of the Vileike *Yizkor* book confirm that "[a]ll we want to bequeath . . . [are] simple, honest stories."[22] What these and many other *Yizkor* books emphasize is the importance of a communal perspective, one that serves both as a collective statement yet also recognizes many of the specific individuals who once contributed to and enlivened a particular Jewish community. While less data driven than the *Oyneg Shabes* archive, which, in contrast to the *Yizkor* books, was implemented by professional historians and writers, the sense of cumulation and individuation marks them both.

Organized chronologically, the majority of *Yizkor* books include essays delineating the history of the Jews in a particular community (often tracing communities with histories as far back as the sixteenth and seventeenth centuries), and conclude with recollections of survivors recounting their experiences during and just after the war. Former residents of the community, both those who emigrated prior to the Holocaust and those who survived it, often created societies (in Yiddish *landsmanshaftn*) that compiled and funded these books. While *Yizkor* books vary widely in style and content, a few features regularly appear, often including, as the interior binding or opening pages of the book, a hand-drawn map of the town's geography just before World War II broke out, and regularly concluding with a necrology that details names and known dates associated with individuals and families who perished in the Holocaust. These two frames of reference—a map that denotes the community's landmarks as a place for Jewish life when it was alive, and a list of the dead that attempts to present a sense of location that, under different circumstances, might have been performed by a cemetery or a series of headstones—encapsulate the sense of *Yizkor* books as sites of memory. As Rae Fust elegiacally notes in her poem: "Let us eternalize the memory of our city, / Which is no longer here. / In a *Yizkor* Book, in a Book of Remembrances. / Let a monument to our city be erected!" Indeed, the *Yizkor* book "is the gravestone for the people from the town who died without one" as well as "the last entry in the town's chronicle."[23]

Number symbolism in *Yizkor* books reveal a sensibility around counting that resonates with that found in the *Oyneg Shabes* archives. Many essays in *Yizkor* books illuminate, as do many of the contributions to the *Oyneg Shabes* archives, a desire to document both numerically and narratively the witnessing of murder. Moreover, *Yizkor* books acknowledge that, in the face of mass murder, the accompanying sense of loss is so vast that it defies the act of counting, on the grounds that, first, it ascribes an unjust sense of objectivity or "thingness" to that which is being counted, and, second, because the very familiarity and ease with which one can count is incompatible with the violence and loss at hand. Unlike the *Oyneg Shabes* archives, however, and largely due to their retrospective nature, shifts between counting and countlessness in *Yizkor* books occur multiple times as authors move from remembering events during the war to considering their effect and meaning postwar.[24]

In his essay "My Experiences under the Germans," part of the Tomaszow-Lubelski *Yizkor* book, Abraham Singer relates watching the murder of twenty-two members of his family and Jewish neighbors from his hiding spot. After the executions, the

> murderers counted up the dead, and saw that their tally was incomplete, because they had 22 dead, and their list showed 23, meaning that one victim was missing. [A local family] examined all the dead, and indicated that *Awrumka* [Abraham] was missing, but that I work in Mechelow, in the sugar production complex, and it was because of this, that they didn't search for me. . . . The bloody corpses lay sprawled about on all sides. . . . In a little while, at this location, several wagons were brought, and the corpses were piled on. Stiffened hands and feet, and bloodied heads, hung down from the wagons, and swayed with the rhythm of the wheels, and along the entire length of the way, human blood continued to drip, which in long red lines, wrote out the sorrowful take of the lost innocent lives. This was the silent language of the spilled Jewish blood that the accursed earth imbibed in it thirst.[25]

Singer's testimony literally recounts the bodies of his brothers, father, mother, and others—not only as they relate to him but also as they are perceived by the murderers—he is the missing 23rd victim; but for a last-ditch (successful) attempt to hide, he, too, would have been counted and checked off the list. The sense of being counted as standing in for being dead connects Singer's testimony to Krzepicki's. Furthermore, as with Krzepicki's description, Singer shifts from numericity to narrativity; the "terrible scene" of mass murder resists counting and instead depends upon the language of tragic abundance in which he describes the magnitude of all he sees, the bodies "sprawled about on all sides," the multitude of swaying limbs and heads as the dead are transported away. Singer's vantage point, unlike Krzepicki's, is colored by his surviving the war. Enabled by his postwar perspective, Singer takes the image of the blood he sees dripping from the bodies of his loved ones and magnifies it to still greater proportions, suggesting that these "long red lines" provide the ink for stories of "spilled Jewish blood" that are both ancient and new.

For Singer, writing as a survivor of the Holocaust, the shift from counting to countlessness involves not only his retrospection of a particular moment, but crosses historical and temporal boundaries, positioning the Holocaust in first particular and then in universal terms. It is important to note that neither Singer nor Krzepicki conflates particularism or universalism, even when reflection on a single scene leads them to statements that recognize both qualities. Rather, their testimony understands the one in relation to the other:

awareness of the universal occurs as a consequence of awareness of the particular.

The counting of bodies in *Yizkor* books, as well as in the *Oyneg Shabes* Archives, is marked as an affiliative act, one that works in multiple, even counter-directions, all of them deeply troubling. On the one hand, the act of counting can only be conducted by the living and both Singer and Krzepicki recognize that it is only by the thinnest of margins that they are in the position to count rather than to be among those counted. Counting in testimony is regarded as necessary to the establishment of factuality, knowledge, and data. On the other hand, the tabulating of bodies was an act carefully and methodically conducted by perpetrators intent on accounting for every Jewish body. Precisely the act of counting, in which the numbers are manipulated as though they are objects themselves, as opposed to adjectives describing real things, reaffirms the Nazi attempt at dehumanization, one that was confirmed linguistically by the use of words such as *stücke*, meaning "pieces" or "scrap," to describe Jewish bodies, living and dead. In contributing to the memorials of their communities, Krzepicki and Singer demonstrate the need both to count—an act that emphasizes individuation and particularity—and to resist counting, an act that recognizes the enormity and incomprehensibility of that which they attempt to describe. By identifying both the universalizing and particularizing aspects of a single scene, Singer and Krzepicki define a space that becomes a site of memory, one marked by a sense of loss both human and incalculable and one that is utterly distinct from the act of knowing accumulation and precision that marked German record keeping.

Both Singer and Krzepicki record the measure of their testimony as survivors—Krzepicki as a survivor of Treblinka and Singer as a survivor who lives to see the end of the war. And yet because Singer writes from, as he calls it, "that oft dreamed of land of our fathers, the Land of Israel," his testimony continues to illustrate a sense of narrative fluidity that is abbreviated in Krzepicki's testimony because of his death (Krzepicki did not survive the liquidation of the Warsaw Ghetto). Shifting from the particular to the universal, Singer then moves from the universal back to the particular.[26] At the end of his essay he notes his return, shortly after the war has ended, to the outskirts of his hometown. There he sees another man, also entering the city. "He looked at me, and I looked at him, each of us terrified of uttering even a single word. In the end, he was the first to speak: One of our people? Yes—I replied. We kissed one another and made each other's acquaintance."[27] Here we see one person facing another, trying to assess the perception or regard that each has for the other. Each man understands both the danger of facing a non-Jew and being recognized as a Jew and, conversely, the significance of finding in the presence of one other person a deep sense of fellowship and, with it, the mitigation of fear.

Singer and Krzepicki demonstrate through their testimony both the limitation and necessity behind the need for numbers as well as the uneasy position associated with countability (that is, the ability to count). Unlike with Holocaust memoirs, sites of memory such as the *Oyneg Shabes* archive and *Yizkor* books are not readily classified as first, second, or third generation. But the qualities that mark the sites of memory created by the generation of survivors—both those who anticipated their own deaths and worked to memorialize their lives in advance, and those who survived and designed memorials retrospectively—undergo a process of transformation when applied to more contemporary sites of memory. More specifically, the symbolism and texture of counting shift from memorials created by survivors to those found in more contemporary Holocaust memorials. The act of *remembering remembering*, so central to more recent sites of memory, transforms the role of numbers and counting as they are read and understood in contexts that are "closer" to the Holocaust. Whereas earlier implementations of numbers and counting contain a resistant and painful quality to them, the shift in the past several decades to routinely incorporate counting into memorials often neglects the larger and more complex meaning behind numbers—one that, as a consequence, tends to collapse the distance between the universal and the particular maintained in earlier memorials.

The recently published book *And Every Single One Was Someone* exhibits an extreme version of just this shift (figures 8.2 and 8.3).[28] Other than the six words comprising the title, each word meant to symbolize, presumably, one of six million Jews, the book is made up of a single word printed six million times: "Jew." Written in minuscule font and lasting 1,250 pages, each page consisting of forty unvarying columns, 120 even rows, the word "Jew" can be read in every direction, 4,800 times per page. The cover of the book features a tallit, or prayer shawl, traditionally the garment that bears witness to every event in a man's life cycle: first worn after the age of thirteen, the age at which boys attain the responsibility of adulthood; and then also held over the heads of a couple in a wedding ceremony; and, finally, used to wrap the body in death. The fact that the cover of the book is not interrupted by words—the title is not found on the cover of the book, but rather first appears on the inside title page—lends itself to the anonymity of its contents. Indeed, the anonymity of each "Jew" in *And Every Single One Was Someone*, contributes to the sense of vastness that the book presents, a vastness that the publisher, who aspires to print and sell six million copies, wishes to magnify. The unvarying nature of the columns and rows, a presentation of data without the inscription of a single number, can only take place in the absence of individuality. And, indeed, the author makes the point that this book presents "how the Nazis viewed their victims: These are not individuals, these are not people, these are just a mass we have to exterminate."[29]

And yet individuality is not absent from the book. Space has been made available on the title page for readers to dedicate the book to a person of their choosing. In the front matter, readers are urged to "Focus on one Jew. Think of that word as one actual Jew. A relative, perhaps, or a friend. Maybe even yourself."[30] The act of reading, then, is intended both to encompass a sense of enormity and, at the same time, is envisioned as an exercise of specificity, where the reader identifies even his or her own self as embodied in a single word produced and re-produced many times on a page. Even the instruction, "Focus on one Jew," becomes problematic; the reader can understand this as an imperative to fix on one printed word that spells out "Jew" and to expand outward from there. But readers can also understand this as a directive that moves in the opposite direction, asking readers to think of a Jew, any person who is Jewish, and then connect them to the text devoted to Jews who perished in the Holocaust. World Jewry becomes limited to 6,000,000 Jews while the individual Jew becomes expanded to the same large group. The sentence deliberately blurs the meaning, just as the memorial blurs its meaning: the symbolism behind the reproduction of the word "Jew" six million times lies in its totality, precisely the element missing from a reader's "focus on one Jew." *And Every Single One Was Someone* strives to meet the condi-

Figure 8.2. Phil Chernofsky, *And Every Single One Was Someone*. Jerusalem: Gefen Publishing, 2013.

Figure 8.3. Phil Chernofsky, *And Every Single One Was Someone*. Jerusalem: Gefen Publishing, 2013.

tions of universalism and particularism simultaneously, collapsing the distance between them. The repetition of a single word, let alone a word that identifies a culture, religion, and identity, cannot, no matter how many times it is duplicated, stand in for a universalist understanding of the Holocaust, where Jewish specificity is replaced by another order, one that is problematically affiliated with a Nazi perspective. Nor is the repetition of one word six million times a version of its oneness. Its very duplication undermines precisely the sense of individuation and specificity required by particularism.

The counting and accumulation of the word "Jew" in *And Every Single One Was Someone* is part of a larger contemporary trend in Holocaust memorialization devoted to what has been called "mass memorialization"; "counting memorials"; "collecting projects"; and "educational memorials." Often initiated by school-age children or with them in mind, the objective of these endeavors is both to collect and count an object that tends to be familiar and recognizable as a means of, as one description states, "commemoration,"[31] or, as another description suggests, "to comprehend the magnitude of the number of Jews killed by the Nazis,"[32] or as still another maintains, "to encourage a better understanding of the indelible lessons created by the horror and magnitude of the number of lives lost during the Holocaust."[33] Objects as diverse as grains of rice, buttons, paper clips, paper butterflies, and pennies have served as means for these memorials. Like many collecting projects, the origins of *And Every Single One Was Someone* are located in an attempt to enable school-age students to grapple with the number six million. The project in its earliest iteration was part of a school assignment: the author assigned his students, in honor of Yom HaShoah, Holocaust Remembrance Day, to spend thirty minutes writing "Jew" as many times as they could. Their combined efforts yielded 40,000 repetitions. From these assembled pages, the author conceived of a book that would compile the number these students were unable to record in the limited time they had.

In his thoughtful study on contemporary counting memorials, Daniel Magilow notes that they often stir the anxiety of viewers and critics who question the appropriateness of symbolizing the extraordinary with the ordinary: "The discomfort with memorial projects arises from an inability to reconcile the radical incongruity between a profane signifier (a button, a penny, or a paper clip) and a sacred signified (the victims of genocide)."[34] Recognizing his voice as maintaining a minority position, Magilow views counting memorials favorably, suggesting that they create a new way to approach the process of remembering, one that is rich in "debate, discussion and reflection," and one that engages a large number of people who otherwise might not invest themselves in the remembering process.[35] This becomes increasingly important, Magilow argues, as the Holocaust recedes in time, creating a need for memory sites in an environment where living memory is gradually diminishing.

Criticism of the relationship between sacred and profane affecting the symbolism of memorials has long existed. Writing in 1949, sociologist Bernard Barber notes that "there is a delicate balance between the sacred and the profane, that there is a contagiousness about them by which they infect each other with their own significance. If some war memorials, expressing sacred sentiments, are contaminated by profane and secular sentiments . . . those war memorials are unsuited to their essential purpose."[36] This kind of symbolic dilution, which can be caused through the physical placement or setting of a memorial, or because of the language or material used in the memorials' construction (among other ways that the ordinary and the hallowed can contaminate each other), is at the core of many discussions regarding memorial design generally and often emerges as a problem during the planning of a memorial. Barber notes the opposition to dedicating college student centers as war memorials for this reason: "Older college graduates tend to feel that it is impossible, not merely difficult, to house sacred war memorials and profane daily activities in the same building."[37] In a more recent example, James Young notes with some trepidation that the site designated by the German authorities for the "Memorial to the Murdered Jews of Europe" is "located at the heart of the Nazi regime's former seat of power. Bordered on one side by the "*Todesstreifen*," or "death-strip" at the foot of the Berlin wall, and on the other by the Tiergarten, the former site of the "Ministerial Gardens" was still a no-man's land in its own right, slightly profaned by its proximity to Hitler's bunker and the Reich's Chancellery."[38] I do not wish to suggest that the mingling of the sacred and profane is not a problem with counting memorials—I believe it is. But other issues compound and even dwarf this one. Counting memorials, which are notably a product of American culture, construct remembrance through commodification and accumulation, implying a direct relationship between collecting and remembering—the more we collect the more we remember. In fact, though, the act of collecting often works to the contrary, overtaking any remembering that it is intended to inspire, and diminishing the painful work of remembrance through the far more familiar activity of collecting and counting. The relationship of the sacred to the profane, then, is not only one that equates a "profane signifier" to a "sacred signified," but also one that replaces remembrance with procurement.

Another source of discomfort generated by Holocaust counting memorials—and here I consider *And Every One Was Someone* in the larger context of counting memorials that typically use material goods—stems not so much from the particular object collected but from the act of collecting and counting itself. In many ways the act of collecting and counting as a means of creating a memorial appeals to viewers and participants because it actively invites them to insert their presence into a historical moment. It is an attempt to make memory more relevant through the active involvement of viewers—the "doing" of collecting being preferred to the passivity associated with remembering. And yet the greatest detractor to collecting projects stems not so much from inadequate signifiers, but from the action of counting itself, which, in all its familiarity, easily loses its connection to the act of remembering. Consequently, while even the title "counting memorials" places the act of counting as subordinate to the act of memorializing, in point of fact, counting often consumes and replaces the very act it is intended to inspire. As evidence of this, many collecting projects exceed their original counting goals, collecting many more "things" than they initially set out to do. It is possible to view this over-accumulation as a sign of the project's success: so many objects have been donated because so many people care. But precisely this excess points to the limitation that is regularly reached with counting projects, namely that the counting takes over the remembering. That is, there is a comfort to be found in counting that easily overtakes the harder—at times unbearable—work of engaging with historical memory. Counting memorials indicate that the number symbolism found in the number "six million" has largely been lost. Using the number as a fixed point around which a memorial is constructed carries with it an implicit acknowledgment of artificiality: few counting memorials investigate how this number was, itself, amassed and, in a corresponding counter-gesture, few counting memorials stop the act of counting or acquisition once this number has been reached. Instead, counting itself, and with it accumulation and consumption, becomes the focus.

The gesture of counting and collecting both joins and separates a textual memorial such as *And Every One Was Someone* from such collecting memorials as the Children's Holocaust Memorial and Paper Clip Project, developed in 1998 by students at Whitwell Middle School in Whitwell, Tennessee, in which more than thirty million paper clips have been amassed. They are now housed on the campus of the school in an original boxcar used to transport Jews and other victims to concentration, labor, and death camps. Or with the Peoria Holocaust Memorial Button Project, a collaborative project initiated by a range of organizations including public and private schools throughout the Midwestern United States. The Peoria Button project is situated in front of an entrance to the Shoppes at Grand Prairie in Peoria, Illinois. They are held in six Star of David containers, each containing one million buttons; five triangular containers hold an additional million buttons each, representing other persecuted minorities. Or with The Holocaust Museum Houston's The Butterfly Project in which more than 1.5 butterflies have been made and collected "to remember the children who perished in the Holocaust."[39] On the one hand, in its repetition of a single word, "Jew," *And Every Single One Was Someone* falls prey to many of the inadequacies that affect other collecting memorials, which are largely dismissed as trivializing the Holocaust and disregarding the real work of remembering even as they claim to bear both universal lessons and influence the lives of those who participate. On the other hand, however, the textuality of *And Every Single One Was Someone* distinguishes it from other collecting memorials, which hold at their core a reverence for objectivity and an obsession for collective collecting. In spite of its many limitations, the word "Jew" is performed in print, a medium that holds a special place in Jewish tradition, and a medium that helps to secure the memorial from secular, ordinary influences of the profane. But perhaps most significantly, the interactivity of this collecting memorial depends on the reader reading, as opposed to the more suspect act of donating, which includes with it a sense of finality, one that marks the interaction, from start to finish, between viewer and memorial. It is this fundamental aspect, as opposed to its show of counting, which links this memorial most closely to earlier and devastatingly powerful memorials such as the *Oyneg Shabes* archive. *And Every Single One Was Someone* literalizes the absence of six million Jews through printing the one-word identity that marked them, it also emphasizes the illegibility of this absence: it is unlikely, unintended, and virtually impossible for any reader to read the book from start to finish, even if its single word is known in its entirety to all readers. And it is this quality of estranged textuality that lends this work, in spite of its many limitations, its sense of meaning and memory.

In contrast to the memorial book *And Every Single One Was Someone*, the memorial project created by German artist Gunter Demnig and entitled "*Stolpersteine*" or "Stumbling Stones," provides another example of textual memory and numerical symbolism. Perhaps the most "monumental" of all the memorials considered here, *Stolpersteine* works to remember victims of the Third Reich by embedding a brass plaque in the pavement in front of the last known self-chosen address of the person being memorialized (figure 8.4). Conceived of in 1992, when he was working on a memorial commemorating the deportation of Sinti and Roma from Cologne, Demnig installed the first personalized *Stolpersteine* in 1996 as a response to a local resident who had lived through the war and insisted that no Sinti or Roma had ever resided in her neighborhood. The stones, most of which open with the statement "Hier Wohnte," or "Here lived," include the personal details about an individual including name, dates of birth, deportation, and death (if known), and place of death (figure 8.5). A stone embedded in the pavement at 7 Bartningallee in Berlin reads: HIER WOHNTE / GITTEL LITTWACK / JG. 1939 / DEPORTIERT 9.12.1942 / ERMORDET IN AUSCHWITZ. "Here lived / Gittel Littwack / Born in the year 1939 / Deported on December 9, 1942 / Murdered in Auschwitz." In many respects, the *Stolpersteine* Memorial Project moves away from the anonymity and focus on accumulation found in memorials such as *And Every Single One Was Someone*. Instead it returns viewers to memorials centered on specificity and the enormous sense of absence that the murder of a single person effects. It is in some ways a push against data, and a move toward narrative. The personalization of each stone is a product not only of its inscription, but also of the stone's location in front of a residence that in every other way would be wholly unremarkable. In this way the *Stolpersteine* Memorial Project lends presence to the invisible history and character of a building as well as to that of an individual, rendering both more legible by inscribing the names of former inhabitants, most of whom were forcibly relocated, on a landscape that otherwise remains largely impersonal. Indeed, scholar Kirsten Harjes compares *Stolpersteine* to a miniature headstone, noting that a "stone with a name and a date of death or deportation recalls the tombstone for a particular historical individual. The stones commemorate individual people rather than large groups or complex events."[40] Demnig, however, resists calling or comparing *Stolpersteine* to headstones, wanting instead to think of them as a way of returning a person's name to their home community and thus connecting the past to the present: "To think about six million victims is abstract, but to think about a murdered family is concrete."[41]

And yet the *Stolpersteine* Memorial Project invokes numbers and counting in ways that connect it to more obvious and self-declared counting memorials. The two-pronged motivation that most frequently leads to the creation of counting memorials, namely an effort to comprehend the magnitude of loss involved in the Holocaust, and a wish to use the site of memory as an opportunity to educate, are both at work in many contemporary memorials that focus on individualism and particularity, such as the *Stolpersteine* Memorial Project. Furthermore, like many collecting memorials, the *Stolpersteine* are catalogued as countermemorials or countermonuments—"memorial spaces conceived to challenge the very premise of the monument—to be ephemeral rather than permanent, to deconstruct rather than displace memory, to be antiredemptive. They would reimpose memorial agency and active involvement on the German public."[42] While *Stolpersteine* are intended to be permanent, their lack of obtrusiveness—they are intentionally a part of the landscape—together with their independence from state-funded or -sponsored memorials (indeed, at €120 or $166 per installation, *Stolpersteine* are relatively inexpensive to sponsor; these costs cover materials, labor, and any research that might need to be done) *Stolpersteine* are democratic in nature and available to the public both as a memorial and in terms of sponsorship. Finally, while Demnig recognizes that the number "six million" will likely never be achieved with his *Stolpersteine* Memorial Project, it stands as a figure that continually urges him forward. Ultimately, the *Stolpersteine* Memorial Project, through denoting singularity, achieves an important sense of a unified and singular site of memory that, at the same time, is necessarily widely dispersed. As a collection, then, the *Stolpersteine* Memorial Project recognizes that the unquantifiable or countless is best understood by reflecting on the more quanitifiable. Demnig comments on these points in a speech he made in 2012:

> When my idea for the "Stolpersteine" was born in 1993, this project for me—as an artist—was a CONCEPTUAL WORK OF ART—an idea I initially filed away in my archive. For faced with the incredible, and yet real numbers of victims during the Nazi dictatorship and the Shoah—I did not think my idea could actually be realized. In the end, it was Kurt Pick—a protestant priest in Cologne—who said to me at one point during our conversation: "Gunter, you will never be able to lay those millions of stones, but you can get started in a small way." . . . One powerful reason for my joy is the interest that many young people are taking in the "Stolpersteine," including pupils and students in different grades and various areas of study . . . maybe because to open a book and read of six million who were herded together by the Nazis in Europe and murdered, this number remains an abstract entity. This is something which I myself still experience, despite being confronted with these destinies on a daily basis and having visited several concentration camps. How much more of an effect this unimaginable number of destroyed human beings must then have on these students and pupils? When all of a sudden they are faced with the personal destiny of a family that might have lived in their immediate vicinity? . . . In this context, then, the young people get more and more interested in these dramatic events and find themselves even more engaged.[43]

Here Demnig acknowledges the power and meaning, even the necessity, of presenting varying modes of reading and counting, modes that resonate both historically and affiliatively. Viewers read the number phrase "six million" (and even the word "Jew" printed six million times) uncomprehendingly because, as so many eyewitness testimonies acknowledge (some with far lower numbers), it conveys a sense of countlessness that, as part of its functional definition, contains within it an inability to conceptualize. In a move that distinguishes his memorial from many others, Demnig approaches the reading of incomprehensibly large numbers from the position of a single figure. Importantly, reading a *Stolperstein* is not limited to the text of the stone, even with its unadorned and simple language—lived, born, deported, murdered. Readers also read the context, suddenly aware that the building in front of which they stand once housed the person whose name they now know, aware also that the path they have walked was once traversed by this person. By creating this larger narrative, the *Stolpersteine* Memorial Project incorporates an entire contemporary and historical geography into the act of reading. As with third-generation literature, it includes the figure of the millennial reader reading a landscape that was once read by the person who has since—tragically, unwillingly—become the subject of reading rather than the reader, the walker, the counter, the rememberer.

The quality of reading and textuality that *Stolpersteine* manage to achieve is in large part a consequence of the memorial's in-between nature. The memorials are located at the intersection of private and public, as seen in their physical presentation: planted in public sidewalks in front of private residences and also as realized in the publicity they generate for an individual

Figure 8.4. Photo by Karin Richert.

who would otherwise remain known only to a small circle. As a memorial, the *Stolpersteine* create historical meaning in a present time where there otherwise is none. Furthermore, their decentralized performance of memory is integral to their role as a single site of memory—as of the end of 2013,

Figure 8.5.   Photo by Karin Richert.

over 43,500 *Stolpersteine* memorial stones can be found in more than 1,000 locations scattered across seventeen countries. "'In a way, my *Stolpersteine* are small,' says Demnig, 'But they are bigger, bigger than the big monument in Berlin [the Berlin Memorial to the Murdered Jews of Europe]. . . . That is a memorial in the center of the city. I'm all over Germany. North, south, east and west. The stones are in front of houses where the people lived, where people live. Every time you step you have to look.'"[44] Demnig makes clear that he is intent on enlarging, with families of Holocaust victims and the communities where they once lived, the *Stolpersteine* Memorial Project, and in so doing not only increasing the number of individuals whose identities are re-inscribed in their onetime neighborhoods, but also increasing the number of interactions between *Stolpersteine* and members of the public who walk past them and pause.

In his well-known sociological work *The Practice of Everyday Life*, Michel de Certeau links walking with reading, declaring it an elementary form of experiencing the city, a means of writing text with the body "without being able to read it."[45] The *Stolpersteine* rely on pedestrians, intent on some further destination, to stop and reflect—an action that is itself positioned as intermediary, requiring them to look down at the ground, up at the residence, and then within (as Hansen notes, one does not actively seek out *Stolpersteine* to visit, rather they visit you).[46] Viewers tend to read spontaneously and inadvertently; their reading, like their visit, is neither planned nor anticipated. The minimalist inscription engraved into *Stolpersteine* echoes the necrology found at the end of so many *Yizkor* books and moving us across and within generations; both bear an encyclopedic quality. The impersonality of the inscribed language is countered by the intimacy of the stone's setting outside a private residence and home. *Stolpersteine* invite an act of reading that causes the walker to pause in the act of walking/writing the city, to momentarily stop the practices, motions, and habits that color everyday life. It is an act of reading that extends beyond the provided text, entering the world of the reader, incorporating it and us into a memorial landscape. Reading here is affiliative, locating the viewer in a geography once occupied by the perished and that, through the stone's engraving, reinserts (in some sense a literal re-membering) the name of the dead on a contemporary landscape. Significantly, the reading of *Stolpersteine* does not come at the expense of the unreadable—of what cannot or will not be known or accessed. Instead, *Stolpersteine* are a piece of a transformed landscape, both marking and contributing to it, and yet at the same time, their proportions—small in size, wide in scope—and their ever growing numbers—a memorial project that will never be completed—recognize the impossibility of being able to do justice to those they memorialize.

The numbers associated with *Stolpersteine* are not infinite but neither are they fixed around a single figure, which becomes itself an object of memory and risks becoming the goal of the memorial in and of itself. "[N]umbers as symbols," writes the music theorist Kazu Nakaseko, "result from the abstraction of the numerical idea from the reality of counting."[47] This is precisely what we trace in the use of numbers in textual memorials created before and after the end of the Holocaust, textual memorials that reflect three generations of readers and viewers. Earlier memorials, as demonstrated by the *Oyneg Shabes* archives and *Yizkor* books, illuminate the impossibility and, yet, the necessity of counting the countless, and with it the need to shift between universalist and particularist conceptions of memory and history. What counting inevitably fails to capture, the vastness of the loss witnessed, these memorials attempt to describe through a narrative sense of the unquantifiable. The number 6,000,000 (or 11,000,000, the total number of estimated victims of the Holocaust) emerged as a postwar symbol and, as memorials that often use them as a starting and end point inadvertently recognize, a contradiction emerges: their very abstraction "from the reality of counting" is what propels these sites of memory to engage in the act of counting itself, which then obviates, at least partly, the symbolism behind the number. Instead, much like the candle in the Yad Vashem Children's memorial that is reflected and refracted countless times, or a *Stolperstein* dedicated to one person, the many contemporary textual memorials that reflect the opposing and yet necessary conceptions of countlessness and the counted, commit their performance of Holocaust memory to universalist terms, addressing the concept of "*tikkun olam*," repairing the fractures of the world, through an

156 Jessica Lang

affiliative act of reading that attends to the role of a single individual, whose name is inscribed and re-inscribed, remembered and re-remembered, counted and re-counted.

NOTES

1. Cynthia Ozick, "A Mercenary," in *Bloodshed* (Syracuse, NY: Syracuse University Press, 1972), 38.
2. As James Young notes, "the most ancient of Jewish memorial media" are words on paper." James Young, *The Texture of Memory: Holocaust Memorials and Meaning* (New Haven, CT: Yale University Press, 1994), 7.
3. I refer here to the John Felstiner translation of "Todesfugue" found in *Selected Poems and Prose of Paul Celan*, trans. John Felstiner (New York: W. W. Norton & Co., 2000).
4. Yehuda Bauer, *Rethinking the Holocaust* (New Haven, CT: Yale University Press, 2002), 2.
5. Alan L. Berger, *Children of Job: American Second-Generation Witnesses to the Holocaust* (Albany, NY: State University of New York Press, 1997), 4.
6. Berel Lang, "From the Particular to the Universal, and Forward," in *Post-Holocaust: Interpretation, Misinterpretation and the Claims of History* (Bloomington: Indiana University Press, 2005), 101.
7. James Young, *The Texture of Memory: Holocaust Memorials and Meaning* (New Haven, CT: Yale University Press, 1993), 4.
8. Young, *The Texture of Memory*, 6–7.
9. Young, *The Texture of Memory*, 14.
10. Young, *The Texture of Memory*, 12, 13.
11. Samuel Kassow, *Who Will Write Our History? Rediscovering a Hidden Archive from the Warsaw Ghetto* (New York: Vintage Books, 2007), 308.
12. Ringelblum Archive, part II, no. 197. Found in Kassow, *Who Will Write Our History?* 308.
13. Kassow, *Who Will Write Our History?* 225.
14. Kassow, *Who Will Write Our History?* 306–07.
15. Abraham Krzepicki, "Eighteen Days in Treblinka," *The Death Camp Treblinka: A Documentary*, ed. Alexander Donat (New York: Holocaust Library, 1979), 85–86.
16. Krzepicki, "Eighteen Days in Treblinka," 88.
17. Krzepicki, "Eighteen Days in Treblinka," 90.
18. Krzepicki, "Eighteen Days in Treblinka," 94.
19. Ringelblum Archive, Part I, no. 1018. Found in Kassow, *Who Will Write Our History?* 4.
20. Rosemary Horowitz, "A History of Yizker Books," *Memorial Books of Eastern European Jewry: Essays on the History and Meanings of Yizker Volumes*, ed. Rosemary Horowitz (Jefferson, NC: McFarland & Company, Inc., 2011), 11.
21. Korczyna Book Editorial Committee, "Some Words from the Publishers of the Korczyner Memorial Book," *Korczyna; sefer zikaron*, ed. Korczyna Relief Committee (New York: Committee of the Korczyna Memorial Book, 1967), 11.
22. The editors, "Foreword," in *Sefer zikaron kehilat Vileike*, ed. K. Faber and J. Se'evri (Tel Aviv: Society of Vileykah and Surroundings, 1972), 326.
23. Horowitz, "A History of Yizker Books," 25.
24. Most *Yizkor* books were compiled and published in the 1960s and 1970s, although a number of them were written in the 1940s (even before the war had ended) and 1950s. Most *Yizkor* books were written in Yiddish and/or Hebrew. In the past decade, these books have increasingly been translated into Hebrew and English for readers unable to access the original language (Horowitz, "A History of Yizker Books," 13, 16–18).
25. Abraham Singer, "My Experiences under the Germans," recorded by Y. Schwartz, *The Tomaszow-Lubelski Memorial Book*, ed. Joseph M. Moskop, originally published in Yiddish by

The Tomashover Relief Committee, New York, 1965. Translated and published by Jacob Solomon Berger, Mahwah, NJ, 2008.

26. In his essay "From the Particular to the Universal, and Forward," Lang suggests a similar staging.

27. Singer, "My Experiences under the Germans," 389.

28. Phil Chernofsky, *And Every Single One Was Someone* (Springfield, NJ: Gefen Books, 2013).

29. Jodi Rudoren, "Holocaust Told in One Word, 6 Million Times," *New York Times*, January 25, 2014.

30. Chernofsky, *And Every Single One Was Someone*.

31. VosIzNeias.com, "Hollywood, FL—Teen Collects 1.5 Million Pennies to Represent Each Child Killed in The Holocaust."

32. *MetroWest Jewish News*, January 12, 1995.

33. "Peoria Holocaust Memorial Button Project," www.peoriaholocaustmemorial.org/about_the-project.html.

34. Daniel Magilow, "Counting to Six Million: Collecting Projects and Holocaust Memorialization," *Jewish Social Studies* 14 (2007): 28.

35. Magilow, "Counting to Six Million," 36.

36. Bernard Barber, "Place, Symbol, and Utilitarian Function in War Memorials," *Social Forces* 28 (1949): 64–68.

37. Barber, "Place, Symbol, and Utilitarian Function in War Memorials," 68.

38. James Young, "Germany's Holocaust Memorial Problem—and Mine," *The Public Historian* 24 (Fall 2002): 70. For a longer history of this memorial site, please see Young, *The Texture of Memory*, chapter 3.

39. www.hmh.org/ed_butterfly1.shtml.

40. Kirsten Harjes, "Stumbling Stones: Holocaust Memorials, National Identity, and Democratic Inclusion in Berlin," *German Politics & Society* 23 (Spring 2005): 46. Harjes uses the term *Stolpersteine* to refer to a larger category of Holocaust countermemorials, including Demnig's project. Here I only use it to refer to the title of Demnig's work. A. H. Hansen also compares *Stolpersteine* to a tombstone for victims who were never granted a burial: A. H. Hansen, "Memorials and memory politics in Hamburg and Haifa," in *Power and Culture: New Perspectives on Spatiality in European History*, ed. P. François, T. Syrjaämaa, and H. Terbo (Pisa: 2008), 163–85.

41. Lois Gilman, "Memory Blocks: Artist Gunter Demnig builds a Holocaust memorial one stone at a time," October 11, 2007, *Smithsonian Magazine*, (http://www.smithsonianmag.com/people-places/memory-blocks-173123976/.

42. Noam Lupu, "Memory Vanished, Absent, and Confined: The Countermemorial Project in 1980s and 1990s Germany," *History & Memory* 15 (2003): 131.

43. Gunter Demnig's Speech at the Dr. Bernard Heller Prize Ceremony at Hebrew Union College-Jewish Institute of Religion/New York Graduation, May 3, 2012, http://huc.edu/news/article/2012/gunter-demnig's-speech-dr-bernard-heller-prize-ceremony-huc-jirny-graduation-may-3.

44. Stacey Perman, "The Right Questions," *Tablet Magazine*, July 25, 2007, http://www.tabletmag.com/jewish-arts-and-culture/719/the-right-questions#undefined.

45. Michel de Certeau, *The Practice of Everyday Life*, trans. Steven Rendall (Berkeley, CA: University of California Press, 1984), 93.

46. Hansen, "Memorials and memory politics in Hamburg and Haifa," 173.

47. Kazu Nakaseko, "Symbolism in Ancient Chinese Music Theory," *Journal of Music Theory* 1 (1957): 159.

Chapter Nine

Against Generational Thinking in Holocaust Studies

Gary Weissman

In the conclusion to his final book, *The Drowned and the Saved*, Primo Levi lamented the deleterious effect that the passage of time was having on remembrance of "the Nazi madness."[1] Writing four decades after the Holocaust, Levi described the waning of public and personal concern with the catastrophic events of the 1930s and 1940s in generational terms:

> The experience that we survivors of the Nazi concentration camps bear witness to is alien to the younger generations in the West, and becoming more so with each passing year. For the young people of the 1950s and '60s, these matters belonged to their parents: they were talked about in the family, and the memories still preserved the freshness of things seen. For the young people of the 1980s, they belong to their grandparents: distant, blurry, "historical."[2]

At the time he was writing, Levi found that young people were concerned not by the catastrophes their grandparents had faced but by "current-day problems." Those he listed appear no less relevant a quarter-century later: "the nuclear threat, unemployment, the depletion of natural resources, the population explosion, and frenetically renewed technologies to which they have to adapt."[3] Piling these problems over those faced by victims of Nazism, Levi described the dissolution of Holocaust consciousness in terms of the tragically limited reach of generational concern with the past—even this past.

If only the relation to Nazism and the Holocaust that Levi located in the family ties between young people and their parents in the 1950s and 1960s could be retained! If only wartime memories that "preserved the freshness of things seen" could be passed on from parents to children to grandchildren, from one generation to the next! Levi's view is certainly bleak; and yet he may have *overstated* the capacity of memories to maintain such "freshness" in the family. According to his biographers, Levi was troubled and saddened by his children's active resistance to hearing him talk about the camp.[4] Not unlike the young people of the 1980s, Lisa and Renzo Levi were more concerned by current-day problems, which, when they came of age in the 1960s and 1970s, included the Vietnam War and Italy's "unfinished" transition from fascism to democracy. Perhaps, then, when Levi described the 1950s and 1960s as a time when events related to the Nazi camps "were talked about in the family" he was expressing a longing for a past that, at least for him, never was. Or perhaps we need to decouple the survivor's children from the young people who, a decade after the war, took great interest in the camps and in Levi himself. Unlike the survivor's children, these young people were born during the war rather than after it.

In 1955, when preparing to speak at an exhibition in Turin commemorating the deportation of Italy's Jews, Levi feared he would be poorly received. After all, his 1947 book recounting his experiences in the camp, *If This Is a Man*, had sold poorly and was now out of print. And yet, writes biographer Ian Thomson, at the event Levi found himself "greeted by a surprisingly young audience, whose enthusiasm to know more about the camps was . . . overwhelming."[5] Buoyed by this reception, Levi convinced his publisher to reissue his memoir. Its republication in 1958 marked "a turning-point" for its author, writes Thomson, such that "[a]s the 1950s drew to a close, Levi became the unofficial representative for Italian deportees, both Jewish and non-Jewish."[6] He became an active speaker, visiting schools around Italy to talk about the camps, giving up this practice only in the 1980s when he found it "more and more difficult . . . to find a language in common with the young."[7] This difficulty is captured in Levi's tale of a fifth-grader who lectured him on what to do should he find himself back in the camp: at night he should slit a guard's throat, don his uniform, run over to the power station, and cut off the electricity to the searchlights and electric fence; after that he could "easily make [his] getaway."[8] For Levi this episode illustrated "the gap, growing wider as the years pass, between the way things were 'down there' and the way they are represented in today's imagination, fueled by inaccurate books, films, and myths."[9]

Levi was writing primarily for Italian readers and then for Western Europeans—that is, for readers living in countries that had been theaters of war, countries where Nazi occupation, incarceration, and the deportation of Jews had occurred. We can only imagine how much more his words apply to postwar generations of Americans who are geographically as well as temporally distanced from those events. Indeed, much ink has been spilled over the fate of Holocaust remembrance in the United States. In a 1997 essay titled "From Explosion to Erosion," Anson Rabinbach observed that "a decade of highly public and institutionally anchored Holocaust memory," culminating with the film *Schindler's List* and the opening of the United States Holocaust Memorial Museum in 1993, appeared to have "only heightened the apprehension of forgetting."[10] That is, rather than preserving memory, the "explosion" of popular depictions of the Nazi genocide of European Jews, much like the "inaccurate books, films, and myths" mentioned by Levi, had put Holocaust remembrance at risk. "It might even be concluded," wrote Rabinbach, "that in America today fear of Holocaust erosion is far more widespread and significant than fear of Holocaust denial."[11]

Alvin H. Rosenfeld has voiced this concern more recently in his book *The End of the Holocaust*. "The very success of the Holocaust's wide dissemination in the public sphere can work to undermine its gravity and render it a more familiar thing," he writes, adding that "this wide exposure hardly guarantees the perpetuation of a historical memory of the Holocaust that will be faithful to the past."[12] Indeed, he warns, these "stories and images of the Nazi crimes [kept] before a vast and receptive public" are more likely to "blunt the horrors of this history and, over time, render them less outrageous, and, ultimately less knowable."[13] Lawrence L. Langer concurs in a review of Rosenfeld's book titled "The Erosion of the Holocaust," writing: "The sad fact is that Holocaust knowledge in this country is waning, not growing.... Far from being obsessed with the subject, American Jews probably know less about the details of the destruction of European Jewry today than ever before." Whether or not this is true, the concern that Langer and others express is deeply felt, as is the desire to identify what he calls "energetic caretakers of Holocaust memory"—and to align oneself with them, at a remove from the public.

If the Holocaust known to the public from popular books, films, television programs, and museums bears little resemblance to the Holocaust that was, and if even American Jews have scant knowledge of the destruction of Europe's Jews, it falls on those *properly* "obsessed with the subject" to serve, in Langer's words, as "counterweights" to the "gradual shrinking of Holocaust consciousness." But who can be counted on to perform this duty? Who if not the survivors themselves, ever dwindling in number, might counter the effects of Holocaust erosion, preventing the Nazi genocide of the Jews from seeming ever less relevant to present-day concerns? Who, if not the producers of the very depictions of the Holocaust that, in their inaccuracy, may only widen the gap between "things as they were" and things as we imagine they might have been under Nazism? Though Langer identifies the caretakers of Holocaust memory with "the scholarly community" that produces books and oversees archives devoted to documenting and studying the Nazi genocide, for many scholars working in the field of Holocaust Studies, most prominently scholars of literature, the answer lies with coteries defined in generational terms: "the second generation," "the post-Holocaust generation," "the postgeneration," "the generation of postmemory," and "the third generation."

Whereas Levi evoked "younger generations" to mark an ever-increasing temporal distance and detachment from the events that took place in Nazi-occupied Europe, these scholars employ generational rhetoric to designate the opposite: namely, a living connection or link to the Holocaust that might transcend time.

Increasingly since the 1990s, Holocaust Studies scholarship largely, but not exclusively, written by literary scholars in English and published by university presses in the United States has treated the so-called intergenerational or transgenerational transmission of Holocaust knowledge, in the guise of trauma, memory, or postmemory, as the medium, engine, and saving remnant of Holocaust consciousness. The generational designations cited in this scholarship serve primarily to connote proximity to the Holocaust, a closeness exemplified by the bond between parent and child—and, increasingly over the last decade, between parent and grandchild. These familial connections to Holocaust survivors are expressed in generational terms that are readily broadened to include persons who lack a direct familial connection to victims of Nazi persecution.

Compounding the generational and the familial, this rhetoric obscures distinctions between individuals who are and are not the children or grandchildren of Holocaust survivors, even as it conceives of these children and grandchildren in reductive, idealized terms as the caretakers of Holocaust memory. The particular form that generational thinking takes in Holocaust Studies allows scholars to employ an idiom of family that is alternately biological and metaphorical, as they write and speak of imagined generational communities through which a proper and privileged relation to the Holocaust, characterized by an intimate bond to events that threaten to disappear with the passing of the survivors, may be, as it were, inherited. Such thinking culminates in notions of an expanded Holocaust survivor family which serves as an enclave for those in the know, providing a space in which "the freshness of things seen" may be preserved in perpetuity. This is a space apart from the public sphere in which widely disseminated "stories and images of the Nazi crimes"[14] undermine the gravity of the Holocaust and blunt its horror.

Here I will discuss some of the presumptions, connotations, benefits, and limitations of such generational thinking by examining its conventional moves and key terms. I argue that while generational thinking and rhetoric in Holocaust Studies is not about to go away—indeed, it is so pervasive that it has come to seem natural and inevitable—scholars and critics should question its dominance by consciously thinking beyond its framework. In making this argument I do not mean to suggest that there are no children and grandchildren of Holocaust survivors, that children and grandchildren of survivors should never be discussed in generational terms, or that generations do not comprise useful and significant social groupings. Nor do I mean to issue a decree against attaching the designations "second generation" or "third generation" to writers or artists who are the sons or daughters, or grandsons or granddaughters, of Holocaust survivors, or to the children and grandchildren of survivors as a group. However, what we do out of convenience or convention should not go unexamined, nor should it come to underlie, as it has, theories concerning how the Holocaust is presently remembered, represented, and "transmitted."

At a moment when scholarly attention is turning from the second generation to the third, if not "pondering the existence of a fourth or even fifth generation of Holocaust descendants" in eager anticipation,[15] this essay calls for supplementing generational thinking in Holocaust Studies with a counter-discourse that would encourage scholars to critically reevaluate the established generational terms in which Holocaust consciousness, memory, literature, and aesthetics have so frequently been thought and discussed for the past three decades.

CLAIMS TO COHERENCE

References to the second generation in nonclinical writings on the Holocaust date back to the 1970s. In her 1979 book *Children of the Holocaust: Conversations with Sons and Daughters of Survivors*, Helen Epstein writes that in New York in 1976 fifteen children of Warsaw Ghetto survivors formed a group called "Second Generation" as "a vehicle for bringing members of the second generation together."[16] Her book's bibliography, which includes such titles as "Concentration Camp Survival: A Pilot Study of Effects on the Second Generation" (1971) and "Manifestations of Concentration Camp Effects on the Second Generation" (1973), indicates that the term was employed in clinical literature prior to this group's formation. That it had not yet entered more popular discourse is reflected by Epstein's book. Whereas Aaron Hass could title his 1996 study of the survivors' sons and daughters *In the Shadow of the Holocaust: The Second Generation*, counting on his readers to know, from the subtitle, who lives in the Holocaust's shadow, Epstein largely eschewed generational troping for more explicitly familial terms: children, sons, and daughters.

As some scholars have noted, the concept of the second generation is not without problems. It is premised on the notion that survivors of the Holocaust comprise a generation despite their varied ages; their various countries of origin and residence after the war; their remarkably diverse prewar, wartime, and postwar experiences; and their wide-ranging religious, political, and philosophical orientations and self-understandings. "Only after the second and third generations have appeared," writes Sigrid Weigel, "can a first generation be identified, and often it is implicitly understood as such without expressly gaining the name 'first generation.' One seldom encounters a discourse in the name of the first generation."[17] That said, in Holocaust Studies literature one finds ample reference to "the survivor generation," "the Holocaust generation," and the like.

In an essay questioning such "generational categorizing,"[18] Susan Rubin Suleiman introduces the playful concept of "the 1.5 generation" to distinguish the youngest survivors of the Holocaust, those who were "too young to have an adult understanding of what was happening to them, but old enough to have *been there* during the Nazi persecution of Jews."[19] She writes that only when the term "child survivor of the Holocaust" entered Holocaust discourse could these particular survivors see themselves as "part of a *collective* experience" and thus develop "a 'delayed' generational consciousness, as evidenced by the multiplication of organized groups and reunions as well as by the outpouring of written and oral remembrances."[20] Still, Suleiman concludes, "it is as *personal, subjective expression* that the experiences of children in the Holocaust can most memorably be communicated," for "[u]ltimately, the meaning of their experience remains, despite the collective nature of the historical event and its official commemorations, individual rather than collective."[21]

The same may be said of the experience of being the son or daughter of a Holocaust survivor or survivors. In *After Such Knowledge* Eva Hoffman writes that when she first heard the term "the second generation" in the early 1980s she responded with mixed feelings of recognition and displeasure.[22] Whereas she had regarded "the post-Holocaust strand of [her] biography" as less defining of her identity than "[o]ther threads of causality, influence, development," the term suggested that "living with it was a palpable enough experience to be overtly recognizable; that it *was* in fact an experience; and that, in some way, it counted."[23] What she had previously regarded as "purely private, or at least personal," now struck her as a shared, group experience. Still, Hoffman asks, "What kind of grouping is the 'second generation,' and what is the basis of its claim to coherence?"[24] Given that the children of survivors "have grown up, in the postwar Jewish dispersion, in different countries and cultures, under very different circumstances," she finds little basis for generational commonality. "If a 'generation' is defined by shared historical experience and certain attitudes or beliefs that follow from it, then the 'second generation' is surely a very tenuous instance of it," she writes.[25]

"The third generation" stands as an even more tenuous instance. In her recent study *Remembering the Holocaust: Generations, Witnessing and Place*, Esther Jilovsky writes that "in contrast to the second generation, where there is a generally accepted and assumed definition . . . the definition of third generation is not only more variable, but there is little consensus on its collective experience and attributes."[26] She explains, "In some ways, it is more difficult to pin down the definition of the third generation, because it includes people with either one, two, three or four grandparents who survived the Holocaust. There is therefore much greater variation in family histories and personal identities of the third generation, who may not identify as third generation or even Jewish."[27] The variation is still greater than this, given that some members of the third generation will have spent significant time with their survivor grandparents and know them well, while others will know them hardly at all, and others will have grown up never knowing survivor grandparents who died before they were born.

In their volume *In the Shadows of Memory: The Holocaust and the Third Generation*, Jilovsky and co-editors Jordana Silverstein and David Slucki "caution against any attempt to homogenize the generation," given that "the third generation is diverse" in its "ideas and approaches, in emotions expressed and histories recounted."[28] What then forms the basis of this grouping's "generational consciousness"? The editors cite "the many grassroots third-generation groups which have emerged in recent years"[29] and the "overwhelming number of responses" they received when they put out a call for submissions to their volume, taking these as clear evidence that "there exists a multitude of people who feel themselves to be part of this sometimes amorphous mass that can be grouped together under the name of 'third generation.'"[30] Despite Jilovsky's inclusion of those "who may not identify as third generation" in the third generation,[31] this grouping's claim to coherence seems based primarily in its members' expressed desire for membership in "the third generation."

Hoffman proposes that the second generation may best be understood as an "imagined community" united not by shared circumstances but by "sets of meanings, symbols, and even literary fictions" that foster "a sense of mutual belonging."[32] The third generation may similarly be understood as an imagined community, albeit one heavily indebted to the stock of images, stories, themes, and meanings associated with the second generation. Hoffman conveys these as follows:

> Over and over again, in second-generation literature, testimony is given to a helpless, automatic identification with parental feelings and their burden of intense despondency. Over and over, the children speak of being permeated by sensations of panic and deadliness, of shame and guilt. And, accompanying the suffusion by parental unhappiness, or absence, there is the need—indeed, the imperative—to perform impossible psychic tasks: to replace dead relatives, or children who have perished; to heal and repair the parents; above all, to rescue the parents.[33]

Alternatives to this image of the survivors' children are hard to come by in "second-generation literature." A notable exception appears in *In the Shadow of the Holocaust*, where Hass, a clinical psychologist who is also the son of survivors, remarks, "To my continual amazement, most second-generation children I encounter have little knowledge of the Holocaust. Many do not want to know. . . . If those closest to the Holocaust's effects do not wish involvement, either intellectual or emotional, who can I rely on to perpetuate its memory?"[34] With his lament Hass describes children who find no place in the "imagined community" that is the second generation, a community exemplified by Artie, the tortured artist who suffers the burden of recording and recounting his crazy-making father's testimony in Art Spiegelman's *Maus: A Survivor's Tale.*

The image of the rattled, Holocaust-obsessed survivor's child corresponds to the "memorial candles" discussed by Dina Wardi in *Memorial Candles: Children of the Holocaust*. She writes that in most survivors' families one child is "designated as a 'memorial candle' for all the relatives that perished in the Holocaust." Charged with the "special mission" of remembering the Holocaust, this child, according to Wardi, is "given the burden of participating in his parents' emotional world to a much greater extent than his brothers or sisters."[35] These brothers and sisters do not produce the literature that Holocaust Studies scholars analyze and from which they draw their understanding of the second generation. As a result, the second generation figures in their scholarship as a collective memorial candle. Drawn to its light, scholars may overidentify the children of survivors with their parents, as Efraim Sicher does when he claims that "[t]he Holocaust's eerie claim on the minds of second-generation survivors, who can return to the camps only through fantasies and the memories of others, is no less unremitting than its habitation of the minds of camp survivors and refugees."[36] Whereas Hoffman describes the second generation's claim to coherence in terms of their relationships to their parents, Sicher and many other scholars suggest that "second-generation survivors" are united by their relationship to the Holocaust, by the hold that it exerts on their minds.

Epstein reports that the idea of the survivors' children having a shared identity had not yet entered public consciousness when she wrote *Children of the Holocaust*. She states that the *New York Times* turned down her proposal to write an article on children of survivors: "There was no indication that such a group existed, I was told."[37] She was commissioned to write the piece in 1977 only after a brief article in *Time* magazine reported Israeli psychiatrist Shamai Davidson's finding that "[t]he effects of the systematic dehumanization are being transmitted from one generation to the next through severe disturbance in the parent-child relationship."[38] But as "the second generation" has become a more familiar term in popular discourse, within Holocaust Studies its meaning has been revised by scholars who would not limit inclusion to the sons and daughters of survivors, much less make "severe disturbance" in the parent-child relationship its basis.

THE BROADEST POSSIBLE VIEW

If, as Sicher suggests, the children of survivors are defined by the Holocaust's "eerie claim on the[ir] minds," how are we to speak of like-minded individuals who are *not* the daughters and sons of survivors but who, like them, "can return to the camps only through fantasies and the memories of others"? Why not grant these fellow travelers an honorary place in the second generation? This is precisely what Ellen S. Fine does in "Transmission of Memory: The Post-Holocaust Generation in the Diaspora," writing:

> Most often the term *second generation* is used to characterize the generation born after the war, generally referring to children of survivors. However, my use of the expression is more comprehensive, encompassing those born both during and after the war, including those who did not directly participate in the Holocaust but who have come to endure the psychic imprint of the trauma. They are designated as "the post-Holocaust generation."[39]

Three moves comprise this passage. First, a standard definition of "second generation" is provided; second, that definition is replaced with a broader one; and third, "second generation" is replaced with another term. We might ask, why redefine "second generation" only to replace it with another term? Why not simply define "the post-Holocaust generation"? In fact, Fine's rhetorical moves are necessary because her conception of the post-Holocaust generation depends upon a particular, prior conception of the survivors' children.

Members of the post-Holocaust generation, Fine writes, "continue to 'remember' an event not lived through. Haunted by history, they feel obliged to accept the burden of *collective memory* that has been passed onto them and to assume the task of sustaining it."[40] Here, as throughout her essay, Fine characterizes the post-Holocaust generation in terms taken from writings by and about the children of Holocaust survivors, such as Epstein's book and Menachem Z. Rosensaft's "Reflections of a Child of Holocaust Survivors." These writings are used to establish the existence of a transgenerationally transmitted Holocaust memory, as when Fine writes that "Rosensaft's and Epstein's references to a 'collective consciousness permeated with echoes of a world we never knew' and a group 'possessed by a history they had never lived' are indications of the presence of a collective memory that has been transmitted to them."[41] How this collective memory may be transmitted to "members of the post-Holocaust generation" who are *not* the children of survivors goes unaddressed. Fine's expansion of the second generation, to include all "those who did not directly participate in the Holocaust but who have come to endure the psychic imprint of the trauma," is not achieved through argument; rather, it is an extension of the presumption that children of survivors endure this "psychic imprint."

In replacing the second-generation experience of growing up with a parent or parents who survived the Nazi genocide with the considerably more abstract and heroic-sounding condition of "endur[ing] the psychic imprint of the trauma," Fine effectively reconceives what it means to be traumatized. Fifteen years ago Weigel observed that "recently trauma has become a sort of *entreebillet* with which every individual, regardless of his or her specific historical position, gains access to the great drama called history."[42] In Fine's essay, as in much generational thinking in Holocaust Studies, trauma loses its meaning as a debilitating psychic wound to become, instead, an identifying mark. It becomes what Erin McGlothlin describes as the "mark of a wound" one did not suffer oneself and the "mark of a history" one did not experience oneself, yet a mark that nevertheless carries with it "a visceral feeling that something critical distinguishes [one] from [one's] contemporaries."[43] Trauma, in short, becomes something desirable: a mark of distinction, a sign that one has earned one's place by the victims—closer, as it were, to the Holocaust.

Fine's "more comprehensive" conception of the second generation has proven less influential than a notably similar one presented by the editor of the 1998 volume in which her essay appears. In his introduction to *Breaking Crystal: Writing and Memory after Auschwitz*, Efraim Sicher writes:

> Some might argue that only children of survivors have the right to speak for the victims; what then, one might ask, of adopted children, children of refugees, or the generation contemporaneous with children of survivors who share many of their psychological, ideological, and theological concerns? . . . I start out from the broadest possible view of the "second generation," . . . and I incorporate all who write "after." . . . [44]

Here Sicher makes a case for including writers who are not the children of survivors within the second generation on the grounds that they should not be denied "the right to speak for the victims." But who would argue that only the children of Holocaust survivors have this right—or that even they may speak on behalf of the millions of victims of Nazi persecution and genocide? In the very act of presenting "the broadest possible view" of the second generation, Sicher ascribes to the children of survivors special attributes—"the right to speak for the victims" and shared "psychological, ideological, and theological concerns" relating to the Holocaust—that are simultaneously extended to "all who write 'after.'" As with Fine, Sicher's expansion of the generational cohort does not challenge a reductive conception of "second-generation survivors" so much as it *relies* on such a conception in order to grant its special qualities to other interested parties.

Sicher provides a name for this broadly viewed second generation in the title of his essay which immediately follows and extends his introduction: "The Burden of Memory: The Writing of the Post-Holocaust Generation."

For Sicher, writers of the post-Holocaust generation inherit from the survivors "the unbearable burden, which history placed on them before their birth, of remembrance."[45] He contends that "the task of witnessing has passed to the next generation, a burden of memory almost too great to bear but inescapable because of its moral obligation."[46] That is to say, "all who write 'after'" do so not because they have developed a personal interest in writing about the Nazi genocide of the Jews, but because they are obligated to bear witness by the Holocaust itself.

Sicher's claim that *not only* the children of survivors are tasked with "the burden of memory" assumes that all children of survivors are so burdened. Moreover, it assumes that the Holocaust they address is the same as that addressed by writers who are not raised in survivor families. Sicher writes that "the phenomenon of the Holocaust is a nagging absence in the personal history of those who were not there," creating in them an "obsessive need to imagine that blank."[47] Certainly one need not have a parent who is a Holocaust survivor to feel troubled by the absence of Holocaust consciousness in a culture characterized by historical amnesia and commercial interests impervious to any lessons learned from this or any other catastrophic event—other than that depictions of these events sell (ergo, "Shoah business"). That said, the "nagging absence" felt by a survivor's child concerns something more particular than a phrase like "the phenomenon of the Holocaust" suggests; it concerns family secrets, the mysteries of a parent's life, identity, and family before and during the Holocaust.

We see this, for instance, in *I was a Child of Holocaust Survivors*, where Bernice Eisenstein describes her interest in watching *Sophie's Choice* as follows: "I wanted to see a replication of Auschwitz and be able to imagine my mother and father standing in the background among the starving inmates. In that way, I thought I could find them."[48] The place of the Holocaust in survivor families varies from family to family, and among children in the same family. Even so, when discussing the sons and daughters of survivors it is important to retain a sense of this familial orientation to the Nazi genocide and distinguish it from knowledge of the Holocaust gained from films, books, testimonies, memorials, and museums. It takes nothing away from reading Holocaust memoirs, visiting museums and historical sites, or listening to survivors to acknowledge that these experiences differ substantially from that of growing up in survivor families. In its effort to distill a privileged relationship to the Holocaust from the complexities of the parent-child relationship in these families, the curious move of expanding and then renaming the second generation obscures this very distinction.

THROUGH THE IMAGINATION

As aforementioned, Sicher's "broadest possible view of the 'second generation'" has proven influential. In her compelling study *Second-Generation Holocaust Literature*, for instance, Erin McGlothlin writes that she uses the term "second generation" not as "fairly narrowly" defined by Alan L. Berger in *Children of Job: American Second-Generation Witnesses to the Holocaust* to refer to "offspring of Jewish Holocaust survivors," but as Sicher "expands it to include other Jewish writers of the same generation."[49] She explains, "I take Sicher's framework as my departure . . . for the texts I include in this study are written by both writers whose families experienced the Holocaust and those whose families were not involved in the Holocaust but who nevertheless take on the perspective of the second generation and access that experience imaginatively."[50] Interestingly, even as she would expand the term "second generation" to include writers not raised in survivor families, McGlothlin excludes them as writers who can only "take on the perspective of the second generation."

She likewise excludes them when describing "the writers of the second generation" in terms of what they have inherited from their parents. "The children of survivors inherit their parents' wounds, or more precisely, they inherit not the wound itself (the direct experience of trauma and physical damage) but the mere mark of the wound," she writes[51]; and "The writers of the second generation thus possess the mark of a history they did not themselves experience, a visceral feeling that something critical distinguishes them from their contemporaries."[52] If, as McGlothlin writes, these second-generation writers attempt "through the process of imaginative writing . . . to explore . . . an event that they do not personally know but that they nevertheless sense by its absence,"[53] it follows that writers of second-generation Holocaust literature who are *not* the children of survivors must engage in a *doubly* imaginative writing process, exploring an event they do not personally know (the Holocaust) by writing about an experience they do not personally know (growing up in a Holocaust survivor family).

Like McGlothlin, Marita Grimwood brings Sicher's conception of the second generation to her study of second-generation literature. Two of the five works she examines in *Holocaust Literature of the Second Generation* are not written by children of survivors. "My concern is with writers whose subject is a pressing, often familial link or concern with the Holocaust," she explains. "In line with Sicher, I take a broad view of the second generation, in which the exact nature of this link varies from writer to writer."[54] Why group these writers under the term "the second generation"? When Grimwood describes them as "writers born after the Holocaust [who] actively explore fictional or autobiographical family relationships to it,"[55] "the second generation" functions not an empirical category but as a description of theme or subject matter. At this point, even the sons and daughters of survivors may be said to belong to the second generation not because their parents are Holocaust survivors, but because they explore familial relationships to the Holocaust in their literary writings. Put another way, *all* second-generation writers are writers who take on the perspective of the second generation.

Grimwood remarks that her book uses the term "second generation" as a "point of departure" because "focusing narrowly within it" is too limiting[56]—in large part because the narrow view is predicated on a false impression that there exists "a psychological and experiential truth shared by all children of survivors."[57] Still, she retains the term, framing the work of assorted writers as a "literature of the second generation." Grimwood concludes by rightly observing that "the 'second generation' is not a small, discrete entity but a contested area," and by calling for "a more differentiated approach to terms like 'second generation' and 'postmemory' that can account for a range of sub-positions that recognize the diversity of literature and experience."[58] But why continue to locate a range of positions within the contested area of the second generation at all? Why continue to apply terms rooted in the familial experiences of the survivors' children to literature not born of those experiences?

One answer may be that second-generation literature is defined not by a writer's parentage but by his or her aesthetic approach to writing about the Holocaust. In "Auto/Biography and Fiction after Auschwitz: Probing the Boundaries of Second-Generation Aesthetics," Sara R. Horowitz writes that whereas survivor testimony is grounded in the "actual experiences of the writer," writings by the children of survivors are not.[59] Much as Sicher notes that "the writing of the post-Holocaust generation" is composed by "writers who were not 'there' and who must access the Holocaust through the imagination,"[60] so Horowitz describes this writing in terms of its incapacity to be survivor testimony or *témoignage*. She writes,

> Post-Holocaust writing becomes less clearly *témoignage* and more historicized or more imaginative as the writers become more distant from the events of the Holocaust. Whether literally and narrowly defined as writing by children of survivors (such as Art Spiegelman) or figuratively and broadly defined as writing by those who were not there (such as Cynthia Ozick), second-generation writing is no longer a matter of eyewitnessing.[61]

Here as elsewhere, the word "post-Holocaust" serves to extend attributes associated with the children of survivors to others. Born in 1928, Ozick was growing up in the Bronx at the time Spiegelman's parents were struggling to survive in Nazi-occupied Poland. She was nearly twenty in 1948 when Spiegelman was born. Her inclusion in a "figuratively and broadly defined" second generation suggests that this group is chiefly defined by authorship:

neither Spiegelman nor Ozick are Holocaust survivors, yet both have authored canonical works of Holocaust literature.

Regardless of whether the second generation is defined broadly or narrowly, what Horowitz calls "second-generation aesthetics" is not specific to writings by the children of survivors. Whether one's work is based on interviewing a parent who survived Auschwitz (as is Spiegelman's *Maus*) or on a sentence in William Shirer's *The Rise and Fall of the Third Reich* (as is Ozick's *The Shawl*), research and imagination are required. Indeed, this is true as well of much work by Holocaust survivors. Horowitz recognizes this, writing that her discussion of "second-generation aesthetics" includes writers who "belong to the survivor generation" because they too write "after" and utilize their imaginations when writing works of Holocaust fiction.[62] "Ida Fink, for example . . . wrote and published her short stories many years later," writes Horowitz, "and in them she frequently adopts points of view patently not her own, writing deliberately of outside her own experiences and imaging her way impossibly to 'the bottom.'"[63] Survivor-writers also frequently integrate historical research to depict events they did not witness or experience themselves, or could not comprehend adequately at the time. Given "the necessarily limited experience any one person could have of the total scope of those events," comments David Mesher, readers of Holocaust survivors' autobiographical writings might consider "the author's use or avoidance of historical information to supplement personal knowledge."[64]

At this point we might ask what sense it makes to describe aesthetic or literary approaches to the Holocaust in generational terms. Why analyze postwar literature about the Holocaust in terms of "second-generation aesthetics" when literary and artistic works about the Holocaust authored by survivors, the children of survivors, and writers (born before, during, and after the war) who are not the descendants of survivors are all "more historicized" and "more imaginative" than nonliterary eyewitness testimony? Why describe a remarkably general approach to writing about the Holocaust, such as utilizing historical research or using one's imagination to depict events one has not witnessed or experienced oneself (the very definition of fiction writing), in generational terms? While an author's identity as the child of Holocaust survivors bears on how we will read her or his work, that information—carrying with it prescriptive notions of what it *means* to be a second-generation writer—does not provide the key to that work's meaning. Nor does an author's generational designation vis-à-vis the Holocaust provide the sole basis, or even the best basis, for classifying his or her writing in terms of aesthetic approach, literary strategy, or genre.

Despite all this, scholars persist in their effort to define the survivors' descendants in purportedly generation-specific terms of how they write about the Holocaust. Effectively taking up Horowitz's notion that writing about the Holocaust becomes "more historicized or more imaginative as the writers become more distant from the events of the Holocaust,"[65] scholars describe third-generation literature as if it is like second-generation literature, *only more so*. If the survivors' children can only imagine what their parents experienced, the survivors' grandchildren, born at a greater remove from the Holocaust, must draw even more on their imaginations. Indeed, from a third-generation vantage point the second generation's distance from the Holocaust may appear overstated. So suggests Caroline Schaumann in *Memory Matters: Generational Reponses to German's Nazi Past in Recent Women's Literature*, as she claims that whereas the survivor's children could "encounter their parents' (traumatic) memories," the grandchildren cannot, and so for them "creative imagination becomes the necessary, appropriate, and imperative approach to the past."[66] For Jilovsky too this distinction is definitive: "While the second generation emphasizes closeness to the Holocaust, a defining feature of the third generation is its comparative distance from the Holocaust."[67]

In a recent essay on third-generation texts, Jessica Lang similarly remarks that "for first-and second-generation Holocaust writers the historical experience 'conveys' a sense of immediacy and impact," as it is only with the third generation that "historical distance . . . transforms these events from a direct experience, the experience of the eyewitness, or even the experience of those closest to them, their children, to an indirect experience."[68] Suddenly, it seems, second-generation writing *is* a matter of eyewitnessing—at least in comparison to third-generation writing. Whereas McGlothlin writes that second-generation writers explore "an event that they do not personally know" through "imaginative writing,"[69] for Lang it is third-generation writers for whom "the Holocaust can become a historical event in the writer's imagination, even if it is not part of her personal history."[70] No matter that all kinds of writers access the Holocaust through the imagination; Jilovsky likewise identifies the central role that imagination plays in third-generation texts as "a direct consequence of the distance in third-generation witnessing."[71] Their remarks place the third generation in the place previously occupied by the second, whose relationship to the Nazi genocide of the Jews—heretofore characterized in terms of belatedness, distance, absence, and imagination—is redefined as one of closeness and connection to the Holocaust.

A SPECIAL PLACE

Even as Jilovsky identifies the grandchildren's "distance from the Holocaust" as "a defining feature" of the third generation,[72] she holds that "[t]he most important characteristic of the third generation is their position as the last living link to the Holocaust."[73] The survivors' grandchildren will make good on this position, according to Jilovsky, if they are indeed "the last generation to know Holocaust survivors and their contemporaries personally,"[74] and if they outlive their parents and grandparents to "one day form the last living link to the eyewitnesses."[75] In short, she foresees a future in which the third generation will be the last people alive to have known Holocaust survivors not through books, films, or video testimonies, but personally—at least as well as grandchildren tend to know their grandparents.

Jilovsky's description of the third generation as "the last living link" appears indebted to a claim made by the founder of a non-profit organization formed to bring the grandchildren of Holocaust survivors together. Jilovsky writes:

> Daniel Brooks, the director of 3GNY, a group based in New York, provides the following description: "We, the grandchildren of Holocaust survivors . . . all share a unique family history. We are also the last living link to Holocaust survivors. It is only through us that future generations will know the actual stories of our grandparents' survival and the unimaginable losses of that generation." This statement poignantly encapsulates the third generation's position in the generational chain.[76]

In actuality, Brooks's statement does no such thing; rather, it expresses a fantasy of one's all-important role as a caretaker of Holocaust memory, at the cost of forgetting the many thousands of written, filmed, videotaped, and digitalized Holocaust survivor testimonies and histories that have been amassed and will continue to be available to future generations. The notion that future generations will have to turn to the grandchildren of Holocaust survivors in order to access the survivors' actual stories—stories recounted in many more books and audio-visual recordings than anyone might read or watch in a lifetime—is bizarre, but no more so than the notion that the children of Holocaust survivors are in large part responsible for these stories. So claims Arlene Stein in *Reluctant Witnesses: Survivors, Their Children, and the Rise of Holocaust Consciousness*. As her book's title suggests, Stein attributes the rise of Holocaust consciousness in the United States to the survivors' children who, by "coaxing the reluctant witnesses to speak," became "coaxers and facilitators of their parents' stories."[77] Stein does not support this claim with evidence so much as take it on faith while at times undercutting it, as when she writes that a "proliferation of books, television shows, and movies about the Holocaust" helped generate "a mass audience for Holocaust stories, encouraging survivors to tell their stories."[78]

Jilovsky attributes not the rise of Holocaust consciousness but the formation of Holocaust Studies to the children of survivors. "The second generation in particular has shaped scholarship in historiography, literature, memory and trauma studies of the Holocaust," she writes. "As the children of survivors, the primary witnesses, the second generation is of course at the centre of non-survivors who write about and otherwise represent the Holocaust and its effect on their lives."[79] Though "of course" the descendants of Holocaust survivors play a central role, Jilovsky manages to cite only six "[s]cholars of the Holocaust who are members of the second generation," and these include a journalist rather than a scholar (Helen Epstein) and a scholar (Margaret Taft) who is unlikely to have shaped the field given that her first book, developed from her PhD thesis, was just published in 2013.[80] Such efforts to position the survivors' children and grandchildren at the center of Holocaust scholarship and representation, making them the central caretakers of Holocaust memory, are all the more striking given the slight evidence on which they are based.

More striking still are descriptions of the second generation as the central caretakers of Holocaust memory provided by those sons and daughters of survivors who "write about and otherwise represent the Holocaust and its effect on their lives" like other "non-survivors" do.[81] Here, for instance, is novelist Melvin Jules Bukiet describing what it means to be second generation in his introduction to the collection *Nothing Makes You Free: Writings by Descendants of Jewish Holocaust Survivors*:

> No one who hasn't grown up in such a household can conceive it, while every 2G has something in common. . . . The Second Generation will never know what the First Generation does in its bones, but what the Second Generation knows better than anyone else is the First Generation. Other kids' parents didn't have numbers on their arms. Other kids' parents didn't talk about massacres as easily as baseball games. Other kids' parents had parents.[82]

Bukiet goes on to identify the survivors' children as owners of "the story" (whether he means the story of growing up with parents who survived the Holocaust, or the story of the Holocaust told by their parents, he does not say) in terms that suggest this is less a burden than a privilege:

> [T]he 2G's occupy a special place. Whatever wisdom others bring to it comes from the heart and head, but for us it's genetic. To be shabbily proprietary, we own it. Our parents owned it, and they gave it to us. . . . We have been given an obscene gift, a subject of predetermined value that no one can deny. It's our job to tell the story, to cry "Never Forget!" despite the fact that we can't remember a thing.[83]

I imagine Bukiet as the second-generation *id*, giving boldly boastful and comic expression to what is normally repressed or suggested in more restrained terms. Despite its claim to exclusivity, his description of the second generation is not unrelated to what scholars have in mind when they evoke the post-Holocaust generation. This is because many scholars will grant the survivors' children a "special place" so long as they may join them there. All that is required is to imagine that what Bukiet calls the "job to tell the story, to cry 'Never Forget!'" is not only handed down by the survivors to their children as part of their "genetic" inheritance, but also imposed by history, indeed by the very magnitude of the Holocaust, upon others who have proven themselves capable and worthy of taking on the burden of memory.

AN IMAGINARY IDENTIFICATION

If Bukiet is the second-generation *id*, Marianne Hirsch may be the second-generation *ego* seeking to moderate his "shabbily proprietary" desire. She writes, "Even the title of Melvin Bukiet's anthology *Nothing Makes You Free* hints at the appropriation of suffering, underscored by the exclusively biological definition of second generation that Bukiet applies in his selection of writers to include."[84] Against the threat of over-identification with survivor-parents, Hirsh would join those scholars who have "tried to find the delicate balance between identification and distance."[85] In this effort she is aided by Eva Hoffman, who, in the role of second-generation *superego*, provides the epigraph with which Hirsch begins her book *The Generation of Postmemory*.

Though Hoffman is measured and contemplative where Bukiet is flippant and blunt, she shares with Bukiet a belief that the survivors' children have inherited something of the Holocaust from their parents. The epigraph taken from Hoffman's *After Such Knowledge* reads:

> The guardianship of the Holocaust is being passed on to us. The second generation is the hinge generation in which received, transferred knowledge of events is being transmuted into history, or into myth. It is also the generation in which we can think about certain questions arising from the Shoah with a sense of living connection.[86]

Hirsch concerns herself with "how that 'sense of living connection' can be maintained and perpetuated even as the generation of survivors leaves our midst, and how, at the very same time, it is being eroded."[87] This erosion involves not the public's knowledge of the Holocaust so much as the second generation's "living connection" to this past. "At stake," writes Hirsch, "is precisely the 'guardianship' of a traumatic personal and generational past with which some of us have a 'living connection,' and that past's passing into history or myth."[88] Not unlike Levi, Hirsch fears what will happen when a felt relation to the Nazi past is lost.

What prevents this past from passing into history or myth, for Hirsch, is the transmission of memory across generations. She writes that this "process of transmission . . . is best described by the notion of memory as opposed to history" because "[m]emory signals an affective link to the past—a sense, precisely, of a material 'living connection.'"[89] It seems that this living connection must be "maintained and perpetuated" lest memory (memories that preserve the freshness of things seen) give way to history (distant, blurry, "historical") and myth (inaccurate).

But if this is what Hirsch suggests, it is not what Hoffman means when she writes that "received, transferred knowledge of events is being transmuted into history, or into myth" in the second generation.[90] What then does she mean? In an interesting restatement of the passage that serves as Hirsch's epigraph, Hoffman writes:

> The generation after atrocity is the hinge generation—the point at which the past is transmuted into history or into myth. It is the second generation, with its intense loyalties to the past, that the danger of turning the realities of historical experience into frozen formulae of collective memory is the greatest; but it is also in that interval that we have the best opportunity of apprehending history in all of its affective and moral complexity.[91]

Here it is not history but memory that threatens Holocaust remembrance. And it is not only large-group collective memory that Hoffman warns against. She cautions survivors' children against adhering to "the parental versions of the past" they construct from the images and stories they came by in childhood,[92] writing that they need to supplement their internal imagery with greater "comprehension of history," locating family stories "in the broader context of events" and bringing to them interpretation and analysis.[93] I assume that Hirsch, an elegant and insightful interpreter of Holocaust literature, would agree; but whereas Hoffman would have children of survivors approach the Holocaust from "the position of the analyst and interpreter,"[94] Hirsch would have analysts and interpreters approach the Holocaust from the position of the child of survivors as members of what she calls "the generation of postmemory."

If, as Weigel has it, "trauma" has come to provide "every individual, regardless of his or her specific historical position . . . access to the great drama called history,"[95] "postmemory" has come to offer every individual, regardless of his or her identity position, access to the great drama called memory. As initially conceived by Hirsch, postmemory concerned the Holocaust as a survivor's child imagines it based on her parents' stories, family photographs, and other traces. But in further developing "postmemory" as a concept, Hirsch expanded its meaning in much the same way that the second-generation category has been expanded, transforming postmemory from a second-generational to a post-Holocaust-generational term. As reconceived, "postmemory is not an identity position, but a space of remembrance"[96]—"an affiliative space of remembrance, available to other subjects external to the immediate family."[97]

Put another way, postmemory *is* an identity position (held by the children of Holocaust survivors) but no longer an exclusive one; now it is open to "other subjects" willing to locate themselves in an auxiliary "space of remembrance." Taking the U.S. Holocaust Memorial Museum as a potential, literalized space of this kind, Hirsch writes:

> The museum was created not primarily for survivors and deeply engaged children of survivors like me, but for an American public with little knowledge of the event. At its best, the museum needs to elicit in its visitors an imaginary identification—the desire to know and to feel, the curiosity and passion that shape the postmemory of survivor children. At its best, it would include all of its visitors in the generation of postmemory.[98]

Though the museum's design encourages visitors to identify with the victims of Nazi persecution and genocide, Hirsch suggests that museum visitors should identify first with the children of survivors, as if it is only by imaginatively adopting their identity position that visitors can desire, truly and deeply, to know about the Holocaust and feel for its victims. Moreover, by identifying with "deeply engaged children of survivors," persons properly interested in the Holocaust can distance themselves from a public that knows little about it.

Of course, "imaginary identification" informs most depictions of the Holocaust aimed at the American public. Jonathan Boyarin has observed that in popular representations of the Holocaust "the particular horror of the Nazi genocide is emphasized by an image of the Jews as normal Europeans, 'just like us.' In fact, we can only empathize with, *feel ourselves into*, those we can imagine as ourselves. Thus in the television docudrama *Holocaust*, the Jewish protagonists are a middle-class . . . nuclear family."[99] The children of survivors—who are "just like us" in having been born after the Holocaust, yet unlike us in having survivor parents—may function, much as the family members in the *Holocaust* miniseries do, as intermediaries through whom those with no familial connection to the Nazi genocide of the European Jews may come to care about and identify with the victims.

Hirsch states that "[t]he idiom of family can become an accessible lingua franca easing identification and projection . . . across distance and difference."[100] While this may be true, the parent-child relationship in survivor families provides an odd model for how those who study, teach, and write about the Holocaust, much less occasional visitors to the Holocaust museum, should approach this history. In making "the postmemory of survivor children" the privileged model of Holocaust remembrance, Hirsch does not address how these children's relationship to the Holocaust is complicated by the parent-child relationship. Whereas Hoffman writes of "impossible psychic tasks" that survivors' children may take on for their parents,[101] and sociologist Simon Gottschalk claims that many survivors' children "feel victimized both by history and, more ambiguously, by their parents who themselves are victims,"[102] in connection to "postmemory" growing up in survivor families seems to instill nothing so much as an energizing curiosity and passion for remembering the Holocaust. It follows that persons who both are and are not the descendants of Holocaust survivors might wish to imaginatively identify themselves with "survivor children" so conceived.

LEGACY MATTERS

Why should anyone seek membership in the generation of postmemory? Elizabeth R. Baer and Hester Baer provide an answer in their essay "Postmemory Envy?" In sections alternately voiced by mother and daughter, the Baers reflect on their experience of discovering, translating, and co-editing a memoir by their distant relative Nanda Herbermann, a survivor of the Ravensbrück concentration camp. Elizabeth Baer writes that as "a non-Jew trained in literature with no facility in German, Polish, Hebrew, or Yiddish," she has often felt "like a trespasser in the field of Holocaust Studies."[103] Somehow the discovery of this chance relation—Herbermann's great-great-grandfather was the brother of her great-great-great-grandfather[104]—offered to change that:

> Finding Herbermann and working on her book gave me "postmemory," a claim to the Holocaust as a legacy that gave me a toehold in a field where legacy matters—even if scholars are reluctant to acknowledge this. . . .
> In Holocaust Studies, postmemory moves a scholar from margin to center. Second-generation scholars can claim legitimacy, inside knowledge, and insight unavailable to those not of the second generation.[105]

In reality, Baer gained knowledge and insight not through finding Herbermann and receiving her entitlement, but through the intensive historical and interpretive work she did on the book. Likewise, the legitimacy of her voice lies not in her "claim to the Holocaust as a legacy," or in a relation to a survivor of the camps that Bukiet might call "genetic," but in the quality of her scholarship. Yet, as Baer's references to the place of legacy in Holocaust Studies indicate, a sense that such legitimacy is a matter of familial or generational inheritance persists.

Baer's statement resonates with Pascale Bos's remarks, in "Positionality and Postmemory in Scholarship on the Holocaust," concerning how, as a young scholar whose name and appearance are not recognizably Jewish, she has often been looked at as an "outsider" at Holocaust Studies forums—that is, unless and until she reveals her identity as a Dutch Jew and the daughter of a Holocaust survivor.[106] Bos writes that with this revelation she and her scholarly work "gain in legitimacy": "[M]y opinion now counts, as my perceived proximity to the Holocaust experience, my 'authenticity,' my personal, familial, connection are seen as an advantage, as a genuine source of knowledge, and as a position from which to assert authority." She comments that while her "knowledge and investment may differ from that of scholars without a familial connection," we need to question the nature of this difference and the effect that positionality has on scholars' work.[107]

Bos questions the legitimacy granted the children of survivors from the privileged position of being "second generation" and a European Jew as well—less removed from the scene of the catastrophe than her American Jewish colleagues. Elizabeth Baer's considerably more haphazard claim to postmemory is complicated not only by her greatly attenuated "generational" connection to Herbermann, but by Herbermann's questionable identity as a Holocaust survivor, given that she was not a Jew but "a devout Catholic and German patriot . . . arrested by the Nazis for her work with an anti-Nazi priest and imprisoned in Ravensbrück for twenty months before she was released upon direct orders from Heinrich Himmler."[108] That she stakes this claim anyway speaks to the desirability of attaining what is "unavailable to those not of the second generation"—namely, a legitimacy rooted in the presumed authenticity and insider knowledge of the second generation.

As Baer sees it, postmemory confers legitimacy and belonging. Hester Baer sharply questions such claims, writing that "we must become increasingly wary of notions of 'authenticity' and circumscriptions surrounding who is authorized to speak in Holocaust Studies."[109] Such circumscriptions, or delineations of group identity arrived at through generational categorizing, rest on what she aptly describes as "essentialized notions of identity" that encourage problematic identifications and discourage critical evaluation. Baer astutely concludes, "Instead of envying the ability to lay claim to postmemory, we should focus on what can be gained from the different critical perspectives that emerge from different positionalities."[110]

Such a shift in focus will involve resisting generational thinking that confers specialness, as well as recognizing the multivaried positionalities—or varieties of identities, histories, experiences, knowledges, and worldviews—that are easily obfuscated when we speak of "the second generation" and "the third generation" (or, for that matter, "the survivor"). One might argue that by expanding the second generation or the third to include those who are not the descendants of survivors, or by granting them affiliate membership in "the generation of postmemory," scholars are opening up previously circumscribed and essentialized identities to difference. But here inclusion involves the assimilation of difference into a prescriptive group identity rather than a critical reassessment of that identity. Put simply, granting others access to an essentialized identity position does not de-essentialize that position. Indeed, scholars offered a space in the second, third, post-Holocaust, or postmemory generation have a vested interest in *not* interrogating the terms that would move them from the margin to the center, from the outside to the inside, granting their voices legitimacy.

Like Grimwood, Bos, Baer, and Baer, I am calling for scholars to challenge the limited and hierarchal range of identity positions that generational thinking has made available to us. But I am also arguing for a more radical rejection of the prevailing rhetoric in Holocaust Studies that functions to generate authenticating identity positions by positing a chain of identification running from the survivors to the second and third generations to the post-Holocaust generation. These terms provide a means of locating ourselves and others vis-à-vis the Holocaust in ways that serve psychological, professional, and personal needs for legitimacy and authenticity, at the cost of misrepresenting the Holocaust and ourselves.

In *Breaking Crystal*, Sicher notes with approval that "[f]or George Steiner, those who live 'after Auschwitz' are in a sense survivors of the Holocaust"[111] and that "[f]or [Norma] Rosen everyone in the United States who had knowledge of what happened 'over there' was a survivor."[112] Steiner's sentiment dates to 1965 and Rosen's to 1974. The honorifics change over time, as do their points of reference. Today it is not the survivors who are taken to epitomize and represent all who live or write "after," but their children and grandchildren. In time this generational rhetoric will likewise appear outdated and quite curious. As the experience of growing up in survivor families, like that of surviving the Holocaust, passes into history, and generational distance from the Holocaust increases exponentially, that familial experience will be recognized in its historical specificity and variety, and not in its emblematic capacity to dramatize the condition of all would-be guardians of Holocaust memory.

NOTES

1. Primo Levi, *The Drowned and the Saved*, trans. Michael F. Moore, in *The Complete Works of Primo Levi*, vol. 3, ed. Ann Goldstein (New York: Liveright, 2015), 2564.
2. Levi, *The Drowned and the Saved*, 2563.
3. Levi, *The Drowned and the Saved*, 2563.
4. Carole Angier, *The Double Bond: Primo Levi: A Biography* (New York: Farrar, Straus and Giroux, 2002), 477–78; Ian Thomson, *Primo Levi: A Life* (New York: Metropolitan, 2002), 334.
5. Thomson, *Primo Levi: A Life*, 257.
6. Thomson, *Primo Levi: A Life*, 266.
7. Primo Levi quoted in Myriam Anissimov, *Primo Levi: Tragedy of an Optimist*, trans. Steve Cox (Woodstock, New York: Overlook, 1996), 388.
8. Levi, *The Drowned and the Saved*, 2527.
9. Levi, *The Drowned and the Saved*, 2527–28.
10. Anson Rabinbach, "From Explosion to Erosion: Holocaust Memorialization in America since Bitburg," *History and Memory* 9.1/2 (October 1997): 227.
11. Rabinbach, "From Explosion to Erosion," 227.
12. Alvin H. Rosenfeld, *The End of the Holocaust* (Bloomington: Indiana University Press, 2011), 11–12.
13. Rosenfeld, *The End of the Holocaust*, 12.
14. Rosenfeld, *The End of the Holocaust*, 12.

15. Esther Jilovsky, *Remembering the Holocaust: Generations, Witnessing and Place* (New York: Bloomsbury, 2015), 24.

16. Helen Epstein, *Children of the Holocaust: Conversations with Sons and Daughters of Survivors* (New York: Penguin, 1979), 338.

17. Sigrid Weigel, "'Generation' as a Symbolic Form: On the Genealogical Discourse of Memory since 1945," *Germanic Review* 77, no. 4 (2002): 265.

18. Susan Rubin Suleiman, "The 1.5 Generation: Thinking about Child Survivors and the Holocaust," *American Imago* 59, no. 3 (2002): 284.

19. Suleiman, "The 1.5 Generation," 277.

20. Suleiman, "The 1.5 Generation," 286.

21. Suleiman, "The 1.5 Generation," 291.

22. Eva Hoffman, *After Such Knowledge: Memory, History, and the Legacy of the Holocaust* (New York: PublicAffairs, 2004), 26.

23. Hoffman, *After Such Knowledge*, 26–27.

24. Hoffman, *After Such Knowledge*, 27.

25. Hoffman, *After Such Knowledge*, 28.

26. Jilovsky, *Remembering the Holocaust*, 21.

27. Jilovsky, *Remembering the Holocaust*, 22.

28. Esther Jilovsky, Jordana Silverstein, and David Slucki, *In the Shadows of Memory: The Holocaust and the Third Generation* (London and Portland: Vallentine Mitchell, 2016), 2.

29. Jilovsky, Silverstein, and Slucki, *In the Shadows of Memory*, 4.

30. Jilovsky, Silverstein, and Slucki, *In the Shadows of Memory*, 309.

31. Jilovsky, *Remembering the Holocaust*, 22.

32. Hoffman, *After Such Knowledge*, 28.

33. Hoffman, *After Such Knowledge*, 63.

34. Aaron Hass, *In the Shadow of the Holocaust: The Second Generation* (Ithaca: Cornell University Press, 1990), 157.

35. Dina Wardi, *Memorial Candles: Children of the Holocaust* (New York: Routledge, 1992), 6.

36. Efraim Sicher, "The Burden of Memory: The Writing of the Post-Holocaust Generation," in *Breaking Crystal: Writing and Memory after Auschwitz* ed. Efraim Sicher (Urbana: University of Illinois Press, 1998), 66.

37. Epstein, *Children of the Holocaust*, 338.

38. Shamai Davidson, "Behavior: Legacy of Terror," *Time*, February 21, 1977, 48; slightly misquoted in Epstein, *Children of the Holocaust*, 338.

39. Ellen S. Fine, "Transmission of Memory: The Post-Holocaust Generation in the Diaspora," in *Breaking Crystal: Writing and Memory after Auschwitz*, ed. Efraim Sicher (Urbana: University of Illinois Press, 1998), 186.

40. Fine, "Transmission of Memory," 187.

41. Fine, "Transmission of Memory," 190.

42. Weigel, "'Generation' as a Symbolic Form," 270.

43. Erin McGlothlin, *Second-Generation Holocaust Literature: Legacies of Survival and Perpetration* (Rochester, NY: Camden House, 2006), 9.

44. Efraim Sicher, "Introduction," in *Breaking Crystal: Writing and Memory after Auschwitz*, ed. Efraim Sicher (Urbana: University of Illinois Press, 1998), 7.

45. Sicher, "The Burden of Memory," 19.

46. Sicher, "The Burden of Memory," 19.

47. Sicher, "Introduction," 7.

48. Bernice Eisenstein, *I was a Child of Holocaust Survivors* (New York: Riverhead, 2006), 21.

49. McGlothlin, *Second-Generation Holocaust Literature*, 13.

50. McGlothlin, *Second-Generation Holocaust Literature*, 14.

51. McGlothlin, *Second-Generation Holocaust Literature*, 8–9.

52. McGlothlin, *Second-Generation Holocaust Literature*, 9.

53. McGlothlin, *Second-Generation Holocaust Literature*, 10.

54. Marita Grimwood, *Holocaust Literature of the Second Generation* (New York: Palgrave Macmillan, 2007), 3.
55. Grimwood, *Holocaust Literature of the Second Generation*, 6.
56. Grimwood, *Holocaust Literature of the Second Generation*, 3.
57. Grimwood, *Holocaust Literature of the Second Generation*, 15.
58. Grimwood, *Holocaust Literature of the Second Generation*, 136.
59. Sara R. Horowitz, "Auto/Biography and Fiction after Auschwitz: Probing the Boundaries of Second-Generation Aesthetics," in *Breaking Crystal: Writing and Memory after Auschwitz*, ed. Efraim Sicher (Urbana: University of Illinois Press, 1998), 277.
60. Sicher, "The Burden of Memory," 19.
61. Horowitz, "Auto/Biography and Fiction after Auschwitz," 278.
62. Horowitz, "Auto/Biography and Fiction after Auschwitz," 279.
63. Horowitz, "Auto/Biography and Fiction after Auschwitz," 279.
64. David R. Mesher, "The Recovered Self: Auschwitz and Autobiography," *Judaism* 45, no. 2 (Spring 1996): 237.
65. Horowitz, "Auto/Biography and Fiction after Auschwitz," 278.
66. Caroline Schaumann, *Memory Matters: Generational Reponses to German's Nazi Past in Recent Women's Literature* (New York: Walter de Gruyter, 2008), 225.
67. Jilovsky, *Remembering the Holocaust*, 103.
68. Jessica Lang, "*The History of Love*, the Contemporary Reader, and the Transmission of Holocaust Memory," *Journal of Modern Literature* 33, no. 1 (2010): 46.
69. McGlothlin, *Second-Generation Holocaust Literature*, 10.
70. Lang, "*The History of Love*," 44.
71. Jilovsky, *Remembering the Holocaust*, 113.
72. Jilovsky, *Remembering the Holocaust*, 103.
73. Jilovsky, *Remembering the Holocaust*, 21.
74. Jilovsky, *Remembering the Holocaust*, 21.
75. Jilovsky, *Remembering the Holocaust*, 103.
76. Jilovsky, *Remembering the Holocaust*, 104.
77. Arlene Stein, *Reluctant Witnesses: Survivors, Their Children, and the Rise of Holocaust Consciousness* (New York: Oxford University Press, 2014), 5.
78. Stein, *Reluctant Witnesses*, 110.
79. Jilovsky, *Remembering the Holocaust*, 14.
80. Jilovsky, *Remembering the Holocaust*, 158n79.
81. Jilovsky, *Remembering the Holocaust*, 14.
82. Melvin Jules Bukiet, "Introduction," in *Nothing Makes You Free: Writings by Descendants of Jewish Holocaust Survivors*, ed. Melvin Jules Bukiet (New York: Norton, 2002), 13–14.
83. Bukiet, "Introduction," 16.
84. Marianne Hirsch, *The Generation of Postmemory: Writing and Visual Culture after the Holocaust* (New York: Columbia University Press, 2012), 20.
85. Hirsch, *The Generation of Postmemory*, 20.
86. Hoffman, *After Such Knowledge*, xv; quoted in Hirsch, *Generation of Postmemory*, 1.
87. Hirsch, *Generation of Postmemory*, 1.
88. Hirsch, *Generation of Postmemory*, 1.
89. Hirsch, *Generation of Postmemory*, 33.
90. Hoffman, *After Such Knowledge*, xv.
91. Hoffman, *After Such Knowledge*, 198.
92. Hoffman, *After Such Knowledge*, 194.
93. Hoffman, *After Such Knowledge*, 196.
94. Hoffman, *After Such Knowledge*, 196.
95. Weigel, "'Generation' as a Symbolic Form," 270.
96. Marianne Hirsch, "Projected Memory: Holocaust Photographs in Personal and Public Fantasy," in *Acts of Memory: Cultural Recall in the Present*, ed. Mieke Bal, Jonathan Crewe, and Leo Spitzer (Hanover, NH: University Press of New England, 1999), 8.
97. Hirsch, *Generation*, 93.

98. Marianne Hirsch, *Family Frames: Photography, Narrative and Postmemory* (Cambridge: Harvard University Press, 1997), 249.

99. Jonathan Boyarin, *Storm from Paradise: The Politics of Jewish Memory* (Minneapolis: University of Minnesota Press, 1992), 86.

100. Hirsch, *Generation of Postmemory*, 39.

101. Hoffman, *After Such Knowledge*, 63.

102. Simon Gottschalk, "Reli(e)ving the Past: Emotion Work in the Holocaust's Second Generation," *Symbolic Interaction* 26, no. 3 (2003): 376.

103. Elizabeth R. Baer and Hester Baer, "Postmemory Envy?" *Women in German Yearbook* 19 (2003): 80.

104. Baer and Baer, "Postmemory Envy?" 78.

105. Baer and Baer, "Postmemory Envy?" 80–81.

106. Pascale Bos, "Positionality and Postmemory in Scholarship on the Holocaust," *Women in German Yearbook* 19 (2003): 53.

107. Bos, "Positionality and Postmemory," 53–54.

108. Baer and Baer, "Postmemory Envy?" 75.

109. Baer and Baer, "Postmemory Envy?" 90.

110. Baer and Baer, "Postmemory Envy?" 90.

111. Sicher, "The Burden of Memory," 19.

112. Sicher, "The Burden of Memory," 23.

Chapter Ten

Simon and Mania

Henri Raczymow,
translated by Alan Astro

[Born in 1948, French writer Henri Raczymow would seem clearly of the second generation. His mother (born in Paris in 1928), along with her brother (born in Germany in 1924) and their Polish immigrant parents, belonged to a category of Jews who were not in hiding but "assigned to residence" in a specific locality. There, they could be arrested at any time; but thankfully for some, the police never came. Thus Raczymow's mother and her parents waited out the war in a rural region of France, but her brother, alternately called Hershl in Yiddish, Heinz in German, and Henri in French, was arrested and murdered at Auschwitz.

At Raczymow's grandparents' insistence, this uncle's first name was given to him; he recounts how he thus became at once the real grandson and substitute son of the same couple. Almost using the difficult postwar years as an excuse to raise their daughter's son, these adoring grandparents cast a shadow on his relationship to his mother.

In this configuration, a second-generation writer also looms as a member of the third. (Regarding the confusion of generations, see my article in this volume, "Avatars of Third-Generation Narrative in French and Spanish.")

Raczymow's oeuvre is wide-ranging and includes essays (most notably, on Proust) and novels (including one on a fantasized relationship between Joyce's Jewish character Bloom and Proust's Bloch). Many of his works reconstruct his family's experience of the Holocaust and its aftermath, either in real terms (in books focusing on his father and the uncle he never met) or fictional form. For example, his Writing the Book of Esther recreates the all-determinant relationship with the uncle Heinz/Henri he never met through the story of a Jewish woman, an aspiring writer who commits suicide, named *for an aunt who was murdered by the Nazis, an aunt with whom she becomes obsessed.*

Simon and Mania *shows Raczymow's inventivity, as he presses the writing of Proust—a scion of the most assimilated, bourgeois branch of French Jewry—into the service of far less fortunate immigrant coreligionists. Thus the evocation of Raczymow's grandparents starts with a divertimento on Proust's definition of two incompatible paths that form the titles of two volumes of his* In Search of Lost Time: Swann's Way *and* Guermantes' Way. *—Trans.]*

To arrive at the Dawidowicz apartment in lower Belleville, from home at 71 rue de la Mare in upper Belleville, there were truly two paths that could be taken, each distinct from and incompatible with the other, each possessing its unadulterable essence. It was one or the other; a choice had to be made: to the left or the right as you left the building, the side leading to the rue des Couronnes or to the rue des Pyrénées. What you chose depended on your state of mind. If you felt positive, you didn't hesitate, you turned right toward the rue des Couronnes. But you really had to feel completely positive, because that way was quite desolate. Neither did you hesitate if you were feeling down: you took the rue de Belleville—lively, colorful, joyous. On that note, I can't resist quoting a passage from a book that I hope you'll like. Here it is, with no further ado:

> For in the environs of Combray there were two "ways" which one could go for a walk. . . . I set between them, much more than their distances in miles, the distance that lay between the two parts of my brain where I thought about them, one of those distances of the mind which not only moves things away from each other, but separates them and puts them on different planes. . . . Our habit of never going both ways on the same day, in a single walk, but one time the Méséglise way, one time the Guermantes way, shut them off, so to speak, far apart from each other. . . .[1]

I would like to quote even more, some additional lines, or pages, or tens of pages, but enough. It wouldn't be quite reasonable of me.

To visit Simon and Mania (and I repeat that they called Simon monsieur Henri, or monsieur Honri,[2] and Mania they called Matl, go figure, that is to say Mania is Polish, that was her legal name, and Matl is her Yiddish name, which also sometimes showed up on her papers, instead of the other, or next to it, that's all rather confusing, I admit), you could go by different paths. You went down rue des Couronnes with on the right, perched up high, with the empty lot on the rue Botha (brings to mind the movie *Casque d'or* with Simone Signoret) that you reached by stairway; and the passage Piat (today it's ugly, full of trees, the empty lot is no longer there, there's a nasty-looking housing development, at least that's what they call it: a development) and on the left, as you looked down, were the tracks of the little belt railway, linking I-don't-know-what to I-don't-know-what, which perhaps went around Paris way back—because now (the now I'm writing about is not the now when I'm writing) the railway had fallen into disuse and it no longer transported any freight or, obviously, passengers (or at least I'd never seen any). Under the bridge of the rue Henri-Chevreau that went over the embankment and under which the Seine did not flow,[3] friends of mine went to smoke some nasty P4 cigarettes unbeknownst to adults or had fun making a "campfire" with whatever pieces of wood, paper, cardboard and old shoes they could find. Willy Ronis would have wanted to photograph these picturesque scenes of urban life and maybe even did so, in the far-off time around my birth.

Sometimes Simon would come see us on the rue de la Mare and mama would ask me if I could walk him back home as night fell, to 34 rue Bisson. But who would walk me back? No one, of course. All alone I'd have to walk back up the sinister rue des Couronnes. But I didn't even ask myself the question; I acquiesced with no hesitation, because I loved Simon as limitlessly as I did my grandmother Matl. So together we'd go down the rue des Couronnes that led to their place. Simon had a particular habit that would have bothered some but not yours truly, which was to go through the trashcans of the metalworking shops lined up on the left side of the street and deserted at that late hour. I imitated him as we snuck under Ali Baba's entryways. Watch me as I rummage and fish out treasures, spools of string, twine and Kraft paper, flat- and round-headed nails and screws, nuts and bolts, flat tailors' chalk, awls, rods and washers (what do you mean? they can always come in handy), not to mention rolls of gift ribbon, bits of string and anything worth saving. Sometimes I beat him to it and dug up things I had not known existed one instant before and immediately seemed useable to me. I couldn't say for what, but my grandfather would certainly know. And he did! It's back then, I suppose, that I acquired a propensity to walk through the streets with my eyes riveted to the ground and the gutter (as others are immersed in their thoughts), hoping to uncover rare jewels, perhaps a shiny new coin or a 20-franc solid-gold Napoleon that I could hardly hold in my palm. But as far as I can recall, that never happened. Alas, the doorways are no longer accessible to the pedestrian, you need entry codes, the same way you don't drop in on acquaintances; you have to inform them duly beforehand, call them, get their okay, make an appointment as though you were going to see a lawyer, everyone acts like a businessman with a packed agenda. That's because there's the telephone. But back when there weren't any, or at least not everyone had one, you could show up at the home of someone you knew, just breeze in, go up the stairs, knock on the door, just like that. If someone was home, they'd invite you in, serve you coffee or tea with cookies from a tin box. If no one was there, into the door you'd stick a note scribbled in the semidarkness, Hi auntie, stopping by, Riri. No big deal.

Whom could one possibly be bothering? Even if they were bent over their Singer sewing-machine, what could stop them from having a good chat, asking about the children, the other members of the mutual aid society of Warsaw Jews, the latest policies of the Party, events in Eretz Israel, the USSR, Indochina, Korea, how great was the risk of there being a third world war, is it good for "us," should we pack up and leave, but go where this time, hadn't we already gone off elsewhere quite enough?

Contrarily, the other route, the rue de Belleville, was usually taken when I was with my mother. It was never gloomy, but rather full of shops, cafés, movie houses, fish stores, toy stores (with lead soldiers for my collection, superb U.S. army military trucks, Dinky toys, but also the Hotchkiss Willys jeep, I was dying to have that one, but let's not get carried away, it costs much too much, mama would never spring for it any more than she would for other pieces to complete my collection, such as the Studebaker Commander, the Plymouth Belvedere, the Lincoln Premiere, just to name a few), butchers' shops replete with pheasants, guinea fowls and partridges, pheasants with long autumnal feathers, even redskins hadn't any so shimmering, hares carved in half and entire boars, calves' heads with milky skin like that of Nordics or as I imagined Moby Dick, the white whale, to have. The nostrils of the calves' heads adorned with parsley were supposed to be appetizing; they stuck out their tongues like so many village idiots; they always reminded me of an insult, making me understanding what the country kids we came across on vacation meant by calling us "Parigots têtes de veaux."[4] (There hardly exist anymore such street shows, a kind of *street art*,[5] as it were, at the butcher's.) Not to mention the sellers of children's books, stories about little cats that go camping and every morning cut their whiskers before a mirror hanging from a low branch while another cat says don't do that, we cats need our whiskers; or big dogs in some snow-covered forest of the Great Canadian North who become friends with the lynxes that the trappers have tamed by tossing them bits of meat.

My mother was never taken aback by my demands. It was always a pleasure on clear days to see the Eiffel Tower off in a distance as in a painting by Monet. On the other hand, I always suffered when Anna ran into a friend, their chatter would go on endlessly even as I tugged at her sleeve. It was a different story when my father, on the same street, came across a pal (another Party member). Now that was interesting; the talk was about the Party line, the political situation, preparations for the chapter's next meeting, the imminent election of a delegate to be sent to the federation, how the sale of passes to the *Humanité* fair[6] was going; talk about Jacques Duclos, Maurice Thorez, Jean Kanapa, Benoît Frachon, Henri Krasucki[7] (his comrades called him Krasu, he was "Krakra" for Étienne, who always had to be different, do things his own way). It has to be admitted: those conversations were on a higher level.

But what was Madame Anna going on about with her acquaintance in the middle of the rue de Belleville, as she was going up toward the Pyrénées métro station as the other was descending toward the boulevard? By what right can I assert that what they were talking about wasn't on the same level? Well, I'll tell you with no further ado: I have no idea. Because when in the middle of the rue de Belleville my mother chatted with someone she knew, I didn't even listen. Her words were like little butterflies flying about, worthy of just so much attention and setting down nowhere in particular. The conversation was like a kind of pretty ballet, yes, a ballet, light, sparkling, colorful, lively, silky, airy, filigreed, you name it. But I simply didn't listen, I tugged at her sleeve while looking at the other side of the street where a Simca Chambord of rare beauty was parked; I whined as impatiently as I could. When she finally decided that we should continue our ascent, as though no interruption had occurred, she abruptly asked me who—she or the other lady—had the better figure, a more petit backside, longer legs. With a shrug of my shoulders I answered: she did, my mother did! Her backside? It was hardly noticeable. What do you mean, hardly noticeable? I mean it's not as enormous as the other lady's. Then Anna was happy, life was once more worth living, we could start climbing again like the mountain goats we were.

When I was sick, my grandmother would come up to see us on the rue de la Mare. She'd sit at my bedside and looked at me. I believe no other woman has ever contemplated me that way. At length, silently, smilingly. In rapture, just like Lol Stein, even more so than Lol Stein.[8] Was she thinking of her son? Something now tells me she was, but of course back then that was the furthest thing from my mind. As a child, you can't imagine that you are loved or that you love somebody as a replacement for someone else. You don't wonder about such remote matters. You believe what you see. When you see love right there in front of you, looking at you, what else can you think? You believe it's real. It's later, sometimes, that you come to doubt, doubt not only love but the world, other people, yourself. One day, fissures appear on the walls of life and tend to deepen. Soon they're the only thing you see.

As I recall, my grandmother was a very silent woman. I've forgotten even the sound of her voice, her Yiddish accent, the words she would say to me. But not her face, her sweetness, the caress of her hand. A woman who did what life demanded of her, I suppose. I can only suppose because most of the time I saw her at the window of the dark storeroom behind which, in the center of the cave, the Dawidowiczes piled up the schmattas that Simon, once a week, would trade, fiercely bargaining for the best terms, in the vast hangars of the northern outskirts, at Saint-Ouen or Asnières, or wherever. She was a woman bereft of elegance. She would "dress up" just two or three times a year, when she attended the galas thrown by the mutual aid society of the Jews from Konskie, the shtetl in central Poland whence they came. After a visit to monsieur Grynspan's beauty salon, where until recently her own daughter had toiled, she would put on her nice black lamé dress and take out her gold pieces: necklace, broach, rings, bracelets. She'd adorn herself with whatever she had, the way some people turn on all the lights in their apartment in darkest winter to ward off gloominess. On those occasions, they'd come pick me up in a taxi on the rue de la Mare, on the way to the great illuminated hall where an orchestra was playing. Then I would perk up and enjoy sliding on the waxed floor and break out in a sweat. Noticing it, they'd have me sit down next to them for a few minutes quietly, *shtil*.

Once. when I had accompanied by grandfather to Saint-Ouen, I heard a buyer, a big fatso, say to him, That's my last price, take it or leave it, monsieur Dawidowicz. I was overcome by a painful feeling, infinite compassion for my grandfather whom I saw distraught, uncharacteristically at a loss for words. Within myself I cursed the fellow with the familiar imprecation *Gay in dr'erd arayn!*,[9] which seemed to me more powerful than a simple *Go drop dead like a mangy dog in hell!* My revolt was all the greater as the guy in the skimpy sleeveless argyle pullover bursting out everywhere—knit no doubt by his mother when he was but a tot (served him right)—had in his possession some ten piles of lousy garments, like so many rotten heaps of waste-rock around a coal mine in the North of France . . . whereas my grandfather had just one. It was the only time, I think, that I saw Simon at wit's end and reduced to silence, but he was up against a much bigger fish than he. This wasn't class struggle, it was a *struggle for life*[10] between unequally matched beasts, that's all, like the confrontation between a tyrannosaurus and a brontosaurus, if you can imagine that on a decorative plaque that even a master artist would refuse to paint.

But generally he was talkative and bubbling, more so than Matl, for example. On Saturday—*shabbos*—he'd get out from under his wife's thumb and escape from his labor to the café run by Moishe Katz (the guy with the wolf-dog). There he'd play *belote*[11] non-stop the whole afternoon, betting small sums but always something. Non-stop, or so it seemed to me, because I would go find him there and tug at this sleeve for us to go to a café on the nearby boulevard de Belleville and order a peppermint soda or grenadine. After which I'd walk him to his workshop in a far corner of the courtyard on the rue Dénoyez, as one accompanies an inveterate alcoholic home, and there he'd give my brother and me our allowances, a different amount for each one of us, which was only fair since Alain was younger and inexplicably never complained.

Hardly loath to brag, Simon recounted his "exploits," usually imaginary ones, the fortune that he had just made at cards or in his "business" dealings, which in actuality were quite minuscule. He would sometimes chalk up successful outcomes to his own merit when things simply worked out on their own. When luck looked the other way, as it invariably did, he took great care not to mention it, especially within the acute earshot of his wife. For

Matl was the one in charge, who made the final decisions, who drove the *shpan*, green or not.[12] So much so that when cancer carried her off before her time—I think I was ten years old—and Simon found himself alone, left to his own devices, with no compass to guide him or railing to keep him from falling, he gambled away the entire household savings, went flat broke, begged for handouts from a prosperous sister and my parents (who soon felt taken advantage of), fell ill in turn and died alone in his apartment on the rue Bisson, leaving debts his son-in-law had to pay, and on the shelves of the cabinets and closets (whence had disappeared even the sheets, pillows, pillowcases, cushions, towels, washcloths, blankets) receipts from the betting parlor and a hole-puncher to mark the horses chosen on the racing forms. He died like a dog in February 1968. No doubt unjustly, I held it against my mother. I had a philosophy class that day that I didn't want to miss and was not inclined to go the Bagneux cemetery to bury my grandfather whom I had until most recently adored; nor did I wish to watch my father droningly repeat word by word the rabbi's recitation of kaddish. Somewhat insincerely I asserted to my mother that the living were to be looked after, not the dead! She ran and threw herself dramatically onto the bed, painfully howling that I was a monster, a monster, you hear that, Étienne, your son is a monster!

Simon neither drank nor smoked. The only time he'd buy a bottle of wine—nasty stuff, Postillon, I think—was when we came to rue Bisson for lunch on Thursdays. It's not that Étienne couldn't do without wine, but Simon must have felt that since his son-in-law was a "real" Frenchman, born in France and speaking French with no accent other than the neighborhood Belleville variety, it was only natural to place a "good" bottle on the table. That day, while the radio played Tino Rossi's *Méditerranée aux îles d'or ensoleillées*,[13] Simon read aloud to Étienne from the *Naye Prese*, the Yiddish communist newspaper. Simon must not have known that the newspaper was communist, because he himself wasn't. Sneakily, Étienne suggested that he buy that paper, or perhaps he even had gotten him a subscription. And Simon really seemed to read it—despite the fact that he had brought from his native Poland, on the heels of his shoes, an ancient hatred for anything related to Russians and Russia; and as far as he was concerned, communists, Soviets, Bolsheviks were all just a brood of Russians. Through the *Naye Prese*, Étienne was hoping to raise, if only by a single notch, his father-in-law's political consciousness—no easy endeavor! In an almost devotional silence we listened as Simon read aloud the news from the great Stalin's homeland, Eretz Israel or an America fatally doomed because imperialism would dig its own grave no less certainly than a storm brings lightning, as the great Lenin had said, or as a sleeping cloud announces a storm, as the great Jaurès had put it.[14]

In the century preceding theirs, thanks to ever-stronger secularizing forces (the future Jewish communists, Zionists and Bundists would be atheists in their immense majority), families in those milieus saw a revolution in marital roles. Before, when religion regulated all aspects of life, men enjoyed power; their wives worked, running for example a small store, to earn their livelihood, place the pot on the stove (if they owned a pot), and put something in the pot, thus allowing men to devote all their time to the study of the Torah.

When the religion ceased playing that role and the men had gradually become politicized, it was their turn to put the pot on the stove, because they weren't going to simply stand around. So they descended from their pedestal, became ordinary and unsacred, lost all aura of sainthood, put away their tallit, tefillin and kippah, cut their side curls and dressed as modern "Germans." They were workers like all others, responsible for bringing in a livelihood. But as this happened, power changed hands. Women began to wear the pants. Something like the matriarchal society of the Bonobo apes was created. Matl and Simon exemplified that change. Simon talked, walked out, came back, preened himself, played cards Saturday afternoons at Moishe Katz's place, gave cubes of sugar to neighborhood dogs (who knew him well and would have called him, as did their masters, "monsieur Henri," had they had the gift of speech). Matl, on the contrary, kept silent, riveted most of the time to her sewing machine, at the prow, as it were, of an unstable ship of which she was nonetheless captain, boss, balabosta.

Grandfather Salomon (Szlama, in Polish style, on his identity papers) was something else altogether. We saw him only on Sunday mornings, when he climbed up to our apartment on the rue de la Mare, then on rue Chapon, which really showed of what mettle he was made. How did he get there? Did he take the bus, the métro, a taxi? Did he come by foot, via the place de la République, the Faubourg du Temple, the rue de Belleville, the rue des Pyrénées? I have no idea. But he always came on time, I mean at the same time, yes, always at the same time, dressed in a nice suit that he no doubt had sewn himself, and I even think he wore a tie. How unlike grandfather Dawidowicz, who, as could be surmised from his allure and attire, belonged to another class, another milieu entirely. His ties, save when he wore one to the mutual aid society gala, served most of all to secure the packages of schmattas to be schlepped here and there. Obviously, he wasn't a native of Warsaw, he didn't have the manners; he came from the country. The soles of his shoes still carried the soil, the mud of Masuria, if that's what his area was called. Or Podolia, or Volhynia, or Galicia; what would be gained by greater precision? In any case, an area with its reputed good fecund sludge. Ultimately, it is possible to say there was a mismatch between my father's and mother's families. They came from the same country, lived on the same streets in Paris, spoke the same landless language, and yet were not of the same milieu.

A tailor and a ragman never sit at the same table . . . unless their children are getting married; then they do what they have to do, what circumstances demand. They force themselves and put on a good face. But I suppose Salomon with his nice suits scorned Simon with his nice . . . nice what? Nice nothing! Simon had nothing nice to put on. Or he didn't really try to, he didn't even realize he was supposed to. But I loved him, that's all there was to it. At least as long as my grandmother was alive. Afterwards, I'm not so sure. Something was fractured, first of all between Simon and his daughter. There emerged a new affect that I clearly perceived, that contaminated my feelings and that did not leave me until his death.

So Salomon would climb up to visit us on the rue de la Mare every Sunday at the same time, bringing the same box of the ten little bottles of chocolate filled with different liqueurs. They were quite nauseating. In our neighborhood, Sunday was characterized by a certain solemnity. Things happened outside our windows only on Sundays. One example was the brass band preceded by majorettes. In martial rhythm, it went up the rue des Couronnes, crossed the little square, passed in front of the Levert school and continued high up onto the rue de la Mare toward the rue des Pyrénées, always followed by families in their Sunday best, veterans, morons. Where they went after the rue des Pyrénées, to the right or the left, I knew little and cared less. Then came the carriage drawn by a nag, with a postillion, a mounted carriage driver, in his carriage-driver uniform, probably advertising Postillon wine: a giant with a whip, a hunting horn, a black hat, a red outfit with golden buttons and black boots. But Sunday marked as well a visit from the neighbor on the fourth floor, whom we called monsieur Vaillant, because he brought us a copy of the *Vaillant* ("the most captivating paper") as well as the Sunday edition of *L'Humanité* (which my father himself was hawking, at that very moment, at a stand at the foot of the rue des Couronnes)*, Light Hours for French Women, Illustrated Roudoudou* and *Illustrated Riquiqui* (for my brother). Each member of the family thus had his or her paper, his or her *class organ*, his or her publication of the working-class to which we supposedly belonged but clearly did not. I never found out monsieur Vaillant's real name. I think it ended in *ski*: Popolski, Shokowski, a name befitting one of us.

 Another constant of Salomon's behavior: while his daughter-in-law, indifferent to his presence, stood at the stove, he would sit at the blue Formica table in the kitchen, always on the same stool made of identical Formica, always in the same position, and we would play the same game. Arms outstretched, I planted my fists in his palms and he tried to lift me by the force of his wrists, which he managed to do quite nicely. Having completed this prowess, he would say to me *immmbecile, bannditt*, which I enjoyed: not so much the innocent imprecations as the expected words coming at the right moment, like the ending of a silly story that one is glad is over. With my grandfather Salomon I don't think I exchanged even three sentences the whole time I knew him. I didn't like him, and I don't think his son did, either.

I remember a spring morning when we had gone to visit his brother Arl-Wolf (dubbed in French Aron-Loup) in his country home at Villepinte (I suppose the area is no longer one of private homes but rather of housing developments; it is now the outskirts of Paris—the *banlieue*—whereas at the time we said we were going to the country). Simon announced to no one in particular that he was going for a walk. My mother—I don't know why, she probably wanted me to get some exercise—told me to accompany him. I acquiesced, unfortunately enough. Not used to being around that rigid, cold grandfather, I simply dared not address a word to him. I waited for him to speak, to ask me questions about school, whether I liked my father or mother better, what was my favorite this or that, whatever. There are so many clever questions one can ask a child. My anxiety was reaching new heights. But from him nothing was forthcoming. Not a question, a word, even a gaze. After a few long silent minutes, he began to whistle a tune that was then often aired on the radio, *I Love Paris*, maybe. It was completely annoying. And my anxiety moved up yet another level, and I wondered if he felt the same thing or nothing at all, if he whistled as a diversionary tactic, to appear composed, to dissipate his unease or simply because he felt like whistling. I've never figured it out. At one moment, he decided we had had enough and could return. Whereupon Anna asked me how it had gone with grandfather. I was surprised that she even asked me that question. That meant she was quite conscious of something particular about that man, her father-in-law, but what? He was odd, uncommunicative. Perhaps she felt remorse over having bid me to join him on the walk. Despite his ultrapunctual Sunday visits, the foreseeable chocolate liqueur bottles, the repeated game whereby he lifted me up, the ritual words devoid of meaning—*immbecile, bannditt* that at least made me smile precisely because they meant so little—nothing forced me, or led me, to love him.

What more have I to say about these people, Simon Dawidowicz and his wife Matl, née Oksenberg? I believe they were first cousins. They were born and grew up together in Konskie, a shtetl in Poland. There was a wooden synagogue there that resembled a Chinese pagoda. I am not sure they attended it very often. They had a cart and would go for rides in the nearby forest where wolves roamed. The synagogue was burned down by the Germans when they invaded Poland in September 1939. Perhaps with people inside. No doubt with people inside. What the Germans did at Oradour-sur-Glane[15] in France, which has left such an indelible impression, and rightly so, they did a hundred times in the East to Jews.

The Dawidowicz newlyweds left Poland in 1918, just as the war ended. They went to Germany, Düsseldorf, where they remained several years. Their son Heinz was born there in 1924. Then, God knows why, they moved to Paris. Heinz became Henri. Szymon became Simon and Mania/Matl stayed Mania/Matl. They set up their household at the far end of a courtyard on the rue Dénoyez in Belleville, a courtyard similar to many that existed in Warsaw, and in Poland generally, that hosted garment-manufacturing shops. In the summer, when windows were open, the radios played the same songs and in between was heard the whir of sewing–machines. Then Anna was born in 1928. Then came the war. They left for the non-occupied zone but were stopped at the demarcation line and ordered to remain in the Charente region. One winter day, two gendarmes came knocking at the door of the prefab (provided for them by the Perrusson tile works) and arrested Heinz/Henri, age 20. What had he done wrong? He wandered from camp to camp in France, Nexon, Gurs, Drancy, before arriving at the last camp, in Poland, near Lublin. Much later, Matl fell ill and after an operation died in a private hospital perched high, overlooking the Buttes-Chaumont Park in Paris, which you had to climb innumerable steps to reach. She had been complaining for some time of stomach pains. The doctor came by, either Dr. Denkberg of the rue des Couronnes or Dr. Edmond Kaufman of the rue Bisson. We went to visit her at home. She was sprawled out on a shapeless bed covered with the huge quilt, the *iberbet* that they had schlepped to Belleville (in the 20th arrondissement of Paris) from Düsseldorf or perhaps even from Konskie, in Poland, at the end of the great war when their shtetl had been invaded in turns by the Germans then the Russians and back again, with each passage of troops accompanied by the Prussian eagle, the Russian bear, back and forth, with some damages thrown in: devastated farmlands, burned houses, corpses lying about like fallen autumn leaves, with black crows hopping about, prospecting. She was slumped on the bed, next to which so often, some years before, I would sleep in their room and face them; facing their large bed, I would hear them, at three paces from my little bed with the bars, as they snored like the steam locomotives of then. They would blow, and whistle, and hum in their sleep, and those sounds reassured me. No, that's not true, those familiar sounds didn't reassure me, because I feared nothing. It was only later, when I spent every night at my parents' on the rue de la Mare, that fear of night haunted me and would keep me long awake, sweating and crying for help despite the nearby presence of my brother who stayed sound asleep and heard nothing.

That day, Matl's skin had such an earthy tone, an absence of color that foretold the earth that would soon entomb her in the vault reserved for the Konskie Jewish mutual aid society. Incredulously I observed that bloodless face, astonished at not seeing her red cheekbones, the *royte bekelekh*[16] that caused my father to say that one of her forbears had been raped by a Cassock, one fine day, or perhaps in the course of a pogrom that they were so good at carrying out; and that said ancestress had been left pregnant with a scion with high Mongolo-Slavic cheekbones. My father asked what the doctor had said. It was that she should be hospitalized, operated on as quickly as possible. Waiting any longer would only worsen things. Étienne was a decisive man, a communist who had performed acts of resistance during the war. Practically a hero, quite the opposite of a luftmentsh. So they took Matl to the Buttes-Chaumont Hospital; they operated on her; and she died. It's good to be able to decide like a communist, like a resistance fighter, I said to myself, though the outcomes are not necessarily any surer.

My mother took me one day to see her in the hospital. She went up to her mother's room. My grandmother soon came down into the lobby dressed in a sort of blue hospital-gown under her bathrobe. She searched her pocket, took out a 100-franc coin, and gave it to me. That was the last time. My mother must have known it, my grandmother too. I didn't. After her mother's death, Anna said that she would experience the same fate, that the same illness would take her away some day, at the same age. That's what happened: the same fate, the same age. When we left the hospital, Anna said to me: You see, your grandmother gave you everything she had. Indeed, I saw. Everything she had.

One winter day, as I came back from school, my father was there, sitting on the convertible sofa in the dining room. You'd think he had been waiting for me. In fact, he was. He had some bad news. My grandmother.—She is dead.—Yes. And then I said something strange. I said, I don't know if I should laugh or cry. My father said nothing. His silence was a way of responding, after all, to my strange remark: It's no joke, it's true, my grandmother is dead. I thought of the ditty, "Ma chandelle est morte, je n'ai plus de feu."[17] That was at least as sad. And then, finally, I cried. My father, there, at the other end of the table, was crying too. My mother, who was in the kitchen, stuck in her head and quickly pulled back. No doubt she wanted to cry alone. I had rarely seen my father cry. I must have said to myself: But why is he crying? It's not his mother. I had to find an explanation for his tears. Perhaps he was crying because he saw me crying. Or then, maybe he was thinking of his mother, whom I had not known—Rywka, about whom he never told me anything and of whose death he was never notified; only her absence, no doubt definitive.[18] The next evening, at the same time, I see all three of us, each in the same spot, my father and myself in the dining room and my mother in the kitchen. And then her uncle Noyekh, Matl's brother, knocked on the door. And then he said something he probably should not have said. And Anna shouted as only she could. I had never heard her shout that way, so shrill and forcefully, at anyone beside myself. Except perhaps twice at a neighbor, once because she had said or done something antisemitic, and the second time because the neighbor had been picking a pointless quarrel with me. Hearing her shout against poor Noyekh, I went into the kitchen and managed to reconstruct their conversation in Yiddish. Noyekh had made the mistake of saying that it was better that way, that Matl had been suffering too much and now she was suffering no longer. That enraged Anna. She screamed at her uncle and threw him out of the house, physically pushed him out the door and onto the landing. I felt bad for my uncle, who was also my godfather. How could anyone treat someone like that?

They didn't take me to the Bagneux cemetery to bury my grandmother. There, I suppose, my father recited the Kaddish in his role as substitute son of the family, as he would some years later for his father-in-law. Maybe this avoidance, for which I was not responsible, made me feel for a long time that my grandmother had not really died, that I could and should expect to see her again someday, coming around the corner, or as I would enter once more into the courtyard of the rue Dénoyez and find her, eternally herself, sitting by the window of the storeroom, at her sewing-machine, making the same measured gestures as always, without grandeur, like a little mouse. And something tells me, today, that the same was true of my father: he no doubt expected to see his mother again, was persuaded that such a thing was possible, even likely, not at all miraculous or fantastic; it was something natural, as when there comes around the bend an old acquaintance from school or the army; something completely within the order of things, as ordinary as it gets, possible, yes, ordinary and possible.

What else is there to say? Matl and Simon Dawidowicz, residing at 34 rue Bisson, Paris, 20th arrondissement; born in Konskie, Poland, at the turn of the 20th century; immigrated to Paris toward 1923, during the roaring twenties they hardly experienced; both 4'11" in height; parents of two children, a boy then a girl; profession: merchants at trade fairs. They were very simple people, in all respects. They worked hard. They loved only their family, those closest to them. They insisted on my being named after their son deported to the East. As a child I felt a closeness to them, a physical, organic, visceral intimacy, an animal-like porosity between them and me, and a practically secret language that we shared and that wasn't secret at all, just a mix of rough French and poor Yiddish, the same they and their son had communicated in some twenty years before I was born. An untranslatable language, with no equivalent, at the intersection of several languages, and yet a language comprehensible from them to me. What else to say? What more to say? How to speak about them more, about them just a bit more?

NOTES

1. Marcel Proust, *Swann's Way*, trans. Lydia Davis (New York: Viking Penguin, 2003), 137–38.
2. "Honri" is Henri in Yiddish-accented French. [All notes are by the translator.]
3. Cf. Guillaume Apollinaire's 1912 poem "Le pont Mirabeau": "Sous le pont Mirabeau coule la Seine" [Under the Mirabeau Bridge flows the Seine].
4. The rhyming insult "Parigots têtes de veaux" means "Parisian calves' heads."
5. "Street art" is in English in the original.
6. *L'Humanité* was the official organ of the French Communist Party; it is still published (though its communist affiliation is no longer explicit) and continues to organize a large yearly fair on the outskirts of Paris.
7. Among these various personalities in the French Communist Party, Henri Krasucki was Jewish, born in the Warsaw area in 1903, immigrated to Paris, and resided in the neighborhood portrayed here. Under the German occupation, Krasucki was active in a largely Jewish immigrant Resistance network set up by the French Communist Party. He survived Auschwitz and continued his work in higher echelons of the communist party and union movements until his death in 2003. Raczymow's father's identification with this French Polish-Jewish communist leader needs no explanation. Krasucki is honored with commemorative square at the intersection of the rues de la Mare and des Couronnes, mentioned in this piece by Raczymow.
8. Cf. the 1964 novel by Marguerite Duras, translated by Richard Seaver as *The Ravishing of Lol Stein*.
9. Yiddish curse, literally "Go into the earth."
10. "Struggle for life": in English in the original.
11. Belote is the most popular card game in France, with a deck of thirty-two.
12. Raczymow seems to be making a complex, and somewhat imprecise, play on words here, between the Yiddish word *shpan* (harness, span) and the common Jewish surname of various spellings such as Greenspan and Grynspan, originally pronounced Grinshpan. Monsieur Grynspan, just mentioned, was the hairdresser Matl occasionally went to and whom her daughter had worked for. The idea is that Matl drove the coach, kept the others in harness (*shpan*), no matter what the harness be, no matter its color, etc.
13. Tino Rossi, French crooner of Corsican origin, most popular in the 1930s and 1940s, received a light sentence for collaborationist activities. The song mentioned here, celebrating sunny Mediterranean islands, is typical of his répertoire.
14. Jean Jaurès (1859–1914), socialist leader, supporter of Dreyfus.
15. On June 10, 1944, in retaliation for Resistance activity, the Germans murdered 642 residents of Oradour-sur-Glane, a town in west-central France. The men were burned alive in barns, the women and children were likewise conflagrated in a church.
16. *Royte bekelekh* (Yiddish): little red cheeks. The words turn up, for example, in a popular Yiddish song, *Di grine kuzine*, about immigrant life in America.
17. "My candle has died, I have no light": lyrics from the classic medieval French song *Au clair de la lune*.
18. Rywka, Raczymow's father's mother, was his sole grandparent murdered by the Nazis.

Index

Aarons, Victoria, 9, 74, 84
absence, 21
Abuelas de Plaza de Mayo (Grandmothers of Plaza de Mayo), 101n7
Adorján, Johanna, 32, 73
Adorno, Theodor, 41
aesthetics, second-generation, 172
affiliative postmemory, 77
After Such Knowledge (Hoffman), 58, 164, 176
agency, 73, 78
Aizenberg, Edna, 116, 117
Amsterdam, 104
And Every Single One Was Someone, 133, 144, 145, 145–147, 146, 148–150
Anielewicz, Mordechai, 119
Antelme, Robert, 116
anti-Semitism, 80
Antopol, Molly, xii, xiii, 40, 48, 49–50
archive fever, 59, 69n19
Argentina, xx, 90, 92, 94, 101n7, 116, 125
Argentine Catholic Church, 89
art, looting of, 45–46
artifacts, material, xix
Aspects of the Novel (Forster), 53
Astro, Alan, xv, xvii, xx
Auerbach, Rachel, 137
Auschwitz, 23, 64
authenticity, 179, 180
Authorized Memory, 41
authorship, 171

"Auto/Biography and Fiction after Auschwitz: Probing the Boundaries of Second-Generation Aesthetics" (Horowitz, S. R.), 171
avatars, 105

Baer, Elizabeth R., 179, 179–180, 181
Baer, Hester, 179, 180, 181
The Balcony (Genet), 107
Barber, Bernard, 148
Bar-On, Dan, 4
Barthes, Roland, 63, 64
Bashert: A Granddaughter's Holocaust Quest (Simon), xiii, 32, 74
Bauer, Yehuda, 132
Bayer, Gerd, 21, 24, 32
Beckett, Samuel, 114, 115
Beit Warszawa, 80
Belarus, xii, 48, 49, 50
Belgium, 110, 125n1
Ben-Atar, Doron, 5
Ben-Atar, Roma Nutkiewicz, 5
Ben-Dror, Graciela, xx, 89, 99
Bereichit, 58–60
Berger, Alan, xx, 133, 170
"Beyond Camps and Forced Labour" (conference), 3
Bible, 115
Bibliothèque Nationale de France, 46
BkMk Press, 13

Index

A Blessing on the Moon (Skibell), 32, 33, 34
Bolechow, mass shootings in, 62, 66
Bollinger, Heidi, 44
Bonert, Kenneth, 55n26
Borges, Jorge Luis, 116
Bos, Pascale, 179, 181
Boym, Svetlana, 19, 26, 35
Breakdowns: Portrait of the Artist as a Young %@&*! (Spiegelman), 28
Breaking Crystal: Writing and Memory after Auschwitz (Sicher), 168, 181
Brodeck (Claudel), 113, 114, 123, 125
Brooks, Daniel, 174
Browning, Christopher, 54n13
Buenos Aires, Argentina, 90, 94
Bukiet, Melvin Jules, 14n2, 23, 40, 41, 43; on second generation, 175
"The Burden of Memory: The Writing of the Post-Holocaust Generation" (Sicher), 168
Butterfly Project, 149

Camera Lucida (*La Chambre claire*) (Barthes), 63
camera obscura, 66–69
Carlotto, Estela, 101n7
Caruth, Cathy, 23, 33
Casque d'or (film), 186
"Cattle Car Complex" (Rosenbaum), 30
Celan, Paul, 132
Centre de Documentation Juive Contemporaine, 46
Cervantes, Miguel de, 119
C'est maintenant du passé (*It's Now Part of the Past*) (Rubinstein), 109
La Chambre claire (*Camera Lucida*) (Barthes), 63
Chejfec, Sergio, 98, 100, 116, 117
Children of Job: American Second-Generation Witnesses to the Holocaust (Berger), 170
Children of the Holocaust: Conversations with Sons and Daughters of Survivors (Epstein), 163, 166
Children's Holocaust Memorial, 149
Chinese boxes, 60–64
Chinski, Malena, xvi, xvii, xx, 117
Claudel, Philippe, 113, 123

Cohen, Jessica, 4
Cohen, Marcel, 105, 106
coherence, 163–166
collecting projects, 147, 151
collective consciousness, 18
collective memory, 35, 43, 167, 177
community: imagined, 165; invisible, 100
consciousness: collective, 18; Holocaust, 42, 174; of trauma, 18
Cortázar, Julio, 119
Council for aid to Jews (Zegota), 86n23
counting, 139, 143
counting memorials, 147, 148; symbolism and, 149
Los crímenes de Moisés Ville (*The Crimes of Moisés Ville*) (Sinay), 124–125
culture, material, 27

Dacosta, Uriel, 124
data, 140
Daughter of Silence (Fingueret), 118–119
Davidson, Shamai, 166
de Certeau, Michel, 154
dehumanization, 143
"Deir Yassin" (Singer, M.), 23
Delbo, Charlotte, 23
Demnig, Gunter, 150–152
Denmark, 113
de Paume Museum, 45
Derrida, Jacques, 69n19
"Deutsches Requiem" (Borges), 116
Diamant, Naomi, 41
direct familial ties, xvi
direct testimony, xvii
displacement, 124
distance, xviii, 33; Mendelsohn and, xvii, 31, 32; second generation and, 31; temporal, xvii
"Double Games and Golden Prisons: Vichy, Washington, and 'Diplomatic Interment' During World War II" (Dreifus), 2
dreams, 84
Dreifus, Erica, xiii, xvi, xix, 1, 20; academic career of, 2; background of, 1–2
Dres, Jérémie, 32, 74, 75, 75–76, 85; Jewish roots and, 77–85
The Drowned and the Saved (Levi, P.), 159

Drozd, Anna Przybyszewska, 82, 83
dual vision, 19
Duclos, Jacques, 188

Edelman, Gwen, 24, 35
educational memorials, 147
Edward Lewis Wallant Award, xix, 9, 40
Eisenstein, Bernice, 169
Eishyshok, Poland, 75
Eliach, Yaffa, 75
Elijah Visible (Rosenbaum), 30
The Elusive Embrace (Mendelsohn), 58, 59, 64–66, 68
emotion, expressions of, 97
The End of the Holocaust (Rosenfeld), 161
epics, 57
Epstein, Helen, 100, 163, 166, 167, 175
Eshel, Amir, 17, 18, 19, 31
"Ever After? History, Healing, and 'Holocaust Fiction' in the Third Generation" (Dreifus), 3
Everything Is Illuminated (Foer), 14n8, 32, 44, 75
An Exclusive Love (Adorján), 32, 73
extended memory, 26
eyewitnessing, 173

Facebook, 12
familial postmemory, 77
fantasy, 35
Far to Go (Pick), 7
Fear and Hope: Three Generations of the Holocaust (Bar-On), 4
Fiction Writers Review, 7, 10, 12
A Fifty-Year Silence (Mouillot), 29, 32
Fils et Filles des Déportés Juifs de France (Sons and Daughters of Jewish Deportees from France), 104, 108
Final Solution, 45
Fine, Ellen S., 167; second generation and, 167–168
Fingueret, Manuela, 118–119, 121, 122
Fink, Ida, 172
Finkielkraut, Alain, 112
first-hand accounts, xvii
Fishman, Boris, 40, 51
Flanzbaum, Hilene, 22, 23
Foer, Jonathan Safran, 14n8, 20, 32, 44, 75
forms of remembering, 21

Forster, E. M., 53
Fortunoff Video Archive, 43
Fourth General Census, 90
Frachon, Benoît, 188
France, xix, 78, 97, 103–110, 125n1; free zone of, 185; immigrants in, 104; writers from, xx
France Info, 74
Franco, Francisco, 101n7
Franklin, Ruth, 41, 42, 54n13
free zone, 185
French Communist Party, 198n7
French Ministry of Education, 113
"From Explosion to Erosion" (Rabinbach), 160
Fust, Rae, 141
The Future of Nostalgia (Boym), 19
futurity, 18–19, 19
Futurity: Contemporary Literature and the Quest for the Past (Eshel), 17

Generaciones de la Shoá (Generations of the Shoah), 90
generational thinking, 162, 180
The Generation of Postmemory (Hirsch), 176
Generations of the Shoah (Generaciones de la Shoá), 90
"generation without grandparents," xx, 89, 90, 97, 99, 101n4
Genesis, 61
Genet, Jean, 106–107
Geneva Convention, 103
Germany, xix
Goldberg, Florinda F., 119
Gospels, 115
Gottschalk, Simon, 178
Grandmothers of Plaza de Mayo (Abuelas de Plaza de Mayo), 101n7
Great House (Krauss), 26
Grimwood, Marita, 181; second generation and, 170–171
Gross, Jan T., 86n23
Grossbart, Meg, 66
Grossman, David, 19, 20, 23
G. S. Sharat Chandra Prize for Short Fiction, 13
Guez, Olivier, 76
Gutfreund, Amir, 4, 5–6, 6–7, 10, 12, 13

Halakhic Jews, 79
Halfon, Eduardo, 10–12, 12, 111, 119–122
Hall, Rachel, 13
Harjes, Kirsten, 151
Hartman, Geoffrey, xv
Hasidei Umot ha-olam (Righteous Among the Nations), 86n23
Hass, Aaron, 163, 165, 166
"Haunted Children," 41
Hebrew Bible, 53
Hebrew Immigrant Aid Society (HIAS), 94
Heirlooms (Hall), 13
Herbermann, Nanda, 179
Herejes (*Heretics*) (Padura), 122–124
HIAS. *See* Hebrew Immigrant Aid Society
HICEM, 94
Hirsch, Marianne, 23, 57, 76, 107, 178; second generation and, 176–177
Histoire des grand-parents que je n'ai pas eus (*History of the grandparents I did not have*) (Jablonka), 97, 106
history, transmission of, 47
Hoffman, Eva, 23, 27, 58, 73, 165, 166, 176, 177; on second generation, 164
Holocaust awareness, 42
Holocaust consciousness, 42, 174
Holocaust fatigue, 112
Holocaust Literature (Roskies and Diamant), 41
Holocaust Literature of the Second Generation (Grimwood), 170
Holocaust Museum Houston, 149
Holocaust Remembrance Day, 147
Holocaust studies, 161–162, 162–163, 168, 180; Jilovsky on, 174; legacy and, 179; second generation and, 166; survivor testimony and, 54n13
"Homecomings" (Dreifus), 15n20
Homer, 61
Hopscotch (Cortázar), 119
Horowitz, Rosemary, 140
Horowitz, Sara R., 171, 172
hostility, 110
Houghteling, Sara, 40, 44, 45, 47
humor, 6
Hungary, xiv, 46, 47, 52
Huyssen, Andreas, 17, 28, 35
hybridity, xviii

identification, 10, 59
identity, xiii, 59, 73, 75, 177, 180, 181; postmodern, 78–85; secularization of, 53
If This Is a Man (Levi, P.), 160
imaginary identification, 176–179
imaginative writing, 173
imagined community, 165
immigrants, 104
Imperial War Museum, 3
individuality, 145
information, 27
intergenerational transmission, of trauma, 40, 76, 162
intersectionality, 78
In the Shadow of the Holocaust: The Second Generation (Hass), 163, 165
In the Shadows of Memory: The Holocaust and the Third Generation (Jilovsky, Silverstein and Slucki), 165
The Invisible Bridge (Orringer), xiv, 7, 24–25, 27, 40, 73–74; dreams and, 84; as literary memorial, 44, 46–48; memory and, 22, 26
invisible community, 100
Israel, 79
Italy, 160
It's Now Part of the Past (*C'est maintenant du passé*) (Rubinstein), 109
I was a Child of Holocaust Survivors (Eisenstein), 169

Jablonka, Ivan, 97, 106–108, 110, 111, 112, 121
Jarecka, Gustawa, 135
JCA. *See* Jewish Colonization Association
Jeunehomme, Marie-Paule, 101n7
Jewish Colonization Association (JCA), 94
Jewish Consistory of Paris, 104
Jewish Historical Centre, 82
Jewish Historical Institute, 135
Jewish roots: discovering, 77–78; postmodern identity and, 78–85
Jewish servicemen, 3
Jewish Telegraphic Agency, 93
Jilovsky, Esther, xvi, 164, 165, 173, 174
Jüdische Wochenschau (newspaper), 93

Kadish, Rachel, 26

Index

Kafka, Franz, 113
Kanapa, Jean, 188
Karen et moi (*Karen and I*) (Skowronek), 110
Kassow, Samuel, 135
Katz, Moishe, 190, 192
Kaufman, Edmond, 195
The Kindly Ones (Littell), 116
kinship, xiii, 2, 7, 9, 10
Klarsfeld, Serge, 104
Klezmer: Tales of the Wild East (Sfar), 22
Kornreich, Rena, 121
Krajewski, Stanislas, 84
Krasucki, Henri, 188, 198n7
Krauss, Nicole, 20, 26
Krzepicki, Abraham Jacob, 138, 138–140, 142, 143–144

labor gangs, 46
Lambert, Josh, 42
landsmannschaftn, 44
Lang, Berel, 133
Lang, Jessica, xviii, xx, 173
Langer, Lawrence, 41, 161
language, 25; Yiddish, 117, 118
The Last Flight of Poxl West (Torday), 34–35, 40, 52–53
late-modernity, 17
Latin America, xix, xx, 100
Law of Compression, 6
Lebanon, 119
Lebensraum (Dreifus), 14n5
Leftist Cause, 122
legacy, 179–181
Lenta biografía (*Slow biography*) (Chejfec), 97–99, 116
letters, unsent, 118
The Letters that Never Came (Rosencof), 117
Levi, Lisa, 160
Levi, Primo, 108, 113, 121, 159–161, 176
Levi, Renzo, 160
Lévy, Paule, xi, xvii, xviii, xix
liberal democracy, 17
The Lion Seeker (Bonert), 55n26
literary memorials, 44, 44–53; *The Invisible Bridge* as, 44, 46–48; *Pictures at an Exhibition* as, 44, 44–46
Littell, Jonathan, 116

"Looking Backward: Third-Generation Fiction Writers and the Holocaust" (Dreifus), 7
looting, of art, 45–46
The Lost: A Search for Six of Six Million (Mendelsohn), xiii–xiv, 31, 32, 57–58, 73, 97, 105; *Bereichit* and, 58–60; camera obscura and, 66–69; Chinese boxes and, 60–64; photographs and, 60–64
Lot, 18

Madame Jacques sur la Croisette (*Madame Jacques on the Cannes Promenade*) (short film), 111
magical realism, 44
Magilow, Daniel, 147
The Maids (Genet), 107
Marty, Eric, 106
mass memorialization, 147
material artifacts, xix
material culture, 27
Maus: A Survivor's Tale (Spiegelman), 23, 28, 85, 166
Max, en apparence (*Max, Seemingly*) (Skowronek), 110
McGlothlin, Erin, 168, 173; on second generation, 170
Méditerranée aux îles d'or ensoleillées (Rossi), 191
Memorial Candles: Children of the Holocaust (Wardi), 166
memorialization, mass, 147
memorials, 135; counting, 147, 148, 149; educational, 147; textual, 131–132, 133–134, 134, 149; war, 148. *See also* literary memorials
"Memorial to the Murdered Jews of Europe," 148
memory, xvii, 28, 45, 169; collective, 35, 43, 167, 177; extended, 26; forms of remembering and, 21; *The Invisible Bridge* and, 22, 26; memory and, 65; Mendelsohn and, 21, 29; multidirectional, 124; prememory, 107; presence of, 22; second generation and, 22; sites of, xviii, xx, 74, 134, 140, 144, 147; symbolism and, 133; transference of, xvii, xviii; transmission of, 176;

trauma and, 65; vagaries of, 50. *See also* postmemory
Memory Matters: Generational Reponses to German's Nazi Past in Recent Women's Literature (Schaumann), 173
Mendelsohn, Daniel, xvi, 20, 23, 34, 60, 61, 65, 112; memory and, 21, 29; proximity and distance and, xvii, 31, 32. *See also specific works*
"A Mercenary" (Ozick), 131
Mesher, David, 172
metanarrative, 116
midrash, 61
military service, 3
milk cans, 135, 136
"Ministerial Gardens," 148
modernity, 19, 20; late, 17; postmodernity, 73
Modiano, Patrick, 112, 127n69
Le Monde Magazine, 76
Monsieur Durand's Shoah (*La Shoah de monsieur Durand*) (Skowronek), 110
Montoya Carlotto, Guido, 101n7
monuments, 134
Mouillot, Miranda Richmond, 29, 32
Mr. Rosenblum Dreams in English (Solomons), 7
multidirectional memory, 124
Munkaszolgálat, 46
"My Experiences under the Germans" (Singer, A.), 142
"My Grandmother Tells Me This Story" (Antopol), xii, 48–51
My Holocaust (Reich), 112

Nakaseko, Kazu, 155
Naye Prese (newspaper), 191
Neighbors: The Destruction of the Jewish Community in Jedwabne, Poland (Gross), 86n23
Netherlands, 103, 104, 125n1
"never again," 113
New Jewish Literature, 9
New Jews, 80
The New Yorker, 50
New York Times, 166
Nicholas, Lynn, 45
Los Nietos (*The Grandchildren*) (documentary), 101n7

Night (Wiesel), 5
9/11 terrorist attacks, 42
noncitizen servicemen, 3
nonwitnesses, 20
nostalgia, 26, 35
Not Everyone Is Lucky Enough to Be an Orphan (*Tout le monde n'a pas la chance d'être orphelin*) (Rubinstein), 109
Nothing Makes You Free: Writings by Descendants of Jewish Holocaust Survivors (Bukiet), 175, 176
numbers, 131, 132; symbolism and, 134, 137, 141, 155

objectivity, 134
Odiner, Edward, 79, 80
On the Edge of Destruction: The Shoah in Latin American Literature and Culture (Aizenberg), 116
On the inner scene (*Sur la scène intérieure*) (Cohen, M.), 105
Orringer, Julie, 7–9, 9, 10, 12, 20, 22, 26, 46, 47. *See also The Invisible Bridge*
Osborne, Monica, 20, 21
otherness, 100
Our Holocaust (Gutfreund), 4, 5–6, 10
outside work, 9
ownership, co-option of, 41
Oyneg Shabes archives, 133, 135, 135–139, 140, 141, 143, 150
Oz, Amos, 113
Ozick, Cynthia, 131, 171, 172

Padura, Eduardo, 122
Paper Clip Project, 149
Paper Love (Wildman), 34
particularism, 134, 142
Patt, Avinoam, xv, xviii, xix
The Pawnbroker (Wallant), 39
Peoria Holocaust Memorial Button Project, 149
Perec, Georges, 104, 105, 112, 117
Perón, Eva, 119
Pew Study, 43
philosophical speculation, 57
photographs, 60–64, 102n24
Pick, Alison, 7

Pictures at an Exhibition (Houghteling), 40, 44, 44–46
Piercy, Marge, 13
pilgrimage, 74, 77
Pinto, Diana, 78
place, 33
Poland, xix, 74, 76, 77, 86n23, 194, 195; as anti-Semitic, 80; Eishyshok, 75; Jewish roots and, 77–85
The Polish Boxer (Halfon), 11–12, 120
Polish Council for Jewish-Christian Relations, 84
Polish Israelite Central Union, 93
Portelli, Alessandro, 91
"Positionality and Postmemory in Holocaust Scholarship" (Bos), 179
Post-Holocaust (Lang, B.), 133
postmemory, 57, 76–77, 107, 178, 179; affiliative, 77; familial, 77; second generation and, 23, 76, 177; trauma and, 23, 177
postmodern identity, 78–85
postmodernity, 73
Potel, Jean-Yves, 75
POWs. *See* prisoners of war
The Practice of Everyday Life (de Certeau), 154
prememory, 107
Di Prese (newspaper), 93
Present Pasts: Urban Palimpsests and the Politics of Memory (Huyssen), 17
prisoners of war (POWs), 103
Proust, Marcel, 185
proximity, xviii, 33; Mendelsohn and, xvii, 31, 32; second generation and, 31
psychoanalysis, 57, 67
Publishers Weekly, 10
punctum, 63

Quiet Americans (Dreifus), xix, 2, 12, 14n5, 15n20

Rabcynska, Anna, 84–85
Rabinbach, Anson, 160, 161
racism, 132
Raczymow, Henri, xviii, xxi, 57, 106, 185–186, 198n7, 198n12
Ran, Amalia, 119
The Rape of Europa (Nicholas), 45

realism, magical, 44
recovered grandchildren, 101n7
"Reflections of a Child of Holocaust Survivors" (Rosensaft), 167
refugees, 3
Reich, Tova, 112
Reisman, Suzanne, 13
Reisner, Yale, 82
Reluctant Witnesses: Survivors, Their Children, and the Rise of Holocaust Consciousness (Stein), 174
remembering, forms of, 21
Remembering the Holocaust: Generations, Witnessing, Place (Jilovsky), 164
repair or restoration of the self (*tikkun atzmi*), xx
repair or restoration of the world (*tikkun olam*), xx, 155
replacement, 107, 124
A Replacement Life (Fishman), 40, 51–52
Répliques (radio program), 112
Rethinking the Holocaust (Bauer), 132
return journeys, xiii
return narratives, 33, 74–76, 85
"The Revival of Polish Jewry" (Guez), 76
Richards, I. A., 124
Righteous Among the Nations (*Hasidei Umot ha-olam*), 86n23
Ringelblum, Emanuel, 135, 137
The Rise and Fall of the Third Reich (Shirer), 172
Rolling Stone (magazine), 125
Ronis, Willy, 187
Rosen, Norma, 181
Rosenbaum, Thane, 9, 17, 30–31, 33, 40, 41, 43, 118
Rosenberg, Paul, 46
Rosencof, Mauricio, 102n24, 117
Rosenfeld, Alvin H., 161
Rosensaft, Menachem Z., 167
Roskies, David, 41
Rossi, Tibo, 191, 198n13
Rubinstein, Marianne, 108–110, 110, 112, 121

sacred space, 84
Saura, Antonio, 105
Sauvage, Pierre, 84
Schaumann, Caroline, 173

Schindler's List (film), 161
Schudrich, Michael, 80
Schuman, Burt, 80, 81
second-and-a-half generation, 13, 104
second generation, xiv, 30, 33, 40; authorship and, 171; Bukiet on, 175; co-option of ownership and, 41; distance and proximity and, 31; eyewitnessing and, 173; Fine and, 167–168; Grimwood and, 170–171; Hirsch and, 176–177; Hoffman on, 164; Holocaust studies and, 166; imaginative writing and, 170; as imagined community, 165; Jilovsky on, 164; legitimacy and, 180; McGlothlin on, 170; memory and, 22; as point of departure, 171; postmemory and, 23, 76, 177; problems with, 163; references to, 163; representation and, 21; Sicher and, 168; time and, 23; translations of, 20; true survivors and, 41
second-generation aesthetics, 172
Second-Generation Holocaust Literature (McGlothlin), 170
"The Secret Miracle" (Borges), 116
secularization, of Jewish identity, 53
Semprun, Jorge, 54n13
servicemen, military, 3
Sfar, Joann, 22
The Shawl (Ozick), 172
Shechner, Mark, 9
Shirer, William, 172
La Shoah de monsieur Durand (*Monsieur Durand's Shoah*) (Skowronek), 110
Shoah Foundation Visual History Archive, 43, 46
Shoah Shelanu (Dreifus), 4–5
Sicher, Efraim, 166, 167, 169, 170, 171, 181; second generation and, 168
Signoret, Simone, 186
silent cues, 23
Silverstein, Jordana, 165
Simon, Andrea, xiii, 32, 74
Sinay, Javier, 125
Singer, Abraham, 142, 143, 144
Singer, Margot, 20, 23, 64
Skibell, Joseph, 20, 32, 33, 34, 35
Skowronek, Nathalie, 110, 111, 112, 120, 125
slave labor camps, 54n13
Slow biography (*Lenta biografía*) (Chejfec), 97–99, 116
Slucki, David, 165
Society for the Protection of Jewish (Soprotimis), 94–95, 95, 96, 97, 98, 99
solidarity networks, 104
Solomons, Natasha, 7
Sons and Daughters of Jewish Deportees from France (Fils et Filles des Déportés Juifs de France), 104, 108
Sontag, Susan, 63, 66
Sophie's Choice (film), 169
Soprotimis. *See* Society for the Protection of Jewish
Sosa, Adriana, 123
South America, 90, 99
Spanish narratives, 116–125
Spanish writers, xx
Spiegelman, Art, 23, 28, 30, 40, 41, 43, 85, 166
Spinoza, Baruch, 114, 124
statistics, 135, 140
Stein, Arlene, 174
Stein, Lol, 189
Steiner, George, 181
stereotypes, 77–78
Stockdale, James, 1
Stolpersteine (*Stumbling Stories*) (Demnig), 133, 150–152, 154, 155
"Street for Arrivals, Street for Departures" (Delbo), 23
studium, 63
Stumbling Stories (*Stolpersteine*) (Demnig), 133, 150–152, 154, 155
subjectivity, 91
Suleiman, Susan, 104, 164
Sur la scène intérieure (*On the inner scene*) (Cohen, M.), 105
survivors, 14n2; searches for, 92–94, 94–97; testimony of, 43, 54n13; true, 41
symbolism, 145, 148; counting memorials and, 149; memory and, 133; numbers and, 134, 137, 141, 155
Syria, 113
Szpilman, Isroel, 82

Tablet Magazine, 42

Taft, Margaret, 175
Tanachs, 115
tattoos, 74, 111, 112, 120
Tec, Nechama, 86n23
Temkine, Pierre, 114
Temkine, Raymonde, 114
Temkine, Valentin, 114, 115
témoignage, 171
temporal distance, xvii
testimony: direct, xvii; of survivors, 43, 54n13
textual memorials, 131–132, 133–134, 134, 149
This Eden Called Warsaw (Reisman), 13
Thomson, Ian, 160
Thorez, Maurice, 188
The Thousand and One Nights (Halfon), 120
A Thousand Darknesses: Truth and Lies in Holocaust Fiction (Franklin), 41
tikkun atzmi (repair or restoration of the self), xx
tikkun olam (repair or restoration of the world), xx, 155
time, 23
Time (magazine), 166
Toby Press, 4
"Todesfuge" (Celan), 132
Torah, 115
Torday, Daniel, 34, 40, 52
Tout le monde n'a pas la chance d'être orphelin (*Not Everyone Is Lucky Enough to Be an Orphan*) (Rubinstein), 109
"Tower of Life" (Eliach), 75
Trachimbrod, 44
The Train to Warsaw (Edelman), 35
"Transmission of Memory: The Post-Holocaust Generation in the Diaspora" (Fine), 167
trauma, xv, 18; consciousness of, 18; generational thinking and, 168; intergenerational transmission of, 40, 76, 162; memory and, 65; postmemory and, 23, 177; transfer of, 22
Treblinka, 137–138
true survivors, 41
TSK, 79, 80, 84
Tsvi, Shabbetai, 124

Twain, Mark, 11
2.5 generation. *See* second-and-a-half generation

Ukraine, xix
UN. *See* United Nations
The UnAmericans, 40, 50
unexpected generation, 78
United Nations (UN), 113
United States (U.S.), xix, 160, 174; military service and, 3
United States Holocaust Memorial Museum, 43, 75, 135, 161, 178
universalism, 132, 134, 142
universalization, 113
unsent letters, 118
Uruguay, 90
U.S. *See* United States
USC Shoah Foundation, 90

Valland, Rose, 45, 46, 55n23
Vietnam War, 160
Virgil, 61, 65
Vishniac, Roman, 63
Visual History Archive, 90
voluntary Jews, 78

Waiting for Godot (Beckett), 114–115
Waiting for Godot: From the Absurd to History (Temkine, P.), 114, 116
Wallant, Edward Lewis, 39–40
Wang, Diana, 102n22
Wardi, Dina, 166
war memorials, 148
War of 1967, 79
Warsaw cemetery, 81–82
Warsaw Ghetto, 24, 118, 121, 135, 137, 163
Weigel, Sigrid, 163, 168, 177
Weissman, Gary, xvi, xx–xxi, 20
We Won't See Auschwitz (Dres), 32, 74, 85
What Time and Sadness Spared: Mother and Son Confront the Holocaust (Ben-Atar, R. N., and Ben-Atar, D.), 5
Whitwell Middle School, 149
Who Will Write Our History? (Kassow), 135
Wiesel, Elie, 5
Wildman, Sarah, 34

women, 97
World Jewish Congress, 93
World War II, 3, 4, 21, 49, 50, 52, 94, 140
Wormser, Georges, 104
W or the Memory of Childhood (Perec), 104, 105, 112
Writing the Book of Esther (Raczymow), 185

xenophobia, 104

Yad Vashem, 86n23
Yahrzeit candle phenomenon, 118
Yale University, 43
Yerushalmi, Yosef Haim, 53
Yiddish language, 117, 118
Yiddish Underground, xii, 48
Di Yidishe Tsaytung, 91, 93
Yizkor books, xviii, 44, 47, 49, 133, 140, 141
Yom HaShoah, 147
Young, James, 134, 135, 148

Zamenhoff, L. L., 82
Zarcynsky, Pinchas, 80
Zegota (Council for aid to Jews), 86n23
Zohar, 52
Zoom (magazine), 79

Contributors

Victoria Aarons is O. R. & Eva Mitchell Distinguished Professor of Literature in the English Department at Trinity University and the author of *A Measure of Memory: Storytelling and Identity in American Jewish Fiction* (1996), *What Happened to Abraham: Reinventing the Covenant in American Jewish Fiction* (2005), and co-editor of *The New Diaspora: The Changing Landscape of American Jewish Fiction* (2015), and *Bernard Malamud: A Centennial Tribute* (2016); she is also the editor of *The Cambridge Companion to Saul Bellow* (2016). She has published over seventy essays in journals and scholarly collections, and serves on the board of *Philip Roth Studies*, *Studies in American Jewish Literature*, *Women in Judaism: A Multidisciplinary Journal*, and *Verbeia, Journal of English and Spanish Studies*. She is a judge for the Edward Lewis Wallant Award.

Alan Astro is professor of modern languages and literatures at Trinity University, San Antonio. He is the author of over thirty articles on writers as diverse as Bashevis, Baudelaire, Beckett, and Borges; a recent piece, published in *Partial Answers*, is a new reading of Élie Wiesel's *Night* in its English, French, and Yiddish versions. Astro is the editor of *Yiddish South of the Border: An Anthology of Latin American Yiddish Writing* (University of New Mexico Press).

Alan L. Berger occupies the Raddock Family Eminent Scholar Chair for Holocaust Studies, the first Holocaust chair established in the state of Florida, and is professor of Judaic Studies at Florida Atlantic University, where he also directs the Center for the Study of Values and Violence after Auschwitz. Among his books are *Crisis and Covenant: The Holocaust in American Jewish Fiction*; *Children of Job: American Second-Generation Witnesses to* *the Holocaust* (foreword by Elie Wiesel); *Jewish American and Holocaust Literature*; and *Trialogue and Terror: Judaism, Christianity, and Islam After 9/11*. His essays and book chapters appear in a variety of places, including *Modern Judaism*, *Modern Language Studies*, *Religion and American Culture*, *Studies in American Jewish Literature*, *Saul Bellow Journal*, *Judaism*, *Literature and Belief*, *Encyclopedia of Jewish-American History and Culture*, and the *Encyclopedia of Genocide*.

Malena Chinski's articles on books and other artifacts of Holocaust memory in Argentina have appeared in such venues as print journals of Tel Aviv University and the Center for Documentation and Research on Leftist Cultures in Argentina, and web publications (for example, *Hypothèses*, edited by the French National Center for Scientific Research). She has presented her work at seminars and conferences at the United States Holocaust Memorial Museum, the Museum of Art and History of Judaism in Paris, New York University, the University of Arizona, the Ibero-Amerikanisches Institut of Berlin, the Federal University of Rio de Janeiro, and the Western Galilee College in Akko. Chinski is currently completing her doctoral dissertation, "Memories in the Plural: The Jews of Buenos Aires in the Face of the Holocaust, 1945–1955," at the National University of General Sarmiento in Argentina.

Erika Dreifus is a writer and editor in New York. She is the author of *Quiet Americans: Stories* (Last Light Studio), which was named an American Library Association/Sophie Brody Medal Honor Title for outstanding achievement in Jewish literature. Her current book project is a poetry manuscript provisionally titled *Double Chai*. She is employed as media editor for Fig Tree Books. Visit Erika online at ErikaDreifus.com and follow her on Twitter @ErikaDreifus, where she tweets about "matters bookish and/or Jewish."

Jessica Lang is associate professor of English and the Newman Director of the Wasserman Jewish Studies Center at Baruch College, CUNY. She has recently completed a book on Holocaust literature that examines the concept of "unreadability" in first-, second-, and third-generation memoir, fiction, and memorial.

Paule Lévy is professor of American literature at the University of Versailles, France. She has widely published in the field of Jewish-American literature. In addition to numerous articles, her book publications include *Figures de l'Artiste: Identité et écriture dans la littérature juive américaine de la deuxième moitié du XXe siècle* (2006), *American Pastoral: La Vie réinventée* (2012), and the edited volumes, *Profils américains: Philip Roth* (2002), *Ecritures contemporaines de la différence* (2003), *Mémoires* *d'Amériques* (2009), *Autour de Saul Bellow* (2010), and *Lectures de Philip Roth: American Pastoral* (2011).

Avinoam Patt is Philip D. Feltman Professor of Modern Jewish History at the Maurice Greenberg Center for Judaic Studies at the University of Hartford, where he is also director of the Museum of Jewish Civilization and administers the Edward Lewis Wallant Award. He is the author of *Finding Home and Homeland: Jewish Youth and Zionism in the Aftermath of the Holocaust* and is co-editor with Michael Berkowitz of *"We Are Here": New Approaches to the Study of Jewish Displaced Persons in Postwar Germany* and, with co-editors Victoria Aarons and Mark Shechner, *The New Diaspora: The Changing Landscape of American Jewish Fiction*. He is a contributor to several projects at the United States Holocaust Memorial Museum and co-author of the recently published source volume *Jewish Responses to Persecution, 1938–1940*.

Henri Raczymov was born in 1948 in Paris from a Jewish Polish family who came to France at the beginning of the 1920s. Two among his many works appeared in the United States: *Writing the Book of Esther*, translated by Dori Katz (Holmes & Meyers, 1995), and *Swan's Way*, translated by Robert Bononno (Northwestern University Press, 2002). A short essay, "Memory Shot Through with Holes," translated by Alan Astro, appeared in *Yale French Studies* 85 (1994). The main part of his work deals with the memory before, during, and after the Shoah.

Gary Weissman is associate professor of English and Comparative Literature at the University of Cincinnati. The author of *Fantasies of Witnessing: Postwar Efforts to Experience the Holocaust* (Cornell University Press, 2004), he has published several articles and book chapters on Holocaust literature, film, and scholarship. His current book project, *The Death and Life of the Mind at Auschwitz*, examines the problematics of representing not atrocity but interiority, the inner lives of camp prisoners and survivor-writers, in Holocaust memoirs.